The Increment

CHRIS RYAN

The Increment

C̄

Century · London

Published by Century in 2004

3 5 7 9 10 8 6 4

First published in the United Kingdom in 2004 by Century
The Random House Group Limited
20 Vauxhall Bridge Road, London SW1V 2SA

Random House Australia (Pty) Limited
20 Alfred Street, Milsons Point, Sydney
New South Wales 2061, Australia

Random House New Zealand Limited
18 Poland Road, Glenfield
Auckland 10, New Zealand

Random House South Africa (Pty) Limited
Endulini, 11a Jubilee Road, Parktown 2193, South Africa

The Random House Group Limited Reg. No. 954009
www.randomhouse.co.uk

A CIP catalogue record for this book
is available from the British Library

Papers used by Random House UK Limited are natural, recyclable products made from wood grown in sustainable forests. The manufacturing processes conform to the environmental regulations of the country of origin

ISBN 1 8441 3383 4 (Cased edition)
ISBN 1 8441 3436 9 (Trade paperback edition)

Typeset by SX Composing DTP, Rayleigh, Essex
Printed in Great Britain by
Clays Limited, St Ives plc

ACKNOWLEDGEMENTS

To my agent Barbara Levy, editor Mark Booth, Hannah Black, Charlotte Bush and all the rest of the team at Century.

PROLOGUE

Gorazde, Bosnia, 1999.

The image of the bullet flying through the air was still rattling through Matt's mind. Already, he knew it would stick with him, filed away in some dark corner. Along with all the images of all the other men he had killed.

My own personal graveyard.

The basement had been dark and squalid. Water was dripping down from the ceiling, and there was a suffocating, lingering smell of human excrement rising up from the floor. Matt moved down the stairs, cautiously at first, adjusting his eyes to the darkness. A few pale cracks of light were bouncing through the coal-hole that looked up to the surface of the street. But there was not a single window, nor any electric light.

The man was chained to the wall. His eyes were drooping. It looked as if he had been beaten unconscious. His black hair was thick with sweat, and there were scars running down the side of his face. The blood was still fresh on his skin.

Matt levelled the Smith & Wesson Magnum Hunter pistol, held it steady in his right hand, lining it up next to his eye. To his left, he could feel Jack Matram looking down on him, his eyes tracking his every move. He squeezed his finger on the trigger.

Keep the aim, he told himself. *If this bullet doesn't finish him, you'll need to fire another round.*

The bullet collided with the centre of the man's forehead. Even at a distance of ten feet, Matt could see the hardened steel skin of the bullet smashing into his skull, breaking through the bone and slicing inside the brain. A trickle of red blood started to seep from the open wound, running down the front of his face. He remained completely silent as his neck gave way, his head falling forwards, and his arms rattling against the chains that still held him to the wall.

'Nice shot,' said Matram softly. 'Now let's get out of here.'

'Who was he?' Matt wondered as they walked swiftly back to the van parked on the street outside. Matram refused to tell him. 'If you want to ask questions, join a bloody philosophy class,' he'd snapped. 'We just pull the triggers.'

'How did I do, then?' asked Matt, as they arrived back at the base. A set of five tents, nestling in the hills just outside the market town of Gorazde, about fifty kilometres south of Sarajevo. The regiment had been stationed there for a month, clearing out some of the bandits and robbers that had been plaguing the United Nations forces for the past year. Their instructions were clear and simple. Find the criminals and eliminate them.

'He was already dead,' said Matram, glancing up at Matt.

'Dead?'

'One of our boys went in this morning to kiss him goodnight. I just took you along to see how you handled yourself in the field. We don't take the interns on proper missions. Too risky.' He looked up at Matt, a sly smile creasing up his lips. 'They might bottle it.'

'I've done ten years in the regiment,' growled Matt.

'And you done about five minutes in the Increment,' answered Matram. 'Nobody here gives a fuck about your record. You prove yourself to us from day one.'

Matt buried his anger, searching deep inside himself to find some space to park his fury. It was a decade now since he had first moved from the regular army to the SAS, and he'd learnt over the years how to deal with the Ruperts. You listened, you obeyed, and sometimes you tactfully suggested there might be some other way they'd like to consider. Still, as the years went by, he was finding it harder and harder to take orders from other men. *And Matram looked as if he was going to be the hardest of them all.*

'I don't need target practice. I already know how to shoot,' said Matt. He paused. 'Sir.'

Matram stood up. He was a tall man, over six foot three, which gave him a couple of inches over Matt. His hair was sandy, dirty blond, and his jaw was square and clean. His nose was fatter than average, and his skin was pitted and rough. But his eyes were clear and blue, and beamed out of his face like a pair of headlamps. His accent retained traces of a Cornish burr, although it had been rubbed away by years working from the regiment's Herefordshire base. 'We'll meet up with the rest of the unit in fifteen minutes. We've got another fish to catch, and this one's alive.'

Matt nodded and walked back to his tent. Already, it had been a long day. It had started with Matram putting him through a gruelling series of physical exercises. Next, one of the regiment shrinks sat him down and started asking him a lot of idiotic questions about his attitude to authority and death. Matt had seen right through that one. All they wanted to know was whether you'd shoot the people you were meant to shoot without asking a lot of irritating questions about who the victims were, or why you'd been sent to punch out their number. Finally, just before the fake assassination, Matram had put him through a series of practical questions. In what depth of water do you drown a man? On what floor of a building do you have to be to make sure you kill a man by dropping him from a window? What is the best type of rope for strangulation? That kind of thing.

Still, reflected Matt, a posting to the Increment was always going to be tough. Even within the SAS, there was no harder assignment.

He hadn't asked for the test, nobody ever did. The Ruperts had put him up for it and, if he was being honest with himself, Matt was flattered to be asked. The Increment was a tiny unit consisting of just six men and two women, each of whom did a two-year tour of duty. It operated in the murky shadow lands between the regiment, the regular army, the intelligence agencies MI5 and MI6, and the Home and Foreign Offices. There were plenty of people who could call upon it to do their dirty work, but nobody who would acknowledge its existence if a job ever went wrong. Its task was assassinations. If there was someone the British state needed killed, the Increment was the unit that put its finger on the trigger.

It was nasty, hard and messy work, usually undercover, usually off the books, and always without back-up. But it was also the fast track. After doing his two years, an Increment man could ask for just about any posting he wanted. And get it.

'How did it go?' asked Reid.

The stocky Geordie, one of Matt's oldest friends in the regiment, was lying back on his camp bed, trying to write the letter home to his fiancée he'd been composing for the last two days.

'I think it was OK,' said Matt cautiously. 'I think I passed the test.'

'Right,' said Cooksley, the third man in the tent. 'But do you *want* to join? That's the question you need to answer.'

Matt paused, turning the question over in his mind. He'd thought about that in the past two days, ever since he was told about the possibility of the posting. He knew it meant they rated him. His performance in tours of Ulster, the Gulf, Bosnia, and then some dirty work in the Philippines and Indonesia had impressed the Ruperts. They thought he was good, otherwise they wouldn't have recommended him. But assassinations? It was never a fair fight, and the targets were usually civilians. Matt had never felt any remorse about killing another soldier, and didn't mind if the fight was fair or not: the less fair the better, if he was being honest. But civilians? With no weapons? That was something else.

'If they want me, I'll do it,' he said. 'It's two years, that's all.'

'Even if it means working for Matram?' said Cooksley.

'How bad is he?'

'Think Saddam Hussein, without the easygoing charm,' said Reid.

'Think Gerry Adams without the happy-go-lucky humour,' chipped in Cooksley.

Matt laughed. 'No, what's he *really* like?'

Cooksley looked up from the Nintendo GameBoy he'd bought in Hereford the day before. 'I only know what I've heard around the mess, same as you. As you know, Increment men stay away from the rest of us, so it's mostly the same old gossip. Second-hand.'

'But . . .'

'He's a hard bastard, obviously . . .'

'Obviously.'

'But he treats it like his own little kingdom. Nasty, sadistic little kingdom, from what I hear. Enjoys it. The killing, I mean.'

'One story I heard, they did a few practice rounds, just to get people in shape,' said Reid. 'Here in Bosnia. They got some of the names off the UN wanted list, then went around knocking them off. Not because anyone had ordered them to, but because they wanted to try out some new assassination techniques.'

Matt took a deep breath. 'But the Increment guys do OK?'

'They go up the ladder, that's for sure,' said Reid. 'You

want to be a Rupert, that's your way in. A couple of years pointlessly wasting lives, while fucking everything up, and generally acting like an arrogant tosser? Just the kind of training to turn you into a grade-A Rupert.'

Matt laughed. They could rib him but if he was going to stay in the regiment, he'd need to start taking life seriously. He was past thirty now, and he had to move on. Or find something better to do with his life.

Get promoted or get out. These are my choices.

He was still mulling those options as he walked back towards Matram's tent. It was a miserable, rain-sodden spring day. The clouds were lying thick and low over the landscape, and a harsh wind was lashing in from the east. Matt could feel it chilling his bones, and dampening his spirits as he climbed into the jeep that Matram had prepared.

They drove for an hour, mostly in silence. There were three men in the back: Abram and Unsworth in the second of their two years in the unit Harton in his first. They sat still during the journey, cleaning and checking their weapons, making sure they were working perfectly.

'The target is down there,' said Matram, climbing out of the jeep and motioning the others to join them on the tarmac.

Matt stood in the blustery wind, pulling the collar of his leather jacket up around his neck. Even out here in Bosnia, the Increment operated in civilian clothes: its jobs were all too sensitive for the regular army. His Smith & Wesson was tucked into his pocket, and a hunting knife was slipped down his trousers. In case anything went wrong, five C-5 rifles were stored in the back of the jeep.

He looked down into the valley. The landscape was waterlogged and sodden, the fields ragged and uncared for. Up in the distance, he could see a small herd of goats, next to them a few chickens clustering around a shack of a farmhouse. But most of the fields had started to go back to the wild: the farmers had all gone away to fight, and many of them hadn't come back.

'War criminal,' said Matram. 'His name is Elvedin Jamakovic. Nasty piece of work. Supposed to be a soldier, but he's mainly interested in the cigarettes and heroin smuggled across the Albanian border. He can be prosecuted, but he won't be convicted because all the locals are too scared to testify. A trial is more trouble than it's worth.' He paused, his eyes resting on Matt. 'So it's going to be a fight-back.'

A fight-back.

Matt was familiar with the term from his time in Ulster. The technique was simple. You went in to capture the suspect, then you made sure he resisted. As you attempted to take him, he got shot. End of story. No trial. No lengthy jail term. And no embarrassing questions.

Abram, Unsworth and Harton all looked back at Matram and nodded. 'Who goes in first?' said Harton.

'You and Unsworth can make the initial entry,' said Matram. 'Shoot down the door, and go straight in.' He held up a picture of a man in his early thirties, with dark brown eyes and curly black hair. 'This is Jamakovic. As soon as you see him, tap him a couple of times. Make sure it's nothing too neat or clean. A couple to the leg, then one or two bullets to the chest, but avoid the heart. Let him bleed to death, so that if anyone does an autopsy later it looks as if he got killed in a struggle.' Matram laughed. 'We don't want anyone thinking we killed him on purpose.'

They nodded, their expressions sullen, and as grey as the clouds sweeping down from the hills. For the Increment, Matt realised, this was just another job.

The village was dirt poor. A single street, with three mud tracks running down from it, the water collecting in big, thick, muddy puddles. In total, there were about twenty houses, three of them still half built, and another two bomb-damaged. A group of small boys were playing football at the

7

end of the street, two old car seats propped up to make the goal posts. One of them looked up at the men tramping down the street, but showed no interest. One of his mates shouted at him to get back in goal.

The kids around here are used to seeing men with guns. It's just like growing up in south London.

Jamakovic's house was at the end of the mud track. Maybe ten years old, it was built in the worker's paradise style of the old Yugoslav regime: a flat two-storey box, made from cheap concrete breeze blocks that had badly stained in the harsh weather. There was a big Toyota SUV on the drive, and a ten-metre satellite dish in the garden.

'Ready?' whispered Matram a step away from the entrance.

Harton and Unsworth both nodded.

'Then go.'

The door gave way easily enough. Two clean shots shattered the locks, and one high kick sent the door flying open. Harton and Unsworth swept through the hallway, their guns primed and ready to fire. Abrams, Matt and Matram moved in behind them. Upstairs, they could hear shouting, and the sound of a woman screaming. The three men started running upstairs.

'In here,' shouted Matram, pointing through the first door off the hallway.

Matt held the Smith & Wesson tight in his right hand, and turned into the sitting room. A television, two DVDs on the floor – cheap-looking pirated copies of *The Mummy Returns* and *Die Another Day*, the titles written in German – and a couple of empty wine bottles. Otherwise empty. He walked through to the kitchen. Empty. The bathroom, the same.

The sound of gunfire echoed through the house: the explosions were muffled by the ceiling, but Matt could still make out the screams as the bullets tore into their victims. He started walking cautiously up the stairs, holding his gun in front of him. A single light bulb was swinging on the landing, but the curtains were closed, and the rooms were shrouded in darkness.

Jamakovic was lying on the bed, his mouth open and his hair matted with blood. One eye has been shot out, and another three bullet holes had punctured his lungs, sending blood spilling out across the black sheets. His girlfriend was lying next to him, clinging on to a pillow, as if it were a shield. She had green eyes, a thin, pale body, and streaked blonde hair: there was a tattoo of a Ferrari just above her belly button, Matt noticed. She was trying to say something, but the terror had paralysed her and the words stuck in her throat: small gasps of air were all she could struggle up to her lips.

'You've done a nice job,' said Matram, smiling towards Harton. 'You can finish her if you like.'

'You want this one quick, sir,' said Harton, 'or should she bleed to death as well?'

Matram shrugged. 'Don't care. She's yours.'

Harton moved towards the girl. He was a short, stocky man, just five foot five, but built like a dog: his muscles bulged from his clothes, and every bone seemed thick and heavy. He yanked the girl by the hair, tugging her neck backwards.

'You look nice,' he whispered. 'We'll make it quick.'

Slowly, he put his Smith & Wesson to her right ear. She struggled, trying to break free, but Harton's thick, meaty palms were already pressing down hard on her shoulders making movement impossible. He squeezed the trigger gently, sending the bullet straight through her brain. A small cloud of dust splattered downwards on to the sheets, as the bullet shattered through her skull and hit the wall behind.

That's not soldiering, thought Matt.

Matram walked across the room, checked she was dead,

then looked back at the men. 'Right then, who wants to get clipped?'

'Someone's getting clipped?' asked Matt.

Matram looked across at him. 'I trust you know what the word means, Browning,' he said, 'or have you only ever played toy soldiers before?'

Clipped, thought Matt, repeating the word to himself. *That means one of us has to take a bullet.*

'I know what it means, sir, I just don't know why it's necessary.'

'Christ, man, this is Bosnia, the place is under UN control and it's bloody crawling with social workers, international inspectors, CNN film crews, and half the do-gooders in Europe,' Matram snapped. 'The reason somebody gets clipped is because if none of us gets wounded, it won't look like there was a proper fight.' He raised an eyebrow. 'Somebody might think we had just assassinated the bastard.'

All five of them were standing in the room, four of them looking straight at Matram. He took a coin from his pocket, tossing it into the air. 'Heads, Harton and Unsworth. Tails, Abram and Browning.' The coin landed on the back of his palm, and Matram glanced down. 'Tails.' He tossed the coin back into the air, watching as it spun upwards. 'Heads, Abram. Tails, Browning.'

The coin landed on his palm. Matram looked down at it, his eyes sparkling with amusement. He looked back up towards Matt. 'My my, tails,' he said slowly. 'Looks like you're the lucky winner. Roll up your trousers, we'll make it a nice easy flesh wound in the calf. After all, we don't want to hurt you.'

Matt held his ground.

He had been shot three times before: an arm wound in the Gulf, then a stomach wound in Bosnia and leg wound in the Philippines. He'd listened to old soldiers in the mess bar back in Hereford boasting about how bullet wounds didn't hurt so much once you got used to them. Good to get a couple under your belt just so you weren't scared of them any more, they would say as they downed the pints. Makes a soldier of you. Matt joined in the laughter, but he knew it was all just mess-room bravado. A bullet was a terrible shot of pain, like nothing you would ever experience again: the metal thudded into your skin, ripping it open, then burnt its way through your flesh, smashing open your veins and nerves. As soon as it hit, a faint, sickly smell of charred, butchered flesh started to rise up to your nostrils, and the sudden loss of blood sent your head spinning, shutting down your vision and clouding your brain.

He didn't mind getting shot at if he had to, if it was in the line of battle. *But this was just public relations.*

'Nobody needs to get clipped, sir.'

Matram walked a pace forward, standing a yard from Matt's face. 'Are you afraid, Browning?'

Matt stood rock steady. 'I just don't think it's necessary, sir. It's not soldiering. We shouldn't be ashamed of what we do.'

Matram stepped another pace forward, his eyes bearing down on Matt. 'You don't know how to deliver a bullet, and you don't know how to take one either,' he said, his tone cold. 'You're not Increment material. Not now, never will be. You're a bloody coward.'

'If you are failing me, you're the bloody coward.'

'You should watch who you level that accusation at.'

'A coward, sir, because you don't want anyone in your unit who might question your judgement.'

Matt could see Matram's muscles flexing: his skin was flushed with anger, and his eyes were full of rage. 'I'll meet you again, on a different battlefield, Browning,' he snarled. 'And then I'll teach you some bloody manners.'

Matt turned round, and walked from the room. He stepped downstairs, and strode out along the muddy dirt track that led away from the village. The wind was blowing harder now, and the rain had started to fall: a fierce, cold sleet that caught up in the air and crashed straight into your face.

He knew he would never be part of the Increment now. That didn't matter, he didn't want to be. If he wanted to, he could stay in the army: he'd just have to ask for a different unit.

But somewhere inside Matt knew that his options were closing down. A decision that had been building up for a year or more was suddenly hardening within him. There was no getting away from it. He couldn't be an ordinary soldier for ever, and yet he couldn't turn himself into a Rupert either.

It doesn't matter what happens. My time in the regiment is coming to a close. The moment to start thinking about the rest of my life has arrived.

ONE

Jack Matram ran his eyes across the two men sitting behind him in the car. Simon Clipper was the taller of the pair: six foot three, with short blond hair, green eyes, and a gentle, sloping smile. In his George jeans from Asda, and a blue cotton T-shirt, he blended in naturally with the neat rows of suburban houses stretching into the background. Frank Trench was shorter: about five foot eight, with jet-black hair, blue eyes, a crooked smile.

They had a rugged, easy charm about them. In civilian clothes, the pair of them looked just like any two men on their way down to the pub. Perfect, decided Matram.

Twelve months into their two-year tour of duty with the Increment, Matram knew he could rely on them. Clipper had eleven assassinations under his belt, Trench eight. All of them had been textbook. Lie in wait, move in quickly, dispatch the target, and come back to base without even breaking into a sweat.

They would do what they were told. Killers didn't come any better trained than these two.

'Barry Legg,' said Matram softly. 'That's the name of tomorrow's target.'

Clipper and Trench looked down at the photo Matram had just handed each of them. Maybe thirty-five, with brown hair and a round face, he looked as unremarkable as the modern housing estate on the outskirts of Swindon where he was now living. Both men folded the picture in half, tucked it into the breast pockets of their shirts, then looked silently back up at Matram.

'On Wednesday, his son Billy has after-school football practice,' said Matram. 'It's about a mile across open fields from this estate to the training ground. The practice finishes at seven, but Legg likes to watch the boys kicking a ball about so he's usually there a bit early. He should be passing this precise spot sometime around six tomorrow evening.'

He paused, pointing out towards the fields. 'You'll be waiting here for him. Follow him into the field, then kill him. He shouldn't give you any trouble.'

Clipper nodded. 'Will he be alone?'

'Almost certainly,' answered Matram. 'If he isn't, you may have to take out whoever is with him as well. But I'll be watching from a distance. If I don't like the look of anything, you'll hear from me.'

'Guns OK?' said Trench. 'Or knives?'

'Guns,' said Matram. 'I want this done fast, and I want it done clean.'

He glanced down at his watch. It was just before seven, and the evening light was already starting to fade. In the distance, he could see a pair of young mothers lugging their buggies home. Past them, two guys were walking towards the pub for an early-evening drink. Another quiet night in the Swindon suburbs.

The sound of glasses being clicked together and of chicken and steaks frying on the grill greeted Matt as he stepped into the back room of the Last Trumpet. He pulled the sweat-stained T-shirt off his back, chucking it towards the pile of dirty clothes stacked up in the washroom.

A shower, and then a beer, he decided. *Looks like a fine evening ahead.*

The run had done him good. It had been a hot start to the summer along the southern Spanish coast. Now it was June,

14

the temperatures were hitting the early forties. A five-mile jog along the beach had left him drained and dehydrated but also sharpened up his mind. That was what Matt liked about running. As you pushed your muscles, you also pushed your mind.

In truth, there wasn't much to worry about, Matt had reflected as his feet pounded against sand that had baked bone dry in the midday sun. There was money in the bank from what he had promised Gill was absolutely the last job he would ever go on. Their debts on the Last Trumpet were all paid off, and although the bar and restaurant only ticked over financially during the winter and spring months, it should start making some real cash over the summer. The hard core of regulars, mostly Londoners who had decamped to the Costa del Sol for a few years, meant it could always break even: the tourists who tumbled off the easyJet flights into Malaga through July and August, their pockets bulging with euros, provided the profits for the year. It was a solid, dependable business, one that could be relied upon to make a good enough living to support a family. And the house they were building half a mile down the coastline was almost finished. True, José and his gang of Moroccans who actually seemed to do all the building work for him had slipped a bit on their deadlines. But a Deptford boy like Matt wasn't going to get worked up about a few cowboy builders. Everyone has to make a living, he told himself. And right now, he could afford a few extra expenses.

I've hit the good groove. All I have to do now is hold that note.

He stepped out of the shower. The water was dripping off his shoulders as he wrapped the towel around himself, and started searching around for a clean pair of chinos. Matt paused, as he felt a pair of warm lips brush against the back of his neck. He remained still, letting her tongue tickle the back of his ear. Slowly, his hands moved backwards, pulling her groin closer towards him.

15

'Let me guess,' he said, still not turning round. 'It's that slapper from Reading I saw at the back of the bar. Fresh off the Luton flight, too many cocktails, not enough sun cream, and now completely off her face even though it's not even sunset. We'll have to make it a quick one, babe. My fiancée's knocking about the place somewhere.'

Gill gripped him tighter, her arms circling around his chest. 'And what would this fiancée of yours say,' she whispered, 'if she caught you with another girl?'

Matt chuckled. 'Chop us both into little pieces. Got a bit of a temper.'

Matt turned round, kissing Gill on the lips. Her fingers ran along his chest, slipping into the towel he had wrapped around his waist. The flimsy white cotton dress she was wearing flapped in the light breeze blowing in from the sea, and as Matt ran his fingers along her back, he could feel her skin softening beneath his touch. He buried his face into her neck, pulling her body tight in close to his. Her hair fell across his face, stroking his skin.

No matter how many times we make love, she is always fresh and different each time. Maybe that's why I'm marrying her.

With one swift movement of his hand, the strap holding the dress broke away. It dropped to the floor, and Gill stood naked before him.

The bar was livelier than Matt had expected. A Tuesday night, you didn't always get that many people. The English along the coast got hammered at the weekend, then slowly nursed themselves back into shape. It wasn't until Wednesday they started drifting back into the bars and restaurants, and it was Friday before they were ready for a long session. They might be a thousand miles from home, but their drinking habits, along with their accents, never changed.

He recognised several of the faces. Bob, an ex-army guy who worked as a security consultant for some of the Russian tycoons who had houses along the coast. Sharing a pint with him was Keith, an old London lawyer who'd spent the first half of his working life as a prosecutor trying to extradite some of the villains who lived out in Spain, and was now spending the second half defending them from getting shipped back home. There were men growing comfortably old while Keith spun out appeal after appeal, and some of them were regulars here as well.

We ask no questions, Matt had decided when he first opened the bar. *Any man who can settle his bill is welcome at the Last Trumpet.*

At one of the tables looking out on to the sea, Matt could see Penelope and Suzie. The more times Suzie dropped the phrase 'late thirties' into her conversation, the more you knew she was never going to blow out that number of candles on her birthday cake again. Both women had been divorced in the last two years, and they were sharing a bottle of Chilean white. Matt didn't need to listen to know what they were talking about. They were complaining about their ex-husbands, and gossiping about any new available men who might get snapped up.

Many of the villains along the Spanish coast traded in their wives every time a fresh job hauled in a new lump of cash. These two were like a pair of late-model Ford Sierras: still useful for getting around in, but there wasn't much demand now their men had all upgraded to Mondeos.

But, of course, whatever their faults, Matt found it hard to dislike anyone who spent money in his bar.

One man he didn't recognise. About forty, running to fat, with sandy-blond hair. He was sitting by himself, drinking a glass of port, a rare drink among the bottled beers and cocktails with bright hats. He was wearing a crisp white linen suit, and a sea-blue cotton shirt, open at the neck, and with the initials GA embroidered into the cuff. He stuck out like a mackerel in a butcher's shop, Matt reflected.

17

A copy of that day's *Wall Street Journal* was lying open on the table, but he wasn't reading it. He was just looking out at the waves, his expression confident and peaceful. Matt could see Suzie throw a glance at the fat man. Checking out the suit and the paper. Nobody reads the *Wall Street Journal* for laughs. It means they have money. *And that's what she finds attractive in a man.*

'You think it's hot here, you should see what it's like back at home,' said Bob, handing Matt a bottle of San Miguel.

He took a hit of his beer, his first of the week. Like most of his customers Matt tried to keep his head clear Sunday and Monday. Back in south London where he grew up, his dad had known lots of men who owned pubs, and he'd passed on some advice when Matt talked about opening this place. 'Nobody ever went broke owning a bar, that is unless they take to the drink themselves.'

'What's happening back in Britain?' said Matt.

With the work he'd been doing, getting the bar's accounts straight, and getting the new house sorted, Matt had hardly opened a newspaper in a week. Prince Charles could have been caught in bed with Posh Spice, and Beckham could have left her for Nancy Dell'Olio for all he knew. Anyway, after checking the City pages to see how his portfolio of shares was coming along, Matt had little time for the papers. The longer he stayed out of Britain, the more trivial many of the headlines seemed. He had his own life out here. He had the sea, fresh air and money in the bank. That was all that mattered.

'Heatwave,' said Bob. 'Phew, what a scorcher and all that! Thirty-nine in London yesterday apparently, the hottest day ever. Couple of tube trains broke down. Hundreds stranded for hours underground.'

'Record jams on the road,' said Keith, looking up from his two-day-old copy of the *Daily Mail*. 'Everyone was heading down to the coast to try and cool off. There were tailbacks of four or five hours on the M32 down to the Kent coast. Ambulances had to come along the hard shoulder giving people bottles of water. Then some soldier somewhere lost it completely, started shooting.'

Bob drained his bottle of beer and ordered another one. 'The whole country's falling apart. We're better off out here. Say what you like about the Spanish, you can move about a bit on the roads.'

'What happened to the soldier?' asked Matt. 'Anyone we know?'

Keith shook his head. 'Can't remember the details. Some guy in Shropshire. Engineers Corps, out a couple of years I think. Topped his wife and stepchild, then did himself.'

Matt gazed out into the sea. The waves were crashing into the rocks in the bay that tumbled down from the foot of the restaurant. In the distance, he could see a pair of trawlers hauling in their nets, making the first catch of the night. The moon was rising in the sky, its light merging with the embers of the sun fast disappearing over the horizon. Some clouds were forming in the distance – the big, thick thunderclouds that drifted across from the North African coastline all through the hot summer months. It doesn't matter what's happening at home, he reflected. We're a long way from it all here.

'When's the wedding, Matt?' said Keith.

'September sixth,' replied Matt. 'A bit cooler by then. Otherwise, I'm going to be sweating like a pig. Gill will get one whiff of me and run screaming from the church.'

'She will anyway,' said Keith, 'if she's got any sense.'

Is there any truth in that? wondered Matt. The wedding was only two months away now. A full-blown affair back in south London where they had grown up together. Matt wasn't particularly looking forward to it. The service was scheduled for four, then a reception that would last all evening. Damien, Gill's brother and Matt's best friend from his childhood, would be the best man. A couple of hundred people were coming. Why so many, Matt wasn't sure. Left to him, the list wouldn't have come to more than a dozen people. But Gill wanted it that way. Second cousins, great-aunts, the girl she did a French exchange with when she was twelve; it seemed vitally important to her that they were all there on the day.

After breaking up with her once, I can't make it difficult for her again.

'Matt Browning.'

From the tone of the voice, it was hard to tell whether it was a question or a statement. Matt looked round. It was the man in the white suit. He was looking straight at him.

'Yes. Who are you?'

'My name is Guy Abbott. We need to talk.' The man paused, looking towards Bob and Keith. 'In private.'

Matt followed him reluctantly towards the back of the restaurant. He didn't like the look of Abbott, and he could feel Penelope's and Suzie's eyes tracking them as he walked across to a table tucked into the far corner of the dining patio. A mosquito was crawling over the table. Without blinking, Matt hammered his fist down on to it.

A way of saying, I wish I could do the same to you.

'Nice place you got here,' said Abbott. He pulled out one of the black metal chairs and sat down. 'If I was a cockney gangster with a taste for leathery blondes and overcooked chicken this would be the place I'd come. Bloody marvellous.'

Matt sat down, resting his forearms on the table. 'Who *are* you?'

'Like I told, you, the name's Guy Abbott. I work for a little outfit based in Vauxhall. Big green and beige building. I think you'd recognise it if you saw it.'

He fished a cigarette from his pocket, sticking it into his

mouth, holding the flame of his lighter a few inches from his face. Its pale light illuminated his blotched, reddish complexion: the skin of a man who spent too much of his time behind a desk. 'You've got an account with our firm, my old fruit. And we'd like you to settle it.'

Matt looked away. The clouds were drawing closer, and somewhere out at sea he could hear the rain starting to fall. The Firm was what everyone in the regiment called it, or British Intelligence to give it its proper title. That was what he was talking about. Of that there could be no question.

I always knew they would come back for me. One day. When they wanted something.

More than a year had passed since the last job had finished. Matt and four men had done a hit on al-Qaeda, organised by the Firm. They had taken thirty million dollars in gold and jewels from a boat running the gear across the Mediterranean for the terrorists. It had been worth ten million after it was fenced. But Matt came within an inch of losing his own life.

We kept the money. And we kept some bad memories as well.

He looked back up at Abbott. 'There's no account. I don't know what you're talking about.'

Abbott smiled, revealing a set of crooked teeth. 'Why don't we get a drink? It's much more civilised to discuss these things over a glass of wine. You must have some decent stuff at the back of the bar somewhere. A nice Rioja, or something.'

Show-off, thought Matt, as he walked back to the bar. He took a bottle of red from the case, and started looking for the corkscrew. He knew exactly where it was, but made a show of searching around. *I need to buy myself some time – decide how to handle this.*

He'd always known there would be a reckoning one day. For himself, he had no regrets about what he'd done. The money was rightfully his. But that didn't mean the Firm would see it that way. The Firm wasn't like that.

Matt wrenched the cork free from the bottle, grabbed two glasses and started walking back towards Abbott. A dozen different thoughts were racing through his mind. What could they want? Another mission? How could they hope to make him cooperate? They knew he wasn't going to go back to fighting. He had money in his bank account, his own business, and he was about to get married. He was his own man now.

Just act like one of those helpline people you call up when your computer's broken. *Whatever he wants, tell him he can't have it.*

'You can have a drink,' said Matt, 'but that's as far as it goes. Whatever it is you want me to do, I'm not interested.'

Abbott poured himself a glass of the wine, swilling it around, then putting it to his lips. He sipped delicately, as a woman might. 'Decent drop, this. You have to come to Spain to get a reliable Rioja, don't you think? The stuff we get at home just tastes like some Aussie muck with a few oak leaves chucked in.'

Matt leant forward on the table. 'If I want a wine guide, I'll buy a book.'

'I know everything, Matt. I know about the raid on the boat. I know about the money that went missing. The lot. It's all back on the files at head office.'

He paused, lighting up another Dunhill. 'And I don't mind. The Firm's not *cross*, Matt. Not in the least. We like your style. You gave a good account of yourself. Al-Qaeda was relieved of a lot of money, and we cracked open their network in Britain. There were a few hiccups along the way, but then who ever heard of a job that ran smoothly. If there wasn't some trouble involved, they wouldn't call it work, would they?' Abbott took a deep drag on his cigarette, blowing the smoke up into the air. 'We like you so much, we were wondering if you might be able to do something else for us.'

'Thanks,' snapped Matt. 'But take a look around. I'm in a different trade now.'

'Ah, yes. The Jamie Oliver of the Costa del Crime. But it's not really you, is it, Matt? You're a man of action. If this was the life you wanted, you'd have signed up for Little Chef instead of the army. You'd have been a regional manager by now.' Abbott took another long, slow sip on his wine. 'But that's not what you want, is it? You know the worst thing a man can do? Some people reckon it's lying, others cowardice, but that's all nonsense. The worst thing a man can do is be untrue to himself. And that's what you're doing, Matt. You're a man of action, not a bloody chef and barman. This is no life for you.'

Matt smiled. A heavier breeze was blowing in from the sea now, and the clouds were drawing closer. Soon the rain would be upon them. 'I didn't realise the Firm was moving into pop psychology. Look, whatever it is you're after, I'm not interested. I've served my country, and I've got the scars to prove it. I look after myself these days.'

'Don't you want to know what it is, Matt?' There was a hint of humour in Abbott's voice, as if he was teasing him. 'At least hear what the job is.'

Matt leant back on his chair. There was something odd about Abbott's manner, something he couldn't quite place. He didn't have much experience of senior intelligence officers, but this was not how they usually appeared. Abbott was less smooth, and a lot more colourful. 'Let me ask you a question.'

'Fire away, old fruit.'

'What's the difference between the Firm and a whorehouse?'

'I think I've heard this one before,' said Abbott.

'I'll tell you,' continued Matt, ignoring him. 'In a whorehouse they take their clothes off before they fuck you.' He leant forward. 'Now, I can say it in Spanish, French, German, any damned language you like. I'm not interested. Understood?'

'OK,' snapped Abbott, 'play it your way, Browning. You got an office around here? Somewhere we can access the Internet? I want to show you something.'

Matt walked slowly back through the bar. It was filling up now, and he nodded to a couple of the regulars sitting down to dinner. One person said something, but Matt walked straight past. He was in no mood for talk. A feeling was already growing in the pit of his stomach: whatever Abbott had to show him, he wasn't going to like it.

The office was a simple annexe to the main kitchen, at the back of the building. Matt kept a desk, plus a swivel chair and a bunch of files. A Spanish accountant came in once a week to handle the books, and Janey, the manageress, did the rest of the paperwork. The papers spread across the desk were mostly architect's drawings for the new house. The computer Matt mainly used for checking his bank accounts and sending emails. He'd played the stock markets in the past but had given that up now. Like everyone else he knew, he'd lost too much money.

'This thing work?' said Abbott, pointing towards the computer.

Matt nodded.

'Switch it on, old fruit. You'll be wanting to check your bank accounts.'

Matt could feel his blood freezing. He leant across the desk, flicking the power switch on the Toshiba laptop. It took a moment to boot itself into life. Matt could hear Abbott breathing behind him, but he didn't want to look round, nor did he want to catch the man's eyes.

If the bastard's messed with my money, he'll be lucky to get out of here alive. The fish in the ocean could always use some fattening up. *There's plenty of spare meat on this guy.*

Matt clicked on to the web connection. 'How do you know I bank on the Internet?' he asked, without looking back at Abbott.

'Just open it.'

'You've looked already, haven't you?' Now Matt turned round to face Abbott. 'You've no bloody right.'

'Like I said, open it,' said Abbott carefully. 'You'll discover my position gives me the right to do anything I damn well please.'

The computer was humming into life. On the screen the HSBC logo was displayed. Matt keyed in his details, then the password. The account came on to the screen. Matt pressed on Statement, the command disappearing down the modem. Within seconds, the total was flashed up on the monitor.

Zero.

He pressed Refresh on the web browser. *Might as well make sure.*

Zero.

Matt drew a deep breath. He clicked on the statement. The last two transactions were the hundred euros he had taken out of the cash machine in town three days ago, and a cheque for £650 he'd sent off three days ago to settle his accountant's bill.

After that, the account just dropped from a balance of £12,287 to nothing. There was no explanation. Just an empty row of noughts.

'Check the other accounts,' said Abbott.

Matt remained silent. He had two other accounts at the bank, both of them accessible online: one was a deposit account where he was keeping some of his spare cash, earning a miserable couple of per cent interest a year. The other was a dealing account, where he'd put the bulk of his money into a series of rock-safe bond funds. It didn't earn much of a return, but at least it was still there. Until now.

'They're empty,' said Matt, not looking away from the screen.

'Empty as the jolly old Gobi Desert on a Sunday afternoon,' said Abbott. Matt could tell he was pleased with the stunt he'd just pulled. Now he was walking round to face Matt, and sitting on the edge of the desk. A small cloud of cigarette smoke was wafting above him.

'Great bunch of boys, al-Qaeda. Ever since the events of September 11, my lot have more power than we know what to do with. Want an account blocked anywhere in the world, you just put in a request and they do it faster than you can say Osama bin Laden. None of that boring old stuff about proving reasonable suspicion.' Abbott leant closer into Matt's face. 'The accounts get frozen, and your bank won't even tell you. Right now, you haven't a penny in the world, old fruit.'

Matt moved back in his chair. Sweat was starting to form on the back of his neck. He'd faced many different types of danger in his life, and most of them he could meet with equanimity. But he'd been born poor, and like many people who started with nothing, he feared going back to the gutter.

I've done my time there, and I don't want to repeat it.

'What do you want me to do?'

'Like I said, there's a job that needs doing. You're the right man for it.'

Matt stood up. He walked across to the window. The rain had moved in further from the coast, and was spitting against the bar. Penelope and Suzie had grabbed their wine bottle and rushed inside. The few customers at the Last Trumpet were huddling for shelter around the bar.

'I've been broke before, and survived,' said Matt. 'Money comes and goes. I've made it before, and can make it again. Doesn't matter how many times you block my account, you can't make me do something I don't want to.'

26

'You're not thinking straight, Matt.' Abbott nodded towards the window. 'It's not just about some money in an account. With just one phone call I can have you charged with murder. Oh, and that pretty little fiancée of yours. Gill. I reckon she must be an accessory to murder as well. At least.'

Matt stepped forward, the veins in his face bulging. 'I risked my life for my country on that job,' he said, his voice low, determined. 'I should have got a bloody medal. But I just wanted to be left alone to get on with the rest of my life.'

Abbott nodded, a smile creasing up his lips. 'Should have asked for the medal, old fruit,' he replied. 'Medals we can do. Glory and honour? That can all be arranged. We might even run up a statue if you ask nicely enough. But leaving people alone?' He shook his head. 'No, we can't do that.'

A fresh cigarette jabbed into his mouth, Abbott moved towards the open door. He pulled the collar of his linen jacket up around his neck to protect him from the rain, then looked back at Matt. 'So here's the deal. You be a good boy and do what we ask you to do. Then we'll unfreeze your accounts, and we'll make sure you get a pardon for any connection you might have had with any unpleasantness. Then again, you can turn me down. You're a free man, and I can't make you do anything you don't want to do. But your money will remain frozen, you'll be a penniless bankrupt, and you and Gill will be charged with murder.' He stepped out into the rain. 'Think it over, and let me know tomorrow.'

Matt turned round, sitting back down at the desk. Taking the mouse in his right hand, he clicked open his account again. Still zero. He clicked on to the other accounts. Zero.

It doesn't matter how many times you look at it. The number's always the same.

His fist smashed down on the side of the desk. The

computer shuddered as the force of the blow ricocheted through the machine, and a pair of folders fell to the floor. He wanted to run after Abbott, and beat some respect back into him. Abbott talked tough, but his flesh looked weak and flabby: a few hard blows would level up the score.

Get a grip, Matt commanded himself. Sure, you could probably kill the jerk with a pair of well-placed bare-knuckle jabs just below the temple. He'd seen it done, and he'd have no qualms about taking Abbott down. But it would make no difference. One Abbott would be followed by another, then another. The Firm had an endless supply of them.

No. If I'm going to fight my way out of this corner, I have to do it with my mind, not just my knuckles.

He stood up, and walked out of the office. Somewhere near the bar he could hear Gill calling for him, but he ignored her. Kicking away his shoes, he took the shirt from his back. Dressed only in his shorts, he jumped down the small, rocky pathway that led down from the restaurant to the sea.

The rain was beating fast against the beach as Matt climbed down. He could feel the tepid water seeping into his skin. *Maybe the storm will come down hard, and blow that bastard away.*

TWO

Matram placed the binoculars back in the glove compartment of his Lexus RX300. A slow smile drifted across his face as he put the windows back up and turned on the air conditioning. So far the mission was playing out perfectly.

The murder was as beautifully engineered as the car he was sitting in.

It was just after seven and the streets on the estate were empty. He had just watched Barry Legg walk out of his house and turn down the quiet road that stretched down past the local pub. It was a hot, steamy night - they were all hot and steamy this summer – and Legg looked slightly ridiculous wearing just shorts, dock shoes and a Liverpool FC football shirt: Steven Gerrard's, unless Matram was mistaken. Legg was alone, and apart from nodding to one man on the other side of the street, nobody seemed to have passed him on the way.

Matram checked his watch. Ten past six. Legg would be a few minutes early to watch his son.

Except he wasn't ever going to arrive.

'Target approaching,' he said into the hands-free mouthpiece he had hooked around his neck. 'Ready?'

'Affirmative,' replied Clipper.

The line was kept open. Matram watched as Legg rounded the corner. His pace was quickening as he stepped down from the main road on to the track that led towards the football pitches. Trench and Clipper started walking alongside him, Trench walking slightly ahead. As Matram watched them turn into the field, he took the car forward, turning the corner so he could keep them in sight. Both men were just ten yards away, out of sight of the houses.

'We're looking for the Fox & Hare,' he heard Trench say. 'Do you know which way?'

His tone was firm, noted Matram. Enough to stop a man and distract his attention, but not loud enough to provoke any suspicion. *Good training.*

'You've passed it,' said Legg. 'A hundred yards back down the lane. Turn right. You can't miss it.'

Matram rolled up his binoculars towards his eyes, and adjusted the focus. Legg was speaking to Trench, but his eyes were looking up towards Clipper. The man was standing with his legs a yard apart. His shoulders were rock steady, and his right arm twisted slightly forwards.

Legg's a military man, reflected Matram. Even a couple of years out of the army, he still recognised the position a man took up when he was about to shoot somebody.

'I've seen you before . . .' said Legg.

'Stand still,' barked Trench, pulling the Smith & Wesson Magnum Hunter pistol free from his jacket.

The Hunter had a ten-and-a-half-inch barrel, much longer than any normal pistol, giving the bullet extra velocity and impact: perfect for a job like this where speed and accuracy were a lot more important than trying to conceal a bulky weapon.

'. . . across the water,' said Legg.

Clipper also pulled his gun from his jacket. He fired first, then Trench, both men delivering two rounds of fire. Four bullets ripped into Legg's body, two blasting through his brain, two severing open his heart. He crumpled to the ground, dead.

Through his binoculars now, Matram watched the small trickle of blood seep out into pathway.

Trench walked towards the corpse. From his pocket, he

took a packet of Pampers baby wipes, and cleaned the traces of blood away from the grass. He stowed the wipe back in his pocket, hoisted the corpse over his shoulder, then walked back towards the car. Matram was waiting for them, the engine already running, and the body was laid in the back of the vehicle.

Matram gunned up the Lexus, and pulled away. By nightfall, the body would have been safely disposed of. His wife would have called the local police in a panic, but it would be a couple of days at least before they showed any interest in what had happened to him. Guys disappeared all the time, and usually they turned up a few days later with a terrible hangover; if the police started chasing all of them they wouldn't have any time to fill in forms.

Matram smiled to himself. By then, all traces of the execution would have been eliminated. The operation was a perfect ten.

One more off the list.

'What's got into you?' asked Gill.

The sentence was delivered in the same tone Matt had heard Gill use at the Dandelion nursery school in Puerto Banus where she worked every morning. Strict, insistent and determined: it worked on the three-year-olds, and it worked on Matt as well.

'You've been skulking in your kennel all day.'

A glass of Nestlé iced tea was sitting in front of him on the terrace of the Last Trumpet, but Matt had hardly touched it. The heatwave that had covered northern Europe over the past two weeks seemed finally to have hit southern Spain. The storms of the night had now blown through to the African coastline, leaving the skies completely clear. It was now almost noon, and the sun was starting to hit its peak. Sweat was forming on his brow, but it wasn't the weather that was responsible.

'I'm in trouble.'

He watched as her eyes sank. He'd seen that look before. A sudden resignation came over her, followed by a flash of anger. 'What is it?'

She sat down opposite him, her hands folded together, and her right index finger playing nervously with the single diamond placed at the centre of her gold engagement ring.

'What is it, Matt?' she repeated, her tone more insistent now.

'It's the Firm,' Matt answered. 'They want me to do a job.'

'No, Matt. You're through with all of that. We agreed.'

Matt paused. How should I tell her? He turned the question over in his mind, remaining silent, examining it from every angle. She's entitled to know the truth: he'd never believed in keeping any secrets from Gill, and anyway she'd always seen through him. But Abbott had threatened her with arrest. And there was no doubting his retaliation would be swift and vicious. The Firm didn't like being turned down.

I can't burden her with that. And whatever happens, my first duty is to protect her.

'It was that man in the bar last night,' persisted Gill. 'The one in the white suit.'

'His name's Guy Abbott. He's an officer with the Firm.'

'What does he want with you?'

'There's a job that needs doing. They reckon I'm the right man for it.'

'You're through with that, Matt,' repeated Gill. 'We agreed. No more missions. We're getting married, maybe having kids.' She paused, a trace of moisture already visible in her eyes. 'Making a life together.'

She's not going to like this.

'I know,' Matt started, his voice steely and grave. 'But there are debts, and now they're getting called in. One job, then he says the slate will be clean.'

Gill shook her head. 'No. We have plenty of money. We don't need them. Tell them to go screw themselves.'

'I already did.' Matt reached out to take Gill's hand. She drew it away. 'They've frozen all my accounts. We're broke.'

'They can't do that,' snapped Gill.

'They can, and they have.'

Gill turned away. 'We don't need the money. We're making money on the restaurant, I have my salary from Dandelion. We don't need to finish the house, it doesn't matter.' She turned to look at him again. The moisture in her eyes had turned into a tear now. 'We can sleep on the beach. So long as we have each other, that's what counts.'

I have to tell her, Matt decided. *There's no way she'll accept anything but the truth.*

'It's not just the money. That's the carrot. I do the job and I get our money back.'

'What's the stick?'

'They'll press charges,' said Matt. 'For murder.'

Gill paused. With her left hand she reached up to wipe away the tear trickling down the side of her cheek. 'It wasn't murder. Fight it. You have to prove your innocence.' She leant forward. 'We can't live like this. There'll be this job, then another one, and another one. You'll be working for the bloody SAS for ever. Until they slam the lid down on your coffin, drape a Union Jack over it, and give me a medal to pin up on the wall. I won't do it, Matt. We fight them here and now.'

'Don't be ridiculous,' snapped Matt. He could feel the temper rising within him, a snarling knot of anger that started in his stomach and worked its way up to his throat. 'It's not just about me. They'll arrest both of us. Don't you understand, they'll break us.' He stood up. 'Just one job. I'll go to London, see what it is, and I'll get guarantees that it's just this once. If it's too dangerous, I'll tell them to get stuffed.'

Gill turned away. Her cheeks were reddening, and she pushed her hair out of her face. 'I tell you, you go to London, and it's over between us.'

'Christ, Gill,' shouted Matt. 'Do you have any idea what they'll do to us? They'll throw us in jail, then arrange one of those convenient accidents so we never get out again. Let's play them along, and see if we can get out of this mess with our freedom, and our money still in the bank.'

Gill took two steps back, her expression a mixture of fear and defiance. 'You haven't changed, Matt,' she said softly. 'I thought I could settle you down, but I see now that I can't. There's always another job, another mission, another adventure. I thought you cared enough for me to give all of that up, but I was wrong. I don't think you can ever have a proper relationship, Matt. Because you'll never know how to put someone else first.'

She turned round, and started walking towards the house. 'I wanted to be your wife, Matt, not your widow. Now I don't want to be either.'

'So what do you the serve the gangster boys for lunch around here, old fruit?' Abbott sat down at the table, glancing through the menu. Matt sat down opposite him, his expression sullen.

'I was hoping for a slice of the old horse's head.' Abbott laughed to himself, and started taking off his jacket. 'But I suppose I'll have to settle for the club sandwich, and a glass of rosé. Don't think I can face the sausage and mash in this heat. But good to see you have all the local specialities.'

'We serve what our customers want,' said Matt irritably.

Abbott wiped his brow with his handkerchief. It looked as if the back of his neck, the only bit of skin he left exposed to the sun, was starting to burn. 'So, you want your money back?'

'Tell me the job, and I'll tell you the answer.'

Abbott took a single sheet of paper from the inside breast pocket of his jacket and handed it across to Matt. 'I've booked you on to the five past ten BA flight back to London tomorrow morning. You can meet me for lunch at my club the day afterwards. I'll tell you then.'

Matt nodded. 'Which club?'

'The Oxford & Cambridge, on the Mall,' said Abbott, taking a sip from the glass of rosé that had just been placed on his table. 'I'm sure you know it.'

THREE

The note felt flimsy in Matt's hands. A single sheet of blue writing paper, covered in a few lines of her familiar, rounded handwriting. Matt read it once, and was about to toss it towards the bin when he paused and read it again.

Dear Matt,
Go to London if you want to. I know you are doing what you think is right, but I also have to do what I think is right. I refuse to spend the rest of my life lying in bed alone at night terrified of what dangers you might be facing. If I'm going to lose you, I'd rather lose you now than later.
    I'm breaking off the engagement, for the last and final time. Don't try to contact me.
    Good luck.
    Love, Gill.

Matt looked over the apartment. It was the same bachelor pad he'd had on leaving the SAS three years ago. Although he had hardly noticed it happening, the place had been girled up: some small beige cushions seemed to be arranged across the sofa; on top of the TV there were pictures of Gill and him together; the bathroom had acquired a new mat; and the hi-fi seemed to have been pushed back into a corner where you could hardly find it.

He put the letter into the magazine rack – something else

that seemed to have turned up that Matt couldn't recall buying – and stepped outside. He still had an hour or so, before he had to be at the airport, and he wanted to check into the bar first. Maybe Gill would be there.

Even though it was just after eight in the morning, the sun was already rising in a smooth arc across the clear blue skies. Matt started walking the five hundred yards from the apartment block to the bar. He was carrying a small case with the few items of clothing he planned to take to London.

She'll be back, he told himself. We've argued before, split up before, and patched things up before. She flares up like a sergeant major, but it blows over soon enough. With any luck, the Firm will have a nice simple job, and we'll be back together in a couple of weeks.

Give her a few days and she'll cool off.

'Seen Gill?' he said to Janey as he stepped into the bar.

The manageress was a woman in her early forties, with streaked blonde hair, and a winning smile. Janey had run one of the best pubs in Chingford before splitting up with her husband, and moving out to the sun. There was very little she didn't know about running a bar. Matt relied on her completely.

'No. Trouble?'

Matt shook his head. 'Just wondering where she's got to.'

'Sorry. Someone was calling for you, though,' continued Janey, closing up the ledger where she had been recording last night's takings. 'Some lady who said she was calling on behalf of Sandy Blackman. Said it was urgent.'

Sandy? Matt turned the thought over in his mind.

In the Parachute Regiment, Sandy's husband, Ken Blackman, had been his closest friend. Matt had served alongside him for five years, before he'd left to join the SAS. Ken had done a couple more years in the forces before handing in his uniform. Then he'd gone back to

Derby where he was born, married his girlfriend Sandy and settled down. He'd been working as a truck driver, mostly hauling stuff up and down the M1 for Tesco. A couple of times he'd done long cross-Continent trips out to Spain, and about nine months ago he'd spent a night at the Last Trumpet. It had been a great session. About ten beers each, finished off with a bottle of port and a rough North African cigar. For a while they'd both been back in a windy, desolate barracks in Aldershot, wondering what they'd signed up for.

Whatever happens to you in life, nothing compares to the frozen, hungry, exhausted misery of your first few weeks in the army. The bonds you make in those few weeks are among the strongest of your life.

Last time he'd seen Sandy had been three years ago. At the christening of their first daughter, Jade. She'd be up and walking around by now, and so would the next one, Callum.

Why wouldn't Ken be calling himself?

He punched the numbers into the phone, looking out to sea as he waited for it to be answered. A man picked up the phone. A man he didn't recognise.

'Tell Sandy it's Matt on the phone,' he said. 'Matt Browning.'

'Haven't you heard what happened?'

Matt hesitated. He knew those words, he'd heard them often enough in the army.

'Look it up on the *Derby Evening Telegraph* website,' the man said.

The phone went dead. Matt checked his watch. Half an hour until he needed to be at the airport. He walked to the back office and fired up his computer. It took a few seconds on Google to find the site for the local paper. He clicked on the link, and watched as the front page of last night's paper downloaded itself. A one per cent hike in council tax, that was the day's news in Derby. That and the threat of some more redundancies at Rolls-Royce.

Maybe it was a few days ago? A crash, a fight? *What could Ken possibly do to get himself in the paper?*

He flicked back a couple of days. The announcement of a new ring road, some revelations about the business associates of the deputy council leader. No. Then, from three days ago, a picture flashed up at him. Ken. At its side, the headline was spelt out in 64-point black type: DERBY MAN IN HORROR KILLING SPREE.

Matt's finger stabbed on to the mouse, scrolling down the page to read the story.

Truck driver Ken Blackman, of Pride Park, Derby, went berserk today in a doctors' surgery, killing two people, injuring two others, then attempting to kill himself.

In a horrific shooting incident, Blackman shot Dorothy Houghton, 56, and Alan Miter, 24, both of whom were waiting for appointments at the surgery of Dr Rondy Toogut and Dr Marjorie Kent on Palmerston Road.

He injured Anthea Mills, 46, the receptionist at the surgery, who was shot in the leg, and Charles Bertram, 41, who was hit in the chest. Both victims are recovering in hospital, and are expected to be discharged in the next few days.

The incident happened just after 11 o'clock this morning at the Palmerston Road Medical Centre. Blackman had asked for an appointment with his GP, complaining that he was suffering from depression. His appointment with Dr Kent was delayed, and after ten minutes of additional waiting, he started shouting angrily at the receptionist. Then he pulled out a gun, and started firing at the other people in the waiting room, before turning the gun on himself.

David Holton, 29, who witnessed the incident, said: "It was just chaos. He started shooting randomly, and everyone started taking cover and trying to get out of the building. Then he just turned the gun on himself. He looked like a man possessed."

According to local police, Blackman is now in a secure room at the City General Hospital on Uttoxeter Road. His condition is described as critical but stable.

Blackman is 38, and a driver for the local haulage operator, E.H. Berris & Sons. An ex-serviceman, he is married with two children, and lives in the Pride Park district of the city. He has no criminal record. His wife could not be contacted today.

Matt leant back in his chair. A memory was playing through his mind. It was a couple of weeks after they'd joined the army, and both of them were just eighteen. Another new recruit, a Scottish kid called Ben, was finding it tough to cope with the daily hammering of military training. They all found it tough, but this boy was on the edge of a breakdown: he was sobbing in his bed every night, and couldn't even focus on getting his kit clean and straight. Matt noticed how Ken got up in the middle of the night and made sure Ben's uniform was straight and his boots polished so the sergeant major wouldn't give him a monstering in the morning. Ken never spoke to Ben or anyone else about it: he just occasionally went out of his way to make life more bearable for the other men.

Ken was one of the kindest, gentlest men you could ever meet. What could possibly make him do something like that?

The temperature in the foyer of the Oxford & Cambridge Club just off St James's in London's West End was surprisingly cool. He'd just worn chinos and a linen jacket – it was thirty-three degrees outside in the London traffic – but he'd stashed a tie in his pocket because he knew he needed one.

A gentle breeze was blowing in from the garden as Matt slipped the tie around his neck and knotted it. He could see the man at the desk casting a pair of disapproving eyes across him, but just turned back to the mirror to check his tie was straight.

Which college? Matt wondered to himself with a wry smile. *The college of getting shot at for your country.*

Abbott was already waiting for him in the restaurant, a bottle of white wine chilling in an ice bucket at his side. He looked down at the ground. 'Better keep your feet under the table, old fruit,' he said disapprovingly. 'The club recommends black brogues. And you're wearing brown.'

Matt looked down at his canvas shoes, then back up at Abbott. 'If they throw me out, we'll just have to go to the pub around the corner.'

Abbott smiled thinly. 'A glass?' he said, as Matt sat down next to him.

Matt shook his head.

When you're lunching with a rattlesnake, keep your head clear.

Abbott shrugged. 'I've already ordered your lunch,' he said. 'And a glass of Italian white. You don't have to drink it if you don't want to.'

'I can order my own food,' snapped Matt. 'Tie my own shoelaces, brush my own teeth, the works.'

'Of course you can, old fruit,' said Abbott, his eye following the hemline of a passing waitress. 'Just trying to hurry things along.'

'So what's the job?' said Matt.

Abbott paused while the waiter put a plate of baked salmon down before him. He picked up the fork and toyed with a mouthful of food. 'There's a company called Tocah Life Science,' he started. 'Big drugs company. They need some help. You know, wet work. I think you'd be just the man for the job, old fruit.'

Matt glanced down at his own food, a fillet steak served with chips. It was a while now since he'd attempted to make any money from playing the stock market, but he'd heard of Tocah – he'd even owned some of the stock for a few months, and it had been one of the few shares in his portfolio that had gone up rather than down. Set up by a Frenchman named Eduardo Lacrierre twenty years ago, it had been one of the big successes of the industry in the last two decades. It specialised in drugs for heart disease, and had grown dramatically. It wasn't quite in the league of GlaxoSmithKline or AstraZeneca, but getting close.

'They are a respectable pharmaceuticals company, with money to burn,' said Matt crisply. 'What do they need with me?'

'Counterfeits. An illegal trade in knock-off copies of some of their best-selling medicines. It's a big and very dangerous business. And they need it stopped at source. To go through all the retailers and stop it that way would take years.'

Matt chewed on a mouthful of steak. 'Real medicines with real ingredients, or just smarties with a different coating on them?'

'They're real all right,' said Abbott, refilling his glass of wine. 'That's what makes it such a clever racket. They steal the formulas for the drugs, then they copy them in some of the corners of the old Soviet Union where nobody minds too much what you do so long as you pay off the local mafia monkeys. Then they smuggle them into Western Europe. Some of these pills are charged at twenty or thirty quid a tablet, mostly paid for by the jolly old taxpayer. You don't need to be Einstein to run the maths on that.'

'And it costs Tocah a lot of money, right?'

Abbott smiled. 'That's what I like about you, Matt. You catch on quick.'

Matt could feel his heart thumping against his chest. *I'd forgotten what it's like to be patronised by the Ruperts.*

Abbott paused, taking a sip on his wine. 'A doctor writes out a prescription for one of Tocah's drugs, then the patient gets it filled out at the pharmacy, all as usual. The doctor is innocent, so is the pharmacist. Neither of them knows anything wrong is happening. But what has happened is that someone at the *wholesaler* has replaced the real drug with the fake one, and the gangsters are creaming off the profits. Like I said, it's clever, but it's dangerous as well. As you may imagine, pharmaceutical drugs are manufactured to exacting standards. The gangsters are using the same basic formula, but obviously they don't take the same care.' Abbott shook his head. 'People could die as a result of this.'

'You can save me the Tony Blair sanctimonious git of the year impression,' said Matt. 'What do you expect me to do about it?'

'Take out the factory.'

Matt looked down. He could see a trickle of blood oozing from the side of his steak. He speared the meat, holding it on his fork a few inches from his mouth.

'It's not a difficult mission, not for a man of your experience. Go in there. Blow it up. Run like hell.'

'Why me?'

Abbott shrugged. From the expression on his face, Matt judged the question bored him. 'Why not you?' he replied. 'Ex-regiment. There aren't so many of you around.'

'There's a few.'

'But they aren't all as good as you, old fruit,' said Abbott. He stood up briskly. 'Let's get coffee in the smoking room.'

Abbott threw his napkin down on the table, and started walking. Matt drained his glass of mineral water, and followed a few yards behind. The smoking room was just a few yards down a corridor that led away from the restaurant. A pair of men in their thirties were holding a discussion over

43

an open laptop, and one man in his sixties was reading a paper. Otherwise, the room was empty.

I don't get it, thought Matt to himself. *Something doesn't add up.*

Matt sat down. 'But if it's a simple job, for which I assume Tocah are willing to pay good money, then why not just ask around on the circuit. There's always a few ex-regiment guys around who are short of a few quid. I was in that boat myself a year ago. Why go to all the bother of leaning on me to do it?'

'Christ, Matt, because you owe us.' Abbott smiled, torching up a Dunhill and blowing the smoke into the air. 'You know how it is at the Firm. We like everything tied up.'

Matt looked out towards the garden. A sprinkler was spraying water on the lawn, trying to put some life back into it. 'Well, what's the Firm doing getting involved in an industrial security issue?' he asked, his tone harsh. 'Tocah are big boys. They can pay for their own muscle.'

'Times are changing, old fruit,' said Abbott, stretching out his legs on a footstool. 'The security services have to reinvent themselves along with everyone else. We're taking a broader view of our role. Tocah is an important investor in Britain, and these gangsters are damaging their business. So, we're helping them out. Strong companies equals strong economy equals strong nation. Simple as that.' Abbott sat forward. 'Look, it's a fair deal. You go in, knock out the factory. You get a team and weapons. Shouldn't take more than a month. Then we unfreeze your accounts, and delete what happened last year from the files.'

'And I'm just meant to trust you?' snapped Matt. 'Forget it. I need a guarantee.'

Abbott paused, stubbing out his cigarette in the ashtray. 'David Luttrell is authorising this mission. Personally.'

'David Luttrell? The head of the Firm?'

'I'll arrange for you to see him. You might not trust me, but you know you can trust him.'

'How soon?'

'Next couple of days,' said Abbott. 'I'll be in touch.' He stood up, and started to leave. 'You might like this,' he said, tossing a Waterstone's bag down on the sofa.

Matt picked up the book, glancing down at the title: a copy of Jeffrey Archer's prison diary.

'Thought you might like to get an idea of what life's like behind bars,' said Abbott.

The hospital car park was almost empty at this time of night. Matram checked his watch. Just after one fifteen in the morning. A nurse was walking back from a night shift towards a blue Vauxhall Corsa parked about thirty yards away. In the distance, he could see an ambulance unloading a patient into the accident and emergency unit. Otherwise the place was completely empty. *Perfect.*

'Ready?' he said.

Before him, Lena Kilander and Geoff Wetherell both nodded. Kilander was dressed as a nurse, in a starched white uniform, with plain nylon tights and flat black leather shoes. She had a folder under her arm: in any organisation, a person carrying papers always looks more official and is less likely to be stopped. Wetherell was kitted out as a consultant surgeon, with a grey suit covered by a white coat. Neither of them was carrying any medical equipment – not unless you counted the six-inch reinforced steel knives each had hidden next to their bodies.

A doctor-and-nurse team, reflected Matram. That was the advantage of having two women alongside the six men in the Increment. There were plenty of situations where a man and woman attracted a lot less attention than two men.

Nobody is threatened by a nice-looking young couple.

Matram handed across two NHS passes, both with fake names stamped on to them. 'These should get you through OK,' he said. 'The National Health has terrible security anyway, so you shouldn't have any trouble. Walk quickly. Wherever you are, so long as you walk quickly through the building, everyone will assume you're very important, so they won't challenge you.'

'Where's the target?' asked Wetherell.

'Second floor, intensive care unit,' said Matram. 'Private room. Turn left out of the lift, and it's about thirty yards. Room EH27. His name – Ken Blackman – should be on the medical charts.'

'If we're stopped?' said Kilander.

'Then use whatever force is necessary.'

Matram glanced back at Kilander. She was an attractive woman, with light freckles scattered over pale Celtic skin and black hair that she let grow to just below her shoulders. Her voice was soft and welcoming, keeping the ice within totally concealed. That was the way he liked women in the Increment to be: attractive enough to fit in, but not so pretty that men started staring at them, and with a manner that was easy and reassuring.

'He's on life support,' said Matram. 'Unconscious. And there's no guard. Disconnect the life-support machine, using your knives to cut the tubes. Then use a pillow to suffocate him just to make sure.'

'And leave the body behind?' asked Wetherell.

'It's a hospital,' said Matram tersely. 'They know what to do with a corpse. We'll meet back here in fifteen minutes, precisely.'

Matram stepped back, climbing back into his Lexus. He watched as his two operatives disappeared into the darkness. There were only eight lamps in the car park, and two of those were broken, leaving a murky, half-light spreading out over the tarmac. A few shadows were flickering out from the hospital building, but Kilander and Wetherell soon disappeared from view. Matram leant back in his car seat, and allowed himself a few moments of relaxation.

FOUR

Matt tossed the prison diary aside, stood up and took his bag from the rack at the top of his train carriage. Abbott could keep his book, and he could keep his job as well.

He hopped down on to the platform, walked quickly towards the taxi rank: might as well beat everyone else on the train to the queue. On the billboard outside the station, there was a headline about a road-rage incident on the M1.

Looks as if the heat is getting to everyone.

It was a ten-minute ride from the station to the hospital. As he stepped out of the car, Matt took a deep breath, preparing himself for the few minutes ahead.

He could remember one of the sergeants when he first joined the army warning him that one of the things a soldier had to get used to was the sight of their friends getting blown to pieces. They had to learn how to look at men laid up in hospital with horrible injuries and know how to shrug it aside.

But it doesn't matter how many times it happens. Every time you see one of your mates with a bullet through his head, it gets to you.

'I'm looking for Ken Blackman,' he told the receptionist, a black woman in her late thirties. 'Intensive care.'

He noticed the woman eyeing him suspiciously. The shooting had been a big story locally. No doubt all the staff knew the psycho was in the building, and were tiptoeing around him as if he was some kind of monster. The receptionist was clearly asking herself: *What kind of friends would he have?*

'Official or just visiting?'

'Just visiting.'

'You'll have to check with security when you reach the ward,' said the receptionist. 'They're not just letting anyone in to see *that* patient.'

He's not just some nutter, thought Matt as he walked away from the desk. *He was a good man, and he was my friend.*

There was nobody guarding the intensive care ward. Matt glanced down the corridor. There were twelve rooms, six on either side, each with a number stencilled on to it in faded grey lettering, and a small ten-square-inch glass window. There was no sign who might be inside. Matt glanced through the first window. An old man, with tubes hooked into his body. The second window, a young women, almost completely covered in bandages.

I need to see him. Doesn't matter whether he can speak to me or not. I just need to look into his eyes, and see if I can find any kind of clue there. Something drove him crazy, something weird and inexplicable.

'Who are you looking for?'

The nurse delivered the sentence sharply, as if there was no answer that would fall within her rule book. She was about thirty, with brown hair. Julie Smollett, it said on the label badge.

'Blackman,' said Matt. 'Ken Blackman.'

That look again, he noticed.

'And you are?'

'My name is Matt Browning.'

The nurse hesitated, running her eyes coolly up and down. 'Come with me,' she said.

Matt followed her towards the back of the corridor. The office was just a small room, painted pale grey, with a desk, and a kettle and collection of mugs. 'Ken Blackman died in the night,' she said. 'If he was a friend of yours, I'm sorry.'

The tone of her voice suggested she didn't mean it.

'What happened?'

Smollett looked down at her notes, as if she was searching for a phone number. 'He had serious injuries,' she said flatly. 'It was always touch and go whether he would pull through. He didn't.'

Matt leant over the desk, looking directly at her. 'No, what happened exactly?' he said. 'What was the cause of death? Blood clot, internal bleeding, heart failure?'

He could see the irritation in her eyes as she looked back at him. 'You'll have to talk to one of the doctors,' she said.

'Give me a name.'

A smile started to spread across her lips. 'I can't tell you that. You'll have to apply to one of the administrators.'

'Can I see the body?'

Smollett shook her head: he could tell she was starting to enjoy saying no to him. 'It's already been taken down to the mortuary,' she replied. 'Access restricted to next of kin.'

Matt turned round and started walking from the building.

My friend has died, and I haven't even been able to say goodbye.

Pride Park was on the outskirts of the city. A modern set of family houses, they ranged from the prosperous to the ragged. A couple of kids were kicking a football across the street, and some teenagers were gathering around the bus stop. As the taxi drew up outside the house, Matt could see the curtains were drawn in Number Sixteen and an officer was sitting in a panda car outside.

He had to ring the bell twice before the door was answered.

'Who are you?'

The man putting the question could have been sixty or more. His eyes were bloodshot, and his skin pale and grey. Matt felt he had seen him somewhere before but he couldn't quite place him: a relative he'd met at the christening, or someone who'd come to see Ken back when they were in the regular army together.

'Matt Browning. I was a friend of Ken's.'

As he stepped into the hallway, Matt felt bad he hadn't brought anything. No flowers, no cards. In his black jeans and blue polo shirt he was hardly even dressed for the occasion. 'I just wanted to see Sandy,' he continued. 'To say how sorry I am.'

'You were in the army with him, weren't you?'

Matt nodded. The old man broke into something approaching a smile. 'I'm Ken's dad, Barry,' he said. 'Maybe we met at the barracks once, back when he was in the forces? Come on through, we're just finalising arrangements for the funeral.'

Matt hesitated. 'But', he started, 'Ken died last night. Surely . . .?'

Barry looked back up at him. 'Not Ken. Sandy.'

'Sandy's dead?'

Barry nodded. 'Two days ago. Ken stabbed her the same day, before he went to the surgery. They didn't find the body until later.'

'I'm so sorry.'

Matt had used those words before, talking to the relatives of men who'd died in the regiment: each time he'd been struck by how little they measured up to the enormity of the sorrow he was confronting. But what else could you say? *The words just didn't exist.*

'Since you're here, come and get a cup of tea.'

Matt followed him towards the kitchen. The back door was open, and a pair of plastic chairs were sitting out on the patio that led into the small, ten-foot-by-eight garden. The woman was sitting alone, and Matt could only see the back of her head. Her long blonde hair was tied back in a ponytail, and her shoulders were slumped forward.

51

'This is Matt Browning,' said Barry towards the patio. 'He was a friend of Ken's in the army.'

The woman looked round. Eleanor, Ken's younger sister. Matt had met her once before, at the christening, but she looked different now. Her eyes were puffed and blotched with tears, and her skin was drawn with worry and exhaustion.

Matt stepped towards the patio, leaning against the spare chair. 'I went to the hospital because I wanted to see him,' he said softly. 'When I got there, they told me he'd died. I'm sorry.'

He could dimly recollect their conversation three years ago. He hadn't known anyone at the christening, and, it turned out, neither did she, apart from her own family. Eleanor was very different from Ken, the way siblings sometimes are: Matt remembered being struck by that at the time. A lot more academic than her brother, she had gone down to London to study psychology at Imperial College. Last time he met her, she had been completing a doctorate in mental illness. Where Ken was naturally cheerful and outgoing, his sister had struck him as intense, relying only on herself. They weren't close, Ken had said to him back when they were spending long nights together on guard duty. She was five years younger than him, and she was moving up in her own very different world.

But whenever he spoke of her, there was a tenderness in his voice.

Eleanor smiled, and for a brief moment the clouds around her eyes started to part. 'It's come as such as shock to us,' she said. 'The last few days have just been hell.'

Barry put the cup of tea down in front of him, and Matt sipped it gratefully, glad to have something to do with his hands. 'What happened to Ken?' said Matt. 'I just can't understand it.'

Eleanor looked up at him sharply. 'You mean the shootings. Or why Ken died?'

'Both.'

'Right now, I really can't imagine,' said Eleanor. She spoke quietly, but Matt could detect the steel in her voice. 'But I'm planning to find out.'

David Luttrell was shorter than Matt had expected. Only one official picture of the head of the Firm had been published in the papers, when he had been appointed to the post two years ago, and that suggested a man of at least six foot or more. In the flesh, Matt judged he was no more than five five, with a slim, wiry frame, and sleek grey hair that was combed away from the sharp, tanned contours of his face.

'Good to meet you, Mr Browning,' he said, looking up from the laptop on his desk. 'Do take a seat.'

The building was protected by a thick set of steel doors, for which Abbott needed three separate passwords to gain access. The room was pleasantly air conditioned, a rarity in a London town house. The Firm's main headquarters was a big modern building on the south side of Vauxhall Bridge. But a year ago, its most senior officials had decamped to a modest-looking Victorian house just across the river in Pimlico. The headquarters was too well known, and too vulnerable to a terrorist attack. A September 11–style attacker could almost certainly crash one of his jets into that building, and no one wanted to have to give the order to shoot down a passenger plane over central London. A determined terrorist could even shoot a missile into it from the river as the PIRA had tried to a few years earlier.

'I've looked at your file, and I'm impressed,' said Luttrell.

He stood up from his desk, and poured three glasses of iced still mineral water from the counter, handing one to both Matt and Abbott.

'You know a man called Ivan Rowe, don't you?'

Ivan, thought Matt. The ex-PIRA bomb-maker who'd

saved his life on the last mission. 'Yes,' he answered cautiously.

'Interesting fellow,' said Luttrell. 'Ever played him at bridge?'

Matt shook his head. 'No, not my game,' he answered. 'You?'

Luttrell laughed. 'Ivan was far too good a player for me. I sat in on a rubber or two with him once. Impressive. He was always several tricks ahead of the game.' Luttrell looked back down at the file on his desk. 'Ten years in the SAS, a Military Cross, recommendations for promotion,' he continued. 'You were a model soldier. You should be working for us, not running a bar out in Marbella.'

'I like the sunshine,' answered Matt crisply.

'I'd have thought you'd have seen enough of it by now.' Luttrell sat down. 'Abbott has a job for you, and tells me you need some persuading. What are your doubts? If I can, I'll try to allay them.'

'My doubts?' Matt laughed. 'I don't like being bullied and threatened.'

'Nature of the work, I'm afraid,' answered Luttrell. 'It's a bit like the press-gangs they used to have in Nelson's day. You'd be walking back from the pub a bit squiffy, you'd get a knock on the head, and you woke up to find yourself doing five years in His Majesty's Navy.' Luttrell chuckled. 'People think the world has changed, but the one lesson everyone in the military or intelligence trade learns pretty early on is that nothing really changes. They are still studying Alexander the Great's battles at Sandhurst because they are just as relevant as they have ever been. What worked for them, will work for us. And, the kind of work we do, if we sat around waiting for volunteers. . . well, you know what I mean.'

There was a feline subtlety to Luttrell's voice, Matt noticed. Nothing to suggest he was being deceitful or dishonest, but a playful, teasing quality that suggested he didn't mind stretching an idea when he needed to. From what Matt knew of his record, he'd served the intelligence services with distinction for thirty years, and he'd made his name as the Firm's senior officer in Belfast through the late eighties and early nineties. By reputation, he was a pretty straight guy, but nobody remained that straight while tip-toeing their way through the minefields of Belfast.

Luttrell leant forward, taking a sip on his mineral water. 'If you think you're being press-ganged, Mr Browning,' he said, 'I'm sorry.'

'You blocked my accounts.'

Luttrell laughed. 'Take it up with the Consumers' Association.'

'You're threatening me with murder charges.'

'You're guilty. Not that it makes any difference.' He sat back in his chair. 'Try to picture a series of rocks, all piled up on top of each other, with cement between them. A brick wall. That's what you're banging your head against.' He stood up, walking towards the window. A fierce midday sun was starting to beat down through the window. Luttrell pulled down the blind. 'Abbott wants you for this job. The Firm wants you for this job. I haven't agreed to see you to haggle. I'm not a negotiating man. I'm just here to confirm what Abbott has already told you.' He turned to face Matt directly, his eyes locking on to him. 'We're making you a fair offer. Take this job, the slate gets wiped clean. All debts are paid on both sides. You have my word on that.' He shrugged, walking back towards his desk. 'It's up to you, but if I were unlucky enough to find myself in your boots, I'd make that deal.'

'There's something I don't understand,' said Matt. 'What's the relationship with Tocah? What do they have that gets this kind of treatment?'

Luttrell smiled. 'Look up the trade statistics sometime,' he said. 'Pharmaceuticals and oil, our two biggest exports. The British economy depends on companies like these.'

The lamb dopiaza tasted good. It was just after nine, and Matt had hardly eaten all day. He shovelled the food on to his plate, mixed it up with some rice, dipped the edge of his nan bread into the sauce, and started eating.

Never try to make a decision on an empty stomach. The hunger stops you from thinking.

After the meeting with Luttrell, he'd taken the tube back to the flat he still owned near Holborn. Abbott had given him a grand in cash to cover him for day-to-day expenses. With his bank accounts frozen, it was impossible for him even to get fifty quid from the cashpoint, although he at least had transport – his Porsche Boxter was still safe in the underground garage.

The flat felt dingy. It had been three months since he'd last been back, and without anyone to clean it a thin layer of dust had started to spread itself across the few items of furniture. The post had piled up, but Matt didn't feel like opening any of it. What's the point? he asked himself. It will just be bills, and I don't have any money to pay them.

He checked the land line. Gill usually called his mobile but perhaps she would call him here if she just wanted to leave a message. 'You have one new message,' intoned the BT 1571 voice. Matt jabbed his finger down on the button, but it was only some prat trying to sell a new credit card. He put the phone down, disappointed, had a quick shower, then went round the corner to the local Indian.

It was several days now since he'd heard from Gill, he reflected as he ate his food. He took a sip on the bottle of Cobra. She'd thrown wobblies before. Was it possible that this time she meant it? *Can she really have left me?*

The trouble is, thought Matt, she doesn't understand how little choice I have. Her world is so different from mine. In my trade, there are no resignations.

Matt smiled as he tried to remember a line from an old Eagles song, something about being able to check out at any time but never being able to leave.

If I had other options, I'd take them. Sure, I could tell Abbott to get stuffed. All my money would disappear, and never be returned. Soon afterwards, I'd lose the house and the bar. Next, they'd arrest me and Gill for murder, and the trial would be about as fair as cup tie between Arsenal and Scunthorpe United. *If it ever came to a trial.*

Matt took another hit of the beer. No. If I don't want to do it, I'll have to run. Get out of town, change my name, my face, start over again somewhere else. It could be done. I've heard of men doing it and getting away with it. But how much of a life is that? No friends, no family, none of the old familiar surroundings. Just a life of constant shadows and threats. You could do it, if you had to, but that was no life for a man.

Right now, I'm clean out of choices. I'll do the job, and I'll get it over and done with. *There's nothing else I can do.*

Inside his pocket, his phone was ringing. Gill. She never goes this long without calling, no matter how bad the argument.

'Yes?' he said, snapping open the Nokia.

'Matt?'

Because he'd been expecting Gill, it took a moment to recognise the voice. Soft, with just enough traces of her Northern roots left in it to stop her from sounding too posh. 'Eleanor?'

'I need to speak to you.'

'I'm listening.'

'No, not on the phone.' She hesitated. 'Can you come and see me? Maybe tomorrow?'

Matt turned away to face the wall: he could already see a waiter glancing in his direction, and he wanted this conversation to remain private. 'What is it? Is everything OK?'

There was a shallow, mirthless laugh on the phone. 'You mean apart from my brother turning into a homicidal maniac, then killing himself?' She paused, and Matt caught the sense that she'd had to screw up her courage to make this call. 'There's just something I wanted to ask you, OK?'

'OK, I'll see you tomorrow,' said Matt.

He put down the phone, and picked up his fork. He took a mouthful of his curry, but found it hard to swallow. *Suddenly I'm not hungry any more.*

FIVE

The tower of glass, steel and chrome rose high into the sky. It was on the A4 heading out to Heathrow. The dazzling noon sun caught the side of the building, sending down shafts of brightly coloured, refracted light. As Matt stepped out of the taxi, he pulled his shades down close over his eyes, wiped a bead of sweat away from his brow, and stepped quickly towards the entrance.

Stay out in this heat for more than a few seconds and you start frying like a slice of bacon.

A blast of fresh air conditioning hit him in the face as he walked through the revolving glass doors. Briefly, he could feel his head spinning as the temperature plunged. He paused, recaptured his focus, then looked across to the receptionist.

'I'm here to see Mr Lacrierre,' he said. 'I have an appointment for twelve.'

The girl looked back up at him. 'And you are?'

'Browning,' he replied. 'Matt Browning.' He was dressed in cream chinos, a blue linen shirt and tasselled loafers. She had probably thought at first that Matt was just a delivery guy. Not a man with an appointment to see the chairman.

'Would you like to take a seat?'

Same as any organisation. When they know you're talking to the top guy, suddenly they treat you with respect.

He sat down on one of the black leather sofas that

stretched along the side of the foyer. Straight in front of him, a poster hit him in the eye. A group of smiling African, Chinese and European children were clustered in groups. Some text down below described how the company had been donating vaccines for children in developing countries as part of its social responsibility programme. TOCAH LIFE SCIENCES ran the slogan. BRINGING PEOPLE TOGETHER FOR A BETTER TOMORROW.

I reckon at this place a man has to eat his way through a plateful of corporate bullshit for breakfast every morning.

'Mr Browning?'

Matt looked up. She was a tall, striking woman, with auburn hair tumbling down the side of her face. Her cheekbones were high, and delicately sculpted, and her clear blue eyes shone out of her lightly-tanned face. *How many men fall in love with you every day?*

'I'm Natalie,' she said in a slight French accent, her lips pursing together elegantly as she spoke. 'One of the chairman's personal assistants.'

One of? There can't be many more like you.

Matt found it impossible not to follow the slow swaying of her hips as she led him into the lift. As the door closed, he caught the fragrance of her perfume drifting from her neck. On the tenth floor there was an additional layer of security. The lift stopped, and two guards steered you through a metal detector before catching another lift up to the top floors. One of the guards wanted to take the back off Matt's mobile phone, but he told him to hold on to it. He'd pick it up on the way out.

He stood to the back of the lift, admiring the curve of her arm as she pressed the button for the twelfth floor. 'Here,' said Natalie, as the doors slid open.

Lacrierre's suite of offices occupied the entire top floor of the building, looking out over London to the east, and Heathrow airport to the west. Matt could see the planes cruising low through the sky as they prepared to land, but the office had total soundproofing.

'The chairman will see you in about five minutes.'

The speaker this time was blonde, about six foot, wearing a red trouser suit, and with a harsh, metallic edge to her accent. Scandinavian, perhaps, reckoned Matt. Or one of the small Baltic states. Natalie seemed to have faded away, disappearing behind an oak writing table, where she was looking up at a black, flat-panel computer screen.

'Would you like to wait over here?' continued the blonde, pointing towards a tanned leather armchair. 'Can I get you a coffee?'

Matt nodded and sat down, casting his eyes over the collection of newspapers on the coffee table: the *FT*, *Wall Street Journal*, *Le Monde*, and the *New York Times*. Then he looked back towards the reception desk. Next to Natalie and the blonde, there was another girl, Chinese, tall and slim, wearing a white dress, and with a single gold and diamond necklace.

Christ. This guy's running a harem up here.

Matt had read through a collection of profiles of Lacrierre that morning. He was forty-seven and had set up Tocah twenty years earlier. It now had sales of twelve billion pounds a year, profits of two million, and the stock market valued the business at nearly thirty billion. Lacrierre still owned a third of the business. He was born in Lyons, an only child, and joined the French Army, then the elite First Paratroopers Marine Infantry Regiment, popularly known as the Marsouins: the unit specialised in beach assaults and was the most common recruiting ground for the French equivalent of the SAS.

But he served only six years, retiring when he was twenty-five to restart his career as a businessman. He made some money dabbling in property, then started Tocah in 1984, just as biotechnology was turning into a big business.

He had been married and divorced twice, had two children by the first wife, and one by the second. According to the papers, he was supposed to be dating a French singer, Nadine Riboud.

If I was Nadine, I'd be watching these secretaries.

'He'll see you now.'

The blonde led the way. Matt followed her through the short glass passageway that led towards the main office. The floor was covered in thick, black stone, and the walls were made from a translucent glass that gathered up light from the entire building. A pair of modern pictures hung on the back wall – maybe a Chagall, Matt couldn't be quite sure – flanking a desk constructed out of a sold granite plinth and a thin sheet of burnished aluminium. On top of it, there was a pair of black Bloomberg terminals, showing real-time share and currency prices from the financial markets.

Lacrierre stood up, walking briskly across to Matt. His handshake was firm: two decades after leaving the services, he still carried himself like a military man. He had thick, curly black hair, greying a touch around the edges, worn so that it was hanging just below the collar of his shirt. The accent was stranded somewhere between Washington and Paris, Matt noticed: mid-Atlantic, but a mix of French and American.

'I'm pleased to see you.'

A Rupert, or a Jean-Pierre, it makes no difference, thought Matt. *They're all the same.*

'You too,' said Matt.

Lacrierre gestured towards a pair of suede black sofas in the corner of the room. The centre of the office featured a clear square of glass, twelve feet by twelve, cut in the floor and replicated on each floor below. Looking down, you could see all twelve floors of the headquarters building spread out below you.

Good to be able to keep an eye on the ants.

'You are two years out of the regiment, yes?' said Lacrierre, pouring himself a glass of Vittel mineral water from the bottle on the coffee table between the two sofas.

Matt nodded.

'And you served tours in Bosnia, in Ulster and in South-East Asia. You must have seen many things. I should like to hear about them one day.'

Matt poured himself a glass of water. Moving from the heat of the day to the chill of an air-conditioned building had left his throat raw and dry. 'That's off-limits,' he said. 'Regiment rules. We don't talk about our work to outsiders.'

Lacrierre nodded, a smile spreading over his lips. 'I quite understand. Maybe when we get to know each other better.'

'Look, I'll be frank with you,' said Matt, leaning forward. 'I don't want to be here. The Firm are twisting my arm. You've got some kind of pull with them. I don't know what it is, but it must be bloody good, because I'm being hit hard. So here I am. I'll do the job, and I'll do it well. Then I'm out of here, OK.'

'I respect your honesty, Matt,' said Lacrierre. 'I'm a businessman, I have no time for flattery. As you come to know me, you'll learn the truth of that. But I suspect your view will soften as well. Maybe as you come to know me, I'll appear less of a monster.'

'Perhaps,' said Matt tersely. 'We'll see.'

Lacrierre leant forward. 'Come on, let's go and meet Orlena.'

'Who's that?'

Lacrierre stood up grinning. 'She's your new assistant,' he said, dropping a hint of mischief into his tone. 'And let me tell you, you're a luckier man than you probably appreciate.' He pressed a button on the top of the table. 'Send her in.'

As the door slid open, Orlena walked into the room with the kind of swagger Matt had rarely seen in a woman. At first he suspected she was just another of the painted airheads he'd seen staffing the reception desk, but a moment later he could see that was a mistake. She walked in not just as if she owned the place, he noticed, but as if she was about to order you from the premises as well.

'Shall I start?' she said glancing across to Lacrierre.

He looked across at Matt. 'Orlena started out in research. She did a doctorate in biochemistry at Kiev University, and joined Tocah five years ago as a research scientist. In the last year, she has switched to working on corporate security. The people we're up against are smart and sophisticated. It's no good just fighting them with muscle. We need brains as well. You two should make a good team.'

I might not want this job, but at least the view will be good.

At the press of the button, the monitors sprang to life. Matt settled back into his chair. Orlena had high cheek-bones, and thick black hair that was cut in a sharp, straight line just below the bottom of her slim neck: she had the classical, sculpted beauty of an Eastern European. Her skin was as white as snow, unmarked by a single blemish. Her lips were thick and red, a jagged line of crimson lipstick smeared across them. And her bright blue eyes lit up the room.

Belarus, realised Matt, looking at the map that had just appeared on the screens. The country was like a small rectangle, suddenly squashed out of shape. Matt knew its reputation from his time back in the regiment: the most criminal, lawless, vicious, chaotic and dangerous of all the former Soviet republics.

The Wild East. A bunch of mafia psychos, retired KGB officers and stray nukes.

'Belarus,' said Orlena, tapping at the monitor with a burgundy-varnished fingernail. 'One of the many republics

64

that broke away from Russia during the break-up of the Soviet Union.'

'We can skip the geography lesson,' said Matt.

Lacrierre glanced first at Matt, then at Orlena. 'He's a soldier, Orlena,' he said, his voice dropping to a low whisper that could not quite hide his irritation. 'From an elite regiment.'

Matt smiled. 'I know where Belarus is, and I also know that anyone who was thinking straight would keep well clear of it.'

Orlena turned back to the monitor, ignoring him and pressing a button on the desk. She was dressed in a thick black skirt that stopped just below her knee, and a crisp, starched white blouse that was buttoned up all the way to her neck. It was the most staid, businesslike outfit you could imagine. But somehow she managed to make it provocative.

A fresh series of images jumped on to the screen: a pile of brightly coloured pills, and a series of maps. 'In the last five years, Belarus has become the centre of the world trade in counterfeit medicines. When it was part of the Soviet Union, it was designated the hub of the pharmaceuticals industry under the old five-year plans. The result? There are lots of factories that can manufacture drugs to a reasonable standard. And there are lots of biochemists with time on their hands and no money.'

Matt admired the slender curve of her thigh as she swivelled to point at a different set of maps.

'A series of Tocah's most profitable heart-disease and cancer drugs have been targeted by the gangs. They know the formulas of our drugs, because we have to file them with the patent office. They can unlock the manufacturing process. They are using factories in Belarus to manufacture fake copies. Then they smuggle them into the West. They sell them to wholesalers, at a fraction of the real price, and they end up in the pharmacies. When you get your prescription filled, you don't know whether you are getting the real medicine or a fake. Tocah loses a sale, and the gangsters make huge profits.'

Lacrierre leant forward on the desk, looking directly at Matt. 'We estimate it's costing us a million a year, maybe a million and half, in lost profits.'

'So,' said Matt, 'what do you want me to do about it? 'I'm not a chemist.'

'But you are a soldier,' said Orlena.

'I believe Mr Luttrell has already told you we want you to take out the factory,' said Lacrierre. 'That's the only way of beating these people. It's no use talking to the politicians or the police in Belarus, they are all in the pay of the gangsters, as you know. The whole country is completely corrupt. So if we are to stop this, we need to stop it at source.'

'We need a small team of men,' says Orlena. 'I have contacts in Kiev who can put together some ex-Red Army men for back-up. But they need leadership, and military expertise. That's your job.'

Getting out of the bloody country alive, thought Matt. *That's my job.*

Up on the screen, Matt could see a large-scale photograph taken from the sky. It had been taken by a low-flying surveillance aircraft covering the territory at about 20,000 feet, he judged, working from the clarity of the picture. At this range, it showed a series of fields and some derelict buildings. Orlena gradually enlarged the photograph, sharpening its focus.

'This is the main factory,' said Orlena. 'It's about sixty kilometres north of Minsk, the capital of Belarus. The outside looks a mess, but the interior is in good working order. That's where the drugs are coming from. We need to get in, destroy it, then get out again.'

Lacrierre looked across at Matt. 'Money is no object,' he

said. 'You can have whatever equipment you need. Just tell us what you want, and Orlena will make sure you have it.'

'How well defended is it?' asked Matt.

Orlena shrugged, her hair flicking away from her shoulders as she did so. 'We've identified this as the source of the drugs, but we haven't done detailed surveillance yet. They'll be armed, we can be sure of that. And they'll fight.' She paused, a smile suddenly creasing up her thick red lips. It was the first Matt had seen. 'But you're ex-SAS, right? You can handle anybody.'

Matt pushed back his chair, standing up. He could feel both sets of eyes following him as he walked close to the screen, looking up at the picture. They had money, nobody could deny that. To take pictures this clear from the air required expensive kit: it must be at least ten million pixels per inch on the camera to stand this kind of enlargement. Back in the regiment, you were lucky if the Ruperts nipped round to Waterstone's to buy you a map.

There were two main buildings to the complex, one of them probably a factory, the other probably a warehouse and offices. He could see the blurred outline of two trucks moving down the track towards the gate: their images on the screen were grainy and indistinct, but he could still make out the heavy grey canvas stretched across its roof.

'When was this taken?'

Orlena glanced back at her computer. 'Twelve days ago.'

'What time?'

'Just after five,' she replied carefully, her tone suggesting she was not sure he was meant to be asking so many questions. 'Five twelve, to be precise.'

Matt rested his thumb over the two trucks. 'This isn't carrying cargo, it's men,' he said flatly. 'It's a cargo truck, but they've put some canvas over the frame so guys can sit in the back. Five is close to dusk. I reckon they bring in reinforcements every night to guard the place.' He looked back towards Orlena and Lacrierre. 'This place is well defended,' he said. 'I'm going to need help.'

Lacrierre spread the palms of his hands out across the table. 'I've said, you can have whatever you want.'

'No, not money, a man,' said Matt. 'I'll do it because I have to, but let's do it right. If we're going to blow this place up, we'll need explosives expertise. I know a guy who can help us.'

Matt could see a frown starting to crinkle up the skin of Lacrierre's perfectly moistured and manicured skin. 'No,' he said quietly. 'You're the only Westerner we want on this assignment. Everyone else you can hire locally. Orlena will help you.'

'No help, no mission,' snapped Matt. He walked away from the screen, and stood a few feet from Lacrierre. 'I don't know how you run this business, but in my line, it doesn't matter what kind of kit you have or how much money you have to splash around, it's the quality of the men on the ground that counts. So, either I get my guy, or you can find someone else to burn up your pills.'

Matt paused, watching the cloud drift across Lacrierre's eyes, then slowly lift. From his time as a bodyguard right after he got out of the SAS, he knew what a strange, isolated world the men who ran big companies lived in. They were surrounded by small armies of flunkies, who spent their entire day agreeing with every crazy whim the boss came up with. They were worse than generals: whole years could go by without anyone ever disagreeing with them.

There was a pause, but Matt couldn't read it. Then Lacrierre said: 'Who is he?'

They actually like it when someone stands up to them, noted Matt.

'Irish fellow,' says Matt. 'Called Ivan. He's blown up

more buildings than you've had croissants for breakfast. Don't worry, you'll like him.'

Lacrierre stood up. 'Orlena will check him out, but if it's all right with her then he's on the team.' He stopped, resting his hand on Matt's forearm. 'I've got a busy day, so I'm going to leave you and Orlena to sort out the details. Your friend will be paid, of course, and paid well. Tocah looks after its people.'

Matt nodded. 'In that case, we'll get along just fine.'

Lacrierre started to open the door, then looked back at Matt. 'I'm going to trust you on this, Matt,' he said. 'But I want you to know one thing. This organisation is not so different from your regiment. We are generous with our friends, but ruthless with our enemies.'

Matt could hear the door shutting behind him. He looked around to see Orlena sitting on the edge of the desk, tightening her skirt over her legs so that no knee was revealed. 'OK, when do we start?' he said.

'Right away, of course,' answered Orlena, sliding off the desk. 'We leave for Kiev the day after tomorrow. Once we're there, I can introduce you to the man who will start assembling the team. This factory needs to be dealt with as quickly as possible.'

Matt grinned, noticing for the first time the way her eyelashes flicked as she concentrated, and the way her skin bunched up around her cheeks as she smiled.

'I'll start packing. Let's hope it's a bit cooler in Kiev. I don't think I can take much more of this summer.'

Orlena stepped towards the door. 'Actually, the Ukraine has hot summers. Most Europeans think it snows all the time.'

'Don't worry,' said Matt. 'I can handle whatever heat you throw at me.'

Her expression changed. 'Let me get one thing straight. I never sleep with anyone who works for me. So don't even think about it.'

'I'm freelance,' said Matt coldly. 'I'm not working for you, and I'm not sleeping with you either.'

'You're a proud man, Mr Browning,' said Orlena, walking out into the brightly lit corridor.

SIX

The smell of old papers drifted from the room, mixing with the distinctive aroma of disinfectants and overboiled potatoes that filled the corridors. I can think of nicer places to work, thought Matt as he walked down the corridor of the Charing Cross Hospital. Each room was marked by a stencilled nameplate, and most seemed to be shut. For the twenty yards of corridor that stretched out in front of him, he couldn't see a single person.

'Hi,' said Matt, leaning against the doorway that led into her small, cramped office. 'You home?'

Eleanor looked round, pushing her hair back from her face. At her side, the pile of papers stacked up next to her laptop wobbled precariously, and her elbow only narrowly missed the coffee cup balanced next to it as she swung round in her swivel chair. Maybe it's her mind that's organised, thought Matt. *Something has to be.*

'Thanks for coming,' she said, standing up.

She looked different from the last time he'd seen her. The grief had drained out of her, replaced by an iron determination. She was wearing black slacks and a blue blouse, with just enough make-up to take away the rough edge of the morning.

'You wanted to talk,' said Matt, stepping inside.

'Not here,' said Eleanor. 'There's a coffee bar across the street.'

The Café Rouge on the Fulham Palace Road was almost

71

empty at this time of the morning. A waitress was sitting over a coffee in the corner, reading a magazine. Matt could see Eleanor was looking around, her eyes darting over the room, as if scanning for some hidden danger.

Whatever she wants to tell me, it's clearly rattled her.

'I'm sorry,' she said, taking the coffee the waitress put in front of her. 'I've been really on edge since Ken died.'

If my brother turned into a killer, I'd be more than on edge, thought Matt. I'd be over the side of the cliff by now. 'Tell me what you found out.'

Eleanor took a deep breath. 'I'm a psychologist, you know that,' she started. 'Research, in child development. But, you see, Ken was my brother. Something fucked up his brain, and it wasn't . . .' She looked up at Matt. 'Excuse my language.'

'I spent ten years in the British Army,' said Matt.

'That's why I wanted to speak to you. It's about the army.'

Matt took a sip on his coffee. 'You think that might have had something to do with what happened to Ken?'

That look again. As if she was frightened. 'When I got back to my office two days ago, I started checking the case files. That's one of the advantages of working in psycho-logical research. You can access the files on all kinds of different conditions. I wanted to find out if anyone had suffered anything similar to Ken, to see if that might provide some clues.'

'And?'

'There have been two other men who have killed people at random, and then tried to kill themselves. All in the last three weeks. All of them former soldiers.'

Matt took a moment for the information to settle in his mind. Three soldiers go crazy and start murdering people. *Could that be a coincidence?*

'The first one was a man called Sam Mentorn, living in

Shropshire. He'd been out of the Engineers Corps for two year, working for Orange fixing mobile-phone masts. He gets back to his house one day, and kills his wife and step-child. There had been no known history of psychological problems.'

'Soldier goes crazy,' said Matt, shrugging. 'It does happen, you know.'

'Right,' says Eleanor. 'I know the statistics. Ex-service-men are twice as prone to mental illness as the average for the population.'

'It's the food.'

Eleanor acknowledged his joke with a smile. 'Listen to the rest of the story,' she said. 'The second was a man called David Helton. He was in the Guards Regiment, but he'd been out for a year. He was working for an estate agent in Coventry. One afternoon, ten days ago, he went crazy at a shopping mall in Solihull. Started ramming people with his car. He killed two people and injured another six. Then he drove his car straight into a wall at high speed, killing himself instantly. Again, there was no history of mental illness with either Helton or any of his family.' She drained her cup of coffee. 'And then there was Ken. Three former soldiers, all in the same month. What do *you* think happened to them?'

'You're the psychologist.'

Eleanor shrugged. 'Well, it's not my area. Maybe it was something that happened to them in the army, some kind of post-combat stress disorder?' Her eyes fluttered up towards Matt. 'Is that possible?'

Matt paused before replying. He wanted to make sure he gave her answers as honest and truthful as possible. That was the least she deserved.

'It happens,' he replied. 'Any soldier who tells you he doesn't always carry the wounds around with him is lying. I have nightmares myself. Not every day, but two, maybe three times a week. Visions of the men who have died. It's the sounds that stay with you. When they know they're dying . . . they lie there in a ditch, the blood seeping out of them, and they weep for their mothers. Always the same, it's their mums they want. It's the most terrifying thing you could ever hear, and it stays with you always.'

'And that might have happened to these men?' asked Eleanor. 'A battlefield experience might have unhinged them?'

Matt shook at 'Many of the guys have those memories. They don't flip out and start shooting people.' He looked out to the queue of snarling, stationary traffic backing up along the Fulham Palace Road. 'Anyway, Ken did a couple of tours over the water, but just routine border patrols, no heavy stuff. His units didn't go to Bosnia, or any of those places. The most stressful thing that happened to him was getting balled out by the sergeant major for leaving his kit in a mess. No,' he continued, looking directly at Eleanor. 'I don't know what happened to those three men, but I doubt it was post-combat stress. It was something else, something we haven't thought of yet.'

Matt looked at Ivan as he put the pint of Guinness down on the table. The wounds, as far as he could tell, had completely healed. The hair was starting to grow back on the left side of his face where the bullet had impacted against him, and the scars it left were almost completely covered. 'You were ugly already,' said Matt. 'Can't say you look any worse.'

'At least I can drink again,' said Ivan, putting the glass to his lips. 'The doctors had me off the old stuff for six months.'

A former IRA man turned Firm informer, Matt hadn't wanted to have anything to do with him at first: he was the enemy, and he was a sarcastic bastard as well. But in the end it was to Ivan that he owed his life. There were several men in the regiment of whom that was also true, but outside there was just Ivan.

'Are you feeling OK?'

'Some headaches, but nothing strange about that. I'm probably just thinking too much.'

'You'd be the first Irishman to have that problem.' Matt took a sip on his orange juice: he'd be driving back to London later tonight, and he needed to keep a clear head. At the end of the last job, Ivan had taken his share of the money, and moved down to the south coast with his wife and two kids. He was living in a village in Dorset, in an old school that had been converted into a house. He had a new name, and a new life: a man of leisure and private means.

'A bit bored, if I'm being honest,' continued Ivan. 'I've been playing a fair bit of bridge, but there are no decent games to be had in England. Nobody's got the money to waste – or the brains. I flew out to Dubai last month for a week-long tournament. That's where all the best action is. It's only the Arabs that still take bridge seriously.'

'There's a job,' interrupted Matt. He knew better than to prevaricate with Ivan. Broaching the issue gently would be a waste of time. The man could see through any conversation like it was a sheet of glass. *That's what I like about him.*

Ivan laughed. 'It's your head that needs to be looked at, not mine.'

Matt took another sip of his drink, remaining silent. The pub was a couple of miles from Ivan's house, a quiet country place, with a faded red carpet and pictures of dogs and grouse on the walls. It was quiet this evening: a pair of old guys were chatting at the bar, and a couple were sitting near the entrance, more engrossed in each other than anything happening around them. They were far enough away for nobody to hear them.

'Jesus,' said Ivan slowly. 'You're serious.'

'Like I said, there's a job.'

'We're out of that game, Matt. I thought we agreed that after the last time. We set ourselves up with a nice pile of money, then we get on with the rest of our life. The biggest risk we're meant to be taking is crossing the road without waiting for the green man.'

'Things change, don't they?' said Matt. 'There's a job, and you'd be just right for it.'

Ivan grinned. 'Last time I worked with you, I got half my skull blown out.' He paused. 'There's something else, isn't there? Something you're not telling me?'

'They've come after me, Ivan, just like we always thought they would.'

Matt started to unravel the story: the meeting with Guy Abbott, the freezing of his account, the job for Tocah. 'So you see, it's not that easy,' he finished. 'Of course, I don't want to do the bloody job. Nobody would. They've taken all my money. If I don't do what they say, I'm going to lose everything.'

'And you think it will end here? One job and you'll be off the hook? They'll want this job, then another one.'

Matt stood up. 'You could be right,' he said. 'Believe me, if I had any other options I'd take them. But right now, I'm fresh out of choices. I risked my life for that money, and I plan to keep it.' He took his car keys from the table and turned towards the door. 'I don't really expect you to come along. Christ, if I were in your shoes, I wouldn't either. But the Firm aren't going to let it go, and you're the best man for this job.'

Ivan rose from his chair, and walked alongside Matt to the car park. 'Don't you get it, Matt? Once they've got you, they *never* let go.'

'You make your own choices,' said Matt, opening the door of his car. 'All I'm saying is I need somebody along on this job. Somebody I can trust.'

★

The flat felt stuffy and lifeless as Matt stepped through the door. The fierce heat of the day had collected in the walls of the building, and without any windows open the temperature stuck in the high twenties.

When this job is done, I'm getting back to the Spanish coast. I need some sea air.

The drive back from Dorset had taken him two hours. Another forty-eight hours, he would be on his way to the Ukraine. He needed some sleep. He checked the 1571 service on the phone. One message. Gill, he told himself. It's three days now since I spoke to her. *That woman can sulk, but her tempers rarely stretch past thirty or forty hours.*

He pressed one and listened to the message.

It took a moment before he recognised the voice: the muffled hysteria made it hard to make out exactly what she was saying.

'Matt, it's Eleanor here.' The voice broke up, and Matt could hear the sobbing on the line. 'Matt, I'm so angry. There isn't even going to be a proper funeral. We went to collect Ken's body from the hospital. But when we got there, he'd already been cremated. They said they were sorry, they had made a mistake, then they handed me this little pot of ashes.'

Another pause on the line, and Matt wondered if she might have ended the message there. Then it started up again. 'They burned him, Matt. Ken always wanted to be buried, I wanted to give him a proper funeral, but they took his body and they burned it. And all they could give me was this stupid little pot of fucking ashes. That's all I have left of him now.'

Matt put the phone down, and laid his head down on the pillow, not even bothering to take his clothes off.

SEVEN

The room was barren of any decoration or ornamentation. The walls were painted a faded, dingy magnolia, with a single tacky picture of a waterfall pinned above the simple wooden desk. There were two chairs, and a sofa that looked as if it had been picked up for a few pounds in a bankruptcy sale. An ashtray, unwashed, and with a pair of stale butts in it, was still sitting on the desk.

Corporations, intelligence agencies, armies, they're all the same, decided Matt. *They like to keep the dirty work off the premises.*

The office was part of an old warehouse building converted into a maze of tiny, serviced offices in one of the streets off Acton Green in west London: about half the rooms were empty, and the other half were occupied by web designers, sales companies, and businesses that looked as if they had no other role than printing up stationery and cards. It was only a few miles from the Tocah headquarters, but could have been in a different country. That building reeked of power, money and success. And this one? The only words you could put next to it were struggle, poverty and defeat.

'Did your friend say he'd do the job?' said Orlena. She sat down at the desk, opening a folder of papers. Her legs were crossed neatly, but her brown suede shoes were hanging off the end of her toes.

'No,' replied Matt. 'He told me to get stuffed.'

A look of pleasure swept across Orlena's face. 'Just as well.

I would prefer you were the only Westerner on this job.'

'He'll be along in a minute,' said Matt. 'He's a moody bugger. Says he won't do something, then he does.'

'Like a woman, perhaps?'

Matt grinned and glanced down at his watch. Eleven ten. True, Ivan had shown no interest in the job. Still, as Matt had left, he'd given him the address and time of the meeting with Orlena. In his gut, Matt felt that Ivan would be here.

Ivan's a bridge player, Matt reminded himself. That's all you need to know about the man. *Once the hand is dealt, he has to see how the tricks play out.*

'We should start,' said Orlena. 'I need to be back at Tocah by lunchtime, and our plane leaves tomorrow.'

'Two minutes,' said Matt.

He could see the irritation in the way Orlena knotted her eyebrows together. A forced smile stretched across her lips, but there was no mystery to what she was thinking: she doesn't want Ivan to be involved, and she doesn't mind if I know it. She was a woman used to getting her own way, and that applied to men in particular.

'No more,' snapped Orlena. 'There are plenty of explosives experts in the Ukraine. If not this man, another will do just as well.'

At the buzz on the intercom, Matt walked swiftly towards the door. Ivan stood in the hallway, casting a quizzical eye over the dimly lit corridor. 'I'd have thought Tocah could afford something better.'

'They can,' replied Matt grinning. 'This is just for the hired muscle. They like to keep us off the premises. In case we scare anyone.'

Ivan nodded. 'At least we'll feel at home.'

Orlena stepped forward and shook Ivan by the hand. He was a tall, thin man, with short black hair cropped close to his head. She let go of his hand, and walked around him, her eyes running across him as if he were a slab of meat lying on a butcher's counter. 'Matt says you're the best,' she said to Ivan, her expression questioning. 'At explosives, I mean.'

'I wouldn't say that,' said Ivan, sitting down on one of the two available chairs. 'There's better than me out there. But I know one end of a stick of Semtex from the other. And I used to work with an outfit across the water. They're out of business now, of course. But they used to know a bit about blowing things up.'

Orlena nodded, glancing up towards Matt. 'I don't think this will be acceptable to Mr Lacrierre,' she said. 'Tocah is one of the most respectable pharmaceuticals companies in the world. We can't be seen to be employing terrorists.'

'Ah well, we always thought of ourselves as freedom fighters.'

'If it ever came out that we had such a man on the payroll, the scandal would be too much.' She looked towards Ivan. 'Thank you for coming here today. But I'm afraid we can't use you.'

'Drop the corporate bollocks,' snapped Matt. 'If Lacrierre is so concerned about his bloody image, then tell him not to ask people to blow up factories. There's no nice way of doing it. Either we do this right, or we don't do it at all.'

Orlena glared up at him. 'I've already told you, we can find an explosives expert in Kiev.'

Matt stood up. 'Have you ever blown anything up?'

Orlena shook her head.

'Or taken part in any kind of military operation?'

Orlena's hair flicked down across her face as she shook her head again.

'Then you have no fucking idea what you're talking about,' growled Matt, his cheeks reddening with anger. 'So just try and use your bloody imagination. This might be a surprise to you, but bombs are bloody dangerous. You don't just want some tosser you met yesterday letting them off. You either get the right guy handling the fireworks, or you might as well start ordering the coffins. Clear? Either he comes, or we all go home. And I don't care what threats the Firm make. I can handle them.'

A silence hung between them. Orlena looked first at Ivan then at Matt, her lashes half covering her eyes. 'You can guarantee his role will never be revealed?'

'I'm not telling anyone,' said Ivan with a shrug.

'Neither am I,' said Matt.

'Then I suppose you're on the team,' said Orlena, collecting up her bag. 'We'll pay you five thousand pounds a day, cash, for your time, starting tomorrow. Plus expenses. I'll book you a ticket for the plane.' She walked towards the door. 'I'll see you both at the airport tomorrow.'

Matt took up the sheet of paper she had left behind her. They were catching the two-twenty BA flight from Heathrow to Kiev tomorrow. It was two hours later that far east, so the plane touched down at seven forty. She'd booked an apartment for them already.

The deal was set. There was no turning back now.

'Thanks,' said Matt, as Ivan started to walk away. 'I thought you'd come.'

'One piece of advice,' said Ivan, turning round to look at Matt. 'Don't sleep with her.'

Matt paused. 'I wasn't planning to,' he said. 'I just want to get out there, get the factory blown, and get back to my life.'

'She's trouble,' said Ivan. 'And the closer you get, the more trouble you'll be in.'

The car park at Brent Cross shopping centre in north London was crowded with early-evening shoppers, some of the women waddling back from the mall laden with bags, others struggling to find somewhere to park amid the sea of Mondeos and Astras.

Matram squeezed the Lexus into a spot, slammed the door shut, and looked out across the grey, stained concrete. Floor

Three, Zone W, he had told them to meet him at. He could see them now, a man and a women climbing out from a pale green Renault Clio. Andy Turnton, and Jackie Snaddon.

Two of my best. They won't let me down.

He nodded in their direction. Turnton and Snaddon walked across to the Lexus, while Matram spread a map out on the bonnet. They were in clear view, but he wasn't going to let that bother him. Car parks were a perfect venue, because you could guarantee that nobody would ever notice anything. *Too busy searching for their car.*

'The target's name is Ben Weston,' said Matram coldly. 'He works here as a night security guard. His shift starts at nine, and carries on to four in the morning. That's when the cleaners come in, and he and the night guards knock off.'

'Has he got a regular patrol?' asked Turnton.

Matram nodded, pointing down to the map. It showed the outlines of the mall, detailing the shops and corridors on each level. Weston was assigned to the third floor, with a stretch that ran between W.H. Smith and Marks & Spencer. There were eighteen night guards in total, but most evenings at least three of them called in sick. Mall guards were on minimum wage, and most a lot poorer than the robbers they were defending the mall from. Reliability couldn't be bought so cheaply.

'Use a knife,' said Matram. 'Any kind of noise is going to bring the whole troop of them down on you.'

'How tough is he?'

Matram glanced across at Snaddon. She was the plainer of the two women in the Increment. Her brown hair was cropped short, her hips were slightly too wide, and her legs slightly too short. But her eyes made up for it. They were clear, and bright green, and as hard as tiny pellets of granite.

'Not as tough as you, Jackie,' answered Matram, his face creasing into a rare smile. 'He never saw any real action. And he won't be expecting you.'

'And the body?' asked Turnton.

'When he's dead, carry it back to the boot of your car,' said Matram. 'I'll give you instructions on how to dispose of it later. I don't want traces left behind. And I don't want any corpses turning up later. Just a commonplace case of a man disappearing from the face of the earth, never to be seen again.'

Eleanor was stirring a single sachet of sugar into her latte. A bead of sweat was dripping from her brow: the temperature had hit forty during the day, and showed no sign of cooling off as the evening progressed. It was just after seven and the Starbucks on Southampton Row just around the corner from Matt's flat had emptied out. The office workers had all hit the pubs, and the tourists were back in their hotel rooms. Apart from one Japanese couple, the place was empty.

'Somebody killed him,' said Matt, opening the bottle of orange juice he'd just bought.

Eleanor looked back up at him. She looked even more determined. Matt had seen that look once or twice before in a woman and he had learnt to respect it: she had the appearance of someone who had set out her path, and was not about to stray from it.

'That's what you think?'

Matt shrugged. 'I think it looks suspicious.'

'No autopsy.'

Matt leant forward on the small wooden table. 'You think that might have revealed something?'

'I don't know,' she replied. 'All I know is that something happened to Ken. Something to make him go mad.'

'Did you get a chance to check out any of the other cases?'

'I've spent the day doing just that. I looked up what units they had served in and tried to get hold of their commanding officers. No luck. Both of them said they couldn't discuss that, and put the phone down on me.'

83

'That's the army for you,' said Matt. 'Never apologise, never explain, particularly with civilians.'

'Then I tried the GPs,' persisted Eleanor. 'I didn't expect the officers to tell me much, but I though the local doctors might know something. I tried Sam Mentorn's GP first, but the guy had only registered with the surgery, he had never actually been in for any treatment. She didn't know anything about him. Next I tried David Helton's GP. He'd been in for a foot injury about a year ago, but since then nothing. The doctor said he'd been in touch with the local police after the incident to see if he could help out with anything, but they didn't seem very interested. He didn't know of any similar episodes, and couldn't think of anything else he could help me with.' Eleanor looked up. 'All the doors are slamming shut in my face, Matt.'

'There's no evidence of a link,' said Matt. 'I mean, it could just be the hot weather. It's making me a bit crazy, that's for sure.'

'That's different,' replied Eleanor. 'Hot weather causes panic and anxiety attacks, particularly in people with high blood pressure. That's because of all the extra work the body has to do to stay cool. But there's quite a difference between an anxiety attack, and driving a car into a group of shoppers.' Her hand reached across the table. 'I'm sorry to do this to you, Matt, but you're the only person I know who's familiar with the military.'

Matt could feel her skin touching his. 'You want me to ask around?'

'Somebody, somewhere, must know something,' she said softly. 'If these incidents are linked, then we can't be the only people who've noticed.'

'I'll do what I can,' replied Matt. 'But I can't promise anything. Who knows, maybe it is just a coincidence?'

'Maybe,' said Eleanor, draining the last of her coffee. 'And maybe we'll put our minds at rest.'

EIGHT

The façade of the apartment building dated back to the nineteenth century, one of the magnificent old tsarist buildings that lined the main streets of Kiev. But inside, the apartment had been completely modernised. Its pale blue carpet looked as if it had never been stepped on, and the paintwork was unblemished.

'I've booked this place for as long as we might need it,' said Orlena as they stepped through the door. 'It'll be our base until the job is finished.'

Better than a barracks. We're going up in the world.

Matt had no idea what part of Kiev he might be in. Somewhere near the centre, judging by the ride into the town. They had touched down at Borispol airport ten minutes early after a smooth flight of just over three hours, and a car had been waiting to bring them into the city. Neither Matt nor Ivan had packed much gear. A spare pair of jeans, some shirts, and a leather jacket in case it was cooler in Kiev than it was in London.

Whatever kit we need for this job, we will source it locally.

'When do we start?' asked Matt.

'Tomorrow,' said Orlena. 'Tonight we sleep, then in the morning we get down to work.'

Matt checked out his bedroom. A small double bed, with a plain blue duvet, and a small lamp. There was nothing on the walls, and no books or magazines. We kip, we fight and then we go home.

'Time for a beer, though,' he said, stepping into the sitting room. 'Where can you get a drink around here?'

'Or a game of chess?' said Ivan.

Orlena looked at him with interest. 'You play?'

Ivan shrugged. 'If I was in Spain, I'd go to a bullfight, if I was in America I'd watch baseball. Chess is the national game, right? Ruslan Ponomariov beat Vasilly Ivanchuk to become the youngest FIDE world champion in history last year. He was just eighteen. So I'd say Kiev was the kind of place you might find a game of chess.'

'People think chess is a Russian game,' said Orlena. 'They're wrong. It's a Ukrainian game. All the best players are Ukrainian.' They stepped out into the street. It had just got dark, and only a few cars were making their way down the street: cheap twelve-year-old VWs and Toyotas mostly, broken up with the occasional gleaming new Mercedes.

'Bridge is a far superior game to chess, naturally,' said Ivan. 'People think of chess as an intellectual sport. They're wrong. You need to be good at maths, and have a lot of processing power, but that's about it. Not much in the way of guile, or cunning, or assessing your opponent. No emotional intelligence. That's why computers are good at chess.'

'Bridge?' snorted Orlena. 'A game for grannies. And for a few greasy Arabs.' She started walking more quickly down the street. 'Chess is the greatest intellectual pursuit man has ever devised. What was it Pascal once said? "Chess is the gymnasium of the mind."'

'No, no,' said Ivan, laughing. 'Chess is just chequers, with better PR. The only really great mind in chess was the 1920s world champion José Raúl Capablanca. "In order to improve your game, you must study the endgame." That was his great saying.' He turned towards Matt, his tone turning sly. 'Study the endgame. Good advice, don't you think?'

'Are we ever going to get a drink?' asked Matt.

Orlena looked at him. 'First we settle the argument, then we drink.'

Great, thought Matt. Stuck with a chess fanatic and a bridge fanatic. And Ivan seems to be getting pretty close to Orlena – too close, maybe, despite his misgivings. *Looks like a fun time ahead.*

Matram looked down at the body. Ben Weston was curled up like a baby, with his arms neatly folded around his chest, and his feet tucked up to his body. A thin line of blood stretched down from the incision cut carefully into his throat, but a scarf had been tightly tied around his neck to staunch the bleeding as much as possible, and his eyes had been closed. He looked at rest.

'A good kill,' he said, looking up towards Turnton and Snaddon.

Both soldiers remained silent. Matram always taught his assassins to say as little as possible, but he could see from their faces they were pleased with the compliment. He drove the Increment hard, and never hesitated to hand out punishments: always when they were merited, sometimes when they weren't, just to remind everyone who was the boss. Every man and woman in the unit had felt the force of his fist against their skin at some point during their tour of duty. Each of them had been threatened with a dishonourable discharge from the regiment. He had told them he would break their careers. But, when it was deserved, he liked to congratulate them on a job well done.

Soldiers are like dogs, Matram sometimes reflected. *You have to punish them hard, but it doesn't hurt to praise them occasionally as well. The tougher the punishment, the more they appreciate the praise.*

He reached down, holding the wrist of the corpse, just to make sure there was no pulse there. Then he shut the boot of the car. 'Packington landfill site, in Warwickshire, just south of Birmingham,' he said. 'You are to take the body there, and dump it.' He handed them two sheets of paper. 'These are Department of Environment passes. They get you through the guards at the site. They'll think you're there to check for methane emissions. They'll keep out of your way, and you just need to go down to the main dump and chuck the body in.'

Turnton and Snaddon took the passes, tucking them into their jacket pockets.

'Packington is the biggest landfill site in Europe,' continued Matram. 'Nobody will ever find a body there.'

'Who's next?' asked Turnton.

'Something more challenging, maybe?' said Snaddon, her hard green eyes shining brightly. 'These kills are practically civilians. There's nothing to get our teeth into.'

'Don't worry,' said Matram softly. 'I'll have some harder game for you to track down in the next few days.'

The mobile rang six times before Matt answered it. He rolled over in bed and picked up the Nokia. He glanced down at the Caller ID screen. Nothing. It didn't work in the Ukraine. No way of telling whether it was Gill finally calling or not.

'Matt, I'm sorry, I hope it's not too late there.'

He recognised the tone. Urgent, sometimes tearful, always tense.

'Eleanor.'

He sat up in bed, and rubbed the sleep from his eyes. They'd only been out for a couple of hours, hitting one bar for a beer, then grabbing a pizza at Vesuvio Pizza on Vulitsya Reytarska, one of the new American-style restaurants that had opened in the city in the past few years. Beer, food, and then bed. That would be the routine until they could get this mission behind them.

'Yes,' she replied. 'It's just that I couldn't think who else to call.'

'What's happened?'

'There's been another one.'

Matt rubbed the back of his palm across his forehead. Another one? Somehow he knew he didn't need to ask another *what*. 'Tell me about it.'

There was a pause on the line, enough time for Matt to form a picture of her in his mind. Sitting by the phone, alone, maybe in a dim light, with her hair tied up around her head, and that intense, determined expression written into the skin on her face. For a moment Matt wished he could be there next to her, able to reach out and put a comforting arm around her shoulders.

'A man called Simon Turnbull, down in Esher in Surrey,' she started, her voice gaining in strength as the sentences progressed. 'A year or so out of the forces. A paratrooper. He'd drifted from job to job since he got out, never settling down to anything, living in bedsits and hostels. He was working at Burger King, he'd been there about a month. He arrived at work yesterday morning, same as usual, worked for about an hour, then lost it.'

'What did he do?' asked Matt.

'Took one of the giant vats of fat they use to fry the chips in, and started throwing it over the staff and customers, causing horrible burns. He killed three people, including a child. Then he stood in the centre of the restaurant, poured the rest of the fat over himself and set himself alight.'

We flame-griddle our burgers, thought Matt, stopping himself from saying it when he realised how inappropriate the joke was.

'He went up like a bomb. Caused more damage, and badly injured one of the chefs. By the time they put the fire out, he was burnt to a cinder.'

'That makes four then,' said Matt. 'First two, then Ken, then this guy.'

89

'In a month, Matt,' said Eleanor, stressing the words. 'All ex-soldiers, all gone crazy.'

'Any link between Turnbull and the other guys?'

'I've got no idea, but I shouldn't think so. Burger King are playing down the whole incident. No surprise there. But so are the local police, apparently. The only reason it came through to the register of psychological incidents is because some of the families of the victims are being treated for post-traumatic stress.'

Matt looked around the room. It was completely silent, and outside the window he could just see the dim glow of a street lamp. 'Another soldier goes crazy, and nobody wants to investigate.'

'It's scary, Matt.'

'I'm going to ask around. If these are the four we know about, then, well, there may be more of them out there.' He put the phone down, then checked his watch. Almost one a.m., they had an early start in the morning. He rolled over and closed his eyes. He would try to sleep, but he knew that it would be tough. Too much was happening for his mind to switch itself off.

I can't see how the pieces fit together.

NINE

Sergei Malenkov was a broad man, with thick shoulders and a short, closely cropped beard that covered his chin and his neck. He was wearing dark canvas trousers and a long grey sweater, and was carrying a small black bag slung over his shoulder.

In the last twenty-four hours, Matt had noticed the streets were full of them. Hard, strong-looking men, drifting around the town, desperately poor, looking for any kind of work they could sign up for. You needed some weapons, you just had to ask.

Kiev was the crime world's car-boot sale.

More like a sailor than a soldier, reflected Matt as he shook the man by the hand. His skin had the tanned, deep grooves of someone who has spent years facing the winds and rains of the ocean, and his eyes had the brightness of a man who has spent a lot of his life peering out into the murky, foggy expanses of the sea.

'SAS,' he said, looking sharply at Matt.

Matt nodded. 'Ten years.'

'And your friend,' he said, glancing towards Ivan.

'A different kind of regiment,' answered Ivan. 'Republican Army, Ireland. I specialised in explosives.'

'And you?' said Matt.

He looked hard at the man, waiting for the answer. I'm going to put my life in this man's hands. *He better know how to handle himself.*

Malenkov looked towards Orlena, then back at Matt. 'Soviet Navy, then the Ukrainian Navy after the break-up. Marine amphibious assault units. I served for twenty years. My main posting was on board the *Hetman Petro Sahaydachny*. That's the flagship of the Ukrainian Navy. You probably haven't heard of the Cossack Hetman. He was the man who liberated the Ukraine in the seventeenth century. Our national hero.'

Orlena sat down, gesturing to the rest of them to take their seats. They were meeting in the apartment, at just after eight in the morning. Ivan put a jug of coffee between them. 'Sergei has been out of the navy for two years,' she said. 'Now he helps to provide security for Western companies investing in the region. Tell him what you need, he'll supply it.'

'Men and kit. Just give me the list,' said Malenkov, a broad grin on his face. 'The men will be cheap, and the weapons expensive, that's the way it is out here.'

'We've only seen some pictures from the sky,' said Matt.

'The surveillance plane tells you everything you need to know,' said Orlena sharply. 'We can plan the mission from that.'

Matt looked upwards, meeting her eyes. 'And how many jobs have you been on, exactly?'

A frosty expression descended on Orlena's face. 'Can we just get on with this?'

'I'll tell you what we're going to do,' answered Matt, controlling the irritation in his voice. 'I want Sergei here to come with me and Ivan, and I want to get up there and take a look at the factory. We don't attack anything until we've had a good hard look at it.'

He glanced sideways, first to Ivan, then to Malenkov. 'Right?'

Both men nodded.

'We can get the plane back,' said Orlena. 'It can be

arranged for later today if necessary. Just speak to the pilot. He'll get any photographs you want, any angle.'

'Nice idea,' said Ivan. 'A spotter plane swooping across the factory all afternoon. That's not going to alert anyone, is it?'

Matt tapped the side of his left eyeball. 'There's only one type of surveillance you need for this job. It's called going to have a bloody look. And we're going to do it tomorrow.'

At one a.m., alone in the small bedroom, Matt pressed the end-call button, killing the line. He paused, taking a sip of water before making the next call. Then he punched in the number. Right now, this was just like any military job. A lot of hanging around waiting for the action to start.

Four calls so far, yielding precisely nothing. *Nobody knows anything.*

'Keith there?' he said into the phone as soon as it was answered.

'Maybe,' replied a man with a West Country accent. 'Who's calling?'

'Matt. Matt Browning.'

In the distance, he could hear the man shouting, *phone, phone.* Keith Picton was an ex-regiment sergeant, now in his fifties, who ran an Outward Bound centre near Barnstaple in north Devon. Lots of ex-forces guys drifted through the place: there was always work there for fit young men who knew how to teach rock climbing or kayaking to a bunch of marketing executives from Staines. Picton took them all in, gave them somewhere to kip down, some food to eat, and paid them only a bit less than the minimum wage for the work. It was hard to tell sometimes if he was running a business, or a charity for old soldiers temporarily at a loose end. Doesn't matter, everyone agreed: he was a diamond, no matter how rough his manner, and everyone knew and respected him.

He's better plugged into the network than any man I know.

'Browning, you old bastard,' said Picton. 'What the hell are you up to now?'

'Same old stuff.'

'Really?' said Picton. 'I heard you were Mr Easy out in Marbella. Big pay day from some dodgy-sounding job for the Firm, nice place by the sea, gorgeous totty hanging off your arm, and about to ruin the whole marvellous thing by getting married to your childhood sweetheart.'

Even though I haven't spoken to him in more than a year he knows everything about me.

'Well, you know how it is, Keith. Roll the dice, and you go up a ladder. Roll it again, you go down a snake.'

'Right. How can I help?'

Matt was hoping this, his fifth call, would reveal something. He'd started out with a couple of the private security firms that operated out of London: they were always hiring guys out of the army, and had a good feel for what was going on. Nothing. Next he'd tried a friend who worked in recruitment, helping forces men find new jobs. He tried Bob Crowden, his first sergeant when he signed up more than a decade ago, and a man who kept in touch with all the men who'd passed through his barracks. Nothing there either.

So far as anyone knew, nothing suspicious was happening to ex-army men anywhere.

'I was just wondering if you'd heard anything, Keith,' started Matt. 'Stories about soldiers going crazy, injuring themselves or other people. Do you think there could be any connection? Anything out of the ordinary?'

'Like what?' Picton replied, eventually. 'A bloke running out on his family, or quitting his job, or getting into a fight after a skinful? Can you be more specific?'

'No, just acting weird. And violent.'

Another pause. 'Nothing that I've heard of,' said Picton,

sounding more definite. 'Tell you what, I'll ask around some of the lads in the centre. We hear anything, we'll let you know.'

'Thanks.'

'What's it about, Matt? Why do you want to know?'

'Just chasing down a theory for a friend,' said Matt. 'If you hear something, call me.'

'You ready?' shouted Orlena from down the hallway. 'The car's here.'

Matt slipped the phone into his pocket.

Nobody knows anything, he reflected as he slung his kitbag over his shoulder. *But maybe that's because there's nothing to know.*

The Land Rover must have been two decades old. One of the old models, Matt noted, back from when it was a military vehicle adapted for farmers, not a yuppie-mobile, running the kids to school and back. The paint looked as if it had been retouched a hundred times, with no thought for its appearance: it had turned the car into a patchwork of dark blues, greens, blacks, with the occasional dash of silver streaked along the underside to cover up spots of rust.

'British car,' said Malenkov approvingly. He slapped the bonnet as if he were patting a favourite horse. 'If you think the Ukrainian roads are bad, wait until you see Belorussia.' A laugh peeled out of his throat. 'You'll get a smoother ride in a washing machine.'

'You take the passenger seat,' said Matt, looking towards Orlena. 'Ivan and I can kip down in the back. We're used to it.'

He tossed his kitbag into the back of the car, and climbed aboard. There were no seats in the back, just an old mattress slung down on the metal surface. It was a long drive, and he knew he would have to make himself as comfortable as possible. Matt put his bag at the top of the mattress, lying down flat on his back, with his head resting on his kit. At his side, he could see Ivan doing the same.

'Funny smell,' said Matt, sitting up.

'Poppies,' said Ivan. 'I think they grow them in southern Ukraine, down near the Black Sea coast, around Odessa. Then process them into heroin. I reckon our friend Mr Malenkov is into lots of different businesses.'

The engine roared into life, shaking the Land Rover as it turned away from the kerb, and started speeding through the light mid-morning traffic in downtown Kiev. Matt had glanced at the map earlier, and had a rough idea of the route they would be taking. From Kiev, they would take the M20, cutting north, and crossing the border just before the steel-and-cement town of Gomel. Then they would turn west, on to the A250, keeping straight on to the road through Bobrujsk until they hit Minsk.

Motorway, thought Matt, some time later as he looked at the cracked surface of the single-tracked road. Even the Cromwell Road on a Friday afternoon was quicker than this. *And I thought that was about as bad as any road could get.*

'How long do you reckon?' he shouted through the glass that separated the back of the Land-Rover from the cabin.

'Ten hours, maybe fifteen,' shouted Malenkov over the roar of the engine.

'Let's stop for lunch,' shouted Ivan.

Orlena turned back to them and smiled. 'I'll see if I can find you some cabbage soup.'

Matt lay back on the mattress, and tried to shut his eyes. As the Land-Rover bounced along the pitted surface of the road, he could feel every vibration and bump knocking right through his spine. Horrible food, funny smells, brutal transport and constant danger. *Welcome back to soldiering, mate.*

The forest was dark and edgy, thick with the smell of pine needles. Matt lay down on the ground, feeling the damp

96

moss close to his skin. Behind him he could hear the low whistling of the breeze rustling through the trees. Up ahead, he could hear the low, sneezy rumble of plant and machinery humming through the night.

'What can you see?' he whispered to Ivan.

'Bugger all.'

It had been a long and tiring drive. Matt had slept fitfully, woken up first for lunch, then for supper: both meals were taken at simple roadside cafés serving cabbage soup and sausages to the truckers who worked the highways between the two cities. Neither Matt nor Ivan spoke while they were eating. They were dressed in some cheap jeans and sweat-shirts Orlena had picked up for them at a market in Kiev: Levi's or even Gap jeans would mark you out as a foreigner here. There was no point in alerting anyone that they were neither Ukrainian nor Belorussian. Along these back roads a foreigner was a rare sight, and would immediately provoke suspicion.

They had stopped briefly at the border. Neither of them had visas for Belarus, but that didn't seem to be an issue. Malenkov had dropped twenty dollars into the palm of the guard, and that whisked them through. By nightfall, they had bypassed Minsk, and made their way north towards Khatyn. The forest was just to the north of the city. A dense thicket of woodland, mostly pine, it covered about fifty square miles, dotted with just a few factories and some logging stations and tiny villages. By the time they arrived, it was already after ten at night.

We'll go and check out the target, Malenkov had suggested. Then get some rest.

'Let's get closer,' whispered Matt.

They had parked the Land-Rover half a mile back, snaking through the forest on foot. Right now, they were five hundred yards from the factory.

Matt started wriggling along the dirt track that ran between the trees. They hadn't seen anyone along the track for the past three hours. The factory was about three hundred yards ahead of them, and the main tarmac road leading up to it eighty yards to their left. The compound covered some four hundred square yards in total, protected with a high fence of barbed wire, reinforced with a strong steel mesh. There was just one set of gates, firmly locked, and protected with what looked like just one sentry. Matt moved slowly around the perimeter to get a better look. At two of the corners of the compound, there was a searchlight built on to a twelve-foot high wooden platform. The light swivelled around, in a slow semicircular arc, flashing its beam along the perimeter of the fence: Ivan timed the motion, calculating it took forty-five seconds to complete an arc, leaving at least fifteen seconds when it was safe to move underneath it. So far as Matt could see, there was one guard operating each light.

He pulled out the pair of binoculars Malenkov had given him and, through the magnified circle of vision, he could see that the two guards were carrying what looked like semi-automatic machine guns. At these distances, he couldn't tell the make or calibre. Kalashnikovs probably. No reason why they wouldn't use the local kit. It's not as if they don't make good guns in this part of the world.

Matt put down the binoculars. *The place is heavily guarded.*

'That's a ditch, isn't it?' said Ivan, pointing to the perimeter of the fence.

Matt nodded. 'Standard defensive procedure. A deep ditch and a high fence is the hardest combination of obstacles to get past. You get trapped in the ditch, then you have to scale the fence. Gives the guy inside a lot of time to pick off the attackers one by one. People have been building military encampments like that since time began.'

Ivan looked ahead. There was just a quarter of a moon

struggling to break through the low-hanging clouds, and he was struggling to adjust his eyes to the murky light. 'I thought it was a factory. Not a military base. . . Maybe they've got something to hide.'

'We'll worry about that when we get inside,' said Matt. He looked towards Malenkov. 'Is it possible to get a better look at the back?'

The Ukrainian led the way. There was a clearing of about forty yards at the front of the compound – enough space, Matt noticed, for the guards to get a good clean shot at anybody who came rushing out of the forest. At the perimeter, there was a short stretch of scrub and bush, then the trees started to grow thickly. Within another twenty yards, you were into thick forest, the trees growing close together in a thick mass of vegetation. The four of them started crawling through the undergrowth, Malenkov leading the way.

That's the weakness, decided Matt. *They are surrounded by covered, not open, ground.*

He paused. They'd crawled towards the back of the compound now. The searchlights were brushing against the edge of the forest, the occasional stray shaft of light breaking through the leaves. In the distance, he could hear some animals moving through the woods: deer, perhaps, or some kind of wild boar. Nothing dangerous. He looked up ahead. At this point, the distance between the wood and the fence narrowed to no more than ten yards. It looked as if they hadn't cut the grass for a few weeks, and the weeds and bushes were starting to grow tall and strong. There was additional cover here if you wanted to rush the compound from behind.

'How many men do you think are inside?' Matt whispered to Malenkov.

'Can't say from here. Could be a dozen, could be more,' he replied. 'We'll stay here a while and see when they change the shift.'

Matt turned round to look at the others. 'Right,' he said. 'After that, get some rest. We can draw up our plan once we know.'

It was no more than a shack. A one-storey building with a flat roof, it was another fifteen-mile drive from the factory, this time to the east of Khatyn. They turned down a side road from the main highway, then turned right on to a dirt track that led through some cornfields. Probably a farmhouse, thought Matt as he glanced across at the building: there was enough space for one family, and a few animals, but it had long since been abandoned.

Malenkov had arranged the accommodation, and, as Matt had expected, he was a man who travelled budget class. The door creaked as he pushed it aside. The scent of dried-out rotting wood hit Matt's nostrils, and as he took his first breath he could feel the dust filtering into his lungs.

There was no electricity. Malenkov strode across the floor using his torch, lighting a kerosene lamp, hanging it from a hook in the centre of the ceiling.

'Home, sweet home,' said Ivan, glancing around the main room.

'It'll do,' said Matt gruffly.

Malenkov walked across to the cooking area: an empty fire, with a pot hanging above it, and a single gas ring attached to a canister by a short plastic tube. From the cupboard, he took out four stained china mugs, and from his pocket a bottle of Ukrainian Zhitomirska vodka. He pulled the top off the distinctive red-and-black bottle, decorated with a picture of a Cossack horseman. 'A drink,' he said, handing a cup first to Orlena, then to Matt and Ivan. 'This will get the damp out of our bones.'

Matt took the cup, closed his eyes briefly, then slung the pale, clean liquid into the back of his throat. It tasted hot and sticky and, as the alcohol hit his bloodstream, he could feel his muscles starting to unwind. It was as hot here in Belarus as it had been back in London and Spain: it was in the thirties all through the day, and even at night the temperature didn't seem to drop below twenty-two or twenty-three degrees. The air was thick with humidity, and Matt could feel the sweat seeping through on to his clothes after a night of crawling through open woodland.

'To the mission,' said Malenkov, raising his cracked cup. 'Whatever the hell it is.'

Matt, held his own cup up. 'And to getting home again.'

Malenkov poured a fresh hit of vodka into Matt's cup. 'Now we rest,' he said. 'There are some bedrooms down the corridor. Not luxurious, but they will do. In the morning we start planning our assault.'

'Fine,' said Ivan. 'The sooner we start, the sooner we finish.'

Malenkov grinned, revealing a set of perfect white teeth. 'Soldiers,' he said. 'It makes no difference which country we are from or whether we are fighting for a government or a corporation. We put our lives on the line, and we are never happy about it. We moan and complain, but we finish the job, or die trying. Isn't that right?'

'I can drink to that,' said Matt.

He threw the rest of the vodka down his throat, then followed Orlena as she stepped down the corridor. It was already past two a.m., and they needed to sleep: tomorrow could be a long and dangerous day. They needed all the rest they could get.

'Four rooms to sleep in,' said Orlena, pointing to the two different sides of the building. 'Ivan, Sergei, you take those two. Matt, you're on the other side.'

He walked towards the room. There was no lamp, but enough moonlight was seeping through the open window for him to make out the contours of the room. The bed was no more than a mattress on the floor, supported by what looked like wooden planks. He sniffed. The room had a dusty feel to it, and in the winter it was probably damp, but right now it seemed dry and clean.

He unfolded the sleeping bag that was perched on the bottom of the bed, pulled off his clothes, and shuffled inside the bag. There was no pillow, so he took his towel from his kitbag and put that under his head. As he started to rest, he could feel a wave of exhaustion starting to roll through him.

Suddenly he sat up. Something was moving. He opened his eyes, his forearm reaching forward. Orlena pressed a finger against his lips. 'Don't speak,' she whispered. 'You'll wake the others.'

She was still wearing the tight, low-slung blue jeans she had been wearing all day. Her finger moved down from his lips, tickling through the hairs on his chest. He could feel her breath, hot and fevered, on his skin. Reaching out, Matt slid his arms around her waist, pulling her body closer to his. He kissed her lips, tasting her lipstick, and the vodka still fresh on her tongue.

Whether he was more surprised by her arrival in his bed, or his own eagerness to take her, Matt couldn't tell. Moving his hands down the length of her body, he started to unbuckle her jeans, unpeeling the trouser legs. She giggled as the buckle scratched against her stomach, then pushed him down on his back, kneading his shoulders and his chest. He could feel his skin tensing as her fingers massaged the nerve endings.

Matt reached up, starting to unclip the back of her bra, and lift her T-shirt free from her shoulders.

'No,' said Orlena. 'We fuck the way I want to, or not at all.'

It was smooth and swift. Orlena steered him expertly towards her own pleasure. Sweat was dripping down the back of her spine, and Matt could feel himself perspiring as they both hit a rough climax. The pleasure, he reflected as she started to subside, was all the greater for being so completely unexpected.

Only when they had finished, did she finally take off her T-shirt and bra, freeing a pair of subtle, delicate breasts. Naked, she was a vision of sculpted loveliness. Some girls look better with their clothes off, others worse, Matt reflected. Some used their clothes and make-up to flatter bodies that were flabby and weak. Others used their clothes to conceal the perfection that lay underneath.

No question which category Orlena comes into.

'I thought you didn't want to sleep with me,' said Orlena, nuzzling her face into his chest as they lay together on the flimsy mattress.

Matt smiled. 'I lied.'

'What else have you lied about?'

'Nothing.' Matt rubbed his tongue across her breasts. 'What have *you* lied about?'

Orlena rolled over. 'Wait and see.'

TEN

When he woke up in the morning, she was already gone. Matt's final memory before he went to sleep was of her resting in his arm, her lips pressed against his chest. As soon as he awoke, he reached out for her, but there was nothing there.

She's not the kind of girl who hangs around to make you a nice cup of tea and a boiled egg in the morning.

Matt walked through to the main room. It was light already, the sky fiercely blue, and the sun streaming through the open doorways. A pot of coffee was steaming on the gas ring, and Ivan and Malenkov had clearly been up a while. A chessboard was spread out between them, and Ivan was pondering his next move, a look of intense concentration on his face.

Matt poured some coffee, swilling it down the back of his throat, then refilling his cup. It was the same mug that had been filled with vodka the night before, and traces of the alcohol mixed with the caffeine to bring him sharply awake.

'Where's Orlena?' he asked as he sat down.

'Gone to get some breakfast,' said Malenkov.

'Maybe she's more domesticated than she looks,' said Ivan.

'Women working like that,' said Malenkov. 'It would never have happened in the old days, I tell you. Women knew their place.'

'The sisterhood never really got its act together in the old Soviet Republic, did it?' said Ivan, grinning.

Malenkov snorted and moved his castle four places forward on the chessboard. 'Your move,' he said, looking back up at Ivan.

Orlena stepped back through the door. She had changed into a black skirt, and a pale grey blouse. She glanced at Matt, smiled knowingly for the briefest fraction of a second, then looked away. In her arms, she was carrying two loaves of thick, black bread, a block of soft cheese and some pickled cucumbers. 'Breakfast,' she said brightly. 'We eat. Then we work.'

Matt tore himself a hunk of the black bread. It was chewy, with a taste of rye and traces of the beer that was used to help bake it. The cheese was ripe, and even the pickled cucumbers didn't taste as bad as he'd expected. Washed down with some more coffee, the food was building up his strength again.

'So how are we going to take out the factory?' asked Orlena.

Matt took out a large sheet of paper and a felt pen, drawing out a rough map of the compound. 'Do we know yet how many men are defending it?' he asked, looking towards Malenkov.

'A dozen,' said the Ukrainian. 'I counted them last night.'

'We need to know what their shifts are. How many are on guard duty at different times of the night. Which of them are vigilant, and which of them are just sitting around picking their noses. All that,' said Ivan.

Malenkov nodded.

'And we need to know how long we have to escape,' said Matt. 'How close are the nearest police and army units? Do they have choppers? How quickly can they get to the factory once the alarm goes off? We don't want to be standing there when the local police turn up.' He glanced at Malenkov. 'About three men should be enough, plus the three of us. First, Ivan. We need some loud bangs, enough to distract everyone, and also to cause plenty of havoc and destruction. Then we'll need some more to blow the whole thing to hell at the end. Think you can manage that?'

Ivan grinned. 'Bombs I know about.'

'Malenkov, you can get your men to us by three this afternoon?'

The Ukrainian smiled. 'They'll be here,' he said. 'Three boys, all ex-army. They'll be good men, don't worry. Brave and hungry, which is the way a soldier should be.'

Matt jabbed his finger down on the map. 'OK, here's what we do. There's a manhole cover outside the compound, and another one just inside. I reckon there's some kind of drainage tunnel taking waste from the factory down to the river, which according to our maps is two miles to the west. Tonight, after dark, we get down into that tunnel and make sure we can get through it. Then we'll leave a guard overnight, just to make sure it hasn't been compromised. Ivan makes us a set of bombs. We sneak two men inside, and place the devices around the main factory. That blows the place up to the sky. The rest of us can move in, and finish off whoever is left, and secure the main administrative building. Once we've finished everyone off inside the building, then we can take that down as well.'

'How about casualties?' asked Ivan. 'Are we bothered about killing these guys?'

Matt paused. As usual, Ivan got straight to the point: that issue had been troubling him as well. 'The factory should be empty at night bar the guards. When it goes off, they can all run away into the woods if they want to. If they stay and fight, they'll have to take their chances. Besides, they look like trained soldiers.'

He looked up towards Malenkov. 'What kind of weapons

can you get us?' he asked. 'AK–47s? There must be plenty of those around this part of the world.'

'There are,' replied Malenkov. 'But I can get hold of some of the newer AN–49s.'

'I've heard of them, but I've never tried one.'

'Nice piece of machinery. It was adopted by the Russian Army as the standard-issue assault rifle in 1994, although they never had enough money to get rid of all their old AKs.

'What's the difference with the AK–47?' asked Ivan.

'A much faster rate of fire,' said Malenkov. 'And much greater accuracy. The recoil has been completely redesigned, so the gun hits back after the bullet has left the chamber. That allows for a far greater hit rate. Don't worry, you'll like it. It's a fine gun.'

'What about the sights?' asked Matt. 'We may be picking targets off from distance.'

'It's got a proper rear-mounted peep sight. Not the old notch and post you had on the AK–47. So long as the man holding it knows how to shoot, the gun won't let him down.'

'I like the sound of it,' said Matt. 'We'll need one for each man, and at least twenty magazines of ammunition per man. Plus we'll need at least one back-up gun each. We're going to use American tactics on this job. Ridiculous and cowardly firepower to overwhelm the opposition. The last thing we want is to take casualties ourselves.' He paused, taking another hunk of the black bread and chewing it quickly. 'Everyone happy?'

Malenkov and Ivan both nodded. Matt looked up towards Orlena. 'Happy?'

'So long as the factory gets destroyed,' she replied. 'That's all that matters.'

'You have two new messages,' intoned the Orange answering-machine voice after a long and tedious wait. 'Press . . .'

Matt hit the button, too impatient to listen to the list of options. The Imarsat satellite phones connected perfectly to Matt's mobile, allowing him to pick up his messages, and make calls. Out here, there was no land line, and no mobile connection. But the satellite phone meant you could stay in touch with the world as easily as if you were in London.

Probably easier.

'Matt, it's Bob here, Bob Crowden,' started a familiar Geordie voice. 'About what we were talking about the other day. I did hear something. Guy down in Swindon, called Barry Legg. Passed through my unit. Lovely fellow. Apparently he disappeared a few days ago. Then he was found dead yesterday. Murdered. Maybe nothing in it. Just a bit odd, that's all. I thought you might be interested.'

Matt pressed three to delete the message. A soldier gets killed down in Swindon? He shrugged to himself. Happens all the time. Could have been muggers. Could have owed some money to the wrong people. Could have been some random psycho who had decided to start killing former soldiers.

Guys get their number called all the time. It doesn't usually mean anything.

He pressed for the next message. 'Matt, it's me.' He recognised the voice immediately. 'I just wanted to see if you were all right.' She paused. 'And I guess I wanted to see if you'd found anything.'

Matt hit the button for redialling the last caller. The phone rang three times before it was answered. Before she even spoke, he could hear the heavy roar of traffic in the background. 'Where are you?' he asked.

'Waiting for the bus,' she answered. 'Fulham Palace Road. You OK?'

Matt couldn't help himself nodding into the phone, even though he knew she couldn't see him. 'OK, yes. I heard something.'

There was a pause on the line, and he could hear the honking of a lorry. 'Tell me,' she said eventually.

'A former soldier down in Swindon, called Barry Legg. He died a few days ago, murdered apparently.'

'Could that have anything to do with the men going crazy?'

'I don't know,' answered Matt. 'That's all I've heard. Maybe it's connected, maybe it isn't.' He paused. 'Look, I'll be back in a couple of days, let's speak then.'

Matt snapped the phone shut. It was almost noon, and the sun was beating down fiercely. The morning breeze had dropped, and the few acres of wheat and barley growing around the empty farmhouse were completely still.

Nikita, Josef and Andrei had arrived twenty minutes earlier, delivered in the back of Malenkov's Land Rover. Nikita was twenty-five, Andrei twenty-nine, but Josef looked younger, maybe nineteen or twenty. All three of them had dark hair, and gentle Slavic looks, but with dark brown eyes and a slope of the shoulders that suggested they could decide for themselves which orders they wanted to obey. He knew they were being well paid. Orlena was giving them a thousand American dollars each, a fortune by local standards. And for that kind of money the job would be rough and dirty.

That's as it should be. A soldier is always entitled to know what sort of risk he's taking. It's his life after all.

'The older two look OK,' said Matt. 'Not Josef, he's too young. We need men, not boys.'

Malenkov glared back at him. 'Josef's OK,' he said. 'He stays.'

'No, someone else.'

Malenkov shook his head, and from the look on his face, Matt could tell he wasn't going to budge. 'He stays,' he said firmly. 'Or else we all go.'

Matt looked up as they completed the second circuit of the field. They stopped by a cattle trough, flooding their faces with the dirty water. He tossed a water canister in their direction. Josef was the slowest, and might be carrying a couple of pounds too many on his stomach, and Andrei might not have kept his muscles as trim as he could, but none of them had flagged during the physical test, and none of them showed any sign of giving up.

They were fit, and they needed the work. What more could you ask of any mercenary?

'OK, we go with these three,' said Matt, looking across to Malenkov. 'Let's run through the plan, then get some kip. We've a long night ahead of us.'

The three men sat in a semicircle, Malenkov translating, while Matt and Ivan ran through the plan. They listened closely, watching as Matt pointed to the map, explaining how they were going to get in, and how they were going to blow the factory.

It was straightforward enough. They all claimed to have been in the Russian Army, and the older two had fought in Chechnya. *By the standards of that war, this shouldn't be much more than punch-up in the playground.*

'OK,' said Matt when he'd finished. 'Let's get some kip. Then when it gets dark we'll see how good we are at squeezing through tunnels.'

The smell was brutal: a stale, fetid mixture of human excrement, rotten food, and the heavy suffocating odour of industrial chemicals. Matt could feel his lungs choking on the air, the fumes crawling into every wrinkle in his clothes.

It's going to take a hundred hot showers to get this stink off my skin.

They had slipped down through the manhole cover they had spotted the night before. The tunnel, as Matt had expected, led due west from the compound towards the river: environmentalists had a chance to clear up Belarus yet, thought Matt with a grin. The tunnel was taking the waste from both the compound and the factory. It measured four feet across, built in a half circle. It had originally been built from concrete, but was now in a bad state of disrepair. Flakes of stone were crumbling from its walls, and thick piles of silt and waste had built up along the sides, making it virtually impassable.

We're going to have to hack our way through, realised Matt as soon as they got inside.

The work was hard and slow, the earth tougher than Matt had expected. It was now past one in the morning, and they had already been digging for two back-breaking hours.

Matt paused for breath, pulling back his shovel. The tunnel was at least ten feet beneath the surface. As the man with the most experience of digging tunnels, he'd taken the lead. He placed a tiny hand-held torch on the ground, positioning it so its beam shone upwards. With a pick, he hacked into the silt blocking the tunnel, letting it crumble and tumble to the floor. Then he kicked it back with his feet, letting Andrei scoop the earth up into a bucket, and pass it back along the line.

Some water started to wash through the tunnel. It ran in a tiny river around his boots, lapping up and drenching his socks. Matt forced himself not to think about what might be in it.

Let's hope those bastards don't keep running to the loo all night.

'*Himmo*,' cried the Ukrainian as he fell backwards.

You don't need to have learnt much of the language to know what that means: *Shit.*

Matt remained completely still. He looked up at Andrei, raising his fingers to his lips. The sound of the fall, and the cry that followed might easily be heard above the ground. He kept his breathing steady and even, waiting and listening. Above, he could hear some feet slow and steady across the ground. One of the guards. From the tread, Matt judged the man was walking slowly towards the fence: he was probably directly above them just now. Not running – that was a good sign – but heading out to take a look.

Matt flashed the torch three times down the tunnel: the prearranged signal that they could have been compromised. Ivan, Malenkov and the rest of them knew to melt away into the wood, and ready themselves for a firefight.

Matt gripped the AN-49 he had slung over his back. He held it between his forearms, his finger ready on the trigger: he'd spent an hour this afternoon in the woods familiarising himself with the weapon, but it was still a new gun for him, and it took a moment to remember where everything was and how it worked.

If we're discovered, our only hope is to shoot our way out of the darkness.

'*Tam*,' shouted the guard.

Even down here in the ground, ten feet beneath the surface, the sound was clear enough. Matt didn't know much Russian, but he'd picked up a few words on a regiment training course: *Who's there?*

'*Tam*,' shouted the guard, louder this time.

Matt remained still. He looked towards Andrei, and could see the boy fingering the trigger of his gun nervously. Matt smiled. He wouldn't claim to know much about commanding a troop of men – only what he'd picked up in the field of combat – but he knew the best way to clam everyone down in a flap was to look relaxed and cheerful yourself. Even when your stomach was churning, and your nerves endings felt like someone had just poured raw alcohol on to them.

Fear spreads quickly. So does confidence.

Another voice. Matt couldn't make out what the man was saying, but he guessed it was one of the other guards asking what was going on. More footsteps. The guard seemed to be moving sideways, along the perimeter of the fence. Then he started walking backwards again, towards the interior of the compound.

Matt took a deep breath, feeling the oxygen fill his lungs. Even the stale air of the tunnel felt good. The guard had decided it was nothing, just a stray wolf or some other animal rampaging through the forest.

We're in the clear. For now.

Matt nodded towards Andrei, and repositioned his torch so its light was shining up to the front of the tunnel. He could see the manhole inside the compound ahead of him, and there was just one more pile of waste to be cleared away before they could reach it. He picked up his shovel, and started hacking into it.

Another five feet and we can get out of this graveyard.

Matt took a hit of the vodka, swilling it around his mouth, enjoying its crisp, chunky flavour before letting it hit his bloodstream.

'We know the guards are doing their jobs,' he said, looking across at Ivan and Malenkov. 'That guy who heard the noise was making a proper check of the area. He's not just some clock-watching security guard sitting around drinking vodka and doing the crossword until he can knock off for the night.'

'We can deal with them,' said Malenkov gruffly. 'Our men are good, and we can take them by surprise.'

'Right,' added Ivan. 'And they can take us by surprise as well.'

'Let's get some sleep then,' said Matt. 'We're going to need our wits about us.'

He checked his watch. It was just after four in the morning. It had taken three hours to dig through the tunnel they needed, and they had left Nikita in the forest to keep watch, and make sure the tunnel wasn't discovered. He'd be relieved by one of the other men after three hours.

'Everyone get as much sleep as they can. We start work again at two tomorrow afternoon.'

Matt walked alone through to his room. Somewhere through the forest he could see the first glimmers of dawn starting to break through. He chucked a towel up against the window, catching it on the lock to block out as much sunshine as possible. Back in the regiment, he could lie down anywhere, close his eyes and go straight to sleep, any time of the day or night. But his body, he realised, had become used to the gentler rhythms of civilian life. He was used to going to bed at night, getting up in the morning, getting on with the day. Breaking back ino the old pattern was disorientating him.

It takes weeks, sometimes months to be combat-ready. Whatever the idiots at the Firm might think, you can't just switch it on and off.

Matt stripped off his clothes, and lay down on the mattress. He could feel his eyes shutting, and as they closed, he thought of Gill. It was so long since he'd heard from her, and he was starting to fear this time the break might be permanent. She had disappeared from his life so suddenly, so completely, it was hard to get used to.

Wait until this job is done. Then I'll know whether we can get back together or not.

He rolled over, his eyes closing. Orlena was somewhere down the hallway, and Matt felt a mixture of guilt and desire as he wondered if she might join him on the mattress. He was listening for the sounds of footsteps in the corridors, but the house was completely silent. Within seconds, he was sleeping.

ELEVEN

The sunset melted slowly into the line of trees stretching out beyond the fields. Matt remained still, watching the light of the day seep away. In the regiment, all his toughest firefights had been at night. In the Philippines, he'd taken a flesh wound in the leg during an attack on a communist camp; in Bosnia, he'd held a man face down in the mud, and put a bullet through his head, even though he wasn't sure he'd got the right man; in Ulster, he'd come under sniper fire during a border patrol, and dived for cover as the man next to him had dropped down stone dead.

For most people, night is a time of peace. For men like us, it's a time of war.

The surveillance of the factory was now complete: Malenkov had made notes of when the shifts of guards at the factory changed, and how many men came on each rota. It was twelve in total. Two were on towers, six in the admin block and four in the factory. They had been carrying a lot more weaponry than Matt had expected: how tough this was going to be, he couldn't say, but he knew he had to prepare for the worst.

He turned towards Ivan. 'Kit OK?'

Ivan grinned. 'It'll do.'

The last two hours had been spent constructing home-made bombs for the job. All they needed was a big, cheap, dirty bang, with lots of smoke and flames, and they'd wanted to keep the ingredients simple so they hadn't had to smuggle

115

anything into the country. Ivan had asked Malenkov to go into town and get two dozen cartons of orange juice in big plastic jars, some packets of old-fashioned hard soapsuds, petrol and plenty of strong fuse wire. That, he told him, would be all they would need.

Together with Nikita and Andrei, Ivan had spent the last hour emptying the orange juice out of the cartons, then filling them with some petrol. Into each carton, they mixed handfuls of soapsuds. It was crude, but it made an effective firebomb. Ivan had drawn them a detailed diagram. Put a fuse to the petrol, and it would blow up immediately. The soap made the petrol stick together in little balls of burning jelly. Those balls would fly off in all directions, sticking to whatever they collided with. They would burn for several minutes, enough to send even the toughest structure up in flames. In this dry weather, the wooden factory should light up like candle. The brick admin building would probably survive, but they would clear that by hand.

'Maximum havoc, for minimum effort,' Ivan explained. 'What more can a bomb-maker ask for?'

Matt took a length of fuse wire between his hands, and measured out a six-foot stretch. Ivan took one end, and Matt the other. Matt checked his watch. As the second hand completed a minute, he signalled to Ivan to light the wire. The fuse started burning, the flame racing down the length of the cord.

'Eight seconds to burn six feet,' said Matt, looking back up at Ivan. 'You can do your calculations from that?'

Ivan nodded. 'Once you know the velocity that a flame travels along the fuse, you can coordinate all the bombs to go off at precisely the same time. It's just a matter of cutting the right length of cord.'

Matt nodded. He'd trust Ivan on that. He was a careful, precise man, who took no more risks than were absolutely

116

essential. Just the way a soldier should be. *Nervous, cautious, and alive.*

The darkness had fallen now, the final dregs of the sunset disappearing beneath the horizon. Matt gathered Malenkov over to his side, telling him to bring Nikita and Andrei as well. Josef was now doing his three-hour shift guarding the tunnel entrance, and would meet them there at midnight. With Ivan at his side, Matt started to run through the plan. At midnight he and Ivan would go through the tunnel first. They would position the bombs around the perimeter of the factory, attaching them to the sides of the building with simple masking tape. They'd connect up the fuse wire, then head back down the tunnel. Meanwhile, Malenkov and Andrei would cut the one telephone wire running into the front of the factory: that would stop them calling for any reinforcements, unless they had a satellite phone. And they'd just have to hope they didn't. There was no way they could know whether they did or not. If they did, Malenkov reckoned they would have an hour maximum before the police showed up: the nearest main police station was sixty kilometres from here, and by road that took at least an hour. By helicopter, it would be quicker, but the nearest police choppers were in Minsk, and that was also an hour away by the time they'd scrambled into action.

The bombs would be blown at fifteen minutes past midnight. They'd wait sixty seconds, enough time for the immediate blast of the firestorm to blow through the building. Then the six of them would rush the compound. Ivan and Nikita would take the factory, and take out the men there. Matt, Josef, Malenkov and Andrei would attack the main admin building. Six of the guards would probably be in there, but at least one of them would come out to see what had happened. They would clip him, then move in to take out the rest. If the guards wanted to flee or to surrender

117

they could, decided Matt. Otherwise, they would have to take whatever fate the gods of war had cooked up for them.

'Target practice,' finished Matt, speaking confidently. 'We have better weapons, and we can take them by surprise. Those are two big advantages on our side.'

Sound confident, make it clear, but don't bullshit them.

'Everyone strip down their guns and check they're in working order,' he continued. 'This is a maximum firepower job. OK. We set off in ten minutes. Twenty-three hundred hours precisely.'

Matt looked back towards Orlena, who was standing two feet behind the rest of the men. 'We'll meet you back here,' he said. 'We'll be out of there by one at the very latest, back here before two. Keep the Land Rover ready.'

Orlena shook her head. 'But I'm coming with you.'

Her voice was quiet but determined, the words delivered with total self-confidence.

'Don't be ridiculous,' snapped Matt. 'There's no room for tourists.'

'My company is paying for this mission. I get to say who stays and who goes.' She paused, looking directly at Matt, taking one step forward. 'And I say I'm coming.'

Matt hesitated. He knew he could have an argument with her, but he would risk losing the respect of the other men. *Better not to start any fights you couldn't win.*

'Fine,' he said. 'You get your fingernails chipped, that's your lookout.' He looked around at the rest of the men. 'Let's go.'

The tunnel was hot and sticky, and Matt could feel his T-shirt clinging to his chest as he peered up to the roof. It was three minutes past midnight. He had blacked up his face with a thick layer of cam cream he'd brought from Britain, painting thick dark lines of black and green across the side of the cheeks. His clothes were black, and he had pulled a black baseball cap over his head. When they emerged, they would be on the ten feet of open ground between the edge of the compound and the factory. In the dark, he was going to be no more than a shadow slipping through the air.

'Ready?' whispered Matt, looking back towards Ivan.

Ivan nodded. 'Let's bloody do it.'

Matt could feel the adrenalin surging through his blood, hitting his heart and pumping up his pulse. He took the pick he had left at the end of the short tunnel, and started scratching at the manhole above him. This was where they would come out in the compound. A layer of dirt had caked up over it. Using his shovel, Matt started to hack into it.

A lump of dirt came free, falling to the ground, hitting Matt in the face. He pressed his lips together to stop it falling into his mouth. Using his shoulder muscles, he struck upwards again. This time, a bigger chunk of earth fell away, collapsing inside the tunnel.

Matt repositioned the torch and, using his hands this time, took down another lump of mud. Opening the manhole cover would have to be done carefully.

Matt stopped. He could feel a whisper of air blowing through the ground above him. He gripped the manhole cover then, pushing all his strength into his hands, he started to prise it loose. Nobody had opened it for several years, he guessed, and it took several hard pushes to start getting it open. One final heave, and it started to slide open. Matt gingerly raised his hands up through the hole.

So long as I don't get my hand shot off in the next minute, we'll be OK.

Using his shoulders to lever himself upwards, Matt raised his head slowly above the ground. He kept his back to the fence, and looked forwards, swivelling his eyes sharply from right to left.

If anyone sees me, I'm going to have to make a rapid retreat back down the tunnel.

119

The compound was empty. Twenty yards in the distance, he could see the guards standing on the watchtowers, their searchlights flashing out on to the road and into the forest. But, as he knew from their observations the previous two nights, there was no guard patrolling this section of the fence.

He pulled himself quickly to the surface of the ground, crouched down low, and ran the ten feet towards the back wall of the main factory building. That would give him cover. There was no need to say anything to Ivan. The fact that Matt had moved forward would tell him the way was clear, and he would follow.

Ivan joined Matt at the wall, throwing down a black kitbag that was slung over his back, holding the first ten one-litre petrol bombs. Another ten were stashed at the bottom of the tunnel. He took five of the bombs, handing them to Matt, along with a length of fuse cord. 'Make them at least twenty yards apart,' he said. 'You move right, and I'll go left.'

Matt started to crawl along the length of the factory. He kept his head down low, pulling himself forward by his elbows. It was seven minutes past midnight now, the air was hot and sticky, and the sweat was starting to drip along his spine.

Keep your eyes out of view, he reminded himself as the arc of the watch light swung past: it was beaming out of the compound, while they were inside, but it could still illumi-nate their position if they weren't careful. *Like the Cat's-eyes on a motorway, they will catch the light and reveal your position.*

He stopped. Taking the carton from his back, he ripped a length of masking tape, placed the bomb next to the wall, then strapped it firmly into place. The building was solidly built, probably no more than five years old. It was going to take all the explosive power they could muster to blow it up. He jammed the cord into the top of the petrol bomb, took a moment to make sure it was securely in place, then crept forward. Beneath his breath, he was counting out the paces. Twenty yards translated into roughly sixty elbow strides. The distance measured, he strapped the second bomb into place, then moved forward again. Ten minutes past midnight, noted Matt. They were making progress.

'OK, another ten, then we're done,' whispered Ivan, as Matt met him back at the meeting point.

Matt took the cartons, then started crawling back along the wall of the factory. He strapped the first bomb into place, then the second, quickly securing the cord in each one. He started moving forwards, aware of the blisters that were going to be boiling on his arms by the morning. A searchlight flashed forward, brushing against his fingers. He stopped, freezing his body, burying his face into the dirt.

They see us now, we're corpses. A man lying on the ground is just target practice.

His breath silent in his chest, Matt waited. He counted to fifteen, waiting to see if the light came back again. Nothing. Trying to bring his breathing back under control, he moved forward again. Faster, he told himself, dragging his body forwards. The sooner we get this done, the sooner we can get out of here.

'We're done,' whispered Ivan, as he met up with him again. 'Let's go.'

Ivan dropped first into the tunnel, Matt following quickly behind him. The darkness suddenly engulfed him and, without a torch, he had to use his fingers to judge where the walls were as he moved painfully forward. He could feel his breath quickening as he approached the exit.

I've never liked dark, enclosed spaces. And knowing there's a dozen guys up there waiting to shoot us like pheasants on a moor doesn't make it any better.

Ivan's hand reached down to grab him, pulling him up through the constricted exit of the tunnel. They were ten yards out of the compound, hidden by the trees. He stood up, shaking the dirt free from his body. Malenkov was standing next to him, with Andrei, Nikita and Josef close by. In the insipid torchlight, he could tell from the pale colour of the men's skin that they were nervous: they had taken on the ghostly appearance of men who knew they might die in the next few minutes.

'Chin up, lads, this is going to be a walk in the park,' whispered Matt.

Malenkov said something in Ukrainian but Matt couldn't judge the tone. *I'll just have to hope he's not telling them to bugger off if it turns rough, and leave the foreigners to face the fire.*

'Set?' he said to Ivan.

Ivan cut a length of cord, put it in place and sat back. 'Just need a match,' he replied.

The voice was brimming with certainty and confidence, but Matt could detect the traces of anxiety underneath. Like surgery, bomb-making looked like a science, but was really an art. You needed intuition as well as knowledge. *And that could mean the difference between life and death.*

It was now thirteen minutes past midnight. 'Back down into the tunnel,' said Matt. 'We wait in there until Ivan blows the fuse. After the explosion settles, we move forwards, with me in the lead.'

He looked around. The men were all nodding. *They understood.*

Matt glanced towards Orlena. She was wearing a black T-shirt and black jeans, plus heavy combat boots. Her hair was pinned back behind her head, and across her cheekbones she had smeared her cam cream with the delicacy and precision of a fine mascara.

You have to admit it. She looks like a peach in combat gear.

'And you?' said Matt, looking at her directly. 'You're sure you don't want to stay here?'

Orlena shook her head.

'OK,' said Matt tersely. 'But be ready, all right. A firefight scares most people witless. I've known brave men crack up, so if you feel yourself fainting, just fall back and we'll try and come back for you later. You get a bullet in you, just bite your tongue, and try to hang on until one of us is ready to help you. But remember, regiment rules apply here. We'll only come back to help you after the main objective has been secured. If that means you die, that's just bad luck.'

Orlena nodded, the trace of a smile on her lips. 'I understand.'

'OK,' said Matt, looking around at the group once more. 'Let's bloody do it.'

Down into the darkness again. Matt slipped back along the tunnel, the contours of the hard mud increasingly familiar to him. The space was constricted, claustrophobic, and Matt could sense himself becoming uneasy as the walls closed in around him. Up ahead, he could smell the air leaking through the hole sliced into the surface of the compound. The fuse was lying at his side, like a vein threading through the ground. Matt heard the sound of a match being struck, then smelt the sulphur and cord as the fuse started to burn. He pressed his back tight against the wall of the tunnel as the flame sped past him, disappearing up through the ground, and across the surface of the compound.

Doesn't matter if the guards see it, he realised. By then it will be too late. *Just time to say a quick prayer.*

Matt steeled himself, taking a deep breath, then relaxed his muscles. When the bombs blew, he knew the shockwave would roll through the compound with the force of a tornado. The fireball that was about to detonate would vaporise anything it touched, sucking all the oxygen out of the air, making it tough to breathe for several minutes.

Get ready. Hell is about to be unleashed.

The explosion burst through the air at sixteen minutes past midnight, splitting Matt's eardrums. The bombs detonated a mere fraction of a second apart, the din of the explosions rising in intensity as each bomb added to the symphony of violent noise. After thirty seconds, the noise of the bombs subsided as suddenly as it had arisen, replaced by the chilled, eerie sound of the firestorm unleashed by gallons of sticky petrol. It was like a deadly breeze, wafting through the air, lapping over and consuming everything it touched.

Will the guards flee as soon as they know they are under attack?

In an instant, the compound turned completely still. Matt opened his mouth, tried to breathe but realised the oxygen had thinned out, and he was taking in mostly carbon monoxide. His lungs contracted as they struggled with the noxious air. A wind had started blowing through the tunnel as the explosion sucked the oxygen out of the compound, the air rustling past Matt's face.

Sixty seconds, he told himself. Let the fire do its damage. *Then we move forwards.*

The time ticked by slowly. He could hear the flames, and somewhere in the distance he could hear the sound of a man screaming. Matt had heard men burn to death before, and had learnt to recognise the terrible music of their slow, agonising demise. The lungs and vocal cords kept on working even as the rest of the body was convulsed by the flames, and the screaming grew louder and louder as the heat incinerated all the internal organs. Then, just as it reached a crescendo, it slowly faded, as the lungs and vocal cords burnt; the screams turned into a wheezy, whistling noise, before the victim finally fell silent.

When I go, let it be a bullet, not a fire that takes me.

'OK,' Matt shouted. 'Move out. Move out.'

Matt could feel his heart pounding like a drill against his chest as he pulled himself clear of the tunnel, and emerged blinking into the compound. The firebombs had lit the place up like a shopping mall on Christmas Eve. The light of the flame was brilliant, dazzling, and in that moment Matt could feel the intense heat singeing his skin. He paused for a split second, adjusting his eyes to the glare, then threw himself on to the ground, holding his AN-49 in front of him.

This is the moment of maximum danger. They know they're under attack, and whoever is left alive will be looking for us right now.

He could sense the other five men following behind them. With one glance, he checked they were all in position, then moved himself into a crouching position and started to edge forwards. His gun was cocked, and his finger tensed on the trigger. In front of him, the main factory building was engulfed in flames: first the main walls started to shake as the fire progressively weakened it, then the roof started to quiver, as the walls stopped supporting its weight. Within less than a minute of the fireball igniting, it was clear the building would not survive the inferno.

'Is that one done?' hissed Matt, looking towards Ivan.

'Finished,' snapped Ivan. 'It'll collapse in the next half-hour or so.'

Matt looked forwards. The admin building was fifty yards away, set behind the factory. The flames were licking up into the sky, but so far had not touched it. He glanced towards the lookout towers. They looked abandoned. The sentries had either been knocked out by the force of the explosion, or retreated inside.

'Send two men to check the towers,' said Matt, looking towards Malenkov. 'The last thing we need is sniper fire from above.'

Malenkov barked at Josef and Andrei. The two men fanned out, their guns held in front of them, firing rounds of bullets into each sentry tower. *If anyone was left there, they should be dead by now.*

Matt watched Josef edge forward, his gun high above his head. He loosened off a couple more rounds of fire, then slung his gun over his back. Standing next to the sentry tower, he gripped the wooden slats that led up towards the turret, climbing slowly.

The explosion rocked through the air, catching Matt off balance. Instinctively, he threw himself back down on the ground. When he looked up again, the watchtower had been reduced to smouldering embers, blown completely apart by the bomb that Josef must have triggered. Of Josef, there was no trace.

He was dead. Probably hanging in a thousand pieces on the trees in the forest, realised Matt. *Poor bastard.*

'Christ, what the fuck was that?' he hissed, looking towards Ivan.

Ivan was crouching next to him on the ground. He looked up, sniffing the air. 'I can't smell anything,' he said. 'So they must have used Semtex. Some kind of soft trigger on the watchtower. A booby trap.'

Andrei was standing next to them now, his face drawn, sweat running down his cheek and his hands shaking. Malenkov hardly appeared to have registered what had happened. He was shouting furiously, dragging Andrei down to the ground. This is going to be tougher than we thought, Matt realised. We should stop worrying about whether we kill the guards or not – this is kill or be killed.

They were waiting, they were prepared – not for us, maybe, but for something.

Only a few moments are left to us, Matt judged. We still have the advantage of surprise. If anyone is left inside there, they are disorientated, confused and frightened. That's the time to strike them.

Matt stood upright, using his arm to motion the rest of the squad forward. They were already one man down, and from now on the plan would have to be changed by the second. This isn't just taking out a factory. *This is a battlefield.*

He skirted to the left, avoiding the sparks spitting out of

the burning factory, his gun held in front of him. A silence had descended over the compound. He looked towards the building and, from the corner of his eye, sensed he saw something moving in one of the windows.

'Take cover,' he barked.

A shot rang out. Matt could see a clump of earth kick up from the ground as the bullet hit the baked mud, ricocheting back up into the sky. He hurled himself on to the ground, rolling behind one of the walls running close to the compound, and let off a volley of fire. The bullets streamed through the night sky, but Matt could tell the guard was just shooting into thin air. The admin building was about eighty feet long and twenty wide, and was built from concrete breeze blocks, with six windows and only one door.

'Covering fire,' he shouted to Malenkov. 'We need to get up close.'

The volley of fire started up immediately, aimed straight at the centre of the admin building. It was enough to deter whoever was trying to shoot from the windows. Shielding his ears from the deafening roar of the gunfire all around him, Matt ran forwards, covering the twenty yards to the main building at a fast clip, then dropped to the ground next to the building. His breath was short and rapid. Ivan was hard behind him, followed by Malenkov, then Andrei and Nikita. Finally, Orlena ran into position behind them. Matt glanced into her eyes, and part of him was pleased to see the fear there. Sweat was running down the side of her face. But her limbs were solid. There was no sign of nervous shaking, or muscular collapse, the two most common signs of people who were about to crack under the stress of combat. She was frightened, but she was holding herself together.

She's tougher than she looks – and she looks pretty tough.

'Clear the building, clear the building,' shouted Matt.

A yard above where he was crouching was one of the windows. The glass had already shattered, fragments lying splintered on the earth around them. Matt pulled himself upwards, threw the barrel of the AN-49 across the ledge of the broken window and sprayed the interior of the room with bullets. His arms moved methodically from right to left, while his head remained tucked just below the window ledge. They had no plan of the inside of the building, and from now on, they were going in blind, with little idea of what resistance they might expect.

'Can we blow it from here?' asked Matt, looking towards Ivan. 'Save ourselves getting shot to pieces.'

Ivan shook his head. 'Can't get the bombs around it,' he answered. 'They'll pick us off from the windows if we try.'

'OK,' said Matt grimly. 'We take the buggers room by room. With luck there's only six guys left, but it could be eight or nine.'

Regiment rules, he reminded himself. *Maximum speed, maximum aggression. You'll have time in heaven to work out a detailed plan.*

The room they were now entering had taken a hundred bullets in two minutes. Even a cockroach would have had trouble surviving in there, Matt decided. He pulled himself upwards, looking above the window ledge. The concrete surface of the wall was pitted with holes from the gunfire, and the empty metal cases were filling the floor like the leaves in the park in autumn. One desk in the corner of the room had been shot to pieces, its wooden legs collapsing.

But no corpses.

Matt vaulted through the window, landing roughly on the concrete. He paused, listening hard for the sound of anyone approaching down the corridor. Fifty yards away, he could hear the roar of the burning factory: there was a crashing that sounded like a wall coming down. But here inside the admin building, it was still quiet. Matt motioned to the others to follow him, and within a minute they had all landed inside the room.

'We'll take the corridors,' said Matt. 'Ivan and I will go right.' He looked towards Malenkov. 'You go left with Andrei. Nikita and Orlena can stay here.'

'We should go back for the wounded man,' said Malenkov.

'Forget him,' snapped Matt. 'He was blown to pieces. There's nothing we can do for him now.' He jammed his fist against the light switch next to the door, but nothing happened. Someone's switched the power off, or the bulbs have all been shot out, it was impossible to tell. He flicked on a pocket torch, and flashed it down the corridor. The walls were made of drab, stained concrete and completely bare, stretching twenty yards to the back of the block, with two more doors leading off it. Matt began to edge quietly forward, his AN-49 gripped tightly in his fists. The first door was ajar an inch. He walked quietly up to it, kicked it wide open, and started to spray the room with bullets. Behind him, Ivan was crouching on his knees, his gun held to his shoulder, letting off another murderous round of fire.

We shoot first and ask questions later. Correct that. We shoot and get the hell out of here. Sod the questions.

Behind him, an explosion rattled through the corridor, the force of the blast throwing Matt off balance. He could feel a sharp pain in his left shoulder where it had struck the ground. The AN-49 had been thrown from his grip. He lifted himself up, aware of the pain in his muscles as he did so, and wiped a thick film of dust from his eyes. 'What the fuck?' he shouted.

Malenkov was already running back down the corridor towards him. His clothes were torn, and there were cuts right across his face and torso. Behind him, Orlena and Nikita.

'Andrei's dead,' said Malenkov, his voice sombre. 'He went over some kind of tripwire, and set off a bomb. Killed him instantly.' He was panting and out of breath, and blood

129

was trickling down the side of the skin. 'The rest of us are lucky to be alive.'

'This place is a bloody death trap,' said Ivan, his voice tensing.

'You think there are more of them out there?' said Matt, looking towards Malenkov.

'How the hell do I know?' answered Malenkov. 'At least six including the one who shot at us earlier. And the place could be stuffed with traps and bombs.'

'Snipers, tripwires,' said Ivan looking towards Matt. 'Room-to-room combat. It's a Russian speciality. Remember Stalingrad?'

Matt paused. 'You think we can blow the place now?'

Ivan nodded. 'We've got the kit back at the tunnel. Hold this room, then destroy the rest of the building with firebombs.'

'OK,' said Matt quickly. 'Let's do it. Fight our way through this place, and the whole fucking lot of us are going to be buried here.'

From the back of the room, Matt could see Orlena stepping forwards. Dust was covering her hair, turning it from black to a whitish grey. And the force of the blast had nicked her left arm, cutting open a small wound. 'No,' she said firmly. 'First we search the place, then we blast it.'

Matt clenched his fists together. In the regiment, he'd taught himself lots of techniques for controlling his anger. As the Ruperts flung ridiculous commands at him, he knew all about taking deep breaths, counting to ten, and biting his tongue as he tried to get on with shooting the enemy rather than his own commanders.

But I've never been told to risk my life by a woman before.

'Search it be damned,' he said, his voice rising. 'We're two men down already, and the whole place is booby-trapped. We're facing a hidden enemy, and we haven't even got a map of the building. It's fucking suicide.'

He watched Orlena closely, but not a single muscle on her face twitched. 'I said we search it,' she repeated coldly.

Matt took a step closer, leaning angrily into her face. 'The job was to destroy the compound,' he shouted. 'So we'll destroy the place, and get the hell out of here.'

Orlena tossed a lock of dusty hair away from her face, and glanced back up at Matt. 'As I might have said once already, I pay the bills, so I give the orders. We search the place, *then* destroy it.'

'What have they got here?' asked Ivan. 'What are we looking for that's so important?'

Orlena kept her eyes trained on Matt. 'Like I told you, it manufactures counterfeit pharmaceuticals. And I need to make sure all the formulas have been destroyed.'

'So how come it's rigged up like the Pentagon?' growled Ivan. He looked towards Malenkov. 'What's in here, Sergei? What are they hiding?'

The Ukrainian shrugged. 'I'm getting paid to fight, not to ask questions,' he replied, his tone guarded. 'So as long I'm on my feet, and I've got a gun in my hand, I'll fight.'

Orlena looked towards Matt, then Ivan. 'If you're running away, so be it. I can't stop you. But I'll tell the Firm you got scared and flunked out of the job. And I'll let them take the appropriate action.'

Matt tossed a gun into Orlena's hand. 'Nobody's damn well scared. But we're two bloody men down already,' he barked, 'so you've just been drafted as the reinforcements.'

TWELVE

Matt could feel his fingers tightening on the trigger of his gun. His skin was warm and sticky, and the metal of the weapon was already wet. He moved carefully forwards, making sure he had checked each inch of ground before taking every step.

There's no way of telling where the next trap is.

Where he was standing, one passage led right, the other left. It was already twenty-five minutes past midnight, he realised. They were about halfway through their safe hour, and the job not half done. *The odds are against us and so is the clock.*

'Here's the plan,' whispered Matt, looking back towards Ivan and Malenkov. 'Ivan and I will take the left side; Sergei, you cover the right. We clear this place room by room and we shoot on sight.' He paused, looking back at Orlena. 'You follow me, but keep ten paces behind us.'

'Just try not to damage anything,' she said sharply.

Matt grimaced. 'We'll worry about that if we're still alive. We're soldiers, not removal men.'

He looked ahead. The admin block split into two passages, both of them about ten yards long. His passage led to what looked like a storeroom, the other to a series of small offices and laboratories. Malenkov and Nikita started crawling rightwards, while he and Ivan went left. Orlena was bringing up the rear. It was pitch black, and Matt was using a torch to inch his way forward. The smell of the explosion was still thick and sulphurous in the air, and the blood of the last guard to die was seeping out across the floor in front of him.

'What are we looking for?' hissed Matt, looking back towards Orlena.

'Computers,' she said. 'You see one, make sure you don't shoot it up.'

A noise. Matt couldn't be certain where it was coming from, but he sensed the unmistakable sound of a man breathing. Ten yards away, maybe fifteen, inside one of the two small rooms that led off the corridor. The acoustics along the narrow passageway made every faint whispering sound reflect back on itself. In the background, the flames still rising from the factory were sending waves of hot air across the building.

Still, no doubts. *There is a man out there somewhere.*

If we had known we were going to get into this kind of battle we would have brought stun grenades, thought Matt.

Matt signalled to Ivan. To flush him out of the room where he was hiding, they were going to have to work as a pair. Matt crouched down low, kneeling close to the concrete surface, while Ivan stood behind him, his gun cocked and ready. A shot splintered through the night air. Matt could feel some dust spitting out from the concrete wall, then hitting the floor. He stopped. Behind him, Ivan had loosed off a volley of fire in the direction of the first door. Matt stopped at the second, crouching on the ground. Ivan was increasing his rate of fire, peppering the first door with bullets. Fuck the computers, Matt thought.

He unhooked his gun, checked the cartridge, then started firing into the second room. The computers might get damaged, but Orlena could worry about that: it wasn't part of the original mission, so she couldn't complain now. Even though the kickback from the gun was light, it was still bruising the shoulder that was already hurting from the last fall. But the weapon was solid and easy to handle. After two magazines were spent, the door fell with a crash to the ground.

It didn't matter now which room the man was in. *Either way, he should be dead.*

'Move in,' shouted Matt. 'Move in.'

He pulled himself up, rushing at the room ahead of him. It measured five foot by ten, its walls made from bare concrete blocks. His gun held high, he squeezed his finger down tight on the trigger of the AN-49 ready to fire: he could feel his nerve endings jamming against the hot steel of the gun. As soon as he entered the room, he threw his back against the wall, taking a moment to survey the scene. One man was standing ten feet ahead of him. In an instant, Matt raised the gun to his eyes, fired once, then twice. The first bullet blew apart his skull, the second tore into his chest.

Matt ran across the room, kneeling to check the man was dead. His finger was still twitching, as he clung on desperately to the last embers of life. Maybe thirty, Matt judged, with soft features and dressed in jeans and a black sweatshirt. Matt took one step forward, put the gun to the side of the man's head, and fired a single bullet into his brain.

This one's not standing up again.

'Room cleared,' he shouted.

Ivan and Orlena appeared in the doorway. 'Nobody in my room,' said Ivan, his voice breathless. 'This must have been the guy that was shooting at us.'

In the distance Matt could hear the sound of gunfire echoing down the corridor. He started running back towards the corridor Malenkov was clearing, his feet pounding against the concrete. Turning sharply left, he dived to the ground as he hit the corridor. A bullet had just struck the wall behind him, and Malenkov had taken up his gun, standing at the centre of the corridor and sending covering fire into the room beyond.

134

'Help the bastard, help the bastard,' shouted Malenkov.

Matt could see Nikita on the floor in front of him. He was lying across the centre of the corridor. Blood was seeping from his leg, pouring from the open wound. Matt didn't want to look too closely, but he could see the man had taken more than a single shot: the bullets had shredded the femoral artery running through the thigh, causing massive haemorrhaging and blood loss. Matt grabbed Nikita's shoulders and started dragging him back. He could see the man wince with pain as he slid along the floor.

'*Matinka, matinka*,' he was muttering through strained and fading vocal cords.

He wants his mum, realised Matt.

'How many men ahead?' Matt shouted to Malenkov.

'One, maybe two, can't tell,' shouted Malenkov.

'Drop back,' yelled Matt.

With a round of rapid fire into the doorway above, Malenkov retreated, throwing himself backwards. His breath was short, and his eyes were sagging: he'd taken a cut on his forehead, and the blood was mixing into the sweat on his hair. 'These guys are even tougher than we thought,' he said.

Matt looked down at Nikita, then across at Ivan. 'Can we do anything for him?'

Ivan was already kneeling next to the man. Ivan had taken the shirt from his back, and had tried to wrap it around the wound. 'I think the bleeding is internal as well as external,' he muttered. 'Unless we can get him to a hospital in the next hour, he's finished.'

'Then we put him out of his misery,' snapped Matt. He checked his watch. Thirty-three minutes past midnight. The clock was ticking away on them. Reinforcements could be here in twenty-five minutes. *And then we are all dead.*

He looked first at Ivan, then at Malenkov. 'Anyone disagree?'

135

Both men shook their heads, their expressions sombre. Matt pointed to the gun in Orlena's hand. 'You do it,' he said quietly. 'One bullet to the head, make it quick for him.'

Matt knew it was a challenge. He couldn't be certain, but he doubted Orlena had ever killed a man before. He could tell from the way she was fingering the trigger of her gun, looking down at the man as if she was wondering where the bullet should go. But there was no fear in her eyes, no sign that the horror of robbing another human being of their life had affected her. This was merely a technical exercise, a task to be understood, then accomplished.

'Don't look in his eyes,' said Matt.

The blood was still flowing from Nikita's leg, even where Ivan had tried to bandage it. His head had rolled to one side, and saliva was drooling from his mouth. '*Matinka, matinka,*' he croaked.

She looked at his eyes, then placed the barrel of her AN-49 gently to the centre of his forehead, squeezing the trigger. The bullet smashed through the man's skull, draining him of what little life remained in just a few seconds. His split-open head slumped to the side.

Once she gets a taste for it, she's going to be a natural.

Malenkov knelt down, kissing the boy on his bloodstained cheek. He wiped the sweat from his own brow, looking back up. The more battle-hardened a soldier was, Matt reflected, the more troubled he was by every needless and pointless death: you see one or two men die, you can take it, but when you see dozens it starts to tear away at your soul.

'This wasn't what we were asked to do,' he said angrily, rising to his feet again. 'I hired three boys, three good boys.' He looked hard at Orlena, the blood rising in his cheeks. 'I told them it would be dangerous. But not that they had little chance of getting out alive.'

'You were paid, they were paid,' said Orlena, spitting the words from her mouth.

'OK,' shouted Matt. 'Let's deal with those fuckers up ahead, before the rest of us get shot.'

They were sheltering at the back of the corridor now, taking cover behind the curve of the corner. That kept them out of the line of the sniper fire from the room ahead. Matt was keeping his AN-49 trained on the door to stop the enemy from rushing them, while Malenkov was protecting their rear.

'There's two, I reckon,' said Malenkov, pointing towards the doorway. 'No more.'

'Any windows?' asked Ivan.

'Two at the back,' said Malenkov.

'They'll be guarding them for sure,' said Matt. 'Anyone tries to come through a window, they'll get shot to shreds.'

'Diversion,' said Malenkov. 'One man puts bombs through the windows, the other men move in.'

Matt nodded. It was ten yards up to the guarded room. To get round the back was thirty yards. The plan wasn't going to get any prizes for sophistication. Put a bomb down, get their attention, then shoot them in the back. It was rough and simple and nasty. But it could work.

'Right,' said Matt firmly. 'Ivan, you do the bombing. Sergei and I will attack.'

Ivan disappeared. There were ten petrol bombs left at the top of the tunnel, and he would need two. In total he had to cover two hundred yards there and back. So far as they knew, the compound had been cleared of snipers in the watchtowers, but unless you made a proper search you couldn't be sure. Ivan would have to move carefully to make sure he didn't get a bullet in the back.

'Give me six minutes,' Ivan had told Matt. Two to get back to the tunnel, two to come back to the admin block, and one for ignition. The other minute was for faffing around and admiring the view.

Matt checked his watch again, the tension rising within

him each time he did so. Midnight thirty-nine. By the time Ivan bombed them, they would have just fifteen minutes to clear the room and get out of here. The strain was starting to tell: his nerves were fraying and it was harder and harder to hold his concentration at the peak levels needed for room-to-room combat.

'Ready?' he said, looking across at Malenkov.

The Ukrainian nodded. 'You shoot high, I'll shoot low. That way we cover the room.'

'Fine,' said Matt. He turned towards Orlena. 'You stay here, and guard our rear. You see or hear anything, you shoot.'

Matt looked forward. Another sixty seconds before the bombs blew. If there were two men in there, he reckoned they were lying in wait. And if just one of them had an AK-47, he could kill them all.

If they're patient, they'll think they can take us down. They've got three of us already.

Ten seconds. Matt could feel the sweat pouring off his back. It was more than a year since he'd been in close combat, and he could no longer be certain his reactions were as sharp as they had once been. A mistake, a mistimed shot or a delayed response, and I'll be buried here.

One second.

Matt steadied himself, tightening up the muscles in his ankles, making himself ready to spring forward.

Nothing.

He looked first at Malenkov, then up along the corridor. Somewhere, he could hear a scratching movement, as if there were rats moving around.

Christ, where's Ivan?

Five more seconds ticked past. The sweat was growing on Matt's palms, and he could feel the blood pumping through his veins.

Get on with it, man.

The explosion rocked through the air. Matt could see a blinding flash of light bursting out from beneath the door, followed by the din of a detonation, so loud he could feel his eardrums cracking open. Instinctively, he flinched, backed away, then looked up again. A wave of heat was rolling down the corridor, and the door had been flung open. A familiar scent was hanging in the air.

The smell of petroleum and soap.

'Go,' he shouted, and he sprang forward in a smooth arc across the floor. He had ten yards to cover without getting shot. His AN-49 was gripped hard to his stomach, the barrel pointing forward. His head was bowed down low, and his eyes fixed on the door in front of him. He ran, then pushed, shoving the door aside, and directing his fire into the room.

A hail of bullets chattered out of the gun. He was holding its tip up high, making sure the ammunition sped through the air at around five feet from the ground. At that height, it would sever the head from anyone unlucky enough to be in its path. A short river of flame was rising up from the windows where Ivan had tossed through the firebombs. Then he caught his first glimpse of the enemy. One man was trying to douse the flames, the other was trying to shoot from the window.

With Malenkov standing right behind him, Matt trained his gun on the man with the rifle. *Drop, you bastard, drop.*

He was as strong as an ox, Matt judged. Despite the punishment his body was taking, he was trying to swivel around on his heels and direct a last, dying round of fire on his assailants. Matt went straight for the hands: he could finish him off later if he had to, but without any hands, he wasn't going to shoot back.

The gun dropped, as the bullets shredded through his hands. Then, an instant later, the man crumpled to his knees, blood pouring from the wounds stretched across his body. At his side, the second man, caught in crossfire from

Malenkov's machine gun, had fallen on to his side, his hair catching alight on the flames still rising from the floor.

He looked up, terror filling his eyes, but his gaze moved beyond Matt to the doorway behind him. 'Orlena,' he muttered, struggling to speak through the pain. 'Orlena.'

Matt spun around. Orlena was standing behind him, the gun attached to her hip. 'He knows you?'

Orlena ignored him. '*Likuvannia*,' she shouted down at the dying guard. '*Likuvannia*.'

The man looked up at her. '*Pishov, pishov*,' he shouted.

Orlena pulled her gun free, pointed it down, then fired twice. Two bullets struck the guard, one in the forehead, the other in the cheek. A muted scream struggled from his damaged throat, but within seconds his body was alight, and the life had drained out of him.

Matt walked across, briefly checking that both men were completely dead. They're only doing their job, just as I am. They didn't deserve to go down like this. *Later, in the still of the night, I will grieve for these men, as I grieve for all the others.*

'Clear?' he barked towards Malenkov.

'Clear,' grunted the Ukrainian.

'How's it looking out there, Ivan?'

'Clear,' shouted Ivan through the window. 'I think we're OK.'

Fifty per cent casualties, thought Matt. *I wouldn't call that OK.*

'Let's get these fires out,' said Orlena, walking into the room. 'I want all the data on these computers transported back to London.'

'We came here to destroy a factory,' snapped Matt. 'Not to play the IT department.'

'You came here to follow my instructions,' said Orlena icily.

Matt glanced across at her. One man was lying on the floor, blood seeping from multiple wounds, another was

140

gently burning. Yet Orlena stepped over them as if they didn't exist. Her eyes moved through the room, looking only at the computers, focused on the final part of the mission.

Like a ready meal that hasn't had long enough in the microwave, thought Matt. *Hot on the surface, but freezing inside.*

'How did he know who you were?' asked Matt looking across at Orlena.

She shrugged: a nonchalant toss of the shoulders that suggested the question did not interest her. 'We were here in a delegation some time ago trying to persuade them to stop counterfeiting our drugs,' she answered coldly. 'I guess I have a memorable face.'

Matt stepped closer to her. 'But what was he asking you about?' he persisted. 'What was the word you used? *Likuvannia*? What the hell does that mean?'

'Nothing,' answered Orlena, moving across the room. 'He was begging for mercy, but it was no use. Everyone here has to die.' She paused, looking back towards Matt. 'A screwdriver? Do you have one?'

'Do I look like Bob the bloody Builder?'

'Never mind, a knife will do,' continued Orlena. 'Take out the casings on all these computers, and remove the hard drives. Get those, then we can leave.'

It was midnight fifty, Matt realised. 'We haven't got time,' he said angrily. 'The police could be here in ten minutes.'

Orlena paused, fixing her gaze on Ivan and Malenkov before turning to face Matt. 'There's always time to obey an order.'

Ivan had joined them in the room now. Matt could see the exhaustion in his face, but also the relief.

That was a closer-run thing than I could ever have imagined.

Matt worked fast and furiously. The cuts on his arms were

141

starting to ache, and he could feel the soreness rippling down his back where he had bruised himself.

It took only two minutes to unpick the computers. There were eight of them, and Orlena, Matt and Ivan were working together. Matt was no expert, but he knew how to unscrew the casing, and the hard drive was easy to locate. A shiny square rectangle of metal, it was sited at the centre of the machine's innards. *Don't worry how you take it out,* Orlena had told him. *The data stored on it can be still be retrieved once we get it back to head office.*

What's on the hard drive that she needs so much? wondered Matt as he ripped the disk free.

The job finished, they ran back into the main compound. Ivan planted his remaining eight firebombs to blow the main admin building into the sky. The fire in the factory was still blazing, the flames licking up into the night sky, creating a warm crimson glow that spread out across the whole area. It was hot and the air was thick with the fumes from the fire. Matt scanned the brightly illuminated sky, searching for helicopters. Midnight fifty-three. If reinforcements were coming, they could be here any moment. They certainly weren't going to have any trouble finding the place: the flames would make it visible for miles.

It would burn for another two or three hours, Matt judged. *And by the morning it would be completely destroyed.*

Malenkov had collected the bodies of Nikita and Andrei, and had laid them out on the hard mud, their heads turned towards the east. In the Russian Orthodox Church, he explained to Matt, everyone was always buried facing east: that was where the sun rose, so that represented light, whereas the west, where the sun set, represented the darkness.

It wasn't possible to bury these two men properly or to return their bodies to their families. But they had fought bravely, and died for pitifully little money. *We should do the best we can for them.*

142

'How long is this going to take?' Matt asked anxiously, looking across at Malenkov.

'They gave us their lives,' answered Malenkov. 'We can spare five minutes to bury them.'

Matt was about to reply, but he swallowed his words. His watch had ticked past one o'clock. He looked up into the sky, but could see only the sparks and flames spitting up towards the stars.

Orlena, Matt and Ivan stood in a small semicircle, while Malenkov sprinkled some petrol over the bodies. Malenkov crossed himself and began to chant. The words were in Ukrainian, and meant nothing to Matt, but then at his side he could hear Orlena slowly whispering them in English as well. 'Be open, O earth, and receive the body that has been created out of you. That which was in the image of God, the Creator has received, and do you receive your body?'

Malenkov tossed a match downwards. A blast of burning petroleum hit Matt in the nostrils, as the flames started to crawl over the two corpses. Malenkov turned away and started walking back towards the forest.

'Josef was my son, you know,' he said, not looking back to the others. 'His mother will never forgive me.'

Matt hesitated. He wanted to say something, but he'd seen enough men die on the battlefield to know there was nothing you could say or do. He followed Malenkov back into the forest, taking the same path they had come in by. As he walked, he was scanning the night sky, his ears listening for the hum of choppers. Nothing. All he could hear was the sound of a light breeze rustling through the leaves of the trees, and the crunch of their feet against the moss, twigs and dirt that made up the floor of the forest. The Land Rover was parked twenty minutes' hike away, hidden among the trees, and they should be able to cover the tracks of their escape route.

The sooner we get out, the better.

'Two hours sleep, then we get moving,' said Matt looking up at Malenkov and Ivan. 'It's a long drive. We need our strength.'

The farmhouse had been empty for years, and was surrounded by thick forest. If the police found the burning factory, Matt calculated, it should be days before the search brought them here, so they were safe for a while at least. Before dawn, they would start their drive back to the Ukrainian border.

He drained the glass of vodka Malenkov had poured for him. It was after three in the morning now, and the night was at its stillest. 'I'm sorry about Josef,' said Matt.

Malenkov nodded, his expression remaining sombre. 'He wasn't a soldier, I shouldn't have brought him,' said Malenkov. 'But we needed the money.'

'The families of the other men who died?' asked Matt.

'They'll be contacted in due course,' answered Malenkov. 'I'll get someone to speak to them.'

'And make sure they get paid.'

Matt walked down the corridor towards his bedroom. His kitbag was still in the corner of the room, and the mattress was lying on the floor. He unpeeled his T-shirt, chucking it to one side. A line of red blood ran along his left arm where he had cut himself, stretching for about eight inches, with a thin scab already starting to cover it.

He took a cup of water from the sink, dipped a tissue into the water, and began to press it against the cut, breaking open the scab. He winced as he did so. The water stung the blood, sending a bolt of pain jabbing up through his arm.

'Here, let me do that for you,' whispered Orlena, suddenly appearing at his side.

He looked round. She had a bottle of vodka in her hand, its cap already unscrewed.

'I already had a drink, thanks,' said Matt.

'Not for drinking.'

Orlena poured some of the vodka on to the tissue, and started to run it along the length of the wound. 'Neat vodka is just about pure alcohol,' she said. 'It makes a good disinfectant.'

Matt tried to relax the muscles in his arm. He could feel his skin starting to sting as the alcohol rubbed into the raw flesh. Orlena worked softly and surprisingly tenderly, dabbing at his skin with the tissue, careful not to make it any more painful than it had to be.

When it was done, she put the bottle down on the floor. Next, he could feel Orlena's soft hands caressing his chest. She took his fist, and pushed it inside her trousers.

'I'm cut, and I'm tired,' he said, looking into her eyes. 'And we just killed a dozen or more men.'

'I don't care,' she replied, pushing him down, and stretching her legs over his. 'Like I told you, we fuck the way I want, when I want to, or not at all.'

Matt lay in her arms, his passion spent and exhausted. He could feel her long legs curling around his and, although the mattress and the single blanket were rough and worn, her skin felt fresh, soft and new next to his. As the first glimmers of dawn started to break shards of light through the window, he held her closely to him, enjoying the smell of her breath, and the taste of her lips.

In her company, even the blood of the men who had died during the night was starting to fade from his memory.

'I know so little about you.'

Orlena shrugged her shoulders. 'I'm a woman,' she replied. 'I'm lying in your bed. What more do you need to know?'

Matt laughed, realising there was something girlish about his line of questioning. Still, she fascinates me. *I want to know more about her.* 'Family?'

'Everyone's got one of those.'

'In the Ukraine?'

'No, in New York,' snapped Orlena, anger flashing up into her eyes. 'My dad's chairman of Goldman Sachs.' She rolled over on to her side.

'You must have *someone*,' persisted Matt, his fingers running down the delicate outline of her spine.

'Nobody.'

'Parents, brothers, sisters?'

Orlena shook her head, and although he could not see her face he sensed she was sad: it was written into the tensing of her shoulder blades, and the way her neck was sagging on to the pillow. 'My parents are dead. I have one brother. Roman.'

'Do you see much of him?'

Orlena turned round, lying flat on her back, her arms folded across her supple, white breasts. 'He fought in Afghanistan, for the Soviets,' she said. 'After he came back, he was, well, never quite the same.'

'Happens to a lot of guys,' said Matt. 'I still have night-mares myself, we all do. It doesn't matter what anyone says, men aren't designed to kill other men. It damages all of us.'

'What else are they designed for?'

'I'll show you.'

Matt leant over and kissed her lips, feeling a wave of pleasure roll through him as her tongue flicked up to meet his.

THIRTEEN

Eleanor looked at Matt suspiciously: he had seen several different expressions on her face in the few times they had met – anger, fear, grief, laughter – but this was the first time he had seen suspicion. Up until now, he felt she trusted him. Now he wasn't so sure.

'What is it you do, *exactly,* Matt?'

Matt looked away. 'I run a bar and restaurant,' he replied. 'On the coast, just outside Marbella. You should come down sometime.'

'No, really,' she repeated.

Matt paused. They were meeting in the Feathered Crown, a pub along the river just down from Hammersmith Bridge. It was still hot, even though it was after eight, and most of the drinkers were sitting outside, stripped down to their T-shirts and bikini tops, drinking pint after pint of beer to stay cool. He and Eleanor had stayed inside: there was more shade, it was quieter, and nobody was likely to overhear their conversation.

'I've told you, I was in the regiment,' said Matt. 'They never let you leave entirely.'

'Do you think maybe *you* have issues with letting go, Matt?' said Eleanor, turning serious. 'That's quite a common psychological reaction, particularly with men who have been very committed to one career. After it ends, they have trouble focusing on the next thing.'

'Actually, I think they have problems letting go of

me.' Matt took a sip on his beer. 'What did you find out?'

'There's been another one.'

The words were delivered calmly, but Matt could see a clear tremble of her lower lip as she spoke. *Not as tough as she makes out.*

'Where? Who?'

'A man called Ken Topley. Lived in Ipswich, in a block of bedsits. He was doing some part-time building work. He got up in the middle of the night, and started attacking the other people in the block with a knife. Killed two people, injured three more, then tried to kill himself. Cut open his wrists but he was overpowered when the police arrived. He's at the local hospital now, under heavy sedation, and on life support.'

'Was he a soldier?'

'Parachute Regiment. Did eight years, and got out two years ago. Divorced last year, with one kid. He didn't seem to have any kind of steady job, and he'd been skipping on child-support payments. But no history of mental illness.'

'Can you go and see him?'

Eleanor shook her head. 'I've asked, but they're clamming up. Ipswich Hospital say he is under police guard. No visitors. So I said I was interested in examining him for some research on mental traumas involving ex-servicemen.'

Matt looked up, suddenly interested. 'Did they listen?'

'They bit my head off.' Eleanor drained the orange juice in her glass. 'They told me a request like that would have to go through official NHS channels. I went to my supervisor at the hospital, but she just kicked me upstairs. Apparently, a request like that had to be made through the regional health authority.'

'Let me guess,' said Matt. 'They weren't helpful.'

'They told me to stop wasting my time,' she said. A tired note of despair was starting to creep into her voice. 'A waste of NHS funds, they said. I don't think I can go much further, Matt. I've got a set of suspicious circumstances, and then nothing. Nobody will help me, nobody will tell me anything about these men. I'm about ready to drop it.'

Matt reached across the table, his fingers brushing against the back of her hand. 'No,' he said firmly. 'Don't give up – not until we've checked everything.'

'I don't know where to go next.'

'There's one more man we can try. He's called Sam Hepher. He was your brother's sergeant back in the forces. A friend of mine, Keith Picton, left me his number on my answer machine last night. Keith knows everyone on the circuit. Says Hepher will speak to us tonight.'

Across the table, Matt could see Eleanor's eyes suddenly sparkle: it was as if a light had been switched on inside her. 'Then let's see him.'

Matt could see the shock on Sam Hepher's face. Like most old soldiers, he was used to death. He'd seen it enough times, its power to surprise had been eroded over time. If I just told him Ken was dead, it would hardly register. But a murderer? That was something Hepher was finding it hard to deal with.

'Ken wouldn't do something like that,' he said slowly.

They were sitting in a Portakabin at the back of a building site in Harrow. Hepher had been out of the army for two years, and was now working for his cousin's building firm, organising the security for the site. Usually he'd be at home by now, but the night guard had called in sick, so Hepher was doing the shift himself.

'That's why we're trying to find out everything we can,' said Eleanor. 'We want to know if something happened to Ken, maybe when he was still in the army?'

'It's funny,' said Hepher. 'I heard of another ex-serviceman who went crazy recently. A guy called Simon Turnbull.'

For a moment, Matt even wondered if Eleanor was

149

about to jump out of her seat. 'There have been several,' she said quickly. 'We're trying to figure out if they might be linked.'

Matt looked closely at Hepher. They were sitting opposite him, with a single forty-watt light bulb shining down on them. He was a neatly dressed man, with crisp white chinos, the seam perfectly ironed, and a plain blue polo shirt. The desk was organised and tidy, even the copy of the *Daily Mail* neatly folded away before he started talking. A line was creasing up his forehead as he burrowed his head in concentration.

He's trying to decide how much to tell us.

'There was something that struck me. It might be nothing.'

Eleanor leant forward in her chair. 'Tell us.'

'About five years ago, Ken took part in some tests. Medical tests. There's a test facility on an airfield down in Wiltshire called the Farm. Heavily guarded, all very hush-hush, but the Ministry of Defence used it to test out new products. A lot of the anti-biological warfare agents used in the Iraq war were tested there.' He paused, glancing towards Matt. 'Anyway, they needed some volunteers. You know what it's like, Matt, soldiers never like to take part in that kind of thing. They think it's all bollocks. Most of them would rather face the enemy than a doctor. So it was my job to rustle up some enthusiasm among the men. Blackman needed some leave, so he could get married, and have some money to pay for the honeymoon. So off he went. Everyone who took part got extra leave, plus five hundred quid. Enough for a fortnight in Spain. He was only there a week, and seemed fine when he came back. He said they just gave them a few pills, but he couldn't talk about what they were for.'

'And now this,' said Eleanor.

Hepher leant back in his chair. 'I wouldn't have thought

anything of it,' he continued. 'But that other fellow, Simon Turnbull. He was there the same week, doing the same tests.'

Matt gripped both the coffees in one hand, and walked back towards Eleanor. She was sitting by herself, alone at the row of tables outside the bar that flanked the ticket office to the Waterloo Eurostar terminal.

'What do you think it means?' he asked, putting the coffees down.

Eleanor dabbed a bead of sweat from her forehead. All around them, people were rushing for the last train of the day to Paris. 'It's connected,' she said firmly. 'Has to be.'

They had driven back from Harrow straight to the station: Matt had agreed to meet up with Orlena and Lacrierre just before the latter left for France. Matt and Eleanor were turning over what they had just heard, neither wanting to talk.

'It could just be a coincidence,' said Matt. 'The army tests drugs on the squaddies all the time, it doesn't necessarily mean anything.'

'I know, I know,' she muttered. 'People suffering from trauma or grief often start believing in conspiracy theories. It's all textbook stuff. The Freudians would tell us it's just a way of the subconscious struggling to come to terms with the loss.' She paused, her expression turning serious. 'But that doesn't mean the conspiracy isn't sometimes real.'

'What do you want to do next?'

'I need to find out more about the Farm,' Eleanor replied. 'I need to know who else was there that week and what drugs were tested on them.'

'Be careful,' said Matt. 'It's MOD. They aren't going to like you poking around too much. You've no idea how secretive that organisation is. Whatever happens at that place, they won't want to tell you about it.'

151

'I'll wear a short skirt, then,' said Eleanor. 'And smile a lot.'

'That should work.'

She leant forward, her lips brushing against the side of his cheek. It was only the briefest contact, over in a fraction of a second. 'Thanks,' she said. 'I'll let you know as soon as I find anything out.'

'Am I interrupting something?' said Orlena, looking down at Eleanor.

Her eyes rolled towards Matt, her expression scornful, as if she were taking pity on him for having to spend time with Eleanor. 'Our meeting is in just a few minutes,' she continued. 'The chairman doesn't like to be kept waiting.'

'This is Eleanor,' said Matt, nodding in her direction. 'And Eleanor, this is Orlena.'

'I won't keep you,' said Eleanor, suddenly flustered and shy. She looked towards Matt. 'I'll let you know what happens.'

Matt nodded. Eleanor looked towards Orlena. 'Bye,' she said brusquely.

'This way,' said Orlena, not replying to Eleanor.

She took Matt by the arm, and started steering him towards the platform. The crowds were thinning out, and Matt could see the security guards starting to pack away their equipment for the night.

'Christ,' said Matt. 'Where are we going?'

'Paris, of course,' answered Orlena.

Matt hesitated. 'The last train left ten minutes ago.'

Orlena looked at him and smiled. 'Lacrierre has his own train, stupid. He doesn't travel by public transport.'

He followed Orlena as she skipped through the one remaining security checkpoint, handed his passport to emigration, and followed her towards Platform 21. 'I've heard of private jets, but not a private train,' said Matt. 'Apart from the Queen's.'

'Why not?' said Orlena with a shrug. 'Eduardo likes to get back to Paris at least once a week. This is the best way for him to travel. Quick and safe.'

The train was waiting for them. Orlena had her own pass, and a key that unlocked the security doors. One Alsthom-built engine, with just two carriages attached, it looked just like a normal international train, only much shorter. His own Eurostar, reflected Matt as he climbed on board. You had to hand it to the guy. *He knew how to live.*

Lacrierre looked down at the picture. Even from the air, it was clear that the devastation was total. The factory had been burnt to the ground, its structure reduced to a few charred remnants. The other building had been shot to pieces. By the time this picture was taken – at least twenty-four hours after they'd hit the place, Matt judged – someone had been in to clean it up. But it was going to be a long time before they could start manufacturing anything there again.

'There,' said Matt. 'Job done.'

They were in Lacrierre's private carriage. The first carriage contained a kitchen, plus a range of office equipment: a pair of satellite phones, two computers, a Bloomberg terminal to keep him in touch with the financial markets, and a range of fax and copier machines. There were seats for two security guards, and one secretary: enough hired muscle to reassure, but not enough to look threatening. The second carriage was fitted out for Lacrierre himself, with long black leather sofas along the walls, soft lighting, a hi-fi and television.

It suddenly dawned on Matt that the train had started to move forwards. 'What the fuck's happening?' he said.

'We're going on a little trip,' said Lacrierre coldly.

'Let me off now,' shouted Matt.

'Calm down, Matt,' interrupted Orlena. 'We're going to Paris. I bought you a toothbrush.'

'Stop the fucking train!' said Matt, but he knew it was

hopeless. He would have to roll with it, for the time being at least.

Right now, they had a prime view of Balham, Matt noticed as the train trundled its way through south London towards the new high-speed link starting halfway through Kent.

In the last thirty-six hours, they had driven back across the border to Kiev, grabbed a few hours sleep, said farewell to Malenkov, then headed straight for the airport. There was no BA flight to London, so they caught the LOT flight to Warsaw, then connected there on to a plane into Heathrow. Ivan had been paid £20,000 in cash by Orlena, and gone back to his family. Matt and Orlena had been summoned to a debriefing.

Lacrierre looked up and smiled triumphantly. The carriage had little furniture, but there were some military prints on the wall and two swords were hanging at the top of the compartment. Both, Matt judged from the fine steelwork around the blades, were the delicately curved sabres carried by Napoleon's Chasseurs à Cheval de la Garde, the Imperial Guard that followed him everywhere.

'Did they fight well?'

'Not well enough, obviously,' said Matt quickly.

A stewardess stepped through from the kitchen – a striking blonde, almost as beautiful as the girls in his office – and placed a teapot and biscuits down on the table in front of them. Lacrierre poured tea for Matt and Orlena, and took a bottle of Volvic water for himself. 'A man can die while fighting well, don't you think?' he said. 'It depends on whether the dice roll for or against him.'

'There's no glory in death,' said Matt. 'You've been a soldier, you should know that.'

Lacrierre said nothing. Matt stirred a sugar lump into the delicate china cup, and took a sip of the tea. 'Anyway,' he continued, 'it doesn't matter. The job's done, the

154

factory destroyed. They aren't going to bother you any more.'

Lacrierre leant forward. 'Not quite,' he said softly. 'Think of it like a hive of ants. You can crush all the ants you want to, but unless you deal with the hive, then they just crawl back out again.' He paused, looking directly at Matt. 'I need you to get the hive.'

'The factory's finished,' said Matt. 'That's what I signed up for, and the job's done.'

Lacrierre stood up. He walked towards the window, glancing out on to the passing lawns. From the desk, he removed a single sheet of paper, then walked back across the carriage and laid it down in front of Matt.

'His name is Serik Leshko.'

Matt looked at the picture. It was a single, closely cropped snapshot printed out in black and white. The man was around forty, thin with black hair, and big round but dark eyes. His nose was probably broken, and his jaws were swollen and puffy.

'He is a Belorussian businessman,' continued Lacrierre. 'An old KGB hack, now working for himself in the private sector. He is the man who built the factory, and has been counterfeiting our drugs. We can blow up his factory, but maybe he will just build another one.' Lacrierre shrugged. 'So we blow up the man.' He sat down again, looking across at Orlena, the glimmer of a smile on his face. 'Like I said, crush the hive.'

'I've completed my mission,' said Matt quickly. 'The job's done. Over.'

Lacrierre unscrewed the bottle of Volvic, poured some into a glass and took a sip. 'From Paris you will go back to Minsk,' he continued. 'He should have been at the factory, but unfortunately he wasn't. So now you will go back and kill him. And then your work will be done.'

'It is done,' snapped Matt. 'Three words, one syllable each. Something hard to understand about that?'

155

Lacrierre looked back at him, puzzled, then amused. 'Your job was to wipe out all traces of the formulas for these counterfeits, so these people will never trouble us again. That means there's still work to do.'

'No,' said Matt, his voice rising. 'I've told you, the Firm leant on me to do this job, and I've done it. No more.'

'Then your Firm will just have to lean on you again,' continued Lacrierre. 'I'll tell you what Napoleon once said: "Victory belongs to the man who perseveres." Well, we want you to persevere until our enemy is completely crushed.'

'Napoleon ended up a prisoner of the English,' said Matt. Then he glanced across at Orlena. 'Unless I fell asleep in my history classes.'

He looked out of the window. He could see the train moving swiftly through Ashford as it approached the Channel Tunnel. Damn you, he thought. If I could jump from this train without killing myself, I would.

'Anyway,' said Lacrierre. 'It will give you a chance to spend more time with Orlena. You two have become such good friends.'

The wind was blowing in hard from the sea, taking some of the edge off the fierce midday sun. Matram sat on the stone sea wall, and slotted his shades down over his eyes. There were a few people along the main road running down into Plymouth Harbour, but the boiling temperatures had persuaded even English tourists to stay inside. It had just hit thirty-eight degrees centigrade, the hottest day ever recorded in Britain, and the heatwave was forecast to last for another fortnight.

Simon Clipper and Frank Trench has just parked the Renault Mégane across the street, and were walking towards him. Both men were dressed in shorts and T-shirts, with shades pulled down over their eyes. To the casual observer, they were just tourists looking for somewhere to have lunch.

'What's the job?' said Clipper, sitting down on the wall next to Matram.

Matram took a can of Coke, pulling it open. 'Two men this time,' he replied. 'A pair of guys called Bob Davidson and Andy Cooper, both local boys. They fish. They've got a little boat in the harbour here. This summer they've been going out in the evening because it's so hot.'

'We get them on the boat?' asked Trench.

Matram nodded. 'That's right. I've arranged a dinghy to take us out. I'll be in charge of the boat, you two need to get into the water, then sink them.'

'Can we use any explosives?' asked Clipper.

'Better not,' said Matram. 'We should be quite far out, so there shouldn't be anyone around. But sound travels a long way at sea. An explosion could easily be heard for miles.'

Matram finished the Coke in one swig, crushing the can between his fists. 'Better to drown them, then scuttle the boat. That way they'll never be found, and even if they are it will look like an accident.'

Matt looked out across the Gare du Nord. It was early evening, and the station was streaming with traffic. Backpackers and students were pouring off the last Eurostar of the day, looking for cheap places to stay. Businessmen were rushing through for the last trains out to Brussels and Cologne.

He cupped the phone close to his ear. 'You do this, old fruit, and then even the encores are over,' said Abbott. 'Trust me. You can get straight back to serving sangria and chips out on the Costa del Crime.'

Just the sound of the man's voice was grating on Matt's nerves: every time he had to speak to him, ripples of annoyance ran down his spine. Lacrierre had dropped them at the station, and Orlena was standing a few yards away. The tickets from Charles de Gaulle airport were already in her hands.

'One hit, another hit,' said Matt angrily. 'I need to know how I can get your claws out of my back.'

'I'm telling you,' repeated Abbott. 'This one, then it's over. I've spoken to Lacrierre. He likes you. He likes the way the factory was taken down, and he just needs someone he can rely on to take out the guy who's organising it. Then it's done. Problem solved.'

Matt took a sip on the coffee he'd bought at the station. 'What's Lacrierre got on you?'

'As soon as you get a chance, check your accounts.'

'Which one?'

'The current account, Matt.' Abbott paused. 'The others are still blocked. It's like magic, you see, old fruit. Matt's a good boy, the account opens. Matt's a bad boy, the account closes.'

'I get my own money back, and I'm supposed to be grateful?'

'That one's just a gesture of goodwill. Get back out east and do the hit, and the rest will be open as well. Like I said, the slate will be wiped clean.'

Matt buried his face in his hand. There was always some trouble somewhere, and the Firm always needed men to sort it out for them. It was just as Ivan had said it would be.

'One more hit, Matt,' repeated Abbott. 'What difference can it make to a man with as much blood on his hands as you?'

Matt leant into the phone. 'Where's Gill? I haven't heard from her . . .'

'The sexy playgroup leader?' he said, a giggle playing on his lips. 'Buggered if I know, old fruit. Probably shagging the waiter back at the Last Strumpet.'

Matt paused. 'It's not like her to be out of contact for so long,' he said. 'I want to know if the Firm have anything to do with that.'

'Do the hit, old fruit,' he said. 'Then you can sort out your love life. It's called prioritising. I can lend you a book on it, if you like.'

Matt was about to respond: the fury was building in his chest, searching around for the words to express it. But the mobile had already gone dead in his hand. Orlena slipped her arms around his waist, pointing towards the taxi rank. 'Come on,' she said softly. 'It's time to go.'

Matram could feel the dinghy swaying beneath him. The breeze had dropped since midday, but it was still gusting strongly through the English Channel, whipping up foam on the top of the waves.

The old pirates along the Devon and Cornish coast had the right idea. *At sea nobody can see you kill a man.*

They had been on the water for almost an hour now, and Matram figured they were about a mile off the coast. Earlier in the day, he had fitted a small electronic tracker to the bottom of the target's boat. It was transmitting a signal up to a GPS satellite, and that was transmitting its precise location back down to him.

We can watch it as if it were right in front of our eyes.

'Another five minutes to impact,' he shouted across the stern of the boat. 'Ready yourselves.'

Clipper and Trench were both kitted out with wetsuits, with only their blacked-up faces visible. On to their backs they had strapped oxygen canisters, and they had flippers on their feet. Both of them had two thick steel hunting knives strapped to their belts, but otherwise they were unarmed. They were sitting calmly at the prow of the boat, looking out to sea as the vessel rocked through the waves.

The moonlight was glancing across the ocean, lighting up the path ahead. No clouds were cluttering up the sky, and Matram judged they would have good visibility for the rest of the night.

He looked down at the GPS display, adjusting the engine to the right to shift the direction of the dinghy. They would take the boat to within a kilometre of the target, then kill the engine.

Matram put a pair of Bushnell 20 × 50 high-powered surveillance binoculars to his eyes. They were designed for birdwatchers, but with a twentyfold magnification, and a thousand-metre range, he found them better than any of the kit the regiment issued. Adjusting the focus, he could see the boat drifting across the horizon. Two men were sitting on its deck, their lines cast out into the water. Like ducks, he thought. *Waiting to get shot at.*

Turning round, Matram killed the engine. 'Go,' he whispered.

Clipper and Trench broke through the surface of the waves with hardly a ripple, then disappeared below the water. As he watched them disappear, Matram checked his watch. Fifteen minutes past midnight. Within ten minutes both men should be dead.

He rested the binoculars on his lap, looking out into the water. To the naked eye, the boat was just a speck on the surface of the water. It could easily be a trick of the light. *I can see them, but they can't see me.*

Putting the Bushnell back up to his eyes, Matram counted down the moments. It was the minute before an assault he enjoyed the most. He could feel the anticipation pricking his skin, and the excitement brought out a gentle sweat on his forehead.

You could taste it a thousand times, but every assassination had its own special flavour.

A shadow broke through the surface of the water. Even at this distance, he could see the boat rock and sway as Clipper and Trench punched through the water, and scrambled on board. He increased the magnification, but at this distance it was impossible to make out much of the detail. He could see one of the men standing, and then another bending over, clutching his stomach in agony as a knife plunged into his stomach. The second man jumped backwards, losing his footing, crashing down to the bottom of the boat. Matram could see a knife slashing down at him. Within a minute, the scene had fallen quiet again. Then he could see weights being strapped to the two corpses as they were tossed into the waves. Next, he could see the boat list from side to side, as Clipper and Trench started to cut away at its side, shipping water into its hull.

A burial at sea, reflected Matram as he watched the boat disappear beneath the waves. They were soldiers once. *They should be grateful for the death we have delivered them.*

FOURTEEN

Malenkov looked at him suspiciously, rubbing his hand into the stubble on his chin. 'The last time I worked with you, my son died,' he said. 'And now you think I should do it again?'

Matt leant across the table. They were back in the apartment in Kiev, having arrived on the flight from Charles de Gaulle less than two hours ago. 'I can't give you a single good reason. If I were you, I wouldn't do it either.' He glanced across to Orlena. 'But she'll give you a lot of money.'

Malenkov looked towards Orlena. She was sitting across the table, a slim leather computer case on her lap. Slowly, she pushed it across the table. Malenkov hesitated, then unzipped the case, slipping his fist inside. He pulled out a bundle of notes, holding them crumpled in his hand.

'Twenty thousand,' said Orlena crisply. 'Ten thousand dollars, ten thousand euros.'

Malenkov laughed. 'I've lost one son already,' he said, the laughter ebbing away on his lips. 'For that amount of money, you want me to lose some more?'

Orlena tapped her fingers on the notes, her nails making a small thud against the thick wads of paper. 'There's more,' she said softly. 'As much as you need.'

Malenkov stood up, his expression suddenly angry. 'And how many men will die for that kind of money?' His voice dropped to a whisper. 'And how many will be betrayed?'

'One man will die,' snapped Orlena. 'Leshko. Serik Leshko.'

Malenkov gave them a hard, penetrating stare. 'You're crazy.'

'I wish,' said Matt. 'But those are the orders.'

'Leshko is one of the richest men in Minsk,' said Malenkov. 'He's the biggest gangster this side of the Don. Everyone is afraid of him, even the government. Knocking off Vladimir Putin, that would be an easier hit.'

'We want to take him, and we want you to help us,' said Matt.

Malenkov patted the case on his lap. 'Then this is just a down payment,' he said. 'Leshko is an evil bastard, so I'd be doing the country a favour. If a man is going to throw away his life, he doesn't want to do it cheaply or pointlessly.'

The office was fiercely lit, with a view that stretched down across the centre of Minsk. It was painted pale blue, and along the back wall there was a series of televisions, all tuned to different sports channels around the world. In front of the screens was a black Labrador tethered to the leg of a desk. On the wall next to them was mounted a series of machine guns: just about every important model ever manufactured in the Soviet Union, reckoned Matt. And from their gleaming, polished appearance, all of them were in perfect working order.

Serik Leshko leant forward. 'What did you say your name was?'

'Perkins,' replied Matt calmly. 'Brian Perkins.'

'Mr Perkins is from England,' explained Malenkov, sitting at his side. 'He is looking for someone to do some manufacturing for him.'

Matt could feel his muscles drawing tighter. They had spent a day travelling by train up from Kiev to Minsk, checking into one of the few smart hotels in the city: the

Best Eastern, just off Independence Square. Orlena had stayed back in Kiev: they figured she might be recognised by Leshko's men, and that would blow their cover immediately.

They had been strip-searched by two security guards on their way into the building, and neither of them was carrying a weapon of any sort. The story had, of course, already been worked out in advance. Malenkov was to arrange an introduction to Leshko, with Matt posing as an English businessman who needed some manufacturing work done. It had taken three days just to get this far. Two meetings with Leshko's henchmen to establish their credentials, and a big sum paid into an offshore bank account to make them look like serious businessmen. Leshko didn't meet just anyone: you had to prove yourself before you got in.

Matt felt certain he had his lines memorised. Yet one slip, and this man would kill them. *And there won't be a damned thing I can do about it, except to take my death with dignity.*

'And what is it you want made?' said Leshko.

'David Beckham shirts, in Real Madrid colours, both home and away,' said Matt. 'I'm told you manufacture just about everything. Gucci shirts, Louis Vuitton handbags, Chanel perfumes, Moschino belts, the lot. A shirt shouldn't be a problem.'

Leshko shook his head, a slow smile spreading across his lips. Behind him sat two striking blondes, who appeared to be there just for ornamentation. 'It's no problem,' he replied. 'You give me the sizes, the design, the colours, and I can get them made for you.'

Matt nodded. 'I'd be looking for about ten thousand a month. I could pay you one pound sterling a shirt. That's ten thousand a month, for as long as I can keep selling them.'

'I can add up for myself,' said Leshko curtly.

'It would be cash on delivery,' said Matt quickly.

Leshko nodded. 'Then it can be done. Delivery to the Belorussian–Polish border. How you get them across Europe is your problem.'

'Agreed,' said Matt. 'I look forward to doing business with you.'

'I would need a deposit,' said Leshko. 'Thirty thousand dollars, in cash. Until I have that, I can't do anything.'

Haggle, thought Matt. If I agree too quickly, it looks suspicious. 'Twenty thousand.'

Leshko stood up. He was wearing a black suit, with a dark blue shirt open at the collar. A silver cross was glittering on his smooth chest. 'I'm not a haggling man, Mr Perkins,' he said. 'I'm not a trader in a street market. I state my price, and I expect to have it paid. In full, and on time.'

'Twenty-five thousand,' said Matt.

'Not a haggling man,' repeated Leshko. Now, you can give me thirty thousand in cash tomorrow, or you can find someone else to make your shirts.'

'Agreed,' said Matt. 'But I need a safe meeting place. Just you and me.'

'Alone.' Leshko laughed. He picked up a dog biscuit from a small case on the desk, and tossed it in the direction of the Labrador. 'I never go anywhere without my guards.'

'How many?'

Malenkov leant forward. 'We just want to make sure that we can hand over the money safely,' he said.

'And if we are to do business together, we're going to have to learn to trust each other,' said Leshko. 'Don't you agree, Brian?'

Matt smiled. 'Agreed. So let's start with you telling me how many guards.'

'Two,' said Leshko. 'And we'll meet by the side of the road. That way you can be sure it will be safe.'

'Which road?' asked Matt.

'Ten miles from here,' said Leshko. 'One of my men will

165

give you a map on the way out. At three o'clock. You bring me the money, I'll get the factories working.'

Matt stood up, and stretched out his hand. 'Good doing business with you.'

Behind him, he could hear the Labrador barking viciously.

The lay-by was hot and desolate, the cracked tarmac of the road surface dried out by the sunshine. Matt stood by the side of the road, looking out across the flat, empty farmland. It was two forty-five. The wheat fields were just approaching harvest, sending ripples of gold stretching out towards the horizon. The air was completely still, with not even a trace of cloud visible in the sky, and the sun was approaching its midday peak.

'Make sure Leshko is standing closer to the road than you are, with his back towards it,' said Malenkov, pointing out the precise spot. 'That way I have a better chance of hitting him not you.'

They were standing on the edge of the A236, one of the main roads heading out of Minsk towards the Polish border. In most countries, it might be heaving with traffic, but Belarus was so poor, there was only a car or a truck every hour or so. *More than enough time to kill a man.*

'You think you can get Leshko and the guards at the same time?'

Malenkov shrugged. 'If you can distract them, I can kill them,' he replied.

The plan had been worked out in detail. Matt would meet Leshko at the place he had demanded: this lay-by, ten miles along the A236. Matt would be standing there by himself, while Leshko drew up in a car. Of his two guards, one would certainly stay in the car, the other would get out and stand with Leshko. Malenkov would approach them slowly in his Land Rover, raising little suspicion. At the last moment, he would accelerate, smashing the vehicle into

Leshko and his guard. Matt would jump out of the way, take an AN-49 from the back of the Land Rover, turning it on the remaining guard.

'Just here,' said Matt, walking two yards to the side of the lay-by. 'This is where I will try to stand.'

Malenkov nodded. 'That should give me a straight run at them from the road.'

Matt paced the length of the lay-by, his heart thumping against his chest, and his blood rattling through his veins. It was the waiting that always got him. It was two minutes to three, and Leshko, he suspected, would be punctual: men were always on time when they were collecting money.

The moments leading up to a hit were full of silent, suffocated anxieties: a dozen different scenarios played themselves out in your mind, and at least half of them wound up with you lying dead on the floor.

Leshko is a professional. No kill is ever easy. But this one could be harder than most.

Malenkov was parked five hundred yards away, in a lay-by obscured by trees. After he saw Leshko drive past, he would wait five minutes before hitting the road. Matt was holding on to a plain black case, with thirty thousand in crisp notes stacked inside.

Suddenly, a car appeared on the horizon. It disappeared for a few minutes in a dip in the road, then there it was, some fifty yards away.

The Mercedes was black, with shaded windows. It pulled slowly into the lay-by, and from the way it braked, Matt judged the skin of the car was reinforced with armour: it juddered to a halt in a way a Merc never would unless it was carrying a lot of extra weight.

Armour, bullet-proof glass, and armed bodyguards. *These guys take their security seriously.*

Matt stepped forward. The window of the car slid down, and Leshko looked out, his eyes darting around the lay-by. 'You alone?' he snapped.

Matt spread out his arms. 'Completely.'

The door opened. The guard stepped out first. A tall man, more than six foot, with broad shoulders and light sandy hair, he walked slowly up to Matt with an arrogant dismissive swagger. He was wearing black jeans, a white T-shirt and boots: from the shape of his trousers, Matt reckoned there was one pistol in his pocket, and another tucked into his shoes.

'Search,' he barked towards Matt. 'Search.'

Matt stood with his hands and legs apart. The guard frisked him roughly, thumping his skin with the back of his palm. He pulled up Matt's shirt, checking the belt of his trousers, then feeling around the edge of his shoes.

Be as rough as you like, pal. You'll be dead in a few minutes.

'Clean,' shouted the guard over his shoulder.

Leshko stepped out of the car. A thin smile was playing on his face. He took two steps towards Matt, looking greedily towards the black plastic case on the ground next to his feet. 'I apologise for the inconvenience,' he said slowly.

'T-shirts are a dangerous business,' said Matt. He allowed himself one glance up the road. Nothing. But the dip in the road meant he would only see the Land Rover as it arrived within fifty yards of the lay-by. Matt judged that Malenkov should be here within one minute.

Just time for some small talk.

He looked back towards Leshko. 'As we get to know each other, I'm sure we'll trust each other more.'

'I hope so,' said Leshko. 'You have my money?'

In his head, Matt was counting down the seconds: thirty, twenty-nine, twenty-eight . . .

'Of course,' he replied calmly. 'As you requested. And when will the shirts be delivered?'

'Within one week,' said Leshko quickly. 'My factories are fast. We can make whatever you want, whenever you want it. So long as we get paid.'

Steady yourself, Matt told himself: twelve, eleven, ten . . .

He picked up the case, and started to pass it across to Leshko. 'Here, you count it.'

Matt took two steps backwards: five, four, three . . .

He didn't want to look up, but he could hear the Land Rover coming over the ridge, and the hum of its engine as it started to accelerate. It was three hundred yards away now. Leshko was opening the case, his attention moment-arily captured by the notes inside. Matt could see his eyes sparkling as he feasted on the thick wedges of notes. He turned, the case in his hand, as if he were about to put it in the car. If he does, Matt realised, he'll see Malenkov.

'Why don't you count the money?' said Matt quickly. 'Then we've wrapped up the deal.'

Leshko grinned. 'Shouldn't I trust you?'

'Just count it.'

The guard was standing next to him, his back to the road too, looking edgily towards Matt. The Land Rover was just a hundred yards behind them now, its speed picking up.

Keep looking the wrong way, mate. Then you won't know what's hitting you.

The tyres on the Land Rover screeched as it pulled hard off the road. It swerved, smashing into the back of the guard with a brutal blow. It impacted just above the waist, crushing hard into his spine, instantly paralysing him. He fell to the ground, the wheel of the vehicle crashing into his head.

In front of them, the guard in the Merc fired off a warning shot in the direction of Malenkov, then slammed the car door shut, and Leshko spun round, a look of terror on his face. The Land Rover had slowed after hitting the guard, but it had not stalled. In the split second available, Leshko

169

tried desperately to save himself, throwing himself to the right, but the vehicle crushed into his left thigh, spinning his body sideways, and sending it high into the air. Matt could hear the snap of bones, where he had been hit: his left leg had definitely gone, maybe his hip and pelvis as well.

Matt jumped forwards. A fraction of a second. *That's all I have to save myself.*

He moved swiftly sideways, running around to the back of the Land Rover and grabbing the AN-49 stored in the open boot. The gun felt solid in his hands as he flicked its safety catch. Kneeling, he raised the gun to his eye, then fired a swift round of bullets into the guard on the floor. The body twitched as the metal tore into his flesh, then it fell still.

Matt moved around to the front of the Land Rover and turned his fire on to the Mercedes. The bullets ripped into the tyres, turning them into loose shreds, but the bullets just bounced off the skin of the car. Matt moved closer, peppering the windows with bullets, but they ricocheted up into the air. With the butt of the rifle, he tried to smash open the window, but the strength of the glass deflected his hardest blows.

'Fuck it,' shouted Matt. 'He's getting away.'

He could hear the engine on the Mercedes roaring into life, as the driver attempted to reverse. In that car, Matt realised, even with the tyres shot to pieces, he stood a good chance.

'Ram him,' shouted Matt towards Malenkov. 'Ram the bastard.'

The Mercedes had roared into action, its engine revving furiously as the driver spun it into gear. It screeched on to the road, sparks flying off the tarmac where the bare metal of its wheels hit the road. It turned, then accelerated towards where Matt was standing. He jumped, then flung himself sideways, a bolt of pain juddering up through his shoulder as he crashed against the tarmac.

But, in trying to hit Matt, the driver had lost the split seconds in which he could have made his own escape.

No moment for loyalty mate, thought Matt. *You're wasting your own life.*

Ahead, Matt could see the Land Rover ramming into the Mercedes, the two vehicles colliding in an inferno of twisting, burning metal. Malenkov had thrown himself from the cabin of his car, landing hard on the concrete surface of the lay-by. Flames were starting to lick through the underside of both machines, as petrol spilt out across the road. The driver's side window slid down, and a shot rang out through the air. The man was unable to aim, Matt realised: he knew that if he stuck his head out of the car, he'd get killed. His bullets were whizzing harmlessly through the air.

Poor, miserable bastard, thought Matt. *He's trying to decide whether to get burnt alive or come out and get shot.*

The door opened. A man staggered out, blood seeping from a cut in his forehead. He took two steps forward, his hands raised in the air, shouting, '*Litasc, litasc.*'

Sorry, pal. *We not in the mercy business.*

Matt raised the AN-49, steadying his aim, then unleashing a volley of fire. The bullets struck the man around the upper torso, then in the neck, sending him rocking back on his heels. Another word screamed from his lips, but above the din of the machine-gun fire, Matt couldn't make it out. His knees buckled, and he collapsed to the floor, his hands reaching up to his throat as the blood poured out of him. Within a minute, he would be dead.

'You OK?' Matt shouted across to Malenkov.

The Ukrainian stood up, still holding his gun. 'OK,' he grunted. 'Just some bruises.'

From the side of the road, Matt could hear the sound of a man groaning in pain. He spun on his heels, running to the edge of the field where Leshko was just regaining consciousness, his eyes blinking in the fierce sunlight. Blood was dribbling down the side of his face, and from the bump in his side it looked as if several bones had been broken. Matt jammed the barrel of his gun tight into the man's throat, already worrying that Leshko might try to pull a gun on him. 'Who would dare to do this?' said Leshko, blood spitting from his tongue as he struggled to speak. 'Who would dare?'

Matt tightened his finger on the barrel of the AN-49, pressing it hard into Leshko's skin. He paused, reflecting that the man had a right to know why he was being killed, and he had an obligation to tell him. *That was one of the differences between being a soldier and a murderer.*

'Eduardo Lacrierre,' he replied. 'You've been faking his company's drugs. Big mistake. Knocking out imitation watches and handbags is one thing, but you've been fucking with some serious people.'

A bolt of pain shot across the man's face. Matt could see him trying to move, but too many bones were broken along the left side of his body for him to flex more than a muscle.

'You're a bloody fool, Englishman. I didn't steal from Lacrierre. He stole from me.'

'What could one of the richest men in Europe want to steal from a two-bit gangster in a craphole like Belarus?'

'Not money,' said Leshko. 'Science.'

'Ridiculous. What science could you possibly have out here that would interest a company like Tocah?'

Leshko tried to laugh, but the pain overwhelmed him; as soon as he creased his lips, a look of agony flashed on to his face. 'Weapons. In Soviet days, there was a lot of military research around here. XP22. That's what he took from me. It was a drug the Russians developed for the Red Army to take in Afghanistan. It makes men brave. But it makes them crazy as well.'

'You're just trying to save your neck,' Matt snapped back. 'I didn't come here for a history lesson.'

Slowly, Leshko raised his head up slightly, looking Matt hard in the eye. 'You can shoot me if you want to, Englishman. The pain I'm in right now, I don't care. But you're an idiot, and I want you to know that. They're using you, and when they're finished, they'll dispose of you.'

Matt pushed the tip of the AN-49 into the side of Leshko's cheek, the hot metal of the gun barrel burning up his skin. 'Enough.'

Leshko coughed up a small clot of blood from the back of his throat. 'You must speak to Leonid Petor,' he said, his voice turning down to a deathly whisper. 'He's old now, and lives outside Kiev. But his mind is still good, he'll tell you about it.'

Matt paused, wiping a bead of sweat from his forehead. The cars were still burning a few yards behind him, sending hot waves of smoke across the field.

'We haven't got time for this,' interrupted Malenkov, looking anxiously up and down the road.

'I'll take you to him,' Leshko wheezed, his voice growing hoarser.

Matt shook his head. He squeezed the trigger softly, released one bullet into the side of the man's head. Leshko was already weak and as the metal ripped through his brain the last spark of life left him. Matt checked he'd stopped breathing, then stood up.

He could feel the blood pumping to his head. What was it Leshko had said?

It makes men brave. But it makes them crazy as well.

He turned to look at Malenkov, his eyes intense. 'You think he was telling the truth?'

The Ukrainian shrugged, slinging his gun over his back and starting to stride out across the field. 'I don't know,' he replied warily. 'But there were rumours of drugs like that being tested on the Red Army in Soviet times.'

Matt looked out across the flat, empty fields stretching out on to the horizon. The sun was beating down, flooding the landscape with a dazzling brightness. Behind him, both the Land Rover and the Mercedes were consumed in flames, thick clouds of smoke swirling upwards. 'Christ,' he said. 'This story isn't what I thought it was at all.'

FIFTEEN

Her touch felt gentle and supple on his skin. Orlena took the vodka, dabbed it on to some cotton wool, then rubbed it on to the cuts sliced into Matt's skin. He had taken an ugly graze down the side of his shoulder, and the bruising was starting to turn purple. Across his back, a pair of cuts stretched in deep crimson lines, and the wound on his cheek from the factory raid had been sliced open again.

I've taken a beating. I need a few days' rest to get back into shape.

From the roadside, they had walked ten miles across country until they reached the next village. Malenkov had already arranged to have a car and driver waiting for them there: a twelve-year-old BMW 3 series, for which they paid two thousand euros, cash. It was double what the car was worth, but that didn't matter. It got them as far as the border, and as soon as they were back in the Ukraine, they ditched it and got a taxi down to Kiev. After sixteen hours of travelling, they were back in the apartment. They were exhausted, their energy drained and their nerves shattered. But they were alive, and the job was done. *There was some comfort in that.*

'You've done so well,' said Orlena. 'Not many men could have got to Leshko and come out alive. Lacrierre will be pleased. Very pleased.'

Matt winced. The cold alcohol was stinging his skin and his blood, sending tremors of pain through his shoulders. 'Is there enough blood in the ground now to make him happy?'

Orlena filled a small glass with vodka. 'He's got what he wanted.'

She put the glass to her lips, swilling the transparent liquid into her cheeks, then leant forward, pressing her lips on to Matt's. She seemed different now: happier, more relaxed and confident than at any time since he'd met her. He could feel the vodka dribbling from her tongue to his as they kissed. They were lying back on the bed, Matt stripped down to just his jeans, but Orlena still wearing a short black skirt, suede thigh-length boots and a tight black sweater through which he could see the outline of her bra. Matt reached up, his hands running along the back of her tights until he was inside her skirt. Her legs swung across him, and with her arms she pushed him back on the bed. Matt grabbed hold of her left boot, his fingers starting to peel away its side zip.

'How many times do I have to tell you, we fuck the way I want to or not at all.'

Matt lay back on the bed, allowing her to smother him with kisses. Her lips ran down his chest, her tongue flicking out across his skin, sending ripples of excitement running down Matt's spine. He closed his eyes, letting the throb of his wounds mix with her caress, turning into a cocktail of pain and pleasure. It was swift, yet still consuming, and when Orlena was finished with him, she lay at his side, her breath slow and sleepy, taking short sips at the open vodka bottle.

Matt was starting to feel closer to Orlena. They were relaxing in each other's company. She might have forced him to come back for the second half of the job, but he had survived that, and there was nothing to hold against her now.

'Leshko said something before he died,' said Matt. 'About

a bravery drug. Produced in Minsk in the old days, he said. And Lacrierre stole it from him. It makes men brave, but it also makes them crazy.' As she lay in his arms, Matt could see Orlena smiling, but he could also feel a sudden bolt of tension in her arms.

'Ridiculous,' she snapped. 'A dying man will tell any story no matter how stupid if he thinks it will save his skin. You're a soldier, you should know that.'

Matt shook his head. 'No,' he said firmly. 'There's one thing you learn on the battlefield. A dying man doesn't lie. It's probably the only moment when a man is completely honest.'

'Forget it,' said Orlena softly. 'Let's go back to England together. Or maybe Spain. I won't always be working for Tocah, and who knows, maybe I'll settle in the West.'

Matt laughed. 'I don't forget,' he answered. 'You'll learn that about me one day.'

Orlena fell silent. She was looking away from him, and Matt sensed that she might be crying: it was not a full-grown tear – she could hold those back until she needed them – but just a touch of moisture around the curved, almond-shaped cusp of her eye. 'Don't even think about the bravery drug,' she said.

Matt backed away. It was not the reaction he'd expected. 'I . . . I have to.'

'No,' said Orlena firmly. 'I said no.'

Matt could feel himself becoming angry. 'It might connect back to something in England,' he said, trying to keep his tone casual. 'I just need to check it out.'

'It *doesn't* connect.'

'Well, until I check, I don't know that.'

Orlena rolled over, gripping his fist. 'Listen, just leave it,' she said. 'This is a dark country, with dark secrets. You're a foreigner. You know nothing about what happens here. Just go home.'

177

Matt shook his head. 'I've told you, I just want to check.'

Suddenly, Orlena silenced him with a kiss. She reached down and started to unzip her boots. 'Then make love with me,' she whispered. 'Like it was your last time on earth.'

Matt double-checked down the street. It was early on a Tuesday morning, and the Kiev commuters were on their way to the office. It was still cool at this time of the morning, and, even though the sun was shining, a pleasant breeze was blowing through the city. It was the first time Matt had felt a comfortable temperature in weeks.

Telling Orlena he needed some air, he'd just stepped out of the apartment for a few minutes. He cupped one ear to block the noise of the traffic, sat down at a pavement café, and put his Nokia to the other ear. 'Eleanor,' he said into the phone. 'That you?'

He could tell it took her a moment to recognise his voice. 'Matt. You OK?'

'Just about. You find anything out?'

'About the Farm? Yes, plenty. I've been surfing the Net.'

Matt stirred a sugar into the coffee he had just ordered from a waitress in the café. He looked back up at her, pointing at the picture of some bacon and eggs on the menu. *It seems like weeks since I had a proper breakfast.*

'What Hepher told us checked out. It's about ten miles south of Chippenham down in Wiltshire,' Eleanor continued. 'All very hush-hush, apparently.'

Matt took a hit of the coffee. 'What really happened there?'

'It was used for early-stage testing by some of the big drugs companies. They'd take compounds fresh from the labs, stuff that was so advanced they didn't want anyone to know about it yet. And then try it out on two or three volunteers, put them under observation, and get an idea of what the effects would be.'

178

'If the patients dropped down dead,' interrupted Matt, 'then they knew not to carry on?'

'They used quite a few prisoners. Lifers who were told they'd get some special treatment if they took part in the experiments. And they used soldiers as well.'

The bacon and eggs arrived at Matt's table, along with a serving of black toast. The bacon was in thin streaky strips; a distant relative of a proper back rasher. Still, it would have to do. 'So the MOD was involved.'

Eleanor replied carefully. 'The place was run by a number of the big pharmaceutical companies. They put up all the money, but the Home Office and the MOD came up with the patients.'

Matt took the first strip of bacon, folded it into a slice of toast and swallowed it hungrily. 'Tocah,' he said decisively. 'I bet one of them was Tocah.'

'Why?'

'A hunch, that's all.' Matt swallowed food. 'I found something out. I don't know why, but I think it might be connected. There was something called a bravery drug, it was developed out here in the old Soviet days.'

'What did it do?'

The same phrase looped through Matt's mind. 'It made men brave, but it made them crazy as well.'

He could visualise the expression on her face: surprise, fear, but also pleasure, the rush of adrenalin to the brain when it makes a connection. 'It makes men brave, but it makes them crazy as well,' she said, repeating the words as slowly as if she were reading them out to a class of three-year-olds. 'A drug that you might test on soldiers, but which might drive them crazy.' She paused. 'My God, Matt. Maybe that's what was tested on the soldiers who went to the Farm. Maybe that's what happened to Ken.'

'Let's not get carried away,' said Matt. 'It might be nothing.'

'Can you find out more about the drug?' she continued, her tone rising. 'We could find out if there were any traces of it in the bodies of the men who went crazy.'

'I can try,' said Matt.

'And I'm going to get down to Wiltshire. Ask around about this Farm place. Maybe somebody will know something about it, maybe I can even get a list of the soldiers who had drugs tested on them.'

'No,' snapped Matt. 'Wait until I get back. If it had anything to do with the MOD, there will be tight security. They won't like people asking questions.'

'Don't worry, I can look after myself. Call me as soon as you get back to London.'

'No, Eleanor, don't go.'

Matt could hear his voice rising, but he knew he was talking into thin air. She'd already rung off. Quickly, he started to redial, but the battery on his Nokia had run dead. The phone was refusing to respond.

She's got no idea what she might be up against here. Nor can she imagine the violence they are capable of.

Matt looked down at the remaining egg and slice of bacon on his plate. He folded the bacon on to his fork, and started to chew on it. But suddenly he wasn't hungry any more.

'Here you are,' said Orlena, handing the weapon across the car seat.

Matt glanced down at the gun: a .38-calibre Russian-manufactured Marakov, it was a precisely tooled gun that would fit neatly just below the belt of his jeans.

'Makes a change from unloading my pistol, I suppose.'

Orlena didn't smile. She had spent an hour this morning trying to persuade Matt to go straight back to London with her. After speaking with Eleanor, Matt had told Orlena he was cancelling his flight back to London. He needed to

180

follow up what Leshko had told him about the bravery drug: it was a personal matter, he explained. Nothing to do with Lacrierre or Tocah. She'd been incredibly angry, trying to insist again they had to get back to London to debrief Lacrierre. You do what you like, Matt had told her: I'm staying here. As his determination became clear, her tone changed. She'd offered to come with him. You'll need someone to speak Ukrainian, she said. And to help you find his address.

Now Matt looked back up at the tower block. They were on the outskirts of Kiev, where the Dnieper River started to twist eastwards, away from the factories, and out into the clear, flat countryside stretching down to the Black Sea coastline. The estate looked of late sixties, early seventies vintage, with twelve tall towers grouped in a semicircle around what might have once been a park but was now just a dump for broken furniture and smashed-up cars. Half the windows in each tower were boarded up, another quarter were broken.

'Nice spot,' said Matt.

'Worker's paradise,' said Orlena. 'Anyone gets nostalgic for the old days, they come here. It reminds them that however bad things might get sometimes, anything is better than socialism.'

Matt climbed out of the car – a Fiat Punto, rented from the local Hertz office – and started walking out across the empty ground. 'This way,' said Orlena, walking quickly past Matt.

To his right, Matt could see a pair of teenage boys taking the engine from an abandoned car. He followed Orlena across the waste ground, towards the back of the last of the tower blocks. There was a row of twenty identical two-storey houses, with a flat on each level. They had been white originally, but were now stained, and covered with the patches of a hundred cheap repairs. But the windows were mostly intact, and a few flowers had been planted along the communal front garden. Compared with the rest of the estate, it looked like a palace.

Orlena stopped outside Number Twelve, ringing the bell. It didn't work. She banged twice, loudly, making the door creak beneath her fist. From inside, Matt could hear a man shouting, then the sound of a series of locks being slowly unfastened.

Three locks, counted Matt. *Maybe he doesn't trust the neighbours.*

Leonid Petor was eighty-five and thin, but still sprightly. His skin was stretched tight over the bones in his face, and his eyes shone brightly across the room. He glanced first at Orlena, then at Matt, his expression wary. '*Dobryy den,*' he muttered.

Orlena spoke to him in Ukrainian, waited for the reply, then looked towards Matt. 'He says we can come in.'

Matt stepped into the hallway. It was neat and tidy, with a blue carpet, and a bunch of dried flowers in a vase on a side table. The hall led through to a living room, with a kitchen at the back, a small bedroom and a shower room. So far as Matt could tell, he lived alone. If there was a Mrs Petor, she had long since died.

'I speak English,' said Petor, looking up at Matt. 'I had to. I was a scientist, and English is the language of science.'

Matt followed him into the main room. One wall was taken up with a bookshelf crammed with dusty old papers and books. There was a picture of a family on the mantel-piece, shot in black and white, and at least twenty years old: Matt recognised Petor, and the woman must have been his wife and the boy his child. Next to it were a series of framed certificates, the writing all in Russian. Matt guessed they were medals or awards of some sort.

Petor was not just any scientist. Either they handed out those awards to everyone, or he was something special.

182

'I need some information,' said Matt, sitting down on the sofa. 'About a drug that was manufactured here, maybe a decade ago, maybe two decades.'

'Then you've come to the right address.'

Petor spoke with a heavy accent, but the words were clear and crisp. His body might be frail, but his mind was still active. From his expression, Matt guessed he was pleased to have someone to talk to. *Being ignored. That's what hurts the old the most.*

'That was your area of research?'

Petor sat down on a faded armchair, its arms covered in coffee stains. 'I was deputy director for the Ukraine division, Biopreparat. Do you know what that was?'

Matt shook his head.

'The chief directorate for biological preparations. It was set up by the Politburo in 1973. We had just signed arms-control treaties with the Americans, banning the development of biological weapons. But the treaties didn't say anything about genetics, or about microbiology, or about mind-altering drugs. So those were the areas we started working on.'

Matt leant forwards. 'Mind-altering drugs?' he said, repeating the words slowly.

'Yes, yes, I know what I just said, I don't need it repeated,' snapped Petor. 'I might be old, but I'm not senile.'

'Sorry. Can you tell me more about them?'

Matt could feel himself being examined. The old man's eyes were scrutinising him carefully, running across his face and looking into his eyes. 'Correct me if I'm mistaken, but you look like a soldier.'

'I'm out now, but I spent ten years in the special forces.'

Petor stood from his chair, and walked closer to Matt. He was peering into his eyes, the way a doctor might study an ailing patient. His voice was rasping. 'You didn't take the drug, did you?' he demanded.

'No, not me,' said Matt. 'But I know of some men who might have taken it.'

Petor turned round, sitting back in his chair. 'It should never have been used, it should never have been used.'

'Tell me about it,' said Matt. 'If I can find out more, maybe I can help the men who took it.'

Petor rolled his eyes upwards, as if he was searching for something hidden away: a memory locked right at the back of his mental filing cabinet. 'The work started around 1970. It was an interesting time. Hippies, the Beatles, Vietnam. We didn't have anything like that in the Soviet Union of course, but we still watched what was happening in the rest of the world, and we reacted to it. Mind- and behaviour-altering drugs were just starting to take. Pharmaco-psychology, that was the term we used. There was Valium, that was the first of them, in the early sixties. Then you had LSD, and amphetamines, and marijuana, and all the rest. And so the question naturally arose: were there any military uses for those kinds of drugs?' He looked towards Orlena. 'Could you get me a glass of water? You'll find a tap in the kitchen.'

'You wanted to make soldiers braver?' asked Matt.

Petor took the glass of water from Orlena, holding it steadily in his hand. 'Well, of course. You've been a soldier, you know what the battlefield is like. Men are afraid. When they are trained, battle-hardened, it doesn't matter so much. They get used to it, they learn how to control and master their fear. But when they are boys of eighteen or nineteen, with six months' training, and they are thrown in battle, what happens?'

'They flap,' said Matt. 'Panic, lose it. Happens all the time, even to good men.'

'Exactly,' answered Petor, taking a sip of the water. 'So what if you could find a drug that would suppress fear, maybe just for a few hours? For an army, that would be quite an achievement. It would make you invincible.'

184

'You got one?'

'XP22,' said Petor flatly. 'That was its name. We concentrated on a hormone called corticotrophin. It's well known that at times of stress, your body releases large quantities of corticotrophin into the bloodstream. What it does exactly, nobody is quite sure. But our theory was that if we could find some way of controlling the production of corticotrophin then you would feel much less stressed, even in the most tense conditions possible. We created a blocker, a chemical that shuts down the production of the hormone. Then we twisted it a bit. We added some high-powered amphetamines, basically a variant on Quaaludes. That gives you a short, intense high, and allows you to think with amazing clarity. Your reaction times are all speeded up. So you had men who felt no stress, no fear, and they could fight like supermen.' Petor looked across at Orlena, a mischievous smile on his face. 'Of course, it also meant the drug couldn't be given to women, because of the well-documented impact of Quaaludes on their sexual appetite. Still, the Red Army never really put women in front-line positions, so that was not much of an issue.'

'And it was used?' asked Matt.

'Of course,' answered Petor. 'We were developing the drug all through the seventies and early eighties. Then it was first used properly in Afghanistan. That was a nasty war, you know. Lots of young conscripts with not much training got shot at by fanatics. You had to be brave in that struggle. So we gave them XP22.'

Matt sighed. Didn't matter which army you belonged to, he reflected. *Whether they were Ruperts or Sergeis, they still treated the men like cattle.*

'Did it work?'

A smile broke out on Petor's thin, wrinkled lips. 'Naturally,' he replied. 'The science was good. Get a man to swallow one pill, and you would see some extraordinary feats of endurance and courage. Of course, the casualties were high, because the men became reckless. They would start storming a position single-handed, with no covering fire. But casualties were expected. Bravery they wanted, and XP22 delivered it. At one point, there were so many heroes around the place, they had to step up the production of Order of Lenin medals to honour them all.'

'But something went wrong?' said Matt, leaning forward again.

Petor cast his eyes down. Matt could tell he took some pleasure in recalling the triumphs of his past: the disappointments were not so firmly lodged in his mind. 'Side effects,' he replied slowly. 'It's like any drug. You get the benefits right away. You get the side effects later on.'

Matt glanced across at Orlena. She was leaning forward too, following every word of Petor's precisely. 'The soldiers went crazy, right?' he said.

Petor nodded. 'Nobody noticed at first,' he replied. 'They took the drug, it lasted about twelve hours, then they went back to normal. Or so we thought. About four years later, we started getting reports of strange incidents around the country. Men were going crazy, murdering their wives or children, or their colleagues at work. It took a while before anyone realised, but they were all ex-soldiers. Then it was narrowed down. They were all soldiers who had taken XP22.'

Matt ground his fists together. *I knew it.*

'It was a kind of temporary madness,' continued Petor. 'Stress was usually the trigger. Something would happen in their lives, and suddenly they became madmen, unable to control themselves.'

'And a man called Eduardo Lacrierre, did he buy up the drug?'

Petor's expression turned serious. 'Look up his history sometime,' he replied. 'Twenty years ago he was just a small-time

French businessman, an import–export merchant. He'd done some business in the Soviet Union, so he knew his way around the system. Then after the regime collapsed, he started buying up all the medical research he could get his hands on. He was paying peanuts, of course, but hard-currency peanuts, and people had nothing to live on, so they took what they were offered. That was the basis of his fortune.'

He paused, looking directly at Matt. Then behind him, Matt heard a movement: the sound of a safety catch being taken off a pistol. He spun round. Orlena was standing up, her legs positioned two feet apart, her back perfectly straight, and her right hand held out one foot in front of her. A Marakov pistol was nestling in the palm of her hand, pointing directly at Petor.

'That's enough,' she barked. 'These are old men's stories. We will listen to them no more.'

Matt looked towards Petor. He could see the surprise in the old man's eyes, but also the defiance. The old are not so afraid of dying, he reflected. They have thought about it, they know it's coming, and they have made their peace with it.

'Shoot me if you must, young woman,' Petor said calmly. 'It makes no difference.'

'Are there any papers left?' shouted Orlena. 'The papers must be destroyed.'

Petor glanced around the room. 'My papers are all around me,' he replied. 'You can do what you like to me, but it will make no difference. If anyone has been given XP22 they have to be treated. Or else there will be a terrible price to pay. I can –'

The sentence was left drifting through the room. The bullet cracked out of the barrel of the gun, impacted against the side of Petor's head, crashing open his skull and sending a cupful of blood splattering against the side of the chair. A tear in the side of his cheek opened up, as if you had ripped through an old and rotten sheet of paper, and his head slumped forward. His eyes had already closed.

A young man sometimes survives a bullet to the head. *An old man has no chance.*

Matt lunged forward. Orlena was standing ten yards from him, the Marakov still in her hand. His own pistol was tucked into his jeans, impossible to get at in the split second he had available. He spun round on his heels, reaching out for her hand. His fingers brushed against her skin, but her reactions were good: she had already jumped back, the gun still in her hand.

'On the floor,' she shouted. 'Stay on the fucking floor.' She paused, capturing her breath. 'I told you not to come. I'll destroy this building, and then I'll destroy you.'

Matt could see the barrel of the gun level with his head. It didn't matter what kind of a shot she was, she was not going to miss from there. Ahead of him, a trickle of Petor's blood had started to seep down from the chair, and was running across the floor towards his face. Now Orlena was opening up a lighter with her other hand, sprinkling its fuel across the bookshelf. She took a match, tossing it into the papers. The heat of the summer meant everything in the room was tinder dry: in seconds, the bookshelf ignited with a roar, the papers turning gold and crimson, as a thick cloud of black smoke filled the room. Orlena stepped back to avoid the heat, and Matt suddenly reached out, snatching the heel of her shoe. Pressuring all the strength in his shoulders on to his fingers, he hanked himself forward. Orlena swayed, her arms flying outwards as she struggled to regain her balance. The gun swung through the air. Matt reached up, smashing his fist hard into her hand. Her grip loosened as the pain swelled through her arm, then collapsed: the pistol spun away, flying through the air, smashing against the wall.

Matt leapt at her, his head bowed, his shoulders crashing

188

hard into her legs. There's not much about unarmed combat that can't be learnt on the rugby pitch, he reflected, as she fell to the ground. *Go in low and go in hard.*

Huge balls of black smoke were already filling the tiny room. Matt could feel his lungs choking on the heavy air. He pulled himself up, stamping his boot down on Orlena's neck, pinning her tight against the floor.

This is no time to be a gentleman.

'What's this job really about?' he shouted, his vocal cords choking on the fumes. 'It was never about drug counterfeiting at all, was it? You wanted something in that factory.'

He could see her eyes looking back at him, her expression insolent and angry. The fury started to rise in his chest. 'Just shoot,' she spat. 'Just shoot if you must, it makes no difference.'

'Tell me,' Matt shouted, squeezing his foot tighter into her neck. 'What is this job about?'

'I'll tell you nothing.'

'I'll kill you if you don't talk.'

'You don't have the guts,' she snapped. 'You're a coward.'

Matt leant down, looking into her eyes. He could smell the anger sweating out of her and see the fury coiled up in her lips. 'Whatever you're hiding, whoever you're protecting, it's not worth it.'

'I'll tell you nothing,' she screamed.

Matt pulled her up and slapped her once across the face. 'It's not worth dying for.'

Orlena's voice turned cold. 'I'll die the way I want to.' She moved back towards the bookcases, which were now a raging inferno, bellowing out great clouds of black smoke.

Matt held the Marakov in his hand, pointed it towards her retreating figure, and fired a single bullet. Orlena's silhouette tumbled towards the flames that were now engulfing the carpet, curtains and chairs, into the thick smoke.

Make that fifty-one ways to leave your lover.

Matt could feel the smoke stinging his eyes, and his stomach was starting to heave as the fumes filled his lungs. He pulled himself up off the ground, and started collecting as many of the papers as he could from the shelves. He tucked a bundle underneath his arms, and started to run towards the front door. The smoke was thicker and blacker, and waves of flames had started to crawl across the ceiling, drowning the apartment in heat. Soon the entire building would be on fire.

In the hallway, the carpet and the door were already burning. He held his breath to stop himself taking in any more smoke, then forced himself forward. The metal of the lock was already glowing from the heat. Matt slammed the bolt backwards, a sharp pain running down his arm as the metal burnt the skin on his fingers. With his foot, he kicked the door back, sending it flying open. A rush of oxygen flooded into the hall, stoking up the flames.

Matt ran outside, gasping for air. He sprinted away from the block, not pausing until he was at least a hundred yards from the building. An armful of papers were clutched tight to his chest. Behind him, he could see people starting to stream from the building, and within a few minutes he knew he would hear the sounds of police sirens and fire engines.

Time to make myself vanish.

He tried to bring his breathing under control, heading out of the compound towards the river and the car. It was time to get out of Kiev. *For ever.*

SIXTEEN

Matram put the picture down on the table. A simple headshot measuring six inches by eight, it showed a woman in her late twenties. She had blonde hair tucked behind her neck, and a look of hidden intelligence concealed within her eyes. Attractive, but not a stunning beauty, reflected Matram.

'Her name is Eleanor Blackman,' he said softly. 'She needs to be eliminated. Immediately.'

Turnton picked up the picture, held it between his fingers, then passed it across to Snaddon. 'Who is she?' he asked, his voice, as always, painfully slow.

'Psychologist,' said Matram. 'It's time for her to check out.'

'Where does she work?' asked Snaddon brightly.

Of all the people in the Increment, Snaddon was always the most cheerful. The manner of a holiday rep, Matram sometimes reflected, but with the cold, dark heart of a natural assassin.

Matram glanced across at her. He had chosen her because he felt a woman would be right for this job. *They know the ways of their own sex. It takes one to kill one.*

'Charing Cross Hospital. In research.'

'Another hospital hit?' asked Snaddon.

Matram shook his head. 'I don't think so. Security may be terrible in those places, but it might be hard to get in and out again without being stopped. She doesn't work nights.' He

191

paused, glancing down at the picture. 'I think it would be better if we could take her on our territory, not hers.'

Matt slammed the phone down. He had just spoken to Janey back at the Last Trumpet.

The bar was doing well: despite the intense heat of the summer, there were still plenty of tourists, and they were staying in the bar for half the night, trying to get enough liquids down their throats to stay cool. But there was still no sign of Gill. She hadn't been into the bar, and she hadn't been to work.

There was no sign of her anywhere.

Where is she? he repeated silently to himself. It doesn't matter how angry she is with me. *She can't just disappear off the face of the earth.*

Matt looked out of the window of the small Holborn flat where he had arrived this afternoon. His bag of kit was still in the hallway, he hadn't felt like unpacking. Outside, sweaty commuters were having a drink before they took the tube home. Matt could hear their laughter, but felt as if he were in another world. In their universe, people worked, had families, built careers and got on with their lives. In my world, I am surrounded by shadows, plots, deceptions and intrigues. *And sometimes I despair of it.*

I thought I was going out on a simple security job. Now, I'm at the centre of a conspiracy. I could walk away, forget about it, ignore the connections between Lacrierre and the soldiers who have been going crazy around Britain. That kind of knowledge is dangerous. It could get me killed. But although you can leave everything else behind, you can't throw away your memories. *I'll always know that I could have done something about it. That will always be with me.*

Eleanor smiled at him as she stepped into the flat. He'd called her as soon as he'd landed at Heathrow, telling her they needed to meet up right away. I'll be over, she'd replied. Just as soon as she could get out of the hospital. He remained silent as he showed her through to the main room.

'Are you OK, Matt?'

'It's worse than we thought,' he answered.

He sat down on the sofa, pulling out a sheaf of paper: the same papers he'd taken from Petor's burning apartment. Eleanor sat next to him, her expression worried. 'The drug was called XP22,' said Matt. 'It was developed back in the Soviet Union in the seventies and eighties. It made soldiers braver, but it had side effects.'

'And they used it on their men? Without testing it properly?'

'Cannon fodder,' snapped Matt.

'And you think it might have been used here?'

Matt rubbed his forehead. 'God knows what they use,' he said. 'In the Gulf, they gave the men all kind of crap. Told us it was to protect us against chemical weapons, but nobody knew what it was. Most of us threw it away.' He paused, walking across to the kitchen to get a glass of water. 'So yes, they might well have used it here.'

Eleanor looked down at the papers, studying them intently. Her eyes squinted at the faded lettering: they had been written on an old-fashioned typewriter, and were at least twenty years old, the black ink starting to fade. 'If only we could figure out the chemical composition of the drug.' She stood up, walking across to Matt. 'Then we could just test the bodies of one of the men who went crazy. I'm sure we'd find traces of this drug.'

'But what else are we going to find?' snapped Matt, his face reddening with anger. 'And then what are we going to do when we find out?'

Eleanor turned away from him. 'My brother died, I want the truth, Matt,' she said, her voice cracking. 'That's an end in itself.'

Matt's mobile was ringing. He picked it up, nodded twice, then said, 'OK, I'll see you then.'

'It's Abbott,' he said looking back at Eleanor. 'I'm going to see him now.'

'No,' said Eleanor, her tone anxious. 'It could be a trap.'

Matt shook his head. 'I need to see him,' he answered. 'I need to find out what he knows.'

The crimson, burning tip of a cigarette broke through the darkness. Matt sniffed the air, recognised the aroma of Dunhill tobacco, and started walking forwards. The car park at the Sainsbury's next to Victoria station was deep underground, three floors below street level. The first two floors were filled with busy shoppers, but this level was used only for unloading the food every morning, and was completely empty at this time of night. Abbott had insisted they had to meet somewhere away from the Firm: somewhere with minimal security, and where there was no chance of their being seen together.

'Abbott,' Matt shouted. 'Where the fuck are you?'

From behind a row of six giant rubbish pails, Abbott emerged. He was dressed in white chinos, a blue shirt open at the collar and a pale cream linen jacket. He looked across at Matt, a half-smile on his face, then tossed his cigarette on to the ground, grinding it out with the heel of his shoe.

'Good choice of camouflage,' said Matt. 'Next to the garbage you blend right in.'

'Watch your manners, old fruit,' said Abbott. 'You don't have to like me, but a little politeness wouldn't hurt.'

'And it wouldn't hurt you to learn about not telling lies to the men you are working with.'

'Lies?' Abbott took a step backwards. 'Maybe you didn't like this job, but I assure you there was no dishonesty involved.' He shrugged, reaching into his pocket and grabbing another cigarette. 'Anyway, it's all over now, old

194

fruit. Our friend out in the wild east is dead. Made quiet a splash in the *Minsk Mail,* or whatever the local rag is called. Good work by you, old fruit. Lacrierre is very pleased. I'm very pleased. The Firm is very pleased. We couldn't be any happier if Cameron Diaz walked into the room asking if any of the chaps would mind if she gave them a blow job.'

'You're wrong. It's not over.'

Abbott looked at him closely. 'Listen to me, old fruit, job done. Time to get back to the Last Strumpet. Get the tapas into the microwave. Get the beer nice and cold. All that.'

'XP22,' said Matt. 'Ever heard of it?'

'Not much of a whizz with the computers,' said Abbott. 'What is it? One of Bill Gates's little wheezes for emptying out our wallets once again?'

Abbott stabbed the cigarette into his mouth. An orange glow from his lighter briefly lit up the space between them, illuminating Abbott's eyes as he shifted them sideways. Smokers, noted Matt. They reach for the nicotine when they're under pressure. *Like when they're lying through their teeth.*

'It's a drug. Used on soldiers in the Soviet Union. To make them brave.'

'Ah, Johnnie Commie,' said Abbott, taking a deep drag on the Dunhill. 'How we miss him now he's gone. Much more civilised class of enemy than all these Arabs we have to deal with nowadays. But what's it got to do with the here and now?'

'Lacrierre bought the drug,' said Matt. 'I don't know why or what for, but he did. And that's what the job was all about. Nothing to do with counterfeiting.' He took a step forward, his tone growing harsher. 'Like I said, you've been lying to me all along.'

'Nobody lied to anybody, Matt. The job's done, over. What does it matter to you what drugs were sold to whom? It was a long time ago. Your account is about to be unfrozen.

You can get back to building that house, marry the school-teacher, knock out a couple of little baby Brownings. Be nice to yourself, old fruit. Christ knows, nobody else bloody well will.'

'I can't,' said Matt bluntly.

'What a pity,' said Abbott.

A dark blue Land Rover Freelander drew up, the driver pulling the vehicle up right next to Abbott. He tossed his cigarette on the floor and climbed into the back seat, his eyes avoiding Matt. 'Cheerio, old fruit,' he said. 'I wanted to give you a pat on the back.' He sighed. 'Now I never will.'

The door clunked shut and the car pulled away, heading up the ramp towards the street.

I've made a mistake, realised Matt, cursing himself as the thought struck home. *I should never have told him I knew.*

As Matt left the car park, Ivan was waiting in a rented Ford Focus. 'Listen, I've been digging around,' he said. 'You want to know more about the bravery drug, then you need to go and speak to Professor Johnson. Old guy. Clever.'

Matt looked at him. 'Who is he?'

'He was a left-wing intellectual, back when the peace movement was big in the 1980s,' said Ivan. 'A lot of those people had contacts with my old lot. That's how I came across him. He's one of the world's greatest experts on chemical and biological warfare. If anyone knows about this drug, he will.'

'Where can I get hold of him?'

'Got a pen?'

Matt nodded.

'Then take down the number,' said Ivan.

'Information like that is dangerous,' said Professor Johnson, sitting back in a brown leather armchair.

Matt looked across at the professor. He was in his early seventies, but his hair was still black, and his skin was clean and soft. He tapped the end of his cigar against the desk, then, using a greasy old lighter, lit up a swathe of flame. The smoke curled away from his face.

'You should be careful what you do with it,' he continued.

According to Ivan, Johnson was one of the military's greatest critics. He had made his name in the early eighties, when he led campaigns on behalf of the servicemen who had witnessed nuclear tests. For years, the claims for compensation for the cancers and other diseases they suffered had been turned down, but Johnson had worked tirelessly on their behalf, until eventually some meagre payments were made to a few frail old men and a collection of angry widows. Next, he'd helped reveal how the government-sponsored laboratories had been used to test chemical and biological weapons. Soldiers had been told they were being given drugs to cure colds: in truth, they were being used as lab rats for weapons programmes.

'You look like a soldier to me,' said Johnson, looking across at Matt. 'Which regiment?'

'The SAS. Ten years. I've been out for two.'

Johnson took another drag on his cigar. 'Ever get anything tested on you?'

Matt shook his head. 'The Ruperts gave us some kit sometimes. We'd rather take our chances with the enemy than any of that rubbish.'

'Very wise,' said Johnson. 'There have been some disturbing reports about some of the chemical agents used in the first Gulf War. Men are coming down with diseases a decade later, and of course the military are denying everything. Then read the reports from Gulf Two, and you'll notice something odd again. The Americans have an abnormally high suicide rate. You always get a few suicides

197

in a combat zone. The stress, a lot of men can't take it. But they are running at four or five times what you'd expect.' He shrugged, a smile on his lips. 'So, maybe something in the water?'

Eleanor looked up through the thick cloud of cigar smoke that had settled around Johnson's face. Even though it was close on forty degrees outside, all the windows in the study were closed, and the professor was still wearing a cardigan. 'Bravery,' she said. 'Is there any history of the military trying to enhance that?'

'Of course, over the centuries, armies have tried to enhance just about aspect of military performance. That's what warfare is all about, getting a tiny edge over your opponent. The Incas were among the first, over a thousand years ago. They used to drill into men's heads, performing surgery on the brain, in the belief that it could banish fear in combat. Then there was alcohol, and tobacco. They have always been distributed liberally on the battlefield. And religion, of course, the greatest of all drugs. Every army has a few tame priests in its caravan, just to reassure the men there is another life out there somewhere, since this one might not last much longer.'

'But have you heard of specific bravery drugs?' persisted Eleanor.

Johnson rolled his cigar around in his fingers, examining the burning tip. 'There have been experiments for years, from what I am told,' he replied. 'It's such an obvious area. Fear is the greatest enemy any general faces. It's hard to get the men to do what you want. In a sense, that's what all military life is about. The square-bashing, the discipline, the peer-pressured comradeship, the flag-waving. It's all about getting men to overcome the most obvious of emotions. Which is that it's bloody frightening being shot at, and the most natural thing in the world is to run away.'

The cigar had started to ebb. Matt was beginning to tire of the history lesson. The professor took out his lighter, igniting it, sending a flame shooting upwards. His eyes darkened behind the crimson light, and just a bead of sweat was apparent on his forehead. 'About five years ago, I heard work in that area was being stepped up. In America, in particular, but in this country as well. At a place called the Farm.'

'That's where we think the drug was tested,' said Matt. 'What do you know about it?'

'All very hush-hush,' said Johnson. 'Places like Porton Down got a lot of publicity, but the Farm was where all the really secret work was done. As I said, about five years ago, they started doing a lot of work on para-psychology. And they had some nasty incidents.'

'Men going crazy?' asked Eleanor.

'I believe so,' replied Johnson. 'A couple of staff died in unpleasant circumstances. Again, nothing on public record. There was a man who used to work there, but he became disenchanted with the place. After that, he got in touch with CND, and that's how I met him. There was something dangerous going on there. He might be able to help you out. He's called George Caldwell. Lives near Chippenham. He can tell you what you need to know.'

'We need all the help we can get,' said Matt. He stood up, taking Eleanor by the arm. It was time for them to go. 'Thanks for your help, Professor,' he said, shaking him by the hand.

'You sure you haven't taken the drug?' said Johnson, looking closely at Matt.

Matt shook his head.

'Because you have to be a very brave man to take this on,' he continued. 'You can be certain of one thing. If the drug was tested in Britain, and if it had the side effects you say it did, then they won't let you live. They can't afford to.'

He looked hard at both of them. 'If you and your friend are determined to investigate this, then you have to take precautions. You probably shouldn't even be talking to me.'

As they drove away, Eleanor said: 'Are we going to see Coldwell?'

'No,' said Matt, 'I'm driving you home. We just got all information we need. It's time to confront Lacrierre.'

The house commanded a wide view over the rolling countryside of the Chilterns. About forty miles from London, and just a couple of miles from Junction Five of the M40, it was a grand Georgian residence, set in ten acres of landscaped parkland. Not much change out of five million, thought Matt, as he parked the Porsche on the circular strip of gravel outside the main entrance.

'And who are you?' said the man who opened the door.

A butler, or some other kind of flunky, Matt couldn't tell. 'I'm here to see Mr Lacrierre,' he said firmly. 'It can't wait.'

The servant looked at him disdainfully.

You can't pull that trick with me, pal. *I'm a soldier. Humiliation doesn't bother me.*

'Mr Lacrierre is busy, sir. He left instructions not to be disturbed. Maybe you could phone his office for an appointment.'

Matt reached out, grabbing the man's right hand. He held it tight between his fists, twisting it around until the veins in his wrist started to bulge. He looked up into the man's eyes, waiting until he could see the moment of maximum pain. 'The time for making appointments has passed,' he said. 'Now give him this message. Tell him Leonid Petor is here to see him.'

'Who?'

Matt gripped his hands together, using all his strength to squeeze the man's twisted hand. 'Just bloody tell him.'

Matt waited in the hallway, while the flunky scuttled

away. The floor was laid with marble tiles, and the walls were decorated with oil paintings. Most were of distinguished-looking Victorian gentlemen, with a few dog-and-horse scenes thrown in.

The butler looked sullen, and was still nursing his hand, as he showed Matt towards the library.

'I haven't heard the name of Leonid Petor for years,' said Lacrierre, walking forward and offering Matt his hand.

'I needed to grab your attention,' said Matt, ignoring his gesture.

Lacrierre stepped away, examining Matt suspiciously. The library was filled with leather-bound books, tucked neatly on to the shelves. From a glance at the spines, Matt could tell most of them were military, in a mixture of English and French: biographies, campaign memoirs, guides to guns and weapons and battleships. *You can read about it all you want. But that doesn't mean you won't shrink when the sound of real gunfire is bursting open your eardrums.*

'He's dead,' said Matt.

'I'm sorry to hear that. He was an intelligent man. One of those men who are obscure, yet brilliant. An interesting type, don't you think?'

'There's nothing interesting about being dead.'

'I suppose not,' answered Lacrierre. 'What happened to him?'

Matt took a step forward. 'Orlena shot him,' he answered. 'That was just a couple of minutes before I shot her.'

He watched closely. He wasn't certain, and it was only there for a fraction of a second, but he thought he could see a flicker of surprise pass across Lacrierre's face.

'So many people appear to have died,' he said. 'I don't know where I'm going to get the wreaths from.'

'Perhaps you should get one for yourself while you're at it.'

Lacrierre attempted a half-smile. 'Do sit down.'

201

'I'd rather stand,' answered Matt.

Lacrierre coughed. 'Orlena was a valued employee. Maybe you could tell me what happened?'

'XP22,' said Matt. 'A drug. It makes men brave, but it makes them crazy. Apparently Petor developed it, then you bought it from Leshko. That's what the whole job was about, wasn't it? It was a cover-up.' He leant forward, so close he could smell the aftershave sweating off Lacrierre's skin. 'I don't know any more than that, but I'd like you to tell me.'

'Don't bother about XP22, Matt,' said Lacrierre. 'It was all a long time ago. A lot of scientific material came out of the old Soviet Union. Some of it was useful, most of it rubbish. It's history.' He stepped aside, his eyes scanning the row of books on the shelves, not looking back at Matt. 'Your work is done, you'll be paid, let's bury it.'

'Men are dying all over the country,' said Matt. 'I can't bury it.'

Lacrierre turned round to face him. His eyes were blazing with anger and his lips drawn tight over his mouth. Matt could see Lacrierre pressing a button. Immediately two men entered the room: tall and stocky, with tousled black hair and dressed in black jeans and blue T-shirts, they looked like former French soldiers.

'Don't try and intimidate me,' snarled Matt. 'It won't work.'

The air between them was thick with anger, and Matt could sense the violence in Lacrierre's expression. Suddenly Lacrierre smiled. 'I suppose I should be grateful to both you and Eleanor,' he said slowly. 'For bringing these disturbing matters to my attention. Now let's see if we can resolve this calmly . . .'

Matt turned away. The two guards were advancing threateningly towards him, and although every instinct within him was telling him to stand and fight, he knew that would be a mistake. They started to push him roughly out of the room towards the front door, and Matt staggered down the steps on to the gravel.

Lacrierre's words had struck home. If Lacrierre knew about Eleanor, then she was in danger, Matt realised. *Terrible danger.*

The streets around this part of Brixton were mostly bedsits and small flats. Old Victorian terraced houses had been split up into rabbit warrens of tiny, nasty apartments, often rented out to asylum seekers by profiteering landlords who knew the government would pay the rent. The roads were covered with litter, broken-down cars, and off-licences with thick metal grilles hanging over the windows to stop anyone stealing the booze.

Matt took one look, then jammed his foot down hard on the accelerator of the Porsche. *If she was here, then she was in danger.*

His eyes scanned down the street, darting left and right. No sign of her. But he could see a car, a Vauxhall Omega, outside the house, and inside it two motionless figures. Waiting.

It's them.

Twenty minutes earlier, he'd been at Charing Cross Hospital, asking one of her colleagues where Eleanor was. Not here, he'd been told. Gone on a house call. A house call? asked Matt. She's a researcher, she doesn't do home visits, she doesn't even see any patients. The man had just shrugged, said he didn't know, but the big cheeses at the hospital wanted her to go take a look. Bollocks, Matt had thought. *It's a trap.*

He'd bullied the address out of the secretary, then climbed back in the car. Eleanor didn't drive, he knew that much. She'd be getting public transport; that gave him a chance of getting there before her. He had battled his way through the traffic into Putney, then turned down towards Brixton, swearing to himself as he struggled to find Wellington Road. As he drove, the same thought was hammering into his head. *What if I'm too late?*

Should have bought a different car, realised Matt, as he steered his Porsche into the side of the road. *Then again, all the drug dealers round here drive Porsches and Mercs. Maybe I just look like a local.*

He slipped out of the car and started walking, his head bowed, taking care not to draw any attention to himself. Dressed in black jeans and a grey polo shirt, he blended easily enough into the drab surroundings. He looked down the road. Number Thirty-One was the house she was meant to be visiting. He stole a glance towards it. The bottom two windows were boarded up, one of the ground floor-windows was shattered, and there was a small stack of phone books and junk mail gathered on the porch.

An empty, abandoned house. *A killing field . . .*

He looked further down the road. It was just after five, and there was an old lady pulling a shopping bag down the other side of the street, and a man standing on the corner talking into his mobile phone. Three spaces down the road, the Vauxhall Omega was still parked on the street. Matt could see two heads, a man and a woman, and yes they were sitting perfectly still.

There's only one kind of person who sits like that: still, inconspicuous, patient. *A trained assassin.*

Suddenly Eleanor came into view. Still thirty feet away on the other side of the Vauxhall, she was turning the corner, a bag swinging at her side. She was glancing up and down the street, searching for the right number, then she started walking quickly towards it. Matt moved swiftly along the street, picking up his pace, trying to judge how quickly he could move without drawing any attention to himself. What are their orders? he wondered to himself. Will they start shooting in daylight? Will they risk injuring innocent bystanders? In the next few minutes, I'll find out.

Too quick, they'll realise I'm trying to rescue her. Too slow, they catch us easily, and we'll both get killed. *That's some choice.*

He could hear a noise as he crossed the road.

'Matt,' she said, looking up at him, the surprise evident in her tone. 'What . . .'

'Shut up, and walk,' he muttered, slipping his arm around her back, keeping his voice down low.

'But, Matt . . .'

He started steering her in the opposite direction.

'Shut the fuck up and walk,' he repeated, slightly louder this time.

'Excessive hostility,' said Eleanor. 'I think you have issues.' She paused, struggling to loosen his grip. 'You're hurting me.'

'Just move,' snapped Matt.

He started to steer her past the Vauxhall. The door was opening, two people, a man and woman were climbing out. Matt looked up, catching the woman's eye. There was something in her manner that he recognised, the steadiness with which she held herself under pressure, the mechanical, practised firmness of her movements.

'Run,' he shouted. 'Run for your life.'

Using all the strength in his shoulders, he yanked Eleanor forwards, dragging her along the street. He could see the look of fear and bewilderment in her expression, but her feet were starting to pick up speed. Behind him, he could hear doors closing and then the sound of the car roaring into life, and the skid of tyres against tarmac as it turned itself round. Fifteen yards, he told himself. That will take us back to the Porsche. *Just a few desperate yards.*

'Get in the car,' he shouted, flinging Eleanor around to the other side of the car. He leapt into the driver's seat, hitting the ignition and jamming his foot down hard on the accelerator. The car was already revving furiously as Eleanor was climbing into the seat next to him. He spun away from the kerb, pushing out on to the road, Eleanor screaming that her door was still open.

'Shut it,' he shouted. 'For Christ's sake, shut it.'

In his mirror, he could see the Vauxhall twenty yards behind him. The road was straight at this point, only starting to curve ten yards ahead. A series of five smaller streets cut across it.

The man was at the wheel, Matt saw. And the woman was lining up her gun. *Pointing right at me.*

In the regiment, Matt had been given basic training in escape driving. Both police and former rally drivers would come to Hereford to instruct recruits on tactics for making a getaway. The knowledge was still there somewhere, Matt decided. *If only I can use it.*

He swerved to the left, turning the Porsche into a side street. The Vauxhall was following hard behind. He checked the mirror. The woman. The gun. *Still there.*

A shot rang out, then another, the bullets blasting through the air. Matt instinctively ducked, shielding himself from impact.

'What was that?' said Eleanor, breathless.

'The car behind,' said Matt. 'They're shooting at us.'

Eleanor started to turn around.

'Don't look around,' said Matt. 'That just makes it easier for them. Get down.'

Matt could hear the sound of another bullet impacting against the car. Then another one. He saw that the driver's side mirror was smashed, and the Porsche had taken a hit somewhere else. He started jamming the car from side to side, accelerating down the narrow street. At his side, Eleanor was screaming.

'Stop, stop, you're going to kill us,' she yelled, tears running down her face.

Matt yanked hard on the handbrake, swivelling left as he did so: that sent the awesome power of the Porsche all into the rear of the vehicle, spinning it hard into the ninety-degree turn. This turn was needed to take him into a very tight corner at high speed. Matt could hear the gears crunching, and the sound of metal tearing against metal. The car spun viciously, its force pinning him back in the seat as if a huge weight had just been thrown against his chest. For a brief moment, he could feel it spinning out of the control, then, pushing his body forward, he gripped the wheel, hurtling it sideways and releasing the handbrake. The engine started to rev, and the Porsche accelerated down the left-hand street towards Brixton Road.

One thought was racing through his mind. *Get out on to the open road where the power of the Porsche can outrun these people.*

The car bumped along the edge of the pavement, swerving and narrowly missing a parked van. Matt checked the mirror. The Vauxhall had been confused by the sudden turn, and the engine had stalled as the driver struggled to spin it round, but it was moving again now, accelerating down the road, the woman leaning out, the gun in her hand.

Matt jammed his foot harder on the accelerator, a surge of power from the engine riding through the car.

Another shot. Matt could hear a bullet impacting against the glass, and through the mirror he could see a crack in the back window. He looked ahead. They were approaching the main road, and he could see a queue of afternoon traffic snaking along the thoroughfare.

'Hold on tight,' he shouted to Eleanor.

The car swerved around the corner, then up on to the edge of the pavement, taking it on to the high street. At this point it was wide enough to take a whole car, but the Porsche only narrowly missed the shop windows. Matt crashed his fist on to the horn. A sheet of white noise was rising up from the car, sending shocked pedestrians scattering in all directions.

'You're going to kill someone,' shouted Eleanor.

Never underestimate how quickly people can react when they are facing extreme danger, Matt reminded himself. That had been a lesson he'd learnt in the regiment, and he'd never forgotten it. When they see an out-of-control Porsche driving down the street, people can move faster than they would have believed possible.

A woman jumped out of the way, and a man was screaming as the car slid across the pavement. Matt steadied the wheel, and steered past two shops. He could hear others screaming at him. Horns were blaring, and one man banged furiously on the roof of the car. Ahead, he could see a red light; in front of it a few precious yards of open space had opened up. Matt accelerated and the car leapt into the space. Matt leant back in his seat. As he raced through the red light, the road was suddenly clear. He pushed the car up to seventy, disappearing into south London.

'You OK?' he said, looking towards Eleanor.

He could see the pale terror written into the skin of her face. She tried to speak, but the words wouldn't come.

Matt looked behind. The Vauxhall was nowhere to be seen. They were safe. *For the next few minutes anyway.*

Eleanor took a sip on the Coke Matt had just bought her, but turned down the chips. They had driven south for ten miles, making sure nobody was on their trail. Then Matt turned round, heading back into town, pulling the car up at the drive-in McDonald's at the roundabout on the south side of Wandsworth Bridge.

Never try to fight or think on an empty stomach. *You won't do either right.*

'We go and see Abbott,' said Matt. 'We have to get

208

Lacrierre's goons called off. Next time they might actually kill us.'

'Why can't we go to the police?' said Eleanor, her tone nervous and edgy. 'Those people just tried to kill us.'

'Trust me,' said Matt.

'Don't be ridiculous,' said Eleanor, getting angrier. 'Since when did the police stop protecting people who are getting shot at?'

'No,' he said. 'This involves the MOD, remember. Only the Firm can help us now.'

SEVENTEEN

The house was larger than Matt had expected. An elegant Victorian villa, double-fronted, with its own garden both front and back, it was on the corner of Carlton Hill, just a short walk from Regent's Park. A new Land Rover was sitting on the driveway, and next to it a bright red Mini Cooper.

I might not be keeping up with London property prices. *But this place wouldn't leave much change out of two million.*

'I'm busy, old fruit,' said Abbott, opening the door only a fraction. 'We'll have to talk another time.'

Matt stepped forward. 'We'll talk now.'

The door was carved from a solid chunk of wood, with at least three sets of bolts running through it. But it swung easily enough when you put pressure on it. Matt pushed with his fist and stepped quickly into the hallway. Eleanor was following close behind.

Abbott can get those assassins called off.

'Like I said, this isn't the right moment, old fruit,' said Abbott, backing away into the hallway. 'Why don't you call my secretary, make an appointment.'

'I've been shot at once today already,' said Matt. 'I need this cleared up and I need it cleared up now.'

Abbott started walking towards the drawing room. It was painted pale yellow, with a pair of hunting prints dominating one wall and huge gilt-framed mirror over the marble fireplace. From the bachelor furnishings, Matt judged that Abbott lived alone.

'Do you want a glass of sherry?' he said, walking towards a silver drinks tray with a set of three decanters on it.

'I want the truth.'

Abbott smiled. 'Nice play on words, old fruit.' He looked across at Eleanor. 'And how about the young lady? I don't believe we've met.'

Eleanor looked up towards him. 'I'm fine, thanks.'

'Who is she, Matt? Your new squeeze?' He paused. 'You certainly seem to get through them.'

'She's the sister of a friend of mine. Guy called Ken Blackman. Do you want to know what happened to him?'

Abbott started pouring himself a drink. 'Not really. Don't go much on family histories, not really my bag. But I've a nasty feeling you're going to tell me.'

'He was a soldier,' said Matt. 'XP22 was tested on him. Down at a place called the Farm in Wiltshire. A couple of weeks ago, he went crazy, killed some people, then killed himself. Same thing has happened to a whole group of soldiers across the country. We reckon XP22 was tested on all of them.'

Abbott took a sip of his drink. 'I do hope you're not going to bore me on the subject of that drug again. What do you think any of this has to do with me?'

'Very simple,' said Eleanor. 'XP22 was developed in the Soviet Union. Lacrierre bought up that technology from a gangster called Serik Leshko. He sold it to the Ministry of Defence, along with God knows what other lethal con-coctions. They tested it on some soldiers. Some of those men have since suffered severe side effects. Next, to cover up what had happened, you sent Matt out to destroy Leshko's operation, and kill him.'

Abbott looked at her and smiled. 'So you're the brains of this little outfit. Sure you don't want that drink?'

211

Eleanor shook her head. 'I told you, I'm fine.'

'You should, you know. You're going to need it.' Abbott walked across the room, pulled aside the curtain, glancing out on to the dark and empty street. 'What do you think I'm going to do now?'

'Have Lacrierre arrested,' snapped Eleanor. 'The man's responsible for dozens of deaths.'

Abbott nodded, as if he were turning the idea over in his head. He lit up a cigarette, the smoke curling away from his face. 'Interesting idea,' he said slowly. 'But I was thinking more along the lines of having you arrested.'

The look of shock took a moment to register on Eleanor's face. Matt could see her brain working furiously.

'Us?'

'And why not?' continued Abbott. 'You seem to have figured out most of the story. It's just the ending you haven't guessed. True, XP22 was acquired from the old Soviet Union. True, it was tested on British servicemen. Very effective it was too. But unfortunately, as you have discovered, the drug has side effects. A few of the fifty men who have taken it – not all, about a third so far – have turned into psychopathic monsters. Many of those on whom it was tested have had to be eliminated.' He paused, taking a long, deep drag on his Dunhill. 'For the good of the wider community, you understand.'

'Ordinary squaddies are always expendable,' said Matt bitterly.

'Quite so,' said Abbott. 'Put with your characteristic verve and wit, Matt. You see, Tocah couldn't be allowed to take responsibility for the experiments with XP22. It's a big important company, and it does a lot of covert biological weapons work for the MOD. Then, of course, the Firm wasn't about to take responsibility either. That's not our bag. So, we needed someone to clear up the mess for us.' He looked towards Matt. 'We chose you.'

'It was a set-up all along,' snapped Matt.

'More an unfortunate misunderstanding,' said Abbott. 'We got you to take out the factory, then to kill Leshko, so we could cover up what had happened in the past. If you'd just done that, you could have gone home and everyone would have been happy.'

He tossed the butt of his cigarette into an ashtray. 'Your mistake, Matt, is that you seem to have stumbled across too much information. You know too much. That's why you've been shot at today.'

'The Increment,' Matt muttered darkly.

'Old friends of yours, I think,' said Abbott. 'Always good to meet up with old pals, have a jolly good get-together.' He chuckled to himself, a small mirthless giggle that rattled up from his throat.

Matt moved across the room. He was standing next to Abbott, leaning into his face. 'You miserable bastard,' he shouted. 'I should never have trusted you, never. I should never have trusted the Firm.'

'Probably not,' replied Abbott. 'Still, thanks for all your help. I would shake your hands to wish you goodnight, but I don't like touching dead people.'

The punch landed hard against the side of Abbott's face, sending him sprawling on to the floor. 'I'll kill you first,' snarled Matt.

'No,' shouted Eleanor. 'Leave him. We'll get the evidence and destroy him that way.'

Matt's fist was poised in front of Abbott's face. His shoulders were drawn back, ready to punch. Abbott looked back at him and smiled. 'I've pressed an alarm button,' he said. 'Why don't you take a seat and wait for you old pals to come and deal with you?' He pulled himself up, retrieving the end of the cigarette, taking a quick nervous drag. Then he got up quickly and walked back towards the window, looking out anxiously on to the street. 'You're good, Browning, I'll grant you that.' He turned again to look at Matt, rubbing the red stain where the blow had landed. 'But you're up against the Increment. It's the most lethal, ruthless killing machine on earth. You haven't got a chance.'

Matt moved forward. His face was red with anger, and his muscles were tense, prepared for violence. 'No,' shouted Eleanor, dragging him backwards. 'He's already called for help.'

Matt started to advance towards Abbott again but he knew Eleanor was right. The Increment would be here in a few moments. *If we're to save ourselves, we have to flee.*

The room was damp and cold. The carpet had been rolled up, and the floorboards were grey and dusty. There was one chair in the corner, and some old net curtains hanging across the windows.

'It's not much,' said Ivan, putting down his kitbag, starting to whistle under his breath. 'But it can be home for a few days. And at least it's safe.'

Matt smelt the air. It could have been years since the place was cleaned. From the kitchen, he could detect some ancient, decayed food, and from the state of the floorboards it looked as if mice had been chewing their way through the place. From what he knew of the safe houses run by the IRA through London, there might well be a couple of corpses rotting out the back.

Nothing would surprise me right now.

'It's fine,' said Eleanor, looking across at Ivan and smiling. 'We'll be OK, thanks.'

'Like I said, it's not much.'

As they'd fled Abbott's house, Matt had called Ivan. From his time in the IRA, Ivan knew of some of the safe houses, and quite a few of them were empty now, abandoned and collecting dust. He'd taken them to this one, a nondescript Victorian terrace in Cambridge Grove, just off Hammersmith Broadway.

If you were fighting the Increment, decided Matt, Ivan was the man to turn to. *He'd waged war on the British Army for half his life.*

Matt was aware that Ivan was putting himself on the line. But, he reflected, if the Increment is coming after me, they'll be after him next. *We're all at risk.*

From his bag, Ivan pulled a few essentials: a kettle, a jar of instant coffee, some sandwiches, packets of crisps, chocolate. He handed a bottle of shampoo to Eleanor. 'Keep you hair clean,' he said, with a smile. 'When you're on the run, hiding out, it helps to wash. Makes you feel human, even when nothing else is pointing in that direction. Trust me, I've been there.'

She took the bottle, putting it to one side. 'Thanks,' she replied.

'What are you going to do now?' said Ivan, looking towards Matt.

Matt walked over to the window. The sun had already set and the sky was clear of clouds. The stars were looking as bright as they ever did through London's haze and smog. 'We fight back,' he answered. He turned to look at Ivan. 'Oh, I know what you're going to say. Maybe we should turn and run? Get ourselves some new identities and get the hell out of the country? Put it all behind us, and start again somewhere else?' He paused. 'If I could, I would. But I don't know how.'

'It's the Increment that's coming after you, Matt,' said Ivan. 'You know what they're like. Even back across the water, we were scared of them.'

'I know, I know,' said Matt. 'But those bastards tested that drug on a bunch of good men. While we still have a chance we have to keep trying.'

215

Ivan sighed. 'Okay, I'll help you anyway I can. But you can't say you weren't warned.'

'I understand.'

'New identities,' said Ivan. 'You'll need those for a start. Remember, the Increment has the whole government machine working for it. Use your credit card, your phone, drive your car, check into a hotel under your own name, they'll be on to you in a flash.'

'You know anyone who can help us?'

Ivan nodded. 'I know some guys,' he said. 'They used to work for my lot, doing forged passports, new credit cards, identity theft. They went freelance after the Troubles ended. I'll organise it for you.

You'll be OK for a couple of days, then, so long as you're lucky.' Ivan paused. 'The issue is what do you do next?'

'We go to the papers,' said Eleanor. 'We expose what's happened.'

Ivan shook his head. 'Not yet,' he replied. 'You haven't got enough.'

'Then we'll get it,' said Matt.

'We'll get a sample from one of the dead men,' said Eleanor. 'If we can get it analysed, then we'll have proof that XP22 was tested on British soldiers.'

Ivan nodded.

'There are only four things the Increment does,' said Matram, looking around the room. 'Killing, killing, killing and killing.' He paused, taking a sip of water. 'And there's just one thing it doesn't do. Failure.' Eight people were sitting in a semicircle around him, the entire Increment gathered in one place.

This was an emergency.

Matram put two photographs down on the desk. They were meeting at the Travelodge just next to Wandsworth Bridge in south London; if you looked out of the window,

216

you could see a B&Q and a McDonald's. It was too sensitive for them to meet at the Firm, and although there were several barracks around London they could have used, he preferred to keep well away from the mainstream army.

We're operating off the books. The less anyone knows about what we're doing right now the better.

Matram held up the first picture between his fingers. 'This man is Matt Browning.' He picked up the second picture. 'And this woman is Eleanor Blackman.'

He paused. 'I want them both dead,' he said, spitting the words out of his mouth like little chunks of gravel. 'Immediately.'

He looked closely into the faces of his unit as he delivered Browning's name. The entire membership of the Increment was turned over every few years, so of the current unit only Harton had served alongside Browning. He, Matram knew, would say nothing to the others. Still, it was possible they might have heard of him, but judging by their expressions none of them had. They showed not even a flicker of recognition. The name meant nothing.

He was history. *And in a few more days they would have buried him.*

Browning, thought Matram. Most jobs were just work, but the great God of soldiering has smiled on me this time. I always wanted to get even with that coward. *This one will be a pleasure.*

Matram glanced at Turnton and Snaddon. 'You were sent to deal with her yesterday. She was lured to a prearranged property where she could have been quietly disposed of. The job went wrong. You must explain what happened.'

Turnton leant back in his chair, his arms behind his head. 'The target was rescued, boss, before the job could be completed.'

Matram rubbed his brow wearily. 'Rescued? What do you think this is, a fucking Bugs Bunny cartoon? People don't get rescued from the Increment, man. They may pointlessly sacrifice their own lives by attempting a rescue, but they only end up dying themselves. I can't believe I have to spell this out to you. If anyone attempts to rescue a target, then they get eliminated as well. Simple as that.'

Snaddon stood up, looking straight ahead at Matram: she'd always believed herself to be his favourite operative within the unit. 'We gave chase, sir,' she said crisply. 'We were waiting for the target to go inside the house, then we were going to deal with her. This man, the one in the picture, started fleeing with her, and jumped into a car. A Porsche Boxter. Fast.'

'I think I'm aware that a Porsche is quite a fast car. Just because I have to work with idiots doesn't mean I like being treated like one.' Matram paused, noting the way she blushed at the insult. 'You gave chase?'

'Of course,' answered Snaddon. 'He was good. He took the car up on to the pavement, then pulled it out on to the open road ahead of some traffic lights. There was no chance of following unless we went on the pavement as well.' She paused, her eyes cast down to the floor. 'Standard operating procedure for the Increment is to avoid civilian casualties, unless intervening to prevent a domestic terrorist incident. Because of that, I didn't think it was right to inflict injuries on bystanders.'

'I'm familiar with the SOPs, thank you,' said Matram coldly. 'I wrote them.'

'I think the man knew them as well,' interrupted Turnton. 'He was aware of the limitation on our actions, and he took advantage of them.'

True, thought Matram to himself. *Browning knows how the Increment works.*

'When I want your opinion, I'll ask for it,' he snapped. 'Your inability to eliminate this man will be noted in the next review. I understand your failure, but I cannot accept it.'

Matram looked towards the rest of the unit. 'Nothing like that is going to happen again, because the rules have just changed. Hunting down these two people has now been reclassified as a counter-terrorist operation. That means the gloves are off. A full-scale terrorist alert has gone out to police forces across the country. Every policeman will be watching out for them. Every credit-card company and bank will be alerting us if they use a card, or withdraw any cash. Every hotel company will tell us if they book a room. These two show their faces anywhere, we're going to know about it. When it happens, the police will notify us. They've been told not to approach them. Too dangerous. The last thing we want is for the boys in blue to starting flapping around, buggering everything up.'

With his hands behind his back, Matram walked across the room in a slow methodical line. 'Since this is classified as counter-terrorism, we can use whatever means are necessary to achieve our objectives. Don't kill any bystanders if you can possibly avoid it, but at the same time don't let them escape. If there has to be collateral damage, so be it.' Matram smiled. 'They can run, and run fast. But not fast enough to evade us. Our eyes are everywhere.'

He paused, looking hard into the eyes of each of the men and women present in the room. 'We stop at nothing until they are dead,' he said. 'Now go do some killing.'

The funeral parlour was among a newsagent's, grocer's, butcher's and pub in a row of shops on the outskirts of Swindon. JACK DAWSON & SONS ran the name above the black stencilled lettering on the sign: FUNERAL DIRECTORS, AND MONUMENTAL HEADSTONE CRAFTSMEN.

It was just after nine in the evening, and every shop in the row was now shut: the pub was still open but there was nobody going in or out. 'You wait here,' said Matt to Eleanor. 'I'll get in round the back.'

It was two weeks now since Barry Legg had been killed, and ten days since his body had been discovered face down in a ditch on the edge of a field three miles from the road where he had last been seen alive. They saw a news report detailing how the body had been released by the police and the funeral was scheduled for the next weekend. Now, the body was here, in a casket. If Legg had traces of XP22 in his body, then they had their case. The drug had been tested on British soldiers, and all the men who had taken it were being methodically eliminated. *By the Increment.*

All they needed was a sample of brain tissue.

Matt stopped. A short alleyway ran down the back of the row of shops. There were some bins outside the butcher's, full of bones and offcuts of meat; the sun of the day had caught the decaying flesh, and it was starting to reek. A cat, chewing on one of the bones, glanced up at Matt, then scampered away. He walked forward. The undertaker's was the third shop in the row, with a single black door leading out on to the alley. There was a Banham lock, and a bolt holding the door in place, but above it there was pane of frosted glass with a mesh grille across it.

Not much security, thought Matt. *Then again, who ever tries to rob an undertaker's?*

He checked above him. To the back of the alley, there was a row of buildings, but none of them had windows directly overlooking the door. Matt took out the crowbar he had equipped himself with earlier, and tapped it against the side of the glass. Soft. Not reinforced. He positioned the crowbar in his fist, and delivered a sharp blow to the centre of the window. Hit glass in the right way, and it crumbles in on itself, Matt reminded himself. You just have to strike at the point of maximum weakness, right at the precise centre of the pane. Now the glass splintered, cracking out from the centre, then falling on to the ground. Matt twisted the crowbar into the metal wire, gripped the handle, then yanked it back. The metal struggled, the bolts securing it to the frame straining. Matt concentrated, directing all his strength towards his shoulders, and yanked it again. One bolt dislodged, then another, and the mesh broke free.

Matt ripped the mesh out, cast it to the floor, and pushed his fist through the opening in the window, undoing the bolt. He wedged the crowbar into the lock, and pulled that open. The door swung free.

They'll know there's been a robbery. They'll just be puzzled that nothing has been taken.

The back door led into a small kitchen area. A kettle was next to the sink, a few unwashed cups at its side. A half-opened packet of sugar stood next to a pack of PG Tips. Matt walked through to the back office. He glanced at the papers, and the computer on the desk, then looked across to the row of five black tailcoats and top hats laid out neatly on a coat rack. There were several tins of black boot polish next to them.

These guys keep their shoes cleaner than the Ruperts on medal day.

The bodies were kept in a long, thin gallery just behind the main shopfront. From the heat of the day, it was still and cool in there. When he stepped into the room, Matt could see three coffins ahead: they were laid three feet apart, all of them closed. He checked them one by one, looking for the name tags. Nothing. Christ, he thought, *I'm going to have to look inside them.*

Matt gently lifted the first coffin lid, the pungent smell of the chemicals used to cleanse and preserve the body hitting his nostrils. A woman, probably in her eighties, was staring back at him. He moved on to the next coffin: this time an elderly man. This must be you, he thought as he pulled up the third lid, and looked down at the corpse inside. A man, in his late thirties, with black hair, his eyes closed, and with his arms resting neatly at his side.

Matt winced. A decade knocking around battlefields had not hardened him to the sight of corpses. Every time he looked at a dead body, he felt painfully aware of how thin were the threads that separated the dead from the living. Some instinct told him not to touch it, if it could be avoided, as if death itself were somehow contagious.

He took the thick syringe Eleanor had given him, and thrust it into the corpse just below the ear. She had explained how the bone of the skull was at its softest there. The needle should be able to find a way through. Matt pushed, jiggling the needle as he did so, helping it thread its passage through the bone. The smell of formaldehyde, the most common embalming fluid, drifted up from the corpse: the body had already been prepared for the funeral. Matt could feel his stomach churning, as the sickly chemicals were sucked into his lungs. He jabbed the syringe forward, feeling the needle sink into the soft tissue of the brain. Pausing, he pulled the syringe back, extracting a sample.

Sorry, pal. If you knew why I was doing this, you'd forgive me.

Matt tucked the syringe into his jacket pocket, and pushed the lid back down on the coffin. He stepped quickly away, ducking back into the alleyway, and out on to the street where Eleanor was waiting for him.

'Got it,' he said, steering her towards the waiting car.

Eleanor took the sample, then leant across, kissing Matt on the cheek. 'All we have to do now is get it tested.'

Membury Service Station on the M4 was close to empty. It was after eleven at night by the time Matt and Eleanor pulled up, filled the car up with fuel, and grabbed themselves a pair of burgers from the café.

'Professor Johnson,' said Eleanor, sitting in the car. 'I'm sure he'll know how we can test this sample.'

Matt dialled the number on the stolen mobile Ivan had

given him. 'I'm sorry, I know it's late,' he said to the woman who answered as soon as she picked up the phone, 'but it's urgent. Could I speak to Professor Johnson?'

'Too late,' said the woman, her tone hostile.

'I know it's late, I said I was sorry to disturb you,' repeated Matt. 'But I really need to speak to him. He won't mind being woken.'

'Who are you?'

Matt hesitated. There was something strange about the woman's tone. 'What's happened?' he asked.

'The professor died this morning,' she answered. 'Who are you?'

'I'm . . .' Matt struggled for the words. 'I'm so sorry.'

'Who are you?' repeated the woman, her voice louder now.

'I'm sorry,' said Matt. 'I can't say.'

He snapped the phone shut. 'The professor is dead.'

Eleanor looked back at Matt. 'He said we shouldn't have been to see him.'

EIGHTEEN

Matram looked down from the window. The sun was blazing down on the car park that lay twelve storeys below his hotel room. He could see a few men, dressed only in shorts, waddling back from the B&Q warehouse with new paddling pools for the kids, and hosepipes for the garden.

Ordinary suburban life, he reflected to himself. It makes me sick.

Behind him, the TV was tuned to Sky News. The newsreader was talking about the heatwave, now stretching into its third week. The government was urging people to stay cool, and to use sun cream. The AA was advising motorists to keep off the roads. Some road-rage incidents had been recorded in the sweltering heat and, up in Hartlepool, someone had gone crazy in Tesco with a knife. 'Coming up after the break,' said the newsreader, 'we ask a leading psychologist how to stay cool in the heat.'

Heat, thought Matram. They know nothing about heat.

Snaddon and Trench were in the room with him. The other six members of the unit had been dispatched around the country. Clipper and Turnton were up in Manchester. Harton and Godsall were down in Bristol. Addison and Marley, who had replaced Kilander and Wetherall in the unit, were in Newcastle. That gave Matram a neat quadrangle. Wherever the target appeared, they would have someone who could be on the spot in a couple of hours.

When he revealed himself, he would be dead the same day.

'They've vanished,' said Snaddon.

Matram leant forwards. 'Bollocks. In fairy stories people vanish. In real life, they are always there somewhere. You just have to track them down.'

A full-scale terrorist alert had gone out on Matt Browning and Eleanor Blackman last night: Matram had made certain of that. Their pictures had been circulated electronically to every police force in the country, with officers told to keep a close watch for both. Their car registrations had been noted: if they so much as passed a speed camera, or went inside the London congestion charging zone, it would be picked up. If they used their credit cards, the police would be immediately notified. If they used their mobiles, the location of the transmission mast used for the call would be sent through to the police. Any suspicious movement on any of the tens of thousands of CCTV cameras on street corners around the country would be examined to see if it resembled the two suspects. We live in an electronic society, Matram reflected as he studied the array of different ways their location could be revealed. *A man can run, but the only place he can hide is six feet underground.*

'Nothing from the police?' he said, looking down at Trench.

A laptop was open on the desk, wired to a secure connection at the headquarters of the counter-terrorism unit at Scotland Yard. Any reports from local forces would be fed through to the police there, but would come through to this terminal simultaneously. They didn't want to waste time because one of the plods was on a tea break when the sighting was made.

'Nothing,' said Trench, shaking his head. 'A couple of false alarms. In Romford, they picked up a guy with some Semtex on him, but he turned out to be just a bank robber. Over in Cheltenham, they thought they got a sighting, but it was just a false alarm. Nothing else.'

'How about the financial system?' said Matram, looking towards Snaddon. 'Money is usually the key. People can survive without most things, but they need cash on the run.'

Snaddon shook her head. Her computer was hooked up to a central clearing system for both Visa and Mastercard. Any payment made by either person would show up the instant it went through the computers, giving the precise location of the cash machine used, or the place where a credit-card payment was made. 'Nothing,' she said. 'Not even a whisper.'

'Well, you know what the sportsmen say,' Matram said slowly. 'If the bird won't come to you, then you just have to shake the tree a little.'

Matt poured himself another coffee, and looked down at the plate of bacon, eggs, sausages and beans in front of him. He felt the caffeine kicking into his veins, and scooped some beans on his fork, stuffing them hungrily into his mouth.

First rule of combat, he reminded himself. Eat as much as you can, when you can. *You don't know when you might eat again.*

Eleanor looked across at his breakfast, lightly spreading some jam on her toast. 'You do realise that binge-eating is a common symptom of anxiety,' she said.

Matt forked another sausage. 'It's also a symptom of being hungry.'

The hotel was on the outskirts of Chippenham: the kind of place that was occupied by travelling salesmen before the new chains of Travel Inns and Travelodges went up. This is the land of the invisible men, thought Matt looking around the breakfast room. Pensioners, tourists on a tight budget, maybe a pair of asylum seekers housed here until they got sent back home. *If you want to disappear, you can do it among these people.*

'I'm scared, Matt,' said Eleanor. 'I don't know the endgame.'

'The endgame?'

'I don't know how we can possibly bring this all together,' she continued. 'What difference does it make when or what we discover? Even if we get the sample tested, who is going to believe us?' From the corner of her eye, Matt could see the outline of a tear starting to tumble down her cheek.

Matt paused. His breakfast was only half eaten, but he put his fork down. 'I remember one of the first really sticky firefights I got into in the regiment. We were in the Philippines. We'd been sent down there to help the local army fight some communist guerrillas out in the jungle. But the local boys didn't want to fight, they wanted to get back home. So we found ourselves holed up, four of us, facing about fifty or sixty heavily armed insurgents. We said our prayers and tried to get some sleep, but we were pretty sure we were all going to get slaughtered in the morning. Then, you know what happened? The monsoon came a week early. Freaky. There was so much rain nobody could see more than a few feet, they certainly couldn't shoot straight. It took us a week, but we crawled our way through the mud and survived.'

'Meaning?'

'Meaning when you are in a war, you don't always know the endgame. You press on, and hope to hell something turns up.'

The car was an eleven-year-old Ford Escort, with cloth seats and a couple of dents in its paintwork. Matt had bought it yesterday, paying three hundred pounds, the last of the cash Abbott had given him for Kiev, at a second-hand car dealer in south London. He knew that part of town, it was where he had grown up: he knew there were plenty of dealers that sold scrappy old motors for cash and didn't ask any questions about who was buying it, or bother filling in any registration papers. *So long as you handed across the folding stuff, no questions were either asked or answered.*

Matt had been on the run before. In Bosnia, he and two other men had been stranded fifty miles into enemy territory, with no radios to call in air evacuation: they had to march for three days through hostile territory, knowing that if anyone saw them they would be shot on sight. In the Philippines, as he'd told Eleanor earlier, he'd had to march for days through the jungle at the start of the monsoon season.

That was different. That was in a war zone. This is in my own country, against my own people.

It's all about staying out of sight, staying anonymous, he reminded himself. So long as they didn't use any cards, or try to get any money from the bank, they couldn't be traced financially. The Porsche had been dumped in London: the car was too conspicuous, and anyway, the number plates would give them away. And Ivan had arranged for them to be supplied with a pair of false passports, in the names of Keith Todd and Helen Nuggett: if the police should happen to stop them and ask who they were, that would at least give them a chance of escape.

The Escort came to a juddering halt. The brake pads felt loose, and you had to give the gearbox a good bashing to get it out of first. The car doesn't matter, Matt told himself. *It will get us around, and no one will know who we are.*

They had pulled up outside Caldwell's house, in the countryside, just outside Chippenham. *We must get to him before the Increment does.*

It was a small cottage, maybe three bedrooms, with about an acre of garden: most of it was given over to a series of colourful, elaborate rose bushes. It was just after ten in the morning, and there was not a cloud in the sky. Another hot day, thought Matt as he climbed out of the car.

228

Caldwell was standing in the garden, dressed only in his shorts, a watering can in his hand. 'They'll be lucky to survive this summer,' said Matt, nodding towards the roses. Matt judged him about sixty, with thinning sandy hair, and running to fat. He looked at Matt with curiosity, but without suspicion.

'You wanting directions?' he asked.

Matt looked about him. There was a farmhouse about half a mile away and, in the valley below them, you could see a village, but otherwise they were completely isolated. 'We're looking for some help.'

'You used to work at the Farm,' said Eleanor, stepping forward. 'Professor Johnson gave us your name. He said you might be able to help.'

'And you are?'

Matt hesitated, running the risk-and-rewards calculations through his head. Tell this man who they were and they might be discovered. Lie to him, and they could lose his trust. 'My name is Matt Browning,' he replied. 'This is Eleanor Blackman. We're trying to find some information about a drug that was tested at the Farm, about five years ago.' He paused, looking at Caldwell intently. 'It might save some lives.'

Caldwell laughed: a dry, hollow laugh rooted in anger, not amusement. 'The Farm?'

'What did you do there, Mr Caldwell?' asked Eleanor.

Her voice was gentle, Matt noticed: she was probing him, trying to put him at his ease, open him up.

'Me? Just a lab assistant, nothing special. I used to deliver the drugs that were being tested, then monitor the results. That's what it was mostly about. Checking for side effects.'

'There was a drug called XP22,' said Matt. 'About five years ago. It would have been tested on soldiers. Were you involved with that?'

Caldwell sighed. A look of sadness drifted across his face,

as if some memories he thought long buried had suddenly been brought back to life. 'XP22?' he said. 'You know about that?' He looked at Matt more closely, suddenly afraid. 'You didn't take it, did you?'

Matt shook his head. 'But a friend of mine did. He died.'

Caldwell bent down. With his gloved right hand, he started gripping the stem of a rose, clipping it with his shears. 'Quite a few men did.'

'How many men had the drug tested on them?' asked Eleanor.

'About fifty,' said Caldwell, turning to look at her. 'All soldiers, all serving. They were brought in, given the drug, then kept under observation for the next week. Of course, there are fewer than that now,' said Caldwell. He clipped the stem of another rose, holding the bright red flower in his hand. 'There were side effects. Five of them became uncontrollable. Monsters. They had to be transferred.'

'Transferred?' said Eleanor, puzzled. 'Where?'

Caldwell laughed: that dry, laugh again. 'That was just the term we used. The Farm was full of euphemisms. When we said they were transferred, what we meant was they were taken away.' He paused. 'And we never heard what happened to them.'

'Shot?' said Matt.

Caldwell shrugged. 'That's all I know about XP22,' he said. 'It was a nasty drug, it should never have been used. Nobody should ever have touched it.'

'There may be other side effects, longer term,' said Eleanor. 'We need to find out who those other men were.'

Caldwell shook his head. 'Then you are on your own,' he replied. 'I never knew the names. The men who came into the Farm didn't have any. They just had numbers.'

'The names,' said Eleanor, her tone more insistent now. 'We have to have the names. How else can we help these men?'

Matt could see a look of fear drifting across Caldwell's face, like a small, dark cloud moving across the face of the sun, blocking out all the light. His expression darkened, and his lips started to tremble. 'I've said enough. It's dangerous.'

'The names,' repeated Eleanor.

'No,' said Caldwell, his tone rising. 'I told you, I've said enough.'

He turned, starting to walk back in the direction of the house.

'We've got a sample from one of the dead men,' Eleanor called after him. 'Will you test it for us?'

'Don't be ridiculous,' said Caldwell. 'I don't have any equipment here.'

In the distance, Matt could see a police car advancing along the brow of the hill. Eleanor was following Caldwell, reaching out to tug on his sleeve.

'We have to go,' Matt barked suddenly.

Eleanor looked round, and saw the determination in Matt's eyes. He was already walking back to the car. 'Quickly,' he shouted. Eleanor followed him, her head bowed down, her expression concentrated.

Behind him, Matt was aware of Caldwell turning round as well, walking more quickly, following Matt and Eleanor towards the car.

'There's only one thing I can tell you. The money,' he said. 'Check out the money.'

Matt turned around. 'The money?'

Caldwell stood close to them, his gardening shears still held in his hands. 'The key thing about XP22 was . . . the way it was being paid for.'

Matt looked towards the hill. There were a dozen questions he still wanted to ask. But the police car was less than half a mile away.

★

The woman was walking by herself. Her head was held up high, looking into the sky. She was wearing a short black skirt, and a black T-shirt: her legs and arms were bare, and her skin had tanned a deep rich brown in the fierce summer sun.

'That's her,' said Matram, pointing from the front seat of his Lexus.

'In the black T-shirt?' said Trench.

Matram nodded. 'Let's wait and see where she goes,' he said. 'Follow her home, and take her there.'

It had not been hard to track Gill down. Abbott had told Matram all about her. Matt's childhood sweetheart, his fiancée, they had split up when he got sent on the Ukraine mission. That didn't matter. If anyone was likely to know where Matt was, it was her. A playschool teacher, thought Matram with a smirk. She might be able to control a rowdy toddler, but I bet she can't control us.

There had been no sign of her at the Last Trumpet. Through the Firm, Abbott asked the local police to check her out. There had been no sign of her in Marbella at all. She had vanished into thin air. But that was not the same as hiding. They had run a credit-card check on her, and she had used her ATM card two days ago. At the Barclays Bank on Putney High Street. And she'd used her mobile phone yesterday: the call transmitted through a base station based on the Upper Richmond Road. That was the key. She was staying somewhere in the Putney area.

Easy, realised Matram. She'd need money again soon: only twenty pounds had been withdrawn last time. She was one of those people who thought they spent less if they didn't take out much cash. If they waited at the bank, they'd find her soon enough.

And when they did, she would lead them to Matt. They would torture the information out of her. And if she didn't, well, Browning would fly to her corpse, the same way a vulture flies to a fresh piece of carrion.

He pulled the Lexus away from the kerb, nudging it slowly down the street. She'd already stopped at Starbucks for a coffee, and picked up a newspaper. Now she was walking about thirty yards ahead of him. She turned at the top of the road, strolling down the Upper Richmond Road, then took a left on to an avenue filled with big, suburban houses. She stopped at Number Twelve, looking around. Matram pulled the Lexus to a halt outside the house.

Gill turned the key in the latch.

'OK,' barked Matram. 'Take her. Now.'

Ivan, Eleanor and Matt were standing in the kitchen of the safe house. They had switched to another building, also one of the old IRA safe houses, but this one in Tooting: Ivan insisted they had to keep moving to maximise their chances of staying alive.

Every other opportunity to test the brain tissue had been blocked. 'If we can't do the test,' said Ivan 'we have to think harder. There's something missing about this story. Something we don't know.'

'What?' demanded Eleanor.

'Think about it,' said Ivan. 'The Increment is slowly killing the men who took the drug. One by one. But if this is really a MOD operation, then you wouldn't do it like that. You get all the guys picked up on the same day, get them sectioned, then deal with them in your own good time.'

'What are you saying?' said Matt.

Ivan shrugged. 'Just that we don't have all the answers yet.'

'Perhaps it is to do with the money?' jumped in Eleanor. 'Caldwell said there was something strange about the way XP22 was paid for.'

Ivan smiled. 'Then that's what you need to find out.'

★

Matt checked the van, scrutinising every inch of the vehicle, making sure nothing could be left to chance. It was a blue Ford Transit, with E.H. STEVENS, CLEANING SERVICES, stencilled on to its side in thick yellow lettering.

'You wait here,' he whispered to Eleanor. 'I'll only be a few minutes.'

He stepped out of the Escort, checked the road, then walked quickly towards the parked van. It was early evening, and the roads around west London were already clogged with traffic. He skipped past a pair of courier bikers, then walked casually along the street. One driver was sitting in the front cab of the van; a black man in his mid-thirties, dressed in blue overalls, sipping a bottle of Orangina. Alone. The radio was playing, tuned into Talksport. Matt could hear the presenters discussing the heatwave: the latest prediction was for it to last right through until September, and two more deaths from heatstroke had been reported. 'Sweltering,' jabbered the presenter. 'I don't think we can take much more.'

Matt checked the pavement. Empty. He doubled back, climbing up into the passenger side of the van. 'Hey.'

The driver looked round, his face a mixture of confusion and surprise as he saw Matt's fist hammering towards him. The punch landed just on the side of his cheek, twisting his head round. The bottle went flying from his hand, crashing against the window, then falling to the floor. 'Fuck,' he shouted. 'Fuck.'

The second blow landed hard on the back of his neck. The flesh was soft, the muscles loose and out of shape, Matt noted, as his fist pushed hard into the nerves. The driver's head fell forward, splitting against the steering wheel. 'Sorry, pal,' muttered Matt as he checked that he had lost consciousness. 'You were the wrong man in the wrong place.'

Taking advantage of the few seconds during which he had lost consciousness Matt bundled the driver over the seat, into the back of the van. He tied some rope around his neck, then slotted a gag into his mouth.

Reaching across the dashboard, Matt grabbed the keys. 'Do you think people are less civil to one another in this unbearable heat?' the Talksport presenter was saying. 'Call and tell us what you think.' Matt walked to the back of the van. Opening it up, there were uniforms, plus buckets, clothes and detergents. Matt took two uniforms, two buckets and a mop, then ran back across the road.

'OK,' he said, climbing back into the Escort. 'We're all set.'

The Tocah building loomed out of the street like a tree in a desert. Matt pulled the Escort up into a parking space, and changed into his overalls. At his side, Eleanor did the same. As she peeled down her trousers to climb into the cleaning gear, Matt couldn't help from noticing the pale softness of her skin, and the tapered perfection with which her thighs melted into her hips.

'You look nice,' he said, looking at her, grinning.

'I scrub up good,' Eleanor replied, waving her mop at him.

They walked steadily across the road. Most of the workers were streaming out of the building, heading towards the tube and the bus stops. The women were dabbing their foreheads as they moved from the air-conditioned building to the sultry early-evening heat; the men were taking off their ties and jackets as they prepared for the journey home on hot, crowded, unreliable trains.

'Ready?' said Matt, looking towards Eleanor.

'Frightened,' she replied.

'It's normal to be afraid,' answered Matt. 'The trick is to control it, confront it, not succumb to it.'

'You've learnt some psychology.'

They stepped away from the main entrance, walking around the side of the building. Cleaners were the underclass of corporate life, Matt noted. Nobody looked at them, nobody spoke to them, and nobody paid them any attention. They slipped into and out of buildings like ghosts: they moved only at night, and to most people they were completely invisible. *Perfect cover.*

'Passes,' snapped a security guard, sitting behind a glass screen, his TV tuned to *Big Brother.*

Matt flashed a pair of passes that had been tucked into the pocket of the stolen overalls. The guard's eyes flicked upwards, his expression bored and contemptuous: even down here in the minimum-wage underground of the organisation, there were subtle grades and distinctions. The guards clearly considered themselves a class above the cleaners, and this one wasn't about to lower himself by taking the trouble to check who they were.

You're in hot water when they discover who you just let into the building, pal.

The works lift ran down the back of the building, all the way to the twelfth floor. Like most modern office blocks, there was a set of main lifts for the executives and their secretaries, and a service lift for the cleaners, guards and manual workers. 'Up one flight of stairs,' said Matt.

They walked together up the concrete stairs. A small doorway was cut into the side of the wall. Matt pushed it aside, looking down. The lift shaft soared thirty floors upwards, a gloomy, dark display of cables and wires, hanging loose in the blackened air. Eleanor gasped. 'Wait for the lift to come down, then jump on top of it,' Matt muttered.

He glanced upwards. All around him, he could hear the sounds of the machinery whirring, and he could smell the oil that greased the levers and pulleys of the lift shaft. 'I did regiment training in counter-terrorist special ops. In case some terrorists took over a building and we had to go in and flush them out. It never happened, thank Christ, but if it had, we were ready for them.'

Eleanor gripped his hand tighter. He could feel the sweat on her palms. Above them, he could hear the lift descending. The chains and levers rattled as it dropped through the shaft, stopping twice then three times; each time the noise of metal clacking into concrete echoed down towards them.

'Use the fear,' whispered Matt into Eleanor's ear.

The lift swished past them, a blast of air pushing out of the door as it raced downwards. It stopped on the ground floor, two yards beneath them. 'Now,' whispered Matt.

He stepped down. He held on tight to Eleanor's hand, forcing her forwards. They landed softly on the metal roof of the lift, Matt's hand rising up to Eleanor's throat to stifle the scream he could feel rising within her. 'Keep totally quiet,' he whispered. 'We're about to move.'

Gill didn't struggle. They don't when you take them by surprise, reflected Matram. Like rabbits trapped in the headlights of an oncoming car, they are paralysed by fear. Their muscles seize, and their brains shut down. They can't move and they can't react.

Snaddon and Trench moved in first, Matram hanging back to guard the street. Gill had the key in the lock, about to open the door. She had turned round, looking up, seeing Snaddon approaching her. She hardly reacted. That was the advantage of having women in the Increment: a woman could approach another woman without provoking fear. Snaddon thrust her hand up towards Gill's mouth, clasping her hand tight over her lips. Trench followed swiftly behind, grabbing her arms, twisting them sharply behind her back. Gill would have screamed in pain, but the hand over her mouth prevented any sound from escaping from her lips: instead, the scream travelled within her, sinking down into her stomach, making her ribcage shake with confusion and anger.

237

At her side, Matram leant down to pick up the keys that had fallen on the floor. He glanced out on to the street, making sure they had not been seen, then calmly opened the door. Snaddon pushed Gill roughly inside, casting her down on the floor, then sitting astride her chest, slapping her sharply across the face.

Matram looked around the apartment. The main room was simply but smartly furnished. There was a sofa, a plasma-screen TV, some shelves, and a reproduction of Andy Warhol's portrait of Jackie Kennedy on the wall. A kitchen led off to the sitting room, and there was a bedroom behind that, leading out on to a small patio garden. From the PlayStation positioned underneath the TV, he judged this was probably a man's apartment. She was just borrowing it for a few days.

There's going to be quite a mess to clean up when he gets home, thought Matram. *You don't see that on your PlayStation.*

Matram walked across the floor, towering above Gill's prostrate body. 'Where's Matt?'

'Piss off,' she spat.

Snaddon slapped her across the face again, pushing her back hard against the floor. The sight of a woman in pain, reflected Matram, was always a pleasure to watch and always instructive. Physiologically, women had a far higher pain threshold than men – they were built to withstand childbirth after all – and their capacity to absorb torture was infinitely superior. If you wanted to learn about beating information out of people, you had to start with a female. *Learn that, and the men were easy.*

'Now,' said Matram, 'I'll ask you again. Where's Matt?'

'Piss off.'

Matram shook his head slowly from side to side. 'That's not the language I'd expect from a playschool teacher.' He chuckled softly as he spoke. 'I'd tell you to go and wash your

238

mouth out with soap if I didn't have something much nastier in mind for you.' He paused, walking away from her. 'Now, I'll ask you once more, and then I'll stop being so nice. Where's Matt?'

Tears were starting to run down Gill's face, and her body was shaking with a mixture of fear and pain. 'I don't know,' she spluttered. 'We split up. I haven't seen him for weeks.'

'Don't lie to me,' snapped Matram. 'You know where he is.'

'I don't, I don't, I swear it.'

Gill looked up, only in time to see the back of Snaddon's hand smacking into the side of her face.

'I don't know where he is,' she screamed, louder this time.

'Enough,' shouted Matram. 'I don't have the time to play games with you. One more chance.' He leant down into her face, his eyes burning with anger. 'Tell me where Matt is.'

'I don't know, I tell you,' sobbed Gill.

Matram's head spun round. 'Give her the injection.'

Gill's eyes swivelled to the left, a new look of fear on her face. From his pocket, Trench had pulled a needle, holding it between his thumb and his forefinger.

'The tongue,' said Matram. 'Inject her in the tongue.'

He watched as Snaddon held her down tightly, forcing her mouth open with her fists. Gill was a fit young woman, but she had no real strength: she had no idea how to fight.

The tongue is the perfect place for an injection, reflected Matram. When the coroner does his autopsy, he won't know what's happened. *Injections on the tongue leave no trace.*

'What is it?' spluttered Gill.

'An anaesthetic called suxamethonium,' answered Matram. 'It's quite common, a muscle relaxant, prescribed in just about every hospital in the world. Got an interesting history though. The Nazis used to use it during interrogations. It encourages the patient to be more truthful. It relaxes every muscle in your body. You won't be able to move. You won't even be able to breathe. You'll know exactly what it feels like to die. I'm going to give you a very small injection, which will wear off after just a few seconds, just so you know . . . what it feels like. Then I'm going to ask you again, and then if you don't tell me what I want to know, I'm going to give you another injection. Do it,' he said, looking at Trench.

The needle jabbed into the side of her tongue, piercing the flesh, the pure liquid in the syringe shooting into the bloodstream. Matram could see her whole body go motionless, expressionless, except for a mortal terror shining out from somewhere deep inside the eyeballs. Then, she came to again, stirring slightly, and her eyes moving madly from side to side as she panicked.

'I've already told you the truth,' she said. Tears were streaming down her face now, and her hands were shaking.

'Tell me again,' said Matram softly.

'He's gone on a job,' said Gill. 'I don't know what it is, and I don't care. A man called Guy Abbott came out to Spain from the Firm. They blocked all his money. Matt was livid. Unless he did this job, he was finished.'

She paused, choking back the tears blocking her throat. 'I was furious. I told him not to do it, that it didn't matter about the money, that it was over between us if he did it. He went anyway. That was it between us. I came back to London. I haven't spoken to him since, and I don't want to.'

Matram sighed. 'More,' he said to Trench.

Snaddon held her mouth open again. Gill tried to wrench her head away, but the woman was too strong for her. 'Still,' Trench shouted as the needle jabbed into her tongue.

Another two millilitres, Matram noted. In less than two

minutes she would be dead: the muscles throughout her body would slow and slow, then her heart would stop beating. He leant forward, so close to her face he could smell the despair on her skin. Her bowels had already gone, and a trickle of urine was running down the side of her leg.

'Tell me again,' he whispered.

'I've told you, I don't know where he is,' whimpered Gill. The words were offered up in a tone of sorrowful resignation. 'I don't know.'

The same old story, thought Matram. Maybe she really doesn't know where he is. *Maybe she's telling the truth. But it makes no difference. I would have killed her anyway.*

The sound of metal striking metal rattled through Matt's ears as the lift rode up into the sky. He sat on the cold surface of the machine, his brow sweating as it slowly made its way through the building. It was dark, with only occasional glimmers of light from the doorways penetrating the gloom of the concrete shaft. Whether they were safe or not, it was impossible to be certain: if there was danger out there, it was too dark to see it.

'How long?' whispered Eleanor.

The lift was moving faster now: Matt could feel some nausea welling up in his stomach from the unfamiliar motion. He could feel her shaking: her shoulders were wobbly, and goose bumps were pricking down the skin of her arms. Matt threw an arm protectively across her, but said nothing. Silence was crucial for the next few minutes.

The lift had stopped. Matt couldn't be sure, maybe it was the sixth or seventh floor. His plan was to use the escape hatch to avoid the extra layer of security which he knew, from his previous visit, lay on the top floor: Lacrierre's. Inside the lift, he could hear people climbing in, conversation drifting upwards. He held his breath, desperate not to make a sound. The weather. They were talking about the

241

weather. Matt relaxed, letting the air out of his lungs. If that was all, they were probably just cleaners travelling up through the building for the evening shift.

The lift juddered to a halt. That was the tenth floor, Matt judged. The cleaners climbed out, then up it went again, climbing into the sky. The noise was getting louder now, the echoes travelling down to the bottom of the shaft, then bouncing back up again. Matt had to focus hard to shut the noise out.

It stopped. The lift fell completely still, and within seconds the echoes had died away. One of the metal ropes was swaying against the wall, but otherwise the lift was as silent as a tomb. 'Stay here,' he whispered to Eleanor.

He looked up. Ten yards above him, there was an escape hatch built into the side of the shaft. 'There's always somewhere to escape from a lift shaft,' whispered Matt. 'Building regulations.'

The hatch measured just five feet by five, enough room for anyone trapped in the building to make their escape down the lift shaft. Along the edge of the shaft was a series of metal railings, each one a step one foot apart. He started climbing, pulling himself up foot by foot. 'Quick,' he whispered down to Eleanor. 'Follow me.'

Matt pulled on a pair of protective gloves. Because the escape hatch was built to allow people trapped on the top floor to get out through the shaft, it was bolted from the outside. But the bolts were weak, and the wire mesh flimsy. Beneath Matt's fist, it gave way easily enough.

Throwing his elbows forward, Matt pulled himself out on to the corridor. He immediately turned round, reaching down for Eleanor, pulling her out on to the carpet. Then, above him, he could hear the sound of a man breathing.

He was standing ten feet in front of him, in the corridor. Neatly dressed, in grey slacks and a pale blue linen shirt, he spun around, looking directly at Matt. He had a cup of coffee in one hand, and a folder of documents in the other.

'Who the fuck are you?' he snapped.

NINETEEN

Matt froze. His muscles stopped moving, and he could feel the blood slowing through his veins. 'Who are you?' said the man, walking swiftly towards them.

Matt pulled himself upright, making sure Eleanor was at his side. His overalls were dirty after climbing out of the lift shaft, and there was still dust clinging to his hair.

'Ch-Ch-Ch,' he stuttered, twisting nervously, as if he was inflicted by a terrible stammer. 'Ca-Ca-Ca,' he continued louder this time.

The man looked at him closely, the styrofoam coffee cup still held in his right hand. Everyone is troubled by people with disabilities, Matt figured: they want to spend as little time with them as possible. 'Ca-Ca-Ca,' he coughed.

'Cleaners,' said the man, trying to be helpful.

'Th-Th-Th,' spluttered Matt.

The man looked towards Eleanor. 'Cleaners, right?'

'Ah-Ah-Ah,' she said, twisting her face into a contortion.

'Cleaning,' shouted Matt, his face suddenly triumphant, his hands resting on the man's shoulder.

'You're filthy!' said the man, pushing Matt's hand away. He dusted off the shoulder of his shirt, as if it might have been contaminated. 'Just get on with it.'

He turned, and disappeared towards his office on the left, collected his jacket and called the lift. He was leaving for the evening.

Bastard, thought Matt.

He walked swiftly down the corridor. Eleanor was following on behind him, as they stepped into the main offices. Matt checked immediately to see if anyone was there. The desk where the drop-dead gorgeous secretaries had sat was empty: Matt could see a copy of *Red* magazine and a packet of Nurofen lying open on the desk. Matt took out his duster, and started wiping down the surface of the desk. 'Start cleaning,' he said. 'Make it look real.'

Behind him, he could see Eleanor starting to dust with one of the cloths they had brought with them. Matt pushed open the door that led directly into Lacrierre's office. The place was empty. Matt started looking around, checking the walls for cameras. Nothing. That can't be right, he told himself. There must be more security. *Perhaps Lacrierre doesn't like to be watched while he is working?*

He stepped up to the desk. A diary was placed on top of it, plus a mobile-phone charger. Next to it was a PC, a standard Dell that you might find in any office. Matt looked at it closely. The machine was switched off, and there was no sign of any cameras hidden inside the monitor. *Safe enough.*

He looked at the keyboard, then the mouse. No wires, he noted. There was nothing physically connecting the peripherals to the computer. That's it, thought Matt. Lots of people installed Bluetooth or one of the other wireless systems to get rid of the clutter of wires linking up to the PC. But they were also a common security device. Tiny broadcast signals allowed the different parts of the machine to talk to each other, but the transmissions could also be linked into a security network.

Anyone touches this piece of kit, it's going to trigger an alarm and a couple of dozen security guards are going to come screaming in here, shooting everything that moves.

Matt looked at the back of the PC. The Bluetooth connection was plugged into the USB port. Carefully, he unplugged it, laying it down on the side of the desk. I shouldn't be risking this, but I don't have any choice. *If the goon squad are not here in ninety seconds, I'm in the clear.*

Matt looked anxiously at his watch. He walked back towards the door, glancing down the corridor. At least the floors were stone, he noted, not carpet. If anyone was approaching, they would hear it a long way away.

Nothing. We're clear.

'Got the disk?' Matt whispered to Eleanor.

She nodded, walking towards the computer. Matt booted it up, waiting while it purred into life. As the Windows logo switched on, he opened up the Start menu, clicking on a series of icons. He had never tried this before, but it had been explained to him on an electronic-warfare course in the regiment, and he just had to hope it worked. On most corporate systems, if you deleted the operating system from a Windows desktop, then reloaded it, you could choose a new password. Once you had done that since, you knew what the password was, you could break into the machine.

'OK,' he whispered.

Eleanor slipped the disk into the CD-ROM drive – a standard Windows installation program – and Matt clicked Install. He could hear the hard disk kicking into life: the familiar whirring sound of data being distributed around the machine. He started to pace the room nervously, walking up and down, pushing his mop in front of him, pretending to clean. He emptied one bin, then walked on, his mind focused on the task ahead of them.

'OK,' whispered Eleanor. 'It's done.'

Matt leant over the computer. Set password, said the computer. Matt hesitated, then tapped in 'Orlena'. Confirm password, asked the machine. 'Orlena,' Matt typed. A message flashed up on the screen: 'The computer is now ready to use.'

It took an effort of will for Matt not to punch the air in

triumph. He steadied himself, squeezed Eleanor's hand, then looked down at the screen. 'We're in.'

'Start looking at the files,' said Eleanor. 'Look for anything to do with XP22.'

Matt started searching. There were several hundred documents stored on the machine, and he knew it was a long shot. But it was the only shot they had. Unless he could find some hard documented evidence that Tocah had been in charge of the XP22 program, then he had nothing at all.

'Here,' said Eleanor, her finger jabbing at the screen. Within 'My Documents', there was a folder called 'Alanbrooke'. 'Just outside the Ministry of Defence building on Whitehall there's a statue of Lord Alanbrooke. I must have walked past it a hundred times.'

Matt clicked on the folder, opening up a dozen files on the screen. 'Transfer them,' he said. 'I'll watch the door.'

Eleanor had already set up a new Hotmail account for herself. Transfer all these files to it by email, and they would have their own copies of them. They could study them at leisure. And if Matt's hunch was right about what was in those documents, they could nail their man.

Matt stood by the door, glancing behind him. At the computer, he could see Eleanor's fingers working feverishly, attaching the documents to emails, then pressing Send. She repeated the same task, again and again. Up ahead, Matt could hear something. It was barely audible at first, but it was growing in strength.

A footstep.

Matt looked back towards Eleanor. 'Quick,' he hissed. 'Someone's coming.'

He could see fear in her expression as she looked back at him. 'Just three more.'

Matt stepped into the corridor, then out into the main reception area. He could see a woman approach, carrying a sheaf of papers beneath her arm. One of the drop-dead gorgeous secretaries: a Natalie or a Natasha or a Nadine.

Maybe she recognises me from the last time I was here, thought Matt, a flash of anxiety running through him. Her eyes ran up and down him, but she appeared to be more concerned by the state of his overalls than his face.

'Who are you?' she said, looking sharply towards Matt.

Matt glanced behind him. Eleanor was still at the computer. He pushed his mop along the floor, then looked back up at the woman. 'Ch-Ch-Ch,' he stuttered.

'What?' she said angrily. 'Speak properly.'

'Ch-Ch-Ch,' said Matt, leaning closer to her.

The woman backed away. 'There are no cleaners allowed into Mr Lacrierre's office,' she commanded. 'Who are you?'

'Ah-Ah-Ah,' stuttered Matt. 'I am . . .' He started coughing violently. 'Ah-Ah-Ah.'

'You'll have to leave immediately,' she said. 'Now.'

Matt glanced backwards: Eleanor was still at the computer, but she had her duster out, pretending to wipe the screen. The woman was walking towards the desk. Matt swung the mop up into the air, holding it above his head, then started to move swiftly across the floor. The woman turned, just in time for her to see the handle of the mop slipping over her neck. Matt held it tight between his forearms, bunching his muscles up. The wood cut into her, pressuring the windpipe, making it impossible for her to breath. 'I'm doing you a favour,' whispered Matt in her ear. 'The shortage of oxygen to your brain will make you unconscious, but it's not going to leave any bruising. I wouldn't want to mess up your face.'

Whether the woman appreciated the gesture, Matt would never know. She slipped to her knees, her skirt riding up around her thighs as she fell. Her head flopped to the side, as her body rolled away. Matt snapped the mop away, checking her pulse. Still breathing. From his pocket, he pulled out a white cloth and a roll of tape. He pushed the cloth into her mouth, then taped it over. Next, he slipped her hands behind her back, and taped them together. She'll be OK until the morning, Matt reflected.

Our luck is holding. But not for much longer.

'Out,' he hissed towards Eleanor. 'Out.'

Eleanor put a coffee and a ham sandwich down at his side. The bread was two days old – part of the supplies Ivan had left for them at the safe house in Hammersmith – but it still tasted good. When you're hungry enough, and frightened enough, any food tastes OK.

'Let's see what we've got,' said Eleanor.

'Yes, let's see . . .' said Ivan.

He walked out of the shadows. Matt looked up from the laptop Ivan had supplied for them.

'Just keeping an eye on you,' said Ivan with a grin.

He sat down on the floor, pouring himself some coffee. Eleanor had already downloaded all the files they had taken from Lacrierre's office. Her face was framed in concentration as she started to scroll through them, her eyes darting from left to right as she tracked the mass of information on the screen.

'It's here,' she said eventually, her voice soft yet determined. 'It's all here.'

Matt walked around her, resting his arms on her shoulders and peering down at the screen.

'Tocah was paid by the Ministry of Defence, all through the 1990s, to produce and develop a bravery drug for NATO. Called XP22.' She stopped, her fingers darting across the keyboard. 'One hundred million pounds, paid out of the defence budget every year, over a period of ten years. That makes one billion pounds.'

'The bastards,' said Matt grimly. 'The government was behind it all along.'

'British secret service,' said Ivan. 'You can't trust them.'

Eleanor pointed at the screen. 'The money wasn't paid directly into Tocah's account. Obviously, they had to keep it secret. It was paid out to a series of dummy companies, based in different locations around Europe. All of them secretly owned by Tocah, and the money was flowing back into the company so that it looked like legitimate income from selling their pharmaceuticals.'

Matt shrugged. 'Makes sense. If you had a bravery drug, you wouldn't want anyone to know about it. Least of all the poor bloody soldiers you were planning to give it to.'

Eleanor scrolled further down the list. 'Here, these are the men they gave it to. A list, their names.' Her fingers ran down the glass surface of the screen. 'Fifty men, just as we were told.' She paused, taking a deep breath. 'Five of them died during the course of the treatment. But look, here are the others. Barry Legg. Simon Turnbull. Sam Mentorn. David Helton. All the names I started out investigating. All the ex-servicemen who started going crazy with no previous history of mental illness. All their names are on this list. And they've all got a capital M next to them.'

'For *mort*,' chipped in Ivan. 'The French for dead.'

'Ken Blackman, in Derby,' said Eleanor. 'His name has been crossed off the list as well. Dealt with.'

'The bastards,' said Matt.

Ivan took a sip on his coffee. 'If the side effects are only coming through now, a few years later, you don't want too many homicidal maniacs springing up around the country. Sooner or later someone is going to start putting the bacon and chicken and lettuce together until they've got themselves a whole club sandwich. Just the way Eleanor started to. No, if they want to keep what they've done a secret, and they have to, then the only thing to do is to eliminate the evidence.' He knelt down, his eyes squinting and his finger pointing at the screen. 'Who are these payments to, then?'

250

Eleanor followed the line of his finger. 'One million each year, from the money generated by the bravery drug,' she said. 'Paid out to two accounts in Luxembourg.'

'Who are they?' said Matt, finishing his sandwich.

'We don't know, just numbers, no names,' said Ivan. 'But I'd say they were the key.'

Matt stood up, walking towards the window. His muscles felt tired, and strained. He was longing for a beach, and the feel of wet sand beneath his feet. He wanted to smell the salt of the ocean, and fill his lungs with the sea air. He was tired of the city, he was tired of hiding.

'But we've got enough, haven't we?' said Matt. 'We know about XP22. We know that Lacrierre imported it to this country, and sold it to the MOD. We know it was tested on British servicemen. We know some of them have gone crazy, a direct result of the medicine they were given. We know they are killing the men it was tested on to cover up what happened. What more do we need? Everything has fallen into place. We've cracked it.'

Ivan walked across the room, standing next to him. He held out a coffee, thrusting it into Matt's face. 'Take a good sniff,' he said. 'It's time you woke up and smelt some of this.'

'Meaning?' snapped Matt, suddenly filled with anger.

'Meaning you don't seem to have figured out what you are going to do with this information. The deeper you get into this, the more trouble you are in. So what's the plan now? Go to the police? They'll arrest you. Go to the Firm? They got you into this mess.'

'A newspaper, as I said before,' interrupted Eleanor. 'They could blow this scandal wide open.'

Ivan chuckled to himself, turning away. 'In a John Grisham book, maybe. Not in the real world. One sniff of this story, a newspaper would get itself shut down. Any journalist who knew even part of the story would be quietly disposed of. They're *deadly* serious about this, Matt. That's why the Increment is already on to you. This stuff is toxic. Anyone who touches it is dead.'

'A foreign newspaper,' persisted Eleanor.

'No,' said Ivan, with a shake of the head. 'You'll look like a nutty conspiracy theorist. They'll think you're raving mad. You've got to tie it all down.' He paused, looking directly at Matt and Eleanor. 'You have to find out who these accounts belong to. Right now they don't mean anything. Until you get that information, you don't have any way to convince anyone of your story.'

Matt was standing by the window, looking out on to the dingy block of council flats opposite. 'It's us against the world, Matt,' said Ivan, resting his hand on Matt's shoulder. 'If they were offering odds on this one down at William Hill, my money would have to be on the world.'

Matram looked down at the corpse. She had stopped breathing some minutes ago, the last breath silent and quiet as the anaesthetic sent her into a deep sleep, and as her heart slowed to a rate at which life could no longer be supported.

He cracked the back of his fist hard against the side of her cheek, his knuckles bruising the skin. 'You stupid bitch,' he muttered, his tone harsh and rasping. 'You should have told me where he was.' He turned round, looking at Trench and Snaddon. 'I want this body moved.'

Trench looked back at him coldly. 'We could leave it here,' he said. 'The apartment is empty. It could be days, even weeks, before anyone finds it.'

'Don't you understand anything, you damned fool?' he said, his voice rising. 'I want the bloody corpse discovered. Get it out of this building, and put it down in the middle of the nearest car park. Anywhere it's going to be found immediately.'

He looked down again at Gill, closing her eyes with his

fingers. 'It's like a worm,' he said. 'The angler digs the poor little animal out of the dirt, kills it, sticks it on his line and casts it out into the river. All so he can use it to catch the fish.'

TWENTY

Eleanor had come into his room. She was wearing a white T-shirt, but beneath it he could see the outline of her breasts, soft and warm. 'I'm frightened,' she said. 'I've been trying to sleep, but I can't.'

Matt looked up towards the window. They were back in the first safe house now: moving every other day made them harder to track. Even now Ivan was off somewhere preparing another house for them. The first light of dawn was breaking through the frosted glass.

'Like we were saying, it's OK to be afraid,' he said. 'Fear is natural.'

He ran his fingers through her hair. Even though she was sweaty, she smelt good. Her skin was stretched and sleepy. Matt held her in his arms, feeling her breath on his chest. They hadn't made love yet, he felt guilty about Gill; but, he reasoned, *she left me*. Something was happening between them, they were drawing closer. Maybe it was just the chase, the sense of common danger. Maybe it was being thrown together in extreme circumstances. Matt couldn't be sure. But he was certain of one thing. Right now, there was no one he would rather be with.

We got into this together, and we'll get out of it together as well.

He slipped away from the bed, washing himself in the bathroom. There was no shower, just a piece of plastic hosing jammed into the tap from which a trickle of rusty water emerged. Only one razor had been left lying in the cupboard, and it had last been used several years ago: the blade was rusty and clogged with dirt, biting into Matt's skin as he dragged it across his face. He washed away the two smears of blood it left on his chin, and looked at the face staring at him from the mirror. He looked older. There were lines around his eyes, his skin was rough, his complexion blotchy, and his hair looked uncut and unkempt. This is taking its toll, he reflected. *If I don't finish this soon, it's going to finish me.*

His jeans were hanging from the back of the chair, his polo shirt next to them. Matt started to slip them on. The mobile in his pocket was ringing. He looked at the machine curiously. It wasn't his normal Nokia: he'd chucked that away since it could be used to track him down. It was a cheap Motorola. Ivan was supplying him with a new one every day to reduce the chances of detection, stolen and fitted with a new SIM card, with a pay-as-you-go account issued in a false name. The phone was safe to carry around, and only Ivan had the number.

Matt picked up the phone, punching the green answer button. 'Matt,' said Ivan. Then there was a pause on the line. 'I just heard from Damien. It's about Gill.'

'What is it?' said Matt quickly.

Another pause. That fateful hesitation Matt had learnt about in the regiment. The delay the Ruperts employ before they tell a mother or a wife or a sister of the death of a man.

'She's dead.'

Matt buried his face in his hand. It had been weeks now since he'd heard from Gill. After that argument back in Marbella, she walked out of his life in a way he'd never imagined possible. One minute they had been about to get married. The next minute she was gone. And all that had come between them was Guy Abbott and his fucking job.

Matt slammed his fist against the wall, shaking loose a tiny cloud of dust. *If I'm in any way responsible for her death, I'll never forgive myself.*

'Where?' said Matt. 'How?'

'Matt, you have to stay calm,' said Ivan.

'I need to see her.'

'No,' said Ivan, raising his tone. 'It's too dangerous. You mustn't go anywhere where they might find you.'

'Just tell me where she is,' snapped Matt, his voice rising.

The phone line was dead. Matt hurled it across the room, pulling on the rest of his clothes. His head was burning with a hundred different emotions. Sorrow, regret, confusion and despair were all mixing together in a lethal cocktail. But one emotion was trumping all of them. *Anger.*

A line has been crossed. This is a different country we've moved into. Bringing them to justice is not enough. *Now I take my revenge in the reddest blood. Or I die trying.*

Matram leant back against the table of the Travelodge. He was chewing on what the front desk described as a 'breakfast selection buffet'. That struck him as a rather grand description for a plastic tray with a rubbery croissant, a carton of processed orange juice and a tub of sweet strawberry yogurt. Still, it was food that would get them through another day.

'This is our moment,' he said, looking out at the Increment. 'The prey is about to fall into our hands.'

Eight faces, silent and passive, looked back at him and nodded. First thing this morning, he had called the other six back from around the country. Today, he sensed, he needed all his people right here. A good general, he judged, ruled by instinct as much as reason: and right now his instincts were telling him that the enemy was closer at hand than he could have imagined. *The bait was about to be taken.*

A quote from General Patton, the American commander in Europe during the Second World War, and Matram's most revered military hero, was rattling through his mind. *A good plan violently executed now is better than a perfect plan next week.*

'Last night, the offices of Eduardo Lacrierre, the chief executive of the pharmaceutical company Tocah, were broken into,' started Matram, looking down at the unit. 'A secretary was found unconscious there this morning, after she interrupted an intruder last night.' He paused. 'I believe that must have been our targets, Browning and Blackman.' Matram ground his fists together. 'I want them found, and I want them found now.'

The unit remained silent, as Matram walked slowly across the room and stood looking out of the window. In the regiment, the rule was that all the men, whether they were squaddies or Ruperts, were equal. When you were out on a job, everyone's voice carried the same weight. That didn't apply in the Increment. It was Matram's unit, and when he told you to do something, you obeyed.

'The woman we took yesterday,' Matram continued. 'That was Browning's fiancée. I'm going to make the assumption that he's heard of her death. And he's going to want to see her, that's the kind of man he is.'

Matt walked silently by himself through Plumstead Common. It was still early in the morning, but the sun was already shining, and the light breeze blowing in from the west was doing nothing to take the heat out of the air. Another scorching day.

In the distance, he could see two mothers playing with their children. The kids were stripped down to their shorts, screaming and splashing water over each other. Matt watched them for a few minutes. *One day I always imagined Gill and I would settle down and have a kid or two. I never thought about it much, but that was what I expected for the future. So long as I didn't get killed in some miserable foreign war, we would eventually be together.*

257

And now she's dead. And that future has turned into ashes and dust.

He could see Damien a hundred yards distant, sitting by himself on a park bench. His shoulders were hunched, and his head bowed, looking intently at the ground. Matt could feel his pace slowing, reluctant to travel the last few yards. Damien was Gill's brother, and Matt's oldest friend: like many siblings, although they looked different, he and Gill had the same voices and mannerisms. Matt and Damien had spent their childhoods together, running in and out of each other's houses. This had been the park where they would come and play, close enough to their houses for them to be allowed out by themselves. There had been countless different wars played out on this turf, and there was a hundred different tunnels, rat runs and mazes they had used as boys when they were escaping from irate policemen, park wardens, bus conductors and ice-cream van drivers.

And although Damien had become a villain while Matt went off to join the army, that had never stood between them: they were both men who fought for a living, and understood that their trade had its own rules. Matt had no closer friend, nor anyone he could rely on more completely. When he and Gill had become engaged, they were about to become brothers-in-law, yet they had been brothers in spirit all their lives. *And now this.*

'What happened?' asked Matt, sitting down on the bench next to Damien.

'Her body was found first thing this morning,' said Damien. His voice was slow and measured, but Matt could hear the cracks in it. 'On Putney Heath. It was taken to the mortuary, and the police have been examining it there. They called me, and I went to see her, to identify the body.' He paused, choking back the words. 'No obvious cause of death. There was some bruising around her cheeks, like someone had been slapping her. But that

258

didn't kill her. Right now, nobody can say what it was.'

Matt's eyes narrowed, looking out across the park. The mums were still playing with their kids in the distance, and he could see a couple out walking their dog. The man was shouting something at the animal, but it didn't seem to be responding: a golden spaniel, it kept bounding on ahead of them. A jogger, the sweat pouring from his face, was just turning the corner, panting along the pathway towards them. 'Are you alone, Damien?' he hissed. 'Are you sure nobody saw you come here?'

Suddenly, Matt could feel Damien's hands around his throat. His knuckles were digging into his skin, and he could feel the supply of oxygen to his brain starting to slow as the pressure on his windpipe increased. 'What the fuck are you up to, Matt?' shouted Damien, his face red with anger. 'Gill's dead, you're sneaking around London like a man on the run. What the fuck's going on?'

His hands broke free from Matt's neck when he could see that he was not fighting back. Matt remained silent.

'You got her involved in another of your bloody money-making schemes, didn't you?' shouted Damien.

'I'm in a mess, Damien. Probably the worst mess I've ever been in.'

'Tell me about it.'

Matt started to talk. He began with Abbott, the job in the Ukraine, then everything that had happened since then, up to the house in Hammersmith where he and Eleanor were hiding. The words came out slowly and painfully, as if Matt were frightened of them himself. When he had finished, he put out an arm, resting it on Damien's shoulder. 'I'm up against the Increment. And you want my guess? I reckon they took Gill because they thought she might lead them to me.'

Matt looked out across the park. The couple with the dog were walking back across the park. The man was still snapping at the animal, the women at his side looked furtively over her shoulder at them. Matt glanced across at Damien, noticing that he too was observing the couple.

'See those two with the dog?' started Matt.

Damien nodded. 'Yes . . . that dog doesn't know who the fuck they are.'

'A decoy,' whispered Matt. 'I thought you said you weren't followed?'

Damien shook his head. 'I didn't realise I would be up against the regiment's finest,' he said bitterly.

Matt hesitated. It was clear now. Gill had been squeezed for information, and when she hadn't given them any, they'd killed her and dumped her body. They knew it would be found. They knew Damien would collect the body, and they knew he would be in touch with Matt. All they had to do was follow him.

You could follow it like the moves on a chessboard. Straight from the murder manual of Jack Matram.

They were in open space. At least two people, the two mothers with their children, could see them – that gave them some cover. He couldn't be certain what rules of engagement the Increment had been given, but the chances were they would avoid a firefight on open ground.

'The sewer,' said Damien.

Matt nodded.

'Start walking,' said Damien.

Matt stood up. He glanced again in the direction of the couple. They were thirty yards across the common. The man was about thirty, with blond hair, and cold, grey eyes. The woman was maybe slightly older, with short dark hair. The dog was still bounding ahead of them, still ignoring their commands.

'I'm going to buy you five seconds,' whispered Damien. 'After that, you're on your own.'

Aged eight or nine, Matt, Damien and some of their mates used to throw eggs at passing buses. They did it every afternoon on the way back from school. Once, the driver stopped, left the bus and started chasing after them. Matt and Damien had escaped, diving into an old disused sewer half a mile across the common that came up behind a garage next to the high street.

That was a quarter of a century ago, reflected Matt. *Would the tunnel still be there?*

Matt tensed himself. In his mind, he had a map of the distance between here and the safe house: it was at least ten miles back to Hammersmith. Eleanor would still be there, alone. If he could just break free of them, he could get to her and move on. Depends how fast I can move, he told himself. *And whether fate is on my side.*

Damien whistled to the dog. From about thirty yards distant, its ears pricked up, and it started running towards him. From their childhood, Matt could recall how Damien had always been good with dogs. He knew the signals and the whistles that would make each breed run towards him. Suddenly, he realised what Damien was doing. It was time to make the break.

'Go,' hissed Damien. 'Go.'

Matt peeled away, his heels digging into the hard tarmac of the walkway that stretched across the common. He switched on to the grass, running up a slope that led towards the sewer. At his side, he could see the dog bounding up towards Damien. He could hear it barking as Damien lifted it clean from the ground, holding it in his arms. And he could hear the sound of the man shouting at him. 'Drop the dog, drop the dog.'

Matt's feet were already pounding against the grass. His blood was starting to pump through his veins, and the oxygen was filling his lungs as he took huge gulps of air.

Behind him, he could hear shouts, scuffles. Don't look

around, he told himself. Every split second counted, every few yards took him further away from their reach.

If a bullet comes, better to take it in the back. At least you won't know about it.

He swerved down the pathway heading towards the bushes that formed the barrier between the street and common. Every muscle straining to push himself further forward. Matt ran every day in Spain, sometimes four miles, sometimes five: but that was along the beach, when he was rested, and had plenty of water. Now, his throat was dry, and the sweat was pouring off his brow.

He could still hear shouting, fighting. He looked back, just long enough to see Damien fleeing in the opposite direction, a trail of anger and confusion in his wake.

Back-up, thought Matt. If they are the Increment, then there will be back-up somewhere. And there may be helicopters overhead within minutes.

He pushed forward into the bushes, dipping out of sight of his pursuers. Diving on to the ground, he threw his hands down into the mud. The spot was as he remembered it. A few planks, now rotting with age, covered by a thick fresh layer of roots and brambles. Matt tore into the ground, cutting his fingers on the brambles as he did so, but the ground opened up, and he pushed the planks aside and squeezed himself into the space.

The sewer had been built in Victorian times, and had been abandoned half a century ago. It had been fine for eight-year-old boys, but it was a tiny space for a grown man, and his shoulders were up tight against the moss-covered brick walls. There was no light and, as Matt plunged forwards, he could feel the darkness surrounding him. Some roots had grown through the tunnel but, after he pushed through those, the way opened up ahead of him: some other boys had found it, he guessed, and had cleared some of the rubbish out of the way.

Not much changes in this part of London. Small boys are always playing at running away from something.

A light. Matt could see a chink at the end of the tunnel. He kicked away the plank that covered it, bursting out into the alleyway. It had been a garage last time he had been here. Now it was the back of a Starbucks: there were a pile of empty coffee bags in the bins, and the smell of cappuccinos drifted out of the building.

He hustled his way down the alleyway that ran down the side of Starbucks and came out on to the street, anxiety still stabbing at his chest. He brushed past a mother pushing her pram, knocking the cigarette from her lips. He could hear her cursing but ignored her. He pushed on, passing a row of shops. Keep going, he told himself. *This is your only chance.*

'You,' shouted a man. 'Where . . .'

Matt pressed on. Don't lead them to the house, he told himself. Wait till you know you've lost them.

He turned down a side street, running hard along the pavement, then ducked into another alley. Nobody seemed to be following. Two more streets, both taken at a hard jog. That led him back down towards the high street. He paused, taking a moment to check behind him.

Nobody.

The street was busy, crowded with people out shopping. Matt hesitated. He was aware the sweat was dripping off his face, and he was gulping down air, trying to get some oxygen back into his lungs. He bent over, taking a moment to rest, and to push some strength back into his muscles.

They think I'm a mugger. They're frightened of me, and who can blame them?

He started walking, then picked up the pace as he turned off the main street. He kept checking behind him, looking out for any signs they were on his tail. He scanned up into the sky, looking to see if there might be a helicopter. And he checked the cars sitting on the street, peering into each one as he passed it, making sure there was nobody sitting, waiting.

A cab. Matt jumped inside, barking out instructions to the driver. It was just after eleven in the morning. For the next twenty minutes, sweat was pouring off him as he checked and double-checked that there was nobody following. Then, after jumping out of the cab, he threw the door of the Hammersmith safe house open, shouting at the top of his lungs. 'Eleanor, Eleanor.'

Eleanor and Damien were sitting in the kitchen. Matt was relieved to see him, and even more relieved to see Eleanor was safe.

'Go,' Matt shouted. 'Go.'

'I'll get my stuff,' said Eleanor, starting to move.

'No,' shouted Matt grabbing the laptop. 'Just go, just go. Now.'

As they had fled the house in Hammersmith, Damien had called one of his gangster friends, and within minutes a black BMW 5 Series had driven up: safe transport to take them where they wanted. From now on, the old IRA safe houses were too risky: if the Increment knew that's where they were hiding, they would search them one by one. It was likely they knew most of the addresses. They would have to try their luck in hotels.

The Holiday Inn Express at Buckhurst Hill in Essex was twenty miles from Stansted airport, and mainly seemed to cater for people flying in and out of east London. There were a few businessmen in transit, and some stewardesses from Ryanair.

We stay half a step ahead. That's the best we can hope for.

He took the keys from the check-in clerk, and walked up the single flight of stairs to their room. Eleanor was following close behind. Ivan had already supplied them with false names and passports plus some more cash. The new identities worked well enough, and the receptionist had not noticed the uncertainty with which Matt signed his new name, Keith Todd.

Pay cash, use different names, and we're still hard to track down.

He closed the door behind him, shutting it softly. There was nothing unusual about the room. Pale blue carpets, pastel duvet, magnolia walls: it was standard corporate design, the same as a thousand hotel rooms right across the country. But for a moment, Matt could feel some of the tension starting to ease out of his limbs. They were alone, unwatched. *They were safe. For now.*

'How else can they get to you?' said Eleanor. 'They got to Gill because they thought they might get to you through her.' She paused. 'Who else is there?'

'There's Damien,' answered Matt, looking back at Eleanor. 'But he already knows they're on to him.' Matt paused, using a towel from the bed to wipe the sweat from his brow. 'Then Ivan. The Firm knows all about Ivan. They're old friends, go back a long way. But he knows how to be careful.'

He threw the towel back on the bed, looking around to see if there was an air-conditioning switch somewhere: the temperature outside seemed to be at least forty degrees, and the air blowing through the hotel was hotter than the fumes from a car exhaust. 'And you? How can they get to you?'

'They know about Ken, but that's no good to them. He's dead, and so is Sandy.'

Matt nodded. 'Who else? Mum? Dad?'

'Mum's dead, Dad went on holiday to Portugal. I don't even know how to get hold of him.'

'How about a boyfriend?'

Matt couldn't be sure, but he sensed Eleanor was blushing: a touch of crimson was flushing through her cheeks. 'No, there's nobody.'

Matt smiled. It was stupid, but he was pleased. 'You're sure? Even an ex. Doesn't matter if it was a couple of years ago. They might still track him down, start trying to beat some information out of him.'

Eleanor shook her head. 'No,' she answered. 'I've been busy, you know, what with the work. It's hard to find the space for other people sometimes.'

'Spare me the woman's magazine article,' said Matt.

He walked towards the window, pushing the curtain aside, already regretting having snapped at her: the tension was eating away at him, and he was taking it out on anyone. The hotel looked over a small garden, then backed on to the car park. In the distance, he could see the planes cruising into Stansted, their thick trails of vapour smudged across the sky. Then he could feel Eleanor's arms snaking around his back, her touch warm against his skin. 'Maybe you're cross,' she said, the hint of a tease in her voice. 'Maybe you were worried about there being someone else?'

Matt turned round, his lips colliding with hers. His tongue pressed down against her lips, and his hands started to ripple down her body, pushing back her long blonde hair, and tugging at the buttons of her blue blouse. Below, he could feel her hands dragging at his jeans, pulling him down on to the bed. Sex and danger, he reflected, as his arms pinned her back down on the mattress, pushing her down. *One inevitably leads to the other.*

TWENTY-ONE

Matt snapped the phone shut. 'That was Ivan,' he said, looking across at Eleanor.

She was dressed only in a white sheet. Her hair was rumpled, and her skin still had a thin layer of sweat covering it. To Matt, she had never looked better.

'What next?' she asked.

'He's been trying to investigate the numbered accounts,' he said. 'He's tried all his contacts. Nothing.'

Eleanor looked exasperated. 'Is there no way of finding out?'

Matt nodded, his expression sombre. 'There's always a way,' he replied. 'If you're prepared to use enough force.'

'Such as?'

'Those two accounts you found on Lacrierre's computer were both registered at the Deschamps Trust: just numbers, no names,' said Matt. 'We have to know who those accounts belong to. Ivan's hacker mates tried to break into the computers but it's too secure. It would take weeks.'

'So how?'

'Regiment rules,' said Matt. 'When you want something bad enough you just go and get it. Somebody stands in your way, you push them aside.' He paused, pulling his T-shirt back on. 'Ivan's got the name and address of the manager of the London branch of the bank. I'm going to pay him a visit.'

★

267

The house was neat suburbia, one of a row on the outskirts of Epping. Nicholl Road was just behind the sports centre, close to the high street. The houses were 1930s semis: neat, ordered boxes, with neat, ordered families, supplying the workforce for the City of London, a few miles to the west.

Matt parked the car, an ancient Volvo he'd picked up from a dealer near the hotel, a hundred yards from the target. Eleanor was back in their room, and Ivan had arranged to meet him later. The avenue was lined with cedar trees and, in the distance, he could see a pair of small girls arguing over which of them should play with the Barbie scooter. Way past your bedtime, he thought. He jammed on the hand-brake, and took a moment to relax himself: breathing deeply, he closed his eyes for a few seconds, shutting out everything but his own thoughts.

The most important moment in any job was the mental preparation. *That, ultimately, determined whether the dice rolled with you or against you.*

He noted it was fast getting dark. Slamming the door shut, he started walking down the street: fast enough to look like he was going somewhere, slow enough that he could examine the house. A light was shining from the front room of Number Seventeen, and a couple of lights were on upstairs. According to the information he had been given, Alan Thurlow lived with his wife and twelve-year-old daughter. Chances were all three of them were going to be home at nine o'clock on a Thursday night.

Let's hope he talks easily, doesn't try to do anything stupid or brave. *The last thing I need is a fight.*

Matt paused outside the house, bending down, pretend-ing to tie his shoelace. In this part of Essex all the big family houses were worth a million, and it was convenient for the office in the City: the train ran straight into Liverpool Street. The windows were open in the front room. Like everyone in Britain, the Thurlows were desperate to get some air into the house. The sound of the television was drifting out into the street. Even from here he could recognise the voices of the actors. Thursday night. That meant *The Bill* on ITV. *A nice regular evening in, for a nice regular family.*

Thurlow worked for the Deschamps Trust, a small private bank headquartered in Luxembourg. A hundred years old, it provided banking and financial advice for a small group of wealthy clients. Like every bank based in Luxembourg, its main strength was secrecy: accounts were numbered, they didn't pay any tax, and there was no way of finding out who owned them.

Not unless you were prepared to bang the door down.

Standing up, Matt started walking towards the end of the street. The two girls were still fighting over the Barbie scooter in their front garden: the bigger one had taken it, but the smaller one was crying, shaking her tiny fists in anger. We're always fighting over something, thought Matt, as he doubled back, walking back down the street in the other direction.

There were different ways into the house. Round the back there would be a garden. Or up on the roof, there was probably a skylight: most houses with large attics had them, so people could see their way around.

Matt scanned the street. At Number Fifteen, there were no lights. Perhaps they were on holiday, he figured. He checked the house. The dustbins were empty as well. Definitely on holiday. He hopped over the bins, and climbed through the wooden gate that led through the back garden. The lawn was parched and drying out. No one to water it, he decided. They're away.

Examining the back of the house, the drainpipe looked the best way up. Looking up, he could see one skylight. If this one had one, so would Number Seventeen. All these houses were identical.

Slipping off his shoes, he climbed the pipe and started to

crawl across the roof: no point in making any more noise than he had to. At the edge of the Number Seventeen, he clung on to the guttering to steady himself. Safe.

The skylight was just a few yards away from him: a five-foot rectangle of glass, framed with metal. There was some rust around the edges. Nobody ever bothered to check their skylight, judged Matt: they couldn't see them so they didn't worry about them. The only people who ever used them were the guys who came around to put your Sky dish on the roof.

This one will break like a piece of jelly.

Matt stabbed his six-inch hunting knife into the space between the frame and slate. The putty was old and flaking, and came away easily enough. A crack opened up between the skylight and roof: enough space for Matt to dig his fingers in, grip, then pull it free. It made a noise, but not enough to be heard over the TV. Levering himself down with his forearms, Matt dropped into the attic.

A mess, he thought, switching on a miniature torch and looking around. The loft had been converted into a spare room, a snooker room and a shower, but it didn't look like anyone came up here very often. He glanced at the old toys, a pram, boxes of papers and books: it looked as if the Thurlows had lived here for years and never thrown anything away. He picked his way through the debris, suppressing a sneeze.

At the back there was a stairway. Matt checked to make sure there was no one below, then scuttled down to the first floor of the house. He glanced along the corridor. Downstairs, he could still hear the noise of the TV: the news was on now, and he could hear something about how Tony Blair was appointing a Heat Tsar to cope with the hot weather. Ahead of him, there was a door displaying a Justin Timberlake poster, and the sound of some music.

Matt approached the door, his breathing slowing. He took another moment to compose himself. The next few minutes were going to be a short, nasty outbreak of anger and pain. There was nothing he could do to soften the suffering he was about to inflict on these people. It was in a greater cause maybe, but that wouldn't make it any better for them. It never does.

It's soldiering, he told himself. *You might have been out of the game for a while, but you still know how to do violence. And sometimes innocent bystanders have to get hurt.*

Matt pushed the door aside. The girl was lying on her bed, listening to some music coming out of her computer. A mobile was in her hand, her fingers tapping out a text message. Twelve, with short black hair, and a soft, chubby face that she still needed a few more years to grow into. Nice normal kid, thought Matt. *She'll get over this one day.*

He moved swiftly across the floor, his hand clamping down on her mouth before she had a chance to scream. Matt could feel her saliva against his palm as he increased the pressure on her lips. Her arms and legs were kicking out, but she had too little strength to inflict any damage worse than a few scratches. With his right hand still stuck over her mouth, Matt flashed the hunting knife out with his left hand, jabbing it towards her, so the point of the blade was tipping into the centre of her throat.

'Do exactly as I say and you will be all right,' he whispered in her ear.

Matram paused in front of the television, turning the sound down. A silence fell over the hotel room, the eight members of the unit looked back at him. 'This is the second time the target has evaded capture,' he said, drawing out the words. 'I want to know what happened.'

Nobody answered.

271

Matram took a step forward, his hands crossed behind his back. 'I said I want to know what happened,' he shouted.

'The target made a clever escape,' said Snaddon, standing up.

'The man we were tasked to follow confronted us,' said Trench, standing up next to her. 'I think they must have realised who we were and what we were there for, sir.'

'The target started running while we were distracted,' added Snaddon. 'By the time we gave chase, he had eluded us.'

Matram folded his arms across his chest. 'That is not good enough,' he said. 'The Increment does not tolerate failure.'

'It was a public space, sir,' said Snaddon nervously. 'The circumstances made it very difficult to take effective action.'

'It was a failure,' shouted Matram, hurling his coffee cup at the wall where it smashed. 'There are no tolerable circumstances for failure. You are the best, the most elite group in the regiment. This is inexcusable. Any more slip-ups like this and you will be out of here and on your way to Iraq faster than you can blink. Understand?' Matram's voice dipped dangerously, 'Now get out of my sight.'

Matt could smell the fear from the girl as he walked her downstairs, his hand still clamped across her throat, his hunting knife still jabbing into her throat. It was sweating out of her, covering her face and her arms in a thin, damp film of cold dread.

She doesn't know who I am or what terrors I might inflict on her, thought Matt. *I could tell her I'm one of the good guys, but right now I don't think she'd believe me.*

Matt shoved her from the back, making her stumble down the stairs. There was a noise as her heel cracked against one of the banisters. 'Lucy?' shouted her mother from the main room. 'That you?'

Another shove. The girl moved faster this time, tumbling

into the hallway. Matt gripped her tighter, edging her towards the doorway.

'Don't move,' he shouted. 'Stay completely still, do exactly what I tell you, and everyone's going to be OK.'

They moved. Alan Thurlow started to rise from the sofa, his wife Alice at his side. Civilians, thought Matt. No brains. Tell them not to move and they start wriggling around like a worm on a hook.

He pushed Lucy into the centre of the room. 'I said stay still.'

They sat back in the sofa, their expression paralysed by shock. Thurlow was a man of almost fifty, in good shape, but with thinning black hair, and glasses that rested on the end of a long, thin nose. Alice was thin, blonde, with sharp blue eyes and an expression that looked to have settled in middle age into permanent disdain. Both of them watched Matt closely, tracking his movements with their eyes, following the blade of his knife as it hovered close to their daughter's throat.

'Just don't hurt her,' said Alice. 'Just leave her alone. We'll do anything you want.' She rose and moved towards Matt, as if she was about to pounce upon him, while her husband was still shrinking back in his chair. When it came to protecting children, Matt noticed, women were always far more courageous than men.

'Get back,' he ordered, and Alice stopped in her tracks.

'Who are you?' stammered Thurlow.

'Doesn't matter who I am, you're better off not knowing,' said Matt. 'I'm not here to hurt you if I don't need to. I just want some information. Give it to me, and this will all be over in a few minutes.'

Matt watched as the man leant forward slightly. That hadn't been the answer he was expecting. A robber, or a rapist maybe: that was what he had taken Matt for. Not a man looking for answers.

'What kind of information?' he said.

Matt pulled on Lucy's hair, so the bare white skin of her throat was thrust up. Better to let her parents get a good look at it: then they could start imagining the kind of damage that would be inflicted on her if they didn't cooperate. 'I'm going to give you the numbers of two accounts with Deschamps Trust.' He paused, looking directly down at the man. 'I want to know who those accounts belong to. Tell me, and I'll be out of here.'

He could see Thurlow looking first at his wife, then at his daughter before looking back at Matt. 'That's impossible,' he said. 'The bank never reveals the names of its account holders.'

'Just do it,' growled Matt.

'Anyway, I'm at home, I couldn't do it from here.'

'We can't,' said the wife. 'We would if we could.'

'Silence,' shouted Matt. He flashed the blade across Lucy's throat, allowing its strengthened steel to press harder into her skin. 'You have a computer, you can access the records from here.' With his left hand, he unfolded a sheet of paper from his breast pocket, pushing it across the room. 'These are the numbers. Now, give me the names.'

Thurlow looked back at Matt, their eyes briefly locking together. He's trying to read me, thought Matt. He's trying to judge how threatening I am. If I was robbing him, or raping his daughter, he'd know. But a man who wants information? *How far will that man go?*

'I'd help you if I could,' said Thurlow. 'But I can't. Now, leave my house, I won't call the police, we can forget about the whole thing.'

Matt yanked Lucy's head back again, a gasp escaping from her lips as the muscles in her neck strained. Cut her, he told himself. That would convince them. Some blood pouring down his daughter's throat. That would start him talking.

274

But she's a bystander, a civilian. It's not her fault she's caught up in all of this, so why should she suffer? *I could get the information, but could I live with the way I got it?*

If I don't hurt the girl, though, Eleanor and I are probably finished. Maybe Damien and Ivan too. He thought back to the day in Bosnia when he had walked out on the Increment. Maybe Matram had been right. *Maybe I don't have the bottle to make those kinds of choices.*

Matt released the pressure on Lucy's throat, letting her fall to the ground, so she was lying just four feet in front of her parents. She was bruised and exhausted, crawling across to her parents, tears smudging themselves across the carpet.

From the kitbag slung around his belt, Matt took out a Tazor as the parents stared at him wide-eyed, both frozen with fear. A small electrical box, powered by its own batteries, the Tazor delivered a short but intense 250,000-volt electric shock. Unless you had a weak heart, it was harmless, leaving no marks, but the pain was horrible, and your skin lit up like a light bulb. So Matt grabbed Lucy's arm. He took a breath then flipped the switch.

The voltage juddered through her body, and her skin briefly shone blue as the power surged into her. She dropped to the floor, collapsing from the waves of pain. Her eyes looped back, and a trickle of urine started to run down her thigh as she lost control of her bladder. She clasped her teeth together, struggling to stop herself from vomiting. It was over in a second, but every nerve ending in her body looked as if it had been set on fire.

'You see,' he said slowly. 'I can inflict as much pain on your family as I want, it makes no difference to me. Now, do as I tell you, and you won't get hurt.'

'Do it, Alan,' hissed the wife. 'He's a psycho. Just do what he says, and get him out of here.'

Thurlow stood up. His expression was blank, as if he was in a trance. 'There's a computer in the study.'

Matt waved the knife at Alice and Lucy. 'You two, follow him,' he shouted.

The two women stood up nervously, holding on to each other. Lucy was undamaged by the shock, but her legs were still wobbling. He watched as they followed Thurlow into the hallway, towards the study. Matt walked swiftly behind them, holding the knife in his right hand.

There was a picture of Lucy on the desk, and another of Alice, taken at least ten years ago when she was younger and prettier: something to remind the guy why he married her. A Dell computer sat in the middle, next to a pile of letters and bills.

'Quick,' hissed Matt.

The computer whirred into life. Thurlow punched up the Internet connection, logging on to a page displaying the Deschamps Trust logo. Alice and Lucy were huddling at the back of the room, Alan still looked blank. 'Two, four, nine, nine, zero, one,' hissed Matt. 'And six, five, four, four, two, eight. Who do those accounts belong to?'

Thurlow turned to look at him, his expression sombre. 'Why do you want to know?'

'Just give the names.'

Thurlow tapped at the screen, then nodded towards Matt. He walked across the study, gripping the knife tightly. Standing behind Thurlow, he rested his hand on the back of the chair.

In thin black letters two names were displayed on the screen of the computer.

'Christ,' whispered Matt. Putting down the knife, he rubbed his aching hand across his forehead. 'This is not what I thought it was.'

TWENTY-TWO

'What happened to you?' said Ivan, looking at Matt's red, bloodshot eyes.

Matt rubbed the sagging, exhausted skin on his face. 'Bad night at the office.'

Matt had driven back from the Thurlow's house in the Volvo. They were meeting at the Little Chef on the Epping Road, just to the north of London. It was just after eleven at night, and they both needed something to eat. Only a few people were in the restaurant at this time: workers from Stansted coming off their shift, and some truckers filling up with food before doing the night run along the M1 to avoid the traffic. At least when they say an all-day breakfast they mean it, decided Matt, as he ordered himself the Olympic Breakfast with an extra egg and some toast on the side.

'You're sure those are the two names the accounts belong to?' said Ivan. 'Abbott and Matram?'

Matt nodded. 'I saw it clearly on the screen,' he replied. 'The man was frightened out of his skin. He wasn't trying to trick me.'

'So it was them all along, in a plot with Lacrierre,' said Ivan drawing out the words. 'That explains why the government hasn't just picked up the men who took the bravery drug. I don't think they even know about the side effects yet. This has been a private-sector operation all along. Lacrierre is using Abbott and Matram to cover up what he's done.'

Matt clenched his fist. 'So we're not fighting the whole government? Just three men.'

Ivan glanced suspiciously around the restaurant. 'You know what you have to do, then?'

Matt nodded, folding some bacon into a piece of toast and stuffing it into his mouth. 'Hit back at them.'

Ivan smiled, tapping the side of his head. 'I might have said this to you before, Matt, but one of these days a little light bulb is going to go off in your head, and you'll start seeing things clearly.'

'Like how?'

'Like this,' said Ivan. He took a sip on the refill of coffee the waitress had just put down on the table. 'There was always something odd about Orlena's involvement. Remember when we were going into the factory? We met a lot more resistance than we expected. Then when we burst into the last room, that boy lying wounded on the floor, he recognised her.'

'He cried out, *Orlena, Orlena,*' interrupted Matt. 'I remember.'

'That's right,' replied Ivan grimly. 'He said something else as well.'

'Some nonsense in Russian or Ukrainian,' said Matt. 'Begging for mercy.'

Ivan shook his head. 'I've been researching this. Orlena used a word back to him. *Likuvannia.*' He stopped, glancing up at the ceiling. '*Likuvannia,*' he repeated. 'Then the man replied, *Pishov, pishov,* and she shot him.'

'Meaning?'

'Likuvannia is Ukrainian. It means cure. Or antidote.'

Matt pushed his plate across the table. 'An antidote? For XP22. You think that's what she was looking for?'

Ivan shrugged. 'I don't know. She was asking the man about that, and he was saying *pishov, pishov.* Meaning it's not here. Then she shot him. That tells me she was looking for something.' Ivan paused. 'And if she was looking for it, you probably should be as well.'

Matt nodded, looking back at Ivan. 'If there was an antidote, then we could save all the men on the list. The men XP22 was tested on . . .'

Ivan grinned.

'We have to go and get it,' continued Matt. 'If the antidote exists, we have to find it.'

Matt looked at Eleanor. He could see the strain in her eyes. Her skin was taut across her face, as if it had been stretched, and her high, solid cheekbones were growing more prominent by the day.

It was morning now, and the light was starting to filter through the window. Matt had glanced up at the sun as he awoke, with the same sensation he remembered from his days out on the battlefield.

You look at the sunrise differently when you keep thinking each day might be your last.

During the night, he'd slept fitfully. After leaving Ivan, he'd come back to the hotel, checking he wasn't being followed, and slipped into the bed next to Eleanor.

Eleanor chewed on one of the croissants that Ivan had just brought them. She was dressed just in a long white T-shirt, her hair pushed out of her face by a clip. Ivan was cradling a cup of coffee in his hands. 'What can we do?' she said, her voice cracking.

'We take the fight to them,' said Matt. 'Tonight, Friday. We close this thing right now. The one lesson I learnt from the regiment was that you always take the fight to the enemy. I tried to take the fight to Lacrierre before, but I didn't have the back-up.'

'And you hadn't thought it *through*,' said Ivan. 'Lacrierre's going to be at his most vulnerable on the train. His house is no good. The office is no good. Both will be crawling with security. A train is much more difficult to defend. On the train we can nail the bastard.'

'It leaves at eight-forty every Friday night,' said Matt. 'I'll speak to Damien and organise some ammo. Ivan, you get home, make sure the family are all right, then help us out with some bombs.'

'And what do we do once we get him on the train?' asked Eleanor.

'We get the antidote,' said Ivan.

'Then we kill him,' said Matt, pronouncing the words with brutal simplicity.

Eleanor winced. 'And me?' she said.

'Stay here,' said Matt. 'You'll be OK. This is work for trained fighters.'

Eleanor was about to speak.

'He's right,' said Ivan. 'I'm usually a big supporter of the sisterhood, but women just get in the way when a battle starts.'

'No,' said Eleanor. 'I need to be there.'

'It's too dangerous,' snapped Matt.

Eleanor's cheeks reddened. 'And which one of you scientific geniuses is going to recognise whether Lacrierre has given you the right antidote?'

A half-smile started to spread across Ivan's face. He glanced across at Matt. 'I'm afraid she's right.'

'Damn it,' muttered Matt. 'We should be doing this by ourselves.'

'You know the trouble with you, Matt?' said Eleanor. 'You're suffering from a hero complex.'

'No,' he replied. 'I'm suffering from a staying-alive-until-the-end-of-the-bloody-day complex.'

A street market was occupying the central square of Sherbourne, a pretty, quiet town of just a few thousand people in Dorset. It was almost midday and the air was filled with the smell of flowers and fresh bread. Matram stopped at a stand, bought himself an ice cream to help cool down, then carried on walking down the high street.

What is it our al-Qaeda pals say to themselves? he asked himself. *If the mountain won't come to Muhammad, them Muhammad must come to the mountain.*

The house was towards the end of the high street. The Happy Times playgroup was scheduled to end at twelve, and from what the local police had told him, Ivan Rowe's son George was always there on Friday morning. His doting father always picked him up, according to the school. You could rely on it.

Matram checked his watch. Two minutes to twelve. *The man would be within his grasp within a few seconds.*

He signalled to Harton and Godsall waiting in a white van across the street: Be ready! The sound of the van's engine roaring to life briefly crossed the street before it dropped back down again.

Matram's eyes scanned up and down the street. There were a few people doing some browsing, but not many: the heat was keeping people indoors, and the shops seemed half empty. He could see a car approach, a three-year-old Audi A4 estate. It pulled up to the side of the street, a man stepped out. Against the mental picture he had filed away in his head, Matram did a quick check. There could be no doubt. It was him. Rowe.

Gripping his Smith & Wesson semi-automatic pistol close to his chest, Matram moved forward. There was one man across the street, but he wasn't looking at them. Matram was standing close to Ivan, their eyes locking on to one another. Swiftly, Matram thrust the pistol forward, jabbing its barrel into Ivan's ribcage, then turning it slightly upwards. He knew enough about guns to know that any bullet fired from that position was going to travel straight up through the ribcage, smash open the heart, then lodge itself in the brain. Nobody could survive.

'There's a white van over there, Irishman,' growled Matram. 'I want you in the back in three seconds. Otherwise you're a nasty stain on the pavement.'

Silently, his head bowed, Ivan started to walk towards the back of the van.

Matt looked over the array of weaponry. The guns were stacked neatly in rows, an armoury that would earn their owner a life sentence if the police ever discovered it. The rifles were mostly Russian: Kalashnikov AK-47s, not the newer AN-49s Matt had been using out in the Ukraine. Next to them were six American-built Winchester X2s, long-range hunting rifles that were also excellent sniping weapons. The handguns were Glocks: two dozen of the small, pocket-sized PI 20569 semi-automatic pistols, and ten of the more powerful PI 35301.

Each gun had a dozen rounds of ammunition stocked next to it, filed away in boxes. Next to them were fifteen crates of Semtex explosives, complete with fuse wires, plus an assortment of flak jackets, and bulletproof vests.

Enough kit to declare war on a medium-sized country.

'So why is it called the North Bank?' Matt asked.

Damien grinned. 'You're spending too much time out of the country, pal. Losing your local knowledge.'

Matt nodded. 'Home supporters' end, Highbury? The North Bank.'

'Right, and this is our Arsenal.'

They were meeting in the cellars of a disused railway arch just outside Chatham, east of London. It was here that Damien kept weaponry that would later be distributed to the gangs of south London: free if you were one of his men, for a heavy charge if you weren't. The kit was shipped in from abroad, usually inside lorries doing the run across from

Belgium or Holland. Both of those countries had a thriving trade in black-market weaponry, either coming across Germany from Eastern Europe, or up from the Middle East through the Balkans. Stick a pair of guns in the cargo of a twenty-two-ton articulated lorry and nobody was going to find it. All the driver had to do was pull up at one of the service stations on the M20, and hand the gear over in the car park. A couple of hundred quid in cash was very handy: Damien's network usually paid out in euros, so the truckers could use it to have some fun while they were abroad without having to tell their wives.

'I need a lot of stuff,' said Matt, pointing at the displays. 'A pair of those Kalashnikovs, plus four pistols. A flak jacket, that would be useful. And as much Semtex as you can spare.'

Damien nodded. 'You're going to go in for them.'

'If anyone's got any other suggestions, I'll take them,' said Matt, his lips creasing into a rough smile. 'But right now I can't think of any.'

Damien took the Kalashnikovs down from the rack, handing them across to Matt. It was the classic 1947 Soviet model, with the slim wooden handle and under-mounting, and the curved thirty-round magazine cartridge: half a century old, but still one of the best weapons ever designed, and one Matt felt comfortable with.

You couldn't rely on much in life, but your AK-47 never let you down.

He loaded up a stack of rounds, then took four of the Glock handguns plus thirty rounds of ammunition. From the cases, he took twenty pounds of Semtex, each one-pound block wrapped in plain greaseproof paper as if it were nothing more dangerous than a lump of lard. He placed them neatly in the plastic rucksack that Ivan had given him: it was going to be a heavy load but his back could handle it.

Get in there, blast them to hell, and get out faster than a rat on roller skates.

Matt hauled the rucksack on to his back. There must have been two hundred pounds of kit in there. Still, it was only two flights of stairs and a couple of hundred yards to his car. Compared with three days of yomping across the Brecon Beacons through the sleeting January rain during his training for the regiment, this was nothing.

As they reached the top of the thick metal staircase that led out of the cellar, Damien gripped Matt by the shoulder. 'What help do you need?' he said. 'I want to repay her blood as much as you do.'

Matt hesitated. He could see the strength and determination written into the man's face, and he could sense the longing for vengeance that was burning within him. 'I need to take out a train,' he replied. 'And I need men. By tonight.'

Damien nodded. 'Then I know just the man who can help you.'

The back of the van was hot and sticky. Matram had ordered all the windows tightly sealed. If Ivan started screaming – and he might – then he didn't want the sound escaping. Even though they were speeding through the countryside, that risked detection.

The van had no air conditioning, and with the midday temperatures getting close to thirty-five degrees outside, the air was pulsing with heat. Nobody could breathe. Harton was up front steering the van through the gentle Dorset countryside, and Godsall was sitting with Matram, guarding the back of the van from any attempt by Ivan to escape.

He's not fighting back yet, but he was a Provo back across the water in the old days. *He'll know how to take a beating.*

'Here,' said Matram.

The van drew up to a halt. From the window, Matram could see they were at the end of a country lane. About two hundred yards away there was a farmhouse, but a row of

284

trees blocked this spot from its view. Only a few sheep grazing in the next field could see him from here.

'Put him on the ground,' said Matram.

Godsall opened the back of the van, pushing Ivan roughly on to the muddy surface of the lane. The mud was caked harder than concrete, and Ivan landed roughly on the side of his shoulder. He rolled over, deflecting the force of the impact, then lay still, his hands tucked in neatly to the side of his chest.

Smart, thought Matram, hopping out of the van and standing next to Ivan. He knows he's going to get a beating, and there's nothing he can do about it. *He's just preparing himself to survive it the best he can.*

'You know what, Irishman, I think you and I could get along just fine if we wanted to,' said Matram slowly.

Ivan remained completely still, his cheek lying flat against the mud.

'A bomb-maker, that's what I heard,' continued Matram, kneeling down next to Ivan. 'Always liked the fireworks boys, myself. Nice big bangs, some pretty lights and not many survivors. That's just the kind of expertise a soldier needs.' He paused. 'So if you and I wanted to be friends, I think we could work something out. Save a lot of unpleasantness.'

'You want a bomb made?' said Ivan. 'I can probably help you.'

Matram shook his head slowly from side to side. 'No, that's not it. I want to know where your friend Matt is.'

'Matt Browning? You've met him?'

'Our paths have crossed.'

'Then you'll know he's a mean fucker,' snapped Ivan, his tone hardening. 'Unless you've got some very fancy medical insurance, you should stay out of his way.'

A boot slammed into Ivan's chest, hitting him just above the heart. His body shuddered under the force of the blow, the pain rippling out from his chest into the centre of his body. He rolled backwards, coughing, as he struggled to refill his lungs with air.

'No jokes, bogtrotter,' snapped Matram. 'Like I said, if you tell me where he is, I can save you a lot of pain.'

'I don't know where he is,' said Ivan, struggling to pronounce the words.

Matram leant closer to his ear. 'We're the Increment,' he said softly. 'I'm sure you know us from the old days across the water. Best bloody fun of our lives, popping across on the BA shuttle and using some bogtrotters as target practice. It was even better when we got to rough them up a bit before we put them underground.' He paused, savouring the words, letting them roll around his tongue. 'Your lot weren't afraid of very much, but they were afraid of us. And so should you be.'

Ivan rolled his eyes upwards. He looked hard at Matram, scrutinising his clean, neatly shaven face, the squashed, flat nose and the narrow, pebble-like eyes that stared intently down. 'I'll take you to him,' he said, stretching out a hand. 'Just help me back up.'

To anyone who just wandered in for a drink, the Two Foxes off Camberwell Church Street looked just like one of a thousand south-London pubs. Faded Victorian coach lamps on the walls, thick stained wood around the bar, beer mats on every table, and the same old pair of geezers sitting in the corner every afternoon nursing their pints and rolling their own smokes. But to anyone in the know, it was an office – a place where the Walters family came to do business.

If we're safe anywhere, we're safe here, reflected Matt. The police won't come in here. *They haven't got the guts.*

Eleanor was staying back at the hotel for the rest of the day: Damien didn't think the people he was about to introduce Matt to would like the idea of bringing a woman on a job. They were old school: in their world, robbing was men's work.

Jack Pointer looked straight across at Matt. A hand-rolled cigarette was dangling from his lower lip. 'Regiment?' he said, pronouncing the word with disgust.

He looked familiar. His head was round and bald, and his skin had the deathly purplish complexion of men who'd spent most of their life in jail. 'Ex,' said Matt. 'Been out for a couple of years.'

'It doesn't matter,' said Pointer. 'You are a ponce in my book.'

'Steady, Jack,' interrupted Damien. 'We're working together on this one.'

Pointer took another sip on his pint of black stout. 'We'll see about that.'

Suddenly Matt realised who he looked like: Harry Pointer, a vicious debt collector who worked for some of the Russian mobsters in Malaga, and dropped into the Last Trumpet occasionally. Matt had owed his people some money once, and had regretted it.

'I think I might know your son Harry,' said Matt. 'Nasty tub of lard, with a vicious criminal mind.'

Pointer smiled. 'That's my boy,' he said. 'Beautiful lad.' He looked up at Matt, his mood softening. 'Damien says you need help?'

'I need a train stopped.'

Pointer grinned. 'Then I'm your man.'

'Ever heard of the Balham job?' said Damien.

Matt shook his head. The gangs were just like the army, he reflected: every regiment had its own history of glorious victories and so did every gang. 'Can't say I have.'

'Seventy-two. Train carrying freshly minted banknotes up to London. Two million of them. Jack and his boys hit it. Got away with the money, as well, back when two million still meant something.'

'So what went wrong?' said Matt, looking across at Pointer. The man was at least sixty, and looked in rough shape.

'Seventy-seven, got shopped,' said Pointer. I got thirty years. Out last year.' He grinned. 'Still got my electronic tag, but I decided to leave it at home today.'

'And you can still stop a train, you reckon?'

Pointer took a pouch of tobacco from his pocket, and started rolling the soft leaves between his grubby fingers. 'Connex South Eastern, British Rail, it makes no difference to me,' he said. 'The one thing you can rely on with a railway in this country is that they won't have bought any new technology. We can stop it the same way we did back in the seventies. By fiddling with the signals.'

He licked the Rizla paper. 'The question is, why do we want to?'

Matt started to speak, but Damien stopped him. 'Because it's regiment you'd be taking out,' he said. He looked back across to Matt. 'There was a bad riot at Brixton nick back in eighty-four. Jack and some of his mates took over a wing for a few days. Barricaded themselves in. The SAS were sent in and started beating the buggers one by one until they gave themselves up. One of his lads suffered brain damage. He's still on a drip.'

'Well, killing some regiment boys,' said Pointer, opening his mouth to reveal two missing front teeth, 'now that is worth getting out of bed for.'

The Volvo was sweating in traffic on the M25. This route had seemed like the quickest way from Camberwell up to Essex, but the motorway had been backed up all the way, and steam was starting to rise from many of the cars. If this ancient car had ever had air conditioning, it had long since broken. Sweat was trickling down Matt's back as he looked up at the angry mess of snarling, stationary traffic stretched out before him.

Christ, a breakdown. That's all I need, thought Matt, watching as the needle pointed towards red on the thermo-stat: *the police coming to help me with a full load of munitions stacked up in the back of the car.*

He glanced at his watch. Ten past four already. Lacrierre's train for Paris left at eight-forty this evening, and would take an hour to make its way down to the Channel Tunnel. In this traffic, he didn't have time to get Eleanor, then get all the way back down to south London to hook up with the train line. There were only four hours left in which to organise the final assault.

Damn the British traffic. It was impossible to get anywhere these days.

He looked across at the mobile lying on the passenger seat. It was the latest model Ivan had supplied. It should be safe, he told himself.

He checked his watch again. Twenty past four. The traffic had inched forwards maybe sixty, seventy yards. At this rate he'd be lucky to get there by next Wednesday.

And the moment of retribution will have escaped me.

Matt wrenched the gear into first, moved forward another eight yards, than jammed his foot on the brake. The lorry in front of him was belching out heavy black fumes, and on the hard shoulder, a pair of cars had broken down, smoke rising from their engines. Caution be damned. The risks I'm running already are so terrifying one more doesn't make much difference. *Either the gods are smiling on me or they aren't.*

He picked up the mobile and punched in the number of the hotel, asking for Room Twelve. Eleanor answered the phone on the second ring. 'You all right?' she asked anxiously.

'So far,' replied Matt tersely. 'You?'

'OK. Just waiting.'

'Listen, I'm not going to make it,' said Matt. 'Too much traffic. You come and meet me in Battersea. Five forty-five on the bridge at the top of Battersea Rise. If I'm not there by six, assume the worst.'

The van was heading up the M3, going past the signs off into Basingstoke and heading into London. Ivan was sitting in the front seat, with Matram at the wheel. Harton and Godsall were sitting in the back, both of them close enough to Ivan to prevent him attempting an escape.

'So give me the name of the hotel,' said Matram.

'The Holiday Inn Express,' said Ivan. 'In Buckhurst Hill, in Essex. Close to Stansted Airport.'

Matram turned to him and grinned. 'Just what I always thought,' he said. 'You PIRA boys were always just a bunch of gangsters. The first sight of blood, you betray your mates. It worked in the old country, and it works here as well.'

Ivan shrugged, remaining silent. He'd been preparing munitions to blow up the train. Fortunately they'd only searched him for guns and knives. He had a tiny sliver of explosive hidden in his trouser pocket wrapped in silver paper to look like a packet of Wrigley's chewing gum. All he had to do was find the right moment to wriggle it down to the floor and stamp on it to trigger the explosion.

'The names, bogtrotter,' snapped Matram. 'I want the names they are checked in under.'

Ivan looked back at him coldly. 'Keith Todd and Helen Nuggett.'

'How do I know you aren't lying?'

'Call them and see,' said Ivan. 'It's a hotel, they'll know who the guests are.'

Matram leant back in his seat, passing a mobile back towards Harton. 'Ring,' he snapped. 'Check they're there.'

Harton took the phone, punching in a number for

directory enquiries, then asking to be put through to the Holiday Inn in Buckhurst Hill. He turned his back, holding the phone close to his ear, shielding the noise of the van as the call was put through.

For a brief second, his back was turned on Ivan, and he was blocking Godsall from moving forward.

Ivan paused. There was a risk he might blow his own leg off in the next few seconds, but that was a chance he'd have to take. The explosive slithered from his trousers, on to the floor in front of him. A mixture of potassium nitrate, available in any agricultural store, and sugar, and packed into an emptied-out Roman candle, it was simple but effective. As the cracker blew, it sent out a huge plume of thick, ugly smoke.

Ivan leant sharply across the seat, his right hand clamping down hard on the steering wheel, tugging it to the right. 'Let's see how you drive, fucker,' he spat up into Matram's face.

The van swerved violently to the right, zagging out into the fast lane of the motorway. All the men in the van were shouting at once. A collision could be heard at the back, as a car winged its left side, sending the van spinning back to the left. It was rocking violently as the huge plume of smoke obscured the view inside and out.

Ivan's hand was still locked to the wheel, yanking it in one direction, while Matram pulled in the other. With his left hand, Ivan reached down, feeling for the handbrake. He grabbed it in his fist, pulling upwards with a single hard movement of his shoulder muscles. The van stopped, the tyres burning against the tarmac, sending both Matram and Ivan hurtling towards the window. It came to a halt, then jolted forwards as something else collided with its back.

Flinging the door open, Ivan jumped down. He landed hard on the tarmac, ducking sideways to avoid an on-rushing car. It screeched to a stop, just six feet short of him, skidding sideways, its horn blaring. Another winged it, turning round, and wobbling on its wheels as it narrowly avoided tipping over. Further behind, a lorry was hammering its brake, a blast of noise rising from its wheels as it struggled to slow down. Amid the fury and the fumes Ivan ducked behind the van and started to run down the central reservation between the two sides of the M3.

Matram pulled himself back out of the seat, then threw open the window. He jumped down on to the tarmac, then looked back down the road. A hundred yards ahead, he could see Ivan disappearing down the centre of the road. Then he could hear a screeching of brakes, as he watched Ivan running across the three lanes of motorway.

Whether he made it to the other side, it was impossible to say. He vanished into a blizzard of cars and lorries and, through the roaring traffic, Matram could see nothing.

Pointer was kneeling down at the side of the track. His hands were running through the gravel, the same way a farmer might run his hands through the soil. 'Here,' he said simply. 'We prepare right here.'

Matt looked behind him. Damien was standing right next to him, and beside him were three other men.

'Where did the goon squad come from?' asked Matt.

'Keith, Perry and Archie,' said Pointer. 'Keith is my other son,' he said, nodding to a man in his twenties with cropped hair, a thick beer gut and a row of tattoos running up his forearm. 'Not a nice quiet boy like Harry. Keith's got a mean streak in him. He was a nasty toddler, and stayed that way ever since. Perry,' he continued, nodding to a man in his forties, with strapping muscles, a huge torso and eyes that shone out of his dark face like two white pearls. 'Perry was with me in Brixton. His best friend got a good hiding at the hands of the SAS. And Archie,' he went on, nodding to a smaller man, nearing fifty, with red hair and a crimson, freckled complexion. 'Archie has come down from Glasgow specially to have a crack at your old mates. He was in Shotts maximum-security prison all through the nineties and it seems your boys mixed it up there as well. It's personal.'

Matt nodded. All three of them were dressed in the bright yellow tunics of railway workers. Matt didn't like the look of any of them. But there was a rule you learnt early in the regiment. In a desperate fight, the enemy of your enemy was your friend. That had never been more true than it was today.

'Gentlemen,' he said, 'when you're all ready, we can begin.'

Matt knelt down by the side of the track, next to Pointer. He was deep in the gully of the tracks, looking down at the rails. They'd chosen this spot because the steep banks from the side of the tracks meant it was not overlooked. The pebbles felt hot to his touch, and the steel of the signal towers had heated up during the midday sun. From the slight vibration on the line, he could tell there was a train coming, but it was still at least a couple of minutes away.

The junction box was at the bottom of the tower. It was protected by a simple padlock. Pointer held it between his fingers. He jabbed the screwdriver into the box, and yanked hard, breaking it free. In front of him, there was a collection of colour-coded wire. The signal was a standard three-light box: one green, one yellow, one red. He needed Lacrierre's train to slow down, as if there was a possibility of a hazard ahead. For that, he needed a red flash, a yellow flash, another yellow flash, then a green flash. 'It's like Morse code,' said Pointer. 'Once you know it, railway codes are simple enough.'

The vibration on the track was growing louder. Pointer slammed the box shut, rolling away from the rails, hiding himself in the dried-out row of bushes that lined the banks of the line. The train started to shunt past, travelling at thirty miles an hour. Matt glanced upwards, looking out at the sweaty rows of commuters. Behind him, the rest of the men were already lying down, protected by the scrubland growing on the side of the banks.

'Job done,' said Pointer, backing away from the track. 'I'll set it back to normal now, for the time being, then back to the red and yellow flashes when the Frenchman's train is due.'

The phone in his pocket was ringing. Matt punched the green button, holding it to his ear. 'Yes?'

'Matt, we've been compromised.'

He recognised the soft Irish accent but not the tone. Ivan had always been calm, unflapped, even in the midst of the hardest battles. Now he sounded rattled, scared, shot up by nerves.

'What happened?'

'They picked me up,' he continued. 'I told them what hotel you were at, what your false names were.'

Matt felt as if he'd been punched in the stomach: he could feel the breath emptying out of him.

'Why the hell . . .'

'I had no choice,' said Ivan angrily. 'I needed to buy some time. I knew you'd be gone by now. And Eleanor is with you, right?'

'That's my life your gambling with,' said Matt, his tone rising. 'And Eleanor's.'

'Eleanor is with you, isn't she?' asked Ivan.

'She's meant to be on her way over to Battersea.' Matt looked around him. Pointer and Damien were discussing some of the finer details of the ambush. 'I'll try to get hold of her.'

'Do that, they might be on her trail,' said Ivan, sounding tense. 'If they get hold of her, they'll . . .' The words faded away on his lips.

Matt punched the red button on the phone, then dialled the Holiday Inn Express, asking to be put straight through to Keith Todd's room. The phone range twelve times, with no answer, before Matt was put through to an automated answering machine. 'To leave a message for this guest please press the star button twice . . .' started the computer.

Matt killed the line, slipping the phone back into his pocket. Eleanor was out there somewhere, alone, vulnerable. He knew he would not feel calm until he could hold her in his arms again.

Matt looked up into the burning hot sky.

I got her into this mess, and it's up to me to get her out again.

Matram held the sheet up to his nose. It was crumpled, with traces of sweat left in it, and the musty aroma of a bed that had been shared by a man and a woman.

Dogs had the right idea, he reflected. *Once you had the smell of your prey, then it couldn't elude you.*

'When did they leave?' he snapped, looking across at the manager.

David Plant was in his late twenties, thin, cheerful, and with an overeager-to-please manner that suggested he had spent too much time on Holiday Inn customer-service courses. 'I can't say *exactly*,' he replied. 'Holiday Inn has an automated check-in service. We introduced it last year under our 'Your Choice, Your Style' customer-service programme. It's very popular with the guests, and obviously it cuts back on check-in staff as well, so it generates value for . . .'

Matram stepped forward, pausing, then leaning into Plant's face. 'I don't give a fuck about your customer-service programme,' he barked. 'If I was looking for cockroaches, this is where I'd start. As it happens I'm looking for two terrorist suspects, a man and a woman. Now, did you see them?'

Plant looked around nervously. Matram was flanked by Harton and Godsall.

'The man left this morning, the woman just over an hour ago,' he said, his face turning red. 'The room was already paid for.'

'They talk to anyone?'

'No.'

'Meet anyone?'

'Not that I know of.'

'Bring anything into or out of the hotel?'

Plant shook his head. 'If they did, I didn't see it.'

'How about phone calls?'

'They got some calls, yes,' said Plant, his tone turning more hopeful. 'Two at least.'

'Now you tell me,' Matram snapped. 'Can we access the records of who called?'

'Oh, yes, the new computer system automatically logs incoming and outgoing calls,' said Plant. 'It's part of a programme designed . . .'

'Just get me the bloody numbers,' roared Matram.

He followed Plant down the one flight of stairs towards the lobby. Plant politely asked the receptionist to take a break, then logged on to the computer. He started tapping into the keyboard, looking back up at Matram.

'This number,' he said. 'It called the room twice. 07456 291186.'

Matram grabbed his own mobile and punched in one of the eight pre-set numbers, one for each member of the Increment. He spelt out the eleven digits he had just been given. 'I want a trace on that mobile,' he snapped. 'Immediately.'

The phone still at his side, Matram paced around the room. He wiped a bead of sweat away from his forehead, then grabbed a glass of water from the lobby desk, throwing it down his throat.

A mobile number, he thought to himself. The idiot. He doesn't realise that we can track incoming calls, and if he's carrying the same phone he used for those calls, then he might as well be carrying a big flag with a target sign on it. Your first big mistake, Browning. *We can take you down the same way we'd take down a fly in this room.*

'Yes?' he said, putting the phone back up to his ear. 'You've got it?' He paused, waiting for the reply. 'Where is he?' Matram nodded, a smile breaking out over his lips. 'We've got him,' he said, looking at Harton and Godsall. 'Same mobile.'

'Battersea?' said Harton, sounding puzzled. 'What's he doing there?'

'We'll find out when we get him,' said Matram. 'But you know what I think.' He paused, slipping his mobile back into his trouser pocket. 'I reckon the bastard is going for the train.'

TWENTY-THREE

Matt walked quickly up and down the street. The afternoon was drawing to a close, and he could see the shadows lengthening on the ground. He was standing at the top of Battersea Rise, a row of smart-looking shops and restaurants leading down towards Clapham. Pointer and his team had been left preparing their positions by the railway tracks. He'd told Eleanor to meet him here, but whether she'd left the hotel before Matram got there, there was no way of knowing. If they caught her, they would know that he would be here now. There was no chance of Eleanor keeping a secret during a beating. Not from the Increment.

Behind him there was a stretch of park leading down towards Wandsworth. Next to him, the railway bridge looked down on the tracks below, a commuter train to the south coast shunting slowly down the track. Matt stared at the roof, looking at the crevices and pits carved into the structure. A moving train can be two things, he reflected. *A weapon or a coffin.*

A man caught his eye, maybe twenty feet ahead of him. He was six foot, dressed in a suit, but with his collar undone and his jacket slung over his shoulder. There was a slowness to the way he was walking, as if he wasn't going anywhere. He strolled along the side of the road, across the bridge, past Emanuel School and on to the pub on the corner. Then he doubled back, walking the same way back again: there was a faint smile on his lips, but also a trace of anxiety, as if he were pumping himself up for action.

Matt looked down at his watch. Four minutes to six. Eleanor should have been here ten minutes ago. *I'll meet you at the bridge at the top of Battersea rise*, he'd told her. *At five forty-five. Wait for me for fifteen minutes, and if I'm not there, assume the worst. I'll be dead, and you'll be on your own.*

I hadn't figured on her not making it.

Matt looked down to the hill. From north of London, how would she get here? By train down to Clapham Junction, then maybe walk. A taxi if she was running late. He scanned the faces of the women walking up the hill, looking for the familiar mane of blonde hair, the bright red lips and the blue eyes that sparkled and shone as they looked into you. He brushed aside the scowls and frowns as the women he was looking at caught sight of his stares. *They think I'm just some idiot ogling babes on a summer evening*, reflected Matt. *I can handle that, just so long as . . .*

Where are you? Please, if one of us is to be captured, let it be me, and not her.

The man again. He had crossed the road again, walking on the same side as Matt now, just ten yards away from him. He was ambling purposelessly, as if he had nowhere to go and all the time in the world to get there. Just the way an assassin might if he was waiting for the moment to unload his bullets. He looked up at Matt, their eyes meeting. Matt sensed a flash of recognition: the look you might get from a man who had been shown your photograph, and told to go out and hunt you down.

Matt felt the pistol in his pocket, his fingers brushing against the sticky metal of the trigger. Silently, he unhooked the safety catch, ready to start firing. He started to glance around the street, assessing the environment, trying to figure out how to minimise the casualties if a firefight broke out in the street.

They can take me if they want to, but with a bullet through the chest, not the back.

'Jack,' shouted a woman, thirty yards behind him.

Matt spun around. Dark-haired, tanned, athletic, and dressed in jeans and a loose blue blouse, she looked like classic Increment material. Matt started to back away, edging himself towards a shop window: there was some space between the window and the door where he might be able to take cover.

'Mary,' said the man, stepping forwards. He gave her a hug, holding on to her hand as they walked together towards the park.

Just a couple meeting up for a date. She was running late, and he thought he'd been stood up. That was why he was looking worried.

Christ, thought Matt. The shadows are everywhere. *And if I don't sharpen up I'll be one of them.*

Inside the train, the air was cool, air conditioned down to a comfortable, steady twenty-three degrees centigrade. Every Tocah office throughout the world was always exactly the same temperature: Lacrierre had read once that twenty-three degrees gave just the right amount of warmth for maximum mental concentration, and insisted the entire empire always operate at that level.

Matram had walked through from the platform into the main compartment, which was still empty. It wasn't due to leave the station until eight-forty this evening, when Lacrierre always returned home to Paris for the weekend. So far as Matram could tell it was clean. No bombs, no trip-wires, no electronic devices — and bulletproof windows. You could never say any vehicle was 100 per cent safe: but if any one was, this was it.

'What makes you think he's coming for the train, old fruit?' said Abbott.

He was looking very comfortable in the leather armchair in the main carriage, next to a desk and a computer screen. The white linen of his suit was looking crumpled, and the sunburnt skin on his nose had started to peel away. A cigarette was dangling from the fingers of his left hand, as yet unlit.

'Figure it out,' growled Matram. 'Matt Browning is somewhere in the Battersea area. This train passes through that area on its way to the Channel Tunnel. So what the hell else would he be doing around there?' He paused, lifting up a pair of chairs, looking underneath them.

'One man against a high-speed locomotive like this,' said Abbott. 'I know you regiment boys like to think of yourself as pretty tough. But that's absurd.'

'One man can do just about anything,' snapped Matram. 'Take over a train, blow it up, whatever. So long as he puts his mind to it, and has a bit of luck.'

Abbott shook his head. 'I think he's on the run,' he replied. 'Deep down, Browning is a coward. That's why he's serving the sangria and chips over in the Costa del Dosh, not doing a proper job. He could have been in charge of the Increment by now if he wanted to.'

'Bollocks,' said Matram. 'He was lucky they ever took him into the regiment. Fucking cowardly scum.'

'Calm down, Matram, I'm sure you're right.' Abbott smiled to himself. 'He's just a glorified Spanish waiter. Shout Manuel, and he'll give you a funny little grin and come running.' He jabbed the unlit cigarette into his mouth. 'So I think he just buggered off. He's probably shagging the little blonde muffin right now, and drawing up a business plan for a little restaurant in Argentina.'

Matram shook his head. 'He's coming for the train,' he said slowly. 'It's the regiment training in him. You can't shake it.'

'Breaking into the open,' said Abbott lighting his cigarette. 'Sounds bloody stupid to me.'

'It's standard operating procedure, drilled into all the men as soon as they start their training. When you're cornered, you break out and hit the enemy. Take the fight to them. It might look crazy, and sometimes it is, but it's the best chance you've got.'

'Then tell Lacrierre to get the bloody plane to Paris,' said Abbott, shifting in his seat. 'Or, sod it, spend the weekend in Britain. How bad can it be?'

Matram walked across to the window, looking down on to the tracks. The train was still in the sidings at Waterloo: it would be another hour before it was shunted on to the main platform ready for its departure. 'No,' he said softly. 'That would make us look nervous.' He turned to look at Abbott. 'And remember, I've dealt with Browning before. He is weak. I can handle him.'

'By yourself?'

Matram shook his head. 'I could of course. But there will be four Increment members on this train, plus me,' he said. 'He's got no chance.'

'What if he tries to blow the train?' said Abbott.

Matram shook his head. 'On a busy track like this you couldn't do it without taking out civilians,' he replied. 'Browning's not ruthless enough. That's always been his problem. He'll try to ambush me and I'll be waiting for him.'

The relief was already flooding through his veins, pushing a surge of energy through him: fast and heady. He saw her walking up the hill, a bag slung over her shoulder, and a trace of sweat down both cheeks. Matt ran straight up to her, kissed her, then started running again.

You don't think about how much you care for someone until you start imagining you might never see them again.

'Quick,' said Matt, grasping her arm, and pulling her along the street. 'There's no time to lose.'

302

'Where are we going?' she said, her voice trailing away in the breeze.

'Down to the railway tracks,' hissed Matt.

They moved swiftly along the side of the street, both remaining silent. It was a quarter past six now, and the rush-hour traffic was starting to calm down. Across the road, Matt could see a collection of beery-looking drinkers gathering outside the Mill Pond pub a hundred yards away, the pints already in their hands, their shirts open to the waist. A gap in the fencing led down to the tracks. Matt pushed through it, guiding Eleanor down with his hands. The fall was steep, and the scrub harsh and dry. Matt stamped his feet into the ground, using his heels to dig into the dirt as he guided himself downwards. A train was just disappearing down the track, leaving a heavy smell of greasy diesel fuel in its wake. He recaptured his balance, walking steadily down the side of the rails. His eyes were fixed on the bush about fifty yards ahead of him: the spot where Damien had dumped his cache of weapons. *So long as that is OK, we're in with a chance.*

'Here,' said Matt, pointing towards the bush.

Eleanor followed him, climbing up a few yards of bank side, then rolling down on to the scrub next to the bush. The others were already there. Damien was lying close to the ground, next to Pointer, Keith, Perry and Archie. They were passing one of Pointer's freshly rolled cigarettes between them, and Archie had a six-pack of Carlsberg Special Brew under his arm.

'Who are they?' whispered Eleanor. 'What are they doing here?'

'They're here to help,' answered Matt. 'We're taking the train, and then we're taking Lacrierre.'

She sat down on the scrub, brushing some of the dust out of the way, introducing herself to each of the men in turn. Damien said hi, but the rest just nodded or grunted. Their expressions suggested they didn't understand what a woman was doing here.

'You stay here,' whispered Matt. 'When the fighting starts, just fall back and keep out of the way.'

'I'm coming with you,' said Eleanor stubbornly. 'Without me, you can't get the antidote.'

'No,' snapped Matt. 'Impossible. Wait until we've taken the train. Then I'll come and get you.'

Eleanor looked away, remaining silent.

'It's too dangerous,' said Matt, his tone softer now. He glanced down at the track. 'We're up against the Increment. It's going to be brutal and bloody.'

'So what do we do now?' asked Eleanor.

'We do what soldiers have always done,' answered Matt. 'We sit around feeling nervous until the action begins.'

Matram looked out across the railway track. He could smell the diesel lingering in the air, mixing with the heat of the evening to fill the atmosphere with a poisonous, sulphurous aroma.

The smell of death. *Like napalm.*

He laid out a map of south London on the ground, jabbing at it with his finger. A circle had been drawn with red ink around two square miles covering Battersea, parts of Clapham High Street, and stretching out across Wandsworth Common. 'Here,' he snapped. 'They are somewhere here.'

The mobile they had identified as belonging to Matt was a pay-as-you-go device operated by T-Mobile: according to the company records it was a Motorola phone, stolen in Leicester six weeks ago. The SIM card and phone might have been swapped over several times since then but that didn't matter. It was transmitting through a base station located just next to Wandsworth Common. The map showed the area in which phones locked on to that base station: move outside that zone, and the phone would automatically search for another base station to lock on to.

Within that circle, covering two square miles, he might be anywhere. But he was somewhere in that space. *That was certain.*

If I was going to hit the train, what spot would I choose? I'd want cover, and high banks, so that I could attack from above. And I'd need to be somewhere where there were no buildings overlooking the track, so I could complete my attack in secret.

'We are looking for anywhere a man might choose to lay himself up for a few hours before making his move.'

'Think he might have a safe house somewhere in the zone?' asked Harton.

'It's possible. We can't be certain of anything. But I think that's unlikely. His main helper seems to be Rowe, and he's ex-PIRA. They had houses around Hammersmith and Kilburn, and over in Docklands, but not much in Battersea. Unless he's got a friend, someone who can take him in for a few hours. No, he's going to find somewhere low-key, somewhere he won't attract any attention. My bet is they'll find him in a pub somewhere, sipping a pint and reading the *Evening Standard.*'

'But we're still searching the rail tracks?' said Godsall.

Matram nodded. 'Maybe he's laying up, maybe he's just waiting for the train. Either way, he can't hide from us for long. I want you to check every inch of this track and make certain he's not hiding on it. No booby traps, no bombs, nothing.'

He looked out down the railway winding its way south from Waterloo station, shielding his eyes from the glare of the sun. 'Any mistakes, and you'll be out of the Increment, and out of the regiment.' He paused. 'And after that, I'll track you down and kill you with my bare hands.'

★

Matt took the bar of Yorkie, broke off a chunk and offered it to Eleanor. It was eight thirty. The sun was close to setting, fierce streaks of red settling down against the dirty, grey sky of south London. The heat of the day was starting to ebb, and at last a gentle breeze was starting to blow in from the east, fanning both their faces.

At their side, Archie had opened up the tins of Special Brew, and each man was drinking one. Villains, thought Matt. They like a beer before they go into action: it's their own version of XP22. In the army, he'd known men carry whisky bottles to gee themselves up before a fight, but most soldiers like to be stone sober on the battlefield.

'You ready?' he said, looking towards Pointer.

'For spilling some regiment blood?' said Pointer, raising an eyebrow. 'Always ready for that.'

Archie chuckled, making some of the foam from his beer spill out over his lips.

A wave of anger rolled through Matt. He was doing what he felt he had to do this evening, but if it meant taking the lives of any of his former comrades he would feel nothing but regret. Fate has some weird twists for us, he reflected. *When I left the Increment, I never imagined I would go into battle against them myself. And not with an army made up of south-London villains.*

'Everyone knows the drill?' he asked.

They had discussed the plan in minute detail. It drew upon all Pointer's experience and knowledge of robbing trains. He had entertained them with the story of how Ronnie Biggs and the Great Train Robbers had completed their famous heist. One of them had climbed a signal mast, and covered the green light with an old leather glove. Then they wired some batteries into the box to activate the red light, bringing the train to a stop. When the driver got out to find a phone to see what was happening, they attacked.

The plan for this evening was similar. Pointer had rigged

up the signal box below to bring the train to a near halt: the flashing red and yellow signal meant slow down, danger ahead. Unlike the old days, the driver wouldn't get out to find a phone: he'd use a radio or a mobile. But as the train slowed, Keith and Perry would sling a branch across the line to bring it to a stop. Then Matt, Pointer, Damien and Archie would launch a barrage of fire from the back of the train, taking down any soldiers who might be on board to defend it. The gunfire would shatter the windows, then they could shoot open the doors and raid the train.

Like any military operation, Matt reflected, it would depend on a combination of surprise and violence to have any chance of success. *And with a bit of luck, it might just work.*

Matt stretched out. The ground felt hard beneath him, but as he started to chew on the chocolate he could feel some of the tension starting to ease out of him. It was always this way, he thought. As the moment of battle approached, you started to calm down. The brain stopped contemplating all the terrible things that might happen, and started concentrating instead on the immediate tasks ahead. Some kind of self-defence, I suppose. *Proof that the human brain is hardwired for combat.*

'You shouldn't be here,' whispered Matt, looking back up at Eleanor.

Eleanor swallowed her chocolate. 'I don't have anywhere else to go. Besides, they killed my brother.'

'And they killed Gill,' said Matt with a shake of his head. For some reason he'd never really told Eleanor about Gill. 'Gill and I grew up together. Our lives went off in different directions sometimes, and we did different things, got involved with different people, whatever. We didn't have much in common really. I was interested in soldiering, she was interested in children and teaching.' He paused, looking beyond Eleanor, down on to the tracks, and into the scrubland of empty warehouses and rusting, decayed rails beyond

307

them. 'Back in the regiment, we used to call it revenge. Simple as that.'

He laughed, and gave Eleanor's arm a secret squeeze.

'There's not just one woman for every man,' she said softly. 'That's just in fairy tales.'

Matram held his ear to the breeze. In the distance, he could hear something. A muttering, the sound of voices, carried down in the air. Up above he could hear a pair of police sirens screeching around a corner. He stopped, straining his ears. There it was again. An animal, maybe. Or just some kids playing. *Or voices.*

Deliver that man to me, he told himself. *So that I can murder him with my bare hands.*

He looked up into the scrublands. He was about two miles past Waterloo now, walking along the edge of the rail. His eyes had been locked on to the track, looking for any signs of disturbance: a scratched rail, some dents in the gravel, some debris lying across the sleepers. Anything that would give him a clue as to whether a trap had been prepared. Anything that would give him an edge in the battle that lay ahead.

There is one crime I shall never be found guilty of: underestimating my enemy.

The voices. Matram cocked his head, then looked up the side of the bank. Some bushes, some dried-up grass, then a barrier of concrete before the rail line gave way to the street. He scanned the horizon. A movement. He started walking, his grip tight on the Smith & Wesson 500 hunting revolver he had strapped to a holster next to his chest. It was ten yards to the bush: a nearly dead collection of brambles and leaves that still covered enough space to hide one maybe two people.

Matram drew the revolver, pointing it in front of him. He edged forward, aware that anyone hiding there might be armed. The bullet, if it came, would fly out of nowhere. *I'd be dead before I even knew about it.*

He paused, knelt and aimed. Three bullets blasted into the bush, then three more. Matram could hear a noise. An impact. Followed by a whimper. He ran into the bush and saw a dog lying on its side. Blood was seeping out of its stomach, but the ground was too hard to absorb it, and the liquid was starting to trickle down the bank side.

Matram reloaded the Smith & Wesson, putting the gun barrel to the dog's head. He fired once, killing it instantly.

Then another noise. He pulled the ringing mobile from his pocket, holding it to his ear. 'The track is clear?' asked Abbott.

Matram nodded. 'I believe so,' he said warily. 'My men have searched the line. Police helicopters have flown over every inch of track.' He glanced down at the dog. 'So far we have found nothing.'

' "Believe so" isn't what I was planning on hearing, old fruit,' snapped Abbott. 'Our friend from the wrong side of the Channel is about to get on the train. We don't want anything happening to him, do we?'

'I said the track has been cleared,' said Matram. 'We'll be monitoring it the whole way. I don't think there's any way Browning can get on to a speeding train. He's not Superman.' He paused, his eyes wandering back down the track. 'Anyway, if he does, we just kill him. End of story.'

'Then get back on this damned train,' snapped Abbott. 'We're already late leaving.'

TWENTY-FOUR

The train should have been there at eight forty-five, five minutes after it left Waterloo, but there was no sign of it. Matt was wondering if it might have been cancelled. *If that happens, we're all done for.*

Then suddenly Matt could feel the steel tracks at his side start to vibrate and tremble as the power surged through them. He could see nothing, except the pale lights of the signal ahead of him starting to change.

It had worked, he realised. Pointer had managed to change the signal.

A line of electrical junction boxes six feet back from the track stretched down to the signal box, and Matt was hiding behind those. For the first phase of the ambush, that would be their cover. The wooden breech of his Kalashnikov was gripped tight in his hands, primed for action. Damien was at his side, and Pointer was running back to join them. Keith and Perry were standing by to put a log on to the tracks. If the signal didn't bring the train to a stop, that would.

If ever there has been a moment to start praying, this is it.

The train was drawing towards them: just a hundred yards away now. Matt glanced behind him. Eleanor was hiding behind a bush twenty yards back. If he died this evening, hopefully she would escape. Ivan had called to say he had to get his wife and children out of the country to make sure they were safe. *This is one battle where we'll have to do without the Irishman.*

The engine was pulling two carriages behind it. As the front of the engine moved past Matt, a roar of mechanical noises washed over him, and a heavy cloud of diesel exhaust spat out into his face, blackening his skin, and filling his lungs with noxious, oily gas, making him choke. He shut his mouth and his eyes briefly, trying to shield himself from the fumes.

Another ten yards forward, and the back carriage would draw level. *Then I can attack.*

'Now!' he shouted.

At his side, Damien, Archie and Pointer stood up, their Kalashnikovs raised to their shoulders. Steadily, they took aim, preparing to unleash a volley of fire into the stranded train.

'What the hell was that?' shouted Abbott as the train wobbled and slowed.

Matram looked out of the window. Both men were sitting in the carriage behind Lacrierre's office. He had work to do and didn't want to be disturbed. Four Increment soldiers were with them: Godsall, Harton, Snaddon and Trench. Each one was equipped with a supply of rifles, knives, handguns and explosives.

Matram felt a flicker of concern. He'd had the whole track searched by police helicopters earlier: it should be clear. He glanced out of the window. He could see nothing but the scrubland rising up to the street above. Then he saw a group of men in luminous yellow jackets moving through the scrub. A single word was rattling through his mind. *Ambush.*

There was a minute of silence. Then Matram decided he had to investigate.

'You,' he said, looking towards Snaddon. 'Check the door.'

Snaddon walked to the side of the carriage. A red lever

was prominently displayed for emergency openings. She yanked on it hard, pulling it down. The door hissed, and a light started flashing. Slowly, the door slid open, and then Snaddon looked down on to the side of the tracks.

'Special delivery,' said Matt, looking up at her. 'For a Mr Jack Matram.'

He pulled the trigger on the Kalashnikov, a round of fire rippling up into her body. The bullets punctured a series of holes in her chest and lungs, cutting through the arteries, and sending blood spilling down the front of her shirt. A cry of pain croaked from her throat, and then she fell forward, dead.

'Move, move, move,' shouted Matram from the back of the carriage.

'Lovely jubbly,' said Pointer, bounding up to Matt's side. 'Stopping a big monster like this. It worked for old Ronnie, and now it's working for old Jack as well.'

Matt looked at him and grinned. Snaddon's corpse was leaking blood over his shoes. The door was still wide open, but apart from the low growl of the engine, the area had fallen silent again. How many men were in there? Four, maybe five, he guessed. The Increment had a total of eight soldiers, but it was unlikely Matram would commit all his forces at the same time. *No commander wants to do that.*

They retreated behind the boxes again, waiting to see if anyone else emerged. It was too dangerous to try to get inside the open door: he would certainly be shot. Damien, Pointer and Archie were lined up behind him, six feet away, also taking cover behind the electrical boxes, their guns at the ready. Keith and Perry were moving down the other sides of the track. The second carriage of the train was completely surrounded.

'Fire,' shouted Matt.

The sound of five machine guns firing in unison suddenly

burst through the still of the evening: a repetitive, chattering sound, like the hum of crickets in summer but magnified a hundred times. The echo bounced back along the steep sides of the tracks, multiplying and replicating the sound of the gunfire until they were lost in a symphony of noise.

Christ, thought Matt. *None of the glass is shattering.* 'Move forward,' he shouted, straining to make himself heard. If they couldn't shoot through the glass of the carriage, they would have to find another way in.

Matt gestured to Damien and they moved quickly to the side of the carriage, flattening themselves against it. No one inside the carriage could shoot at them without emerging from the door, in which case they'd be mown down by Pointer and the others. Now, they moved along the side until they could jam their Kalashnikovs into the doorway Snaddon had left open, twising rightwards to spray the inside of the carriage with bullets. An answering hail of bullets came back at them. There was no way in.

'Back,' shouted Matt. 'Move back,' as he and Damien retreated behind the boxes again.

At the front of the second carriage, a door had briefly opened and a hand grenade arced out into the sky. Matt turned his gun to fire on the window, but it was too late. It had already closed. The grenade skitted to the far side of the train, bouncing across the scrubland behind them. Matt was about to yell a warning when the device exploded. A huge ball of flame licked up into the night sky. The smell of gunpowder hung heavily in the air. As the smoke started to clear, Matt could see Perry lying on the ground, one arm and one leg both severed clean from his body. Keith was staggering towards them, his face cut through. Pointer rushed forwards, grabbing hold of his son, holding him up by the arms, and dragging him across the tracks.

'Get him back up the bank,' shouted Matt. 'Eleanor can deal with his wounds.'

'He's my boy,' grunted Pointer. 'I'll look after him.'

'She's a doctor,' yelled Matt. 'We've got a battle to fight.'

Another grenade tumbled out of the carriage, bouncing along the side of the track, and nestling into scrub. 'Take cover,' shouted Matt.

He dived to the ground, dragging Damien down with him. The grenade exploded with a deafening, ear-splitting roar. Gravel from the track kicked up high into the air, then started raining down, as a thousand hard pebbles dropped out of the sky. Across the track, he could see that Archie had been hit in the blast, taking a wound across the stomach, from which blood was pouring.

Two men down, and we've hardly even started.

'There, there,' shouted Matt, pointing to the window from which both grenades had been tossed. Pointer had left Keith on the bank side, where Eleanor has stripped off his T-shirt and was using it to bandage his wounds. Pointer raised his machine gun to the window, letting off a murderous round of fire, preventing any more grenades from getting out.

Matt and Damien started to crawl across the track to the far side of the train. They had to find another way into the carriage to stand any chance of fighting back. Otherwise, they were just going to get bombed to pieces.

Silence descended upon the tracks again. Matt knew that whoever moved first would make themselves vulnerable. This is turning into a war of nerves, he realised.

Then suddenly Damien ran forward, towards the open door again, and Matt followed just an inch behind him. He admired his friend's guts under fire. Suddenly Trench looked out of the open door, his eyes swivelling from side to side. Matt raised his Kalashnikov to eye level, lining up the sights, then letting off a round of fire. Trench fell to the ground, his neck sagging away from his head, the skin ripped up by bullet holes.

Two down, thought Matt. *But I still don't know how many are left in there.*

Matt and Damien threw themselves on the ground. Maybe they could smash the window from here. They kept firing, but bullets were bouncing off the carriage. 'It's no bloody good,' shouted Damien. 'We can't get in here.'

Underneath the carriage, Matt could see three pairs of feet. They must have climbed down from the train. 'They are coming to get us,' he muttered towards Damien.

Matt let off a round of bullets, aiming to fire under the train and shoot the feet from under the three men. The bullets smashed into the ground, but they were too quick. All Matt could see was the feet fleeing up the side of the bank leading away from the tracks.

Taking cover, he realised. Up in the high ground. At the top of the railway banks, where it meets the street. From there they can shoot down at us from over the roof of the train. *They can pick us off one by one.*

Matt cast his eyes to Eleanor's position. She was badly exposed. If they saw her, they would kill her. 'We're fucked,' he muttered, looking towards Damien.

'I'm standing and fighting,' said Damien grimly.

'Don't be an idiot, you'll just get shot to bloody pieces.'

Damien shrugged. 'I'll take my chances.'

Matt shook his head. 'No,' he said, his tone turning serious. 'Even in the regiment, we knew when to retreat. Get out of here, regroup, and plan the next assault.'

Suddenly he heard a helicopter approaching. Matram had called in reinforcements. Then at his side, he could feel the train juddering to life. A vibration rippled through the several tons of metal, and the wheels strained as they started to turn. The stink of diesel filled the air.

'Fuck it,' shouted Matt. 'They're getting away.'

The train was starting to move again. Its massive engine had broken across the log blocking the track, crushing it into

315

a million splintered fragments of wood. Eleanor was running down the hill, her breath short and furious. 'We're losing them,' she shouted.

'Get back, get back,' he yelled, his face red with fury.

But Eleanor kept moving. A bullet clipped the ground, and Matt reached out, dragging her behind the moving train to get her out of range.

The train was starting to accelerate, dust spitting up from its metal wheels. Thick clouds of diesel fumes blew out from its engine, obscuring Matt's vision. He started running, pulling level with the open doorway.

She can't survive out here herself. Not for a minute. She'll be picked off with the others. I'll have to take her with me.

His right fist reached up, grabbing the handle of the swinging door. With his left hand, Matt reached back and grabbed Eleanor's arm. The momentum of the train was gathering pace, and his arm locked on to the side of the train. He could feel the muscles in his arm being stretched. A sudden burst of acceleration tore his feet clean from the air, and for a moment it felt as if his shoulder was about to be split in two.

Matt twisted his shoulder, pushing all his strength into his arm, and pulled himself and Eleanor forward. He grabbed the side of the door, pulling them both on to the carriage floor. Then he slammed the door behind them. The train was moving faster now. A corpse was lying face down on the pale beige carpet that ran down the length of the carriage, a pool of blood oozing from his wounded gut.

Apart from that they were alone.

Matt took the Glock from his pocket, jabbing it forwards. How many enemies are left on the train? he asked himself.

He hauled Eleanor to her feet. 'Ready?' he whispered.

She nodded, wiping away some of Keith's blood that was still splattered across her T-shirt. 'Let's go make a deal.'

★

The helicopter took off again, flying low, swooping out over the streets of south London. It turned up into the sky over Wandsworth Bridge, then headed due south until it hit the railway line running down towards the south coast.

'There,' snapped Matram. 'There's the train.'

'I can't see anything?' said Abbott. 'You certain he's on board?'

'Let's get down lower,' said Matram. 'I want to take a closer look.'

The automatic door on the front carriage slid smoothly open. Matt positioned the Glock in his right hand, checked the safety catch was released, placed his finger over the trigger and stepped foward. *I'm going to spill some more blood on this smart new carpet.*

Lacrierre was sitting in the leather armchair. The laptop was open on his desk. Some music was playing loud on the speakers – the opera *Manon* – drowning out the sound of the train. He was looking out of his window, his fingers tapping out the melody of the aria.

Matt reached down to switch the music off.

Lacrierre glanced upward, meeting Matt's eyes with his. His face was calm, yet intensely calculating: was he busy trying to figure out how Matt could have got inside the train? Surely he must have heard the gun battle? Perhaps he had been completely confident that Matram would win it for him? Or perhaps this was a trap?

'The English,' said Lacrierre, a sneer in his voice. 'Not a musical race.'

Matt stepped across the floor of the carriage. The train was accelerating away, picking up speed as it moved out into the suburbs of south London. He stood in front of the chair, resting the tip of his Glock pistol against Lacrierre's forehead. One of the lessons he had learnt in the regiment flashed through his mind. *If you want to negotiate with a man,*

317

let him feel the cold, rounded steel of a gun barrel against his skin.

'Let me guess,' said Lacrierre. 'You're about to make me an offer I can't refuse?'

Matt smiled. 'You can refuse if you like,' he answered, his voice calm and measured. He tapped the gun barrel twice against Lacrierre's forehead. 'But there are six reasons in here why you should think very carefully before you do.'

'I'm a businessman, I know about negotiation. Tell me what you want.'

Eleanor stepped forward. 'We know about XP22,' she said. 'We know how you bought it, tested it and made money from it. Everything. With proof. And we know that all the men it was tested on are being eliminated one by one to stop the truth about its side effects ever being revealed.'

Lacrierre spread out his hands. 'Then you know everything,' he said. 'There is surely nothing else I can help you with?'

'The antidote,' persisted Eleanor. 'We want to know where the antidote is.'

'An antidote?' Lacrierre pushed back in his chair, a slow laugh starting to rise from his throat. 'There is no such thing.'

'Really?' said Matt. 'Orlena was looking for it in that factory in Belarus.'

'Perhaps,' said Lacrierre cautiously. 'But her mission, and yours as well, Matt, was just to destroy the factory. Simple as that.' He looked up towards Matt. 'You're a soldier, and soldiers fight. They don't get involved in any of the bigger questions, that's not their role. Now let's finish this right here, right now. If you want more money, tell me the amount, and we can settle it today.'

'We told you, we want the antidote,' barked Matt.

'And I just told you, no such thing exists.'

'*Likuvannia*,' snapped Matt. 'That was the word Orlena was shouting in the factory.'

'My Ukrainian is not what it should be . . .'

'It means cure,' said Matt. 'Or antidote.'

'And an antidote is what you need,' said Eleanor. 'Without one, XP22 is useless. You can do nothing with it. You've already tested it and, as you've discovered this year, the men that take it turn into monsters. No army is ever going to administer it again.' She paused. 'But once you have an antidote to cover the side effects, then it can be used full-scale. Tocah stands to make a fortune.'

Lacrierre ran his thin, bony fingers through his hair. He looked up at Eleanor, examining her, his eyes running up her body, then resting on her face. 'And you are?'

'My name is Eleanor Blackman. My brother was Ken Blackman. XP22 was tested on him, then a few weeks ago he went crazy and killed some people. He's dead now.' Eleanor paused, the words catching in her throat.

'Normally I judge a woman solely by her appearance,' said Lacrierre coldly. 'In your case I may make an exception. You look stupid, but I don't think you are.'

He stood up from the chair, walking over to the window, looking out. He scratched his chin, then turned round to look at Matt and Eleanor. 'Maybe there is an antidote.'

Matram put down the pair of binoculars he had been holding to his eyes. 'Yes,' he snapped. 'Browning's managed to get on board the train.'

Abbott looked across, straining to make out the words over the roar of the blades just a few feet away above him. The helicopter was swaying through the air like a bubble tossed around in the wind as the pilot strained to keep it just a few yards above the train. Abbott was turning pale.

'You sure?' he shouted.

'Look for yourself,' shouted Matram, handing across the binoculars.

'Damn it,' shouted Abbott.

Matram looked up towards the pilot. 'Send a signal to the rail operator to slow the train down,' he snapped. 'Then bring us down low enough over the roof so that we can get on board.'

He looked back towards Abbott. 'I hope you know how to jump on to a moving object because we're about to get on board.'

Abbott turned a shade paler, clutching on to the side of the helicopter as it tipped on its side, and swerved down low in the direction of the speeding train.

Matram laughed. 'At last we've got him where we want him. Trapped like a fish in a bowl.'

'Where is it?' said Matt.

He had stepped forward two paces, holding the Glock to Lacrierre's head, forcing him to sit back down on the chair. The barrel of the gun was squeezed tight against his forehead, leaving a tiny, circular imprint in his skin. 'I said we want it.'

'It's useless to you,' said Lacrierre. 'We retrieved some interesting material from the computers you and Orlena brought back from the factory. There's a *possibility* of an antidote. Another drug that would stop the side effects of XP22 ever manifesting themselves in the men who took it. But it's still very experimental.' He glanced towards Eleanor. 'There isn't some nice little blue pill I can give you.'

Matt could feel the train slowing. He moved the gun aside, then slapped Lacrierre hard across the cheek. His knuckles collided hard with the skin just above his cheek-bone, sending a bolt of pain down into the neck. Matt could feel the bruising in his own knuckles, but the blow had hurt Lacrierre more: he was ageing, his bones turning brittle, without the suppleness that allowed a younger man to absorb far harder punches. 'Do I look like I'm here for a

320

fucking conversation?' Matt barked. 'Now give us what we've asked for. Then I can get on with deciding whether to kill you or not.'

Lacrierre was rubbing the side of his cheek, nursing the swelling. He looked back up, moving his head away from the pistol that was still just a few inches away from his face. 'I just told you, it's useless, you can't use it.'

'On the list there are fifty men who the drug was tested on,' said Eleanor. 'Five of them disappeared. About another ten or fifteen have killed themselves, or been murdered. That leaves at least thirty men. Their lives could be saved if we had the antidote.'

'Soldiers,' said Lacrierre, his eyes rolling upwards, and his shoulders cast back in a shrug. 'They sign up to die for their governments. They shouldn't start complaining about the method their government chooses to dispose of them.' He looked back up at Matt. 'Unless, of course, they are, maybe, *lâches.*' He paused, rolling his eyes. 'Excuse me, that's French. The English word, I believe, is coward.'

Matt smashed his hand back into Lacrierre's face, his knuckles colliding with the same section of cheek. The swelling reddened, and Lacrierre flinched as the pain swelled up in his neck. If you want to hurt a man, you just keep punching him in the same place again and again, Matt reflected. The pain started to multiply, until it became unbearable. *It was simple, brutal and effective.*

'Fuck you,' spat Matt.

'Give us the information,' said Eleanor. 'Now.'

The hydraulics within the carriage hissed, then squealed as the automatic doors through while Matt and Eleanor had come slid open again. Matt glanced round anxiously. With his left forearm he pulled tight against Lacrierre's neck, jerking him backwards. With his right arm, he jammed the Glock against the side of his head, pointing the gun an inch below the ear.

321

Matram walked into the carriage. He strode confidently into the narrow chamber, followed by Abbott and two other men. Matt recognised one of them: Harton had been there that day in Bosnia when he'd walked out of the Increment. Both of them had the hard, detached look of professional soldiers, high on the adrenalin of the battle.

Between the, they were carrying enough munitions to wipe out a medium-sized town.

A single thought rattled through Matt's mind. *I'm done for.*

'Drop him, Browning,' barked Matram. 'Drop him right now, or I'll blow both of your bloody brains out.'

Their eyes met briefly. It had been four years since they'd last set eyes on each other: the last time, Matt had been on his way out of the Increment. Matram's expression was cold and unyielding, but behind the mask of indifference, Matt felt certain he could detect a blind, furious hatred.

Whatever else happens here, he's determined that I should end my day as a corpse.

Matt took a step backwards, dragging Lacrierre by the throat. A few feet ahead of him Eleanor, too, was edging nervously towards the back of the carriage, where two of Lacrierre's heavy Napoleonic swords were hanging in open frames on the wall.

If I'm going to go, we're *all* going to go, decided Matt. *We can finish this party in hell.*

'Really, old fruit, this is all getting a trifle tiresome,' said Abbot. 'You need to learn to rub along with people a little better.' He paused, fishing a packet of Dunhill from his pocket, jabbing a cigarette into his mouth. 'Now do what the man says, and we can finish this nice and quick.'

Matt looked first at Abbott, then across to Matram, then behind to Harton and Godsall. Matram was carrying a Smith & Wesson pistol, and both Harton and Godsall were carrying standard-issue MP-5 sub-machine guns. From his time in the Increment, Matt guessed they would both have pistols tucked into their clothing somewhere, and at least one knife as well. Abbott was not holding a weapon in his hand, but that meant nothing: he could have a gun concealed somewhere within that crumpled linen suit.

He jabbed the Glock harder into Lacrierre's head. 'Anyone touches me or her, you're about to discover what this guy's brain looks like when it's splattered across the floor.'

Matram lifted his right arm, the elongated Smith & Wesson pointing straight outwards. He was standing just five feet away. If he looked closely, Matt could see right down the centre of the barrel, into the inner workings of the weapon.

'Who says I care, Browning?' snapped Matram. 'Drop him if you want to. It's your brains that will be joining his on the floor.'

'Nice try, Matram,' said Matt. 'But I'm not buying. You need him. You see, this was never a job for the Firm. It was never a job for the Increment. It was a conspiracy all along between you and Abbott and Lacrierre.' He paused. 'And he's the boss. He has been all along. You need him. He's your paymaster.'

Matt could see the frown on Matram's face: the anger was surging through him, like a wave crashing against a beach. He inched fowards, the pistol still trained on Matt's forehead. A thin trickle of sweat started to drip down Matt's spine. This is not working, he told himself. The bastard is going to kill me.

I don't mind dying if I have to. *But not from his hand.*

A tense, unsteady silence hung through the carriage: Matt could hear the wheels of the train beating against the track, and the breathing of Lacrierre's strangled throat next to his arms, but otherwise nothing. Then, six feet to the left, Matt could see Abbott lighting his cigarette, blowing a thick cloud of smoke up into the already fetid air.

Then with sudden, unexpected agility, Abbott darted

swiftly towards Eleanor, knocking her sideways. Behind him, Harton and Godsall stepped forward one pace, holding their MP-5s at shoulder level, their fingers poised on the triggers. A scream erupted from Eleanor's lips as Abbott punched her hard in the stomach. She doubled over in pain, and by the time her eyes rolled upwards, Abbott's fist was jammed hard into her throat.

He glanced back at Matt and smiled. 'The muffins, old fruit, that's your weakness,' he said softly. 'Just the jolly old Sir Lancelot. All very nifty with the spear, but show him a bit of hemline and he was all over the place.' The cigarette, still alight, was dangling from his lips. With his right hand squeezed into Eleanor's throat, Abbott took the Dunhill from his mouth with his left hand, flicking the ash down the front of her T-shirt. 'Give up, old fruit,' he said. 'You played a good innings, but your time at the crease is done. Now, you know we're going to execute you. I won't piss about saying we might spare you, because we won't and you know it. But the muffin.' He looked down at Eleanor. 'There's no need to blow this pretty little head apart. So you be a good boy, and put that gun down. We'll make it nice and quick for you, then we can all get out of here.'

Matt looked into Eleanor's eyes. He could see the fear written into the bloodshot rims of her eyes, into the trembling of her lips and the nervous quivering of her hands. An hour ago, she was all bravado and defiance, but now that had all evaporated. She was not a soldier, Matt reflected. She never been to that abyss, never looked down at her own mortality, and she had no idea how to handle it.

With her right hand, Eleanor pushed Abbott's hand away from her mouth. 'Don't listen to him, Matt,' she said weakly. 'Don't listen.'

There's no end to the lies we tell each other, thought Matt. You can say it, but you can't mean it. *Your life is more precious than that.*

Matt started to remove the Glock from the side of Lacrierre's head. He loosed the pressure on his left fore-arm, letting Lacrierre slip free of his grip, and he could hear him choking as he filled his lungs with breath. He glanced up towards Harton and Godsall. The two men were standing with their legs a few inches apart, their expressions motionless and their rifles still trained on him. 'You're not working for the regiment, you know,' he said.

Both men remained silent, their eyes still and dead.

Matt looked straight at them, his eyes unflinching. *I've got one card. I have to play it right.*

'I only met you once, Harton,' he said. '*You* I don't know it all, but we're all regiment. We know the code we sign up for, and we never forget it. We fight rough and dirty. We don't bother about the rules, and the less fair the battle the more we like it. We just get on with winning it, that's our job. But there's some lines we don't cross. We aren't bandits, and we're not freelancers, at least not until we pick up our cards and start working for ourselves. We don't rape the local girls, and we don't loot places. We fight for our unit, nobody else.'

He paused, looking straight ahead: neither man showed any flicker of emotion or even interest. 'Today, you're not working for your unit. You're not working for the regiment. You're just executing two innocent people to protect three gangsters who are out to make a fortune for themselves.'

Matt kept his eyes locked on the two men. He could see nothing on Godsall's face, but Harton showed a flicker of something: if you looked closely, his grip on the trigger of the MP-5 had loosened just a fraction.

Abbott tossed the remains of his cigarette on to the ground, stubbing it out on the carpet with the heel of his shoe. 'Very nice, old fruit,' he snapped. 'Now can we skip

325

the matey bollocks please and get on with the executions. I'll repeat my offer once more, Matt. Put your gun down. Let Lacrierre go, and you can be knocking on the Pearly Gates in time for supper. We'll kill you but we'll let Eleanor go.'

Suddenly Harton began to speak. 'You're a coward, Browning. You bottled the job back in Bosnia because you were scared of getting clipped. Now you're still just trying to save your own skin.'

'No, the Increment is just being used to do the dirty work for these three men.' Matt paused, punching home the next sentence. 'If you go to that computer, I'll give you the account number for a private bank in Luxembourg called the Deschamps Trust. you can look it up, and you'll see ten million pounds paid into two accounts by Tocah. The names on the accounts?' Matt paused again, his eyes switching from Harton to Godsall, then back to Harton. 'Guy Abbott and Jack Matram.'

Harton started to lower his gun from his shoulder. He glanced first at Matram, then towards the computer. Slowly, he started walking towards it.

'Stop right there,' barked Matram. 'That's an order.'

Matt looked towards him. 'You can obey him,' he said, nodding towards Matram. 'Or you can obey your conscience.' He focused directly on Harton. 'I'm telling the truth. You kill me, your lives will be ruined. You'll be in prison until the day you die.'

'He's a madman,' said Abbott. 'He's got a grudge against the regiment. You shouldn't listen to a word he says.'

'We drummed him out of the Increment, don't you remember?' said Matram. 'He wasn't our sort. White skin, but yellow blood.'

Matt kept looking straight at the man. 'You can believe me, or you can believe them,' he said. 'Or you can just take a look, then believe the evidence of your own eyes.'

Without looking back, Harton kept walking towards the computer.

'Don't dare to disobey me,' shouted Matram.

TWENTY-FIVE

A single shot rang out, its noise echoing through the confined space of the carriage. It ripped though Matt's eardrums, briefly disorientating him.

Harton was lying dead on the floor, a single bullet hole through his forehead. A trickle of blood was seeping from the wound, spreading itself out across the beige carpet. A few painful breaths were still struggling up from his lungs, but his eyes had already closed.

For a split second, the room was quiet, and Matt felt as if he could watch events in slow motion. Time itself seemed to have stopped. *In this brief moment, I can attack.*

Matt gripped the Glock in his right hand, using his left hand to hold tighter on to Lacrierre. He steadied himself, rooting his feet to the floor, and locked his elbow into position, holding the gun straight out in front of him. Through its slim, metal sight he could see the bone of Matram's hand, his gun still pointing towards Harton. He squeezed the trigger, taking the recoil in his shoulder.

The bullet smashed into the Smith & Wesson. As the gun spun to the floor, the barrel broke apart. Matram flinched as the bullet grazed the skin of his palm, but his expression remained rock steady.

In front of him, Matt could see Godsall step forward, training his MP-5 on Matram and Abbott. 'Hold it right there,' he shouted. He looked towards Matt and Eleanor. 'I want to check that account.'

Matram was standing dead still, looking at the gun Godsall had pointed at him.

Inwardly Matt grinned, although his face remained unchanged. *If you've got just one roll of the dice, better make it a good one.*

Godsall was standing over the laptop next to Lacrierre's chair. 'Go to www.deschampstrust.com,' said Matt. 'Then click on Account.'

He watched as Godsall's fingers moved across the keyboard. His eyes were locked on to the screen, tracking the page as it downloaded on to the computer. 'Now this number for the account,' said Matt. He read out the twelve-digit number, following Godsall's reactions as he delivered the information. His gun was still jammed into the side of Lacrierre's head. *If I can turn him, we can still get out of here alive.*

'It's blocked,' said Godsall. 'You need a password.'

Matt listed another twelve digits. 'That'll get you through.'

Godsall hammered the numbers into the keyboard, then hit return. The train was accelerating. It had moved free of south London, and was hitting the new fast stretch of track that took it down to the tunnel. Within five minutes it would be getting up to 130 miles an hour. A steel set of doors connected the engine to this carriage, Matt had observed. The driver would remain unaware of what was happening just a few yards away from him.

We're alone here, as if we were on a different planet. Just the six of us to sort this out among ourselves.

'Got it?' snapped Matt, looking back at Godsall.

He could see the man nodding.

Matt caught a breath. He could feel the sweat still trickling down his back. 'What does it say?'

Matram and Abbott were looking at him. So too was Lacrierre, his head twisting from Matt's grip, with the Glock still pressed hard to the side of his skin.

'There are two accounts listed here.'

'The names,' barked Matt. 'What are the names?'

Godsall raised the MP-5 up into his arm. He held it in front of him, the muzzle of the semi-automatic weapon pointing outwards. From this distance, he could spray the carriage with bullets, leaving no one alive but himself. '. . . Jack Matram and Guy Abbott.'

Matt could feel relief flooding through him. Surely there could be no doubt now? The man could see that Matram had been using them, that he had taken them on a mission to enrich himself personally. At the expense of his own men.

That broke the most basic of all regiment rules. *If there were to be any spoils of a battle, you shared them equally. You took the same risks, you got the same rewards.*

'How much?' said Matt.

Godsall was still staring at the screen, the calculator inside his mind crunching the numbers laid out before him. 'Ten million,' he said. 'Five each.'

Matt smiled. He tightened the grip around Lacrierre's throat, the gun still pressed against his head. 'You got the score?' he barked.

As he spoke, he could see the shock written into Godsall's face, but also the anger: for the past few weeks, he and his colleagues had been systematically murdering men around the country. He wouldn't mind that: it was what he was paid to do. But now he could see he hadn't been working for the government: he'd been working for Matram. *The blood was starting to feel heavy on his hands.*

'As I told you, this is not regiment work, it's private business,' Matt continued. 'There aren't many rules in the regiment, but that's one of them. He just broke it.'

He looked at Matram now, but the man seemed entirely calm. Even though blood was still dripping from his right hand, there was not a flicker of fear or emotion on his face.

He had many faults, Matt reflected, *but he could hold his nerve under fire.*

'Is there anything you want to say, Jack?' said Godsall.

Matram's expression remained as still and placid as the surface of a lake on a perfect summer's day. 'There's a third account,' he said. 'Keep looking.'

'A third account?' said Godsall.

'Something wrong with your bloody ears?' snapped Matram. 'Look under the account in my name. You'll see a payment out.'

Matt glanced across at Godsall. 'It's a trick, you idiot.'

'Look at the account,' snapped Matram, his eyes still fixed on Matt. 'Two weeks ago precisely.'

'Don't move,' said Godsall.

Matt could feel the sweat rolling off the back of his neck. Godsall looked back down at the screen of the laptop. His right hand moved swiftly over the keypad, his expression focused and determined. 'A payment of four million,' he said. 'Made to a separate account set up in the name of Raul Causeland.'

The trace of a smile flashed across Matram's lips, and in his steely eyes Matt could see a hint of amusement there: a sardonic flash of his teeth, as if he were relishing some private joke.

'How many men are in the Increment?' asked Matram.

Godsall nodded. 'Eight, sir.'

'Good answer,' said Matram. 'And four million divided by eight makes half a million each. Now, who is Raul Causeland?'

'Joke name,' said Godsall, his eyes flashing towards Matt. 'The Increment goes out for a few beers, it's Raul who gets the drinks in. Who is he? Nobody. Or rather, all of us.'

'So you see, a big chunk of the money goes to you guys,' said Matram. 'Half a million each, sitting waiting in a private numbered account in Luxembourg. Makes a nice, tidy little pension. Better than scrambling around looking for security work. Or getting your balls shot off protecting American oil executives out in Iraq.' He nodded towards Matt, the smile on his face widening. 'Or serving up warm beer and cold chips to the gangsters on the Costa del Crime.'

Godsall's expression changed. The strain and tension of the last minutes lifted, replaced by the first flicker of a smile. He lifted the MP-5, raising it back up to his shoulder, his finger jammed tight over the trigger. 'I understand.'

Matram nodded, looking hard towards Matt. 'So, Browning, what's it to be? Granite, sandstone, marble? One of those nice fancy surrounds, or just a plain slab of rock with a Bible quote on it? I always like to see a regiment man getting a decent headstone. Particularly when you want to make sure the bastard doesn't crawl out and start giving you any trouble.'

Within his right forearm Matt could feel Lacrierre starting to relax too, the tension on the man's skin easing down. Ahead of him, a sly grin was starting to spread out across Abbott's face. A Dunhill was dangling from the edge of his lips, its smoke settling in a small cloud clinging to the ceiling of the carriage.

Outside, another train was flashing past in the opposite direction, the vibrations rattling the train. At the speed both trains were passing each other, it would have been impossible for any of the passengers to see what was happening in this carriage.

So Matram cut the rest of the Increment in on his scheme, reflected Matt. I should have guessed that. Every commander has been doing that from Julius Caesar onwards. You go in, take your loot, but even though you might take the bulk of the gold and diamonds for yourself, you make sure the men have just enough to keep them loyal.

'Come on, Browning,' sneered Matram. 'You must

already know what kind of tombstone you want. Every regiment man has the answer to that question in his head.'

'A white wooden cross will suit me just fine,' said Matt softly.

Matram nodded. 'The unknown soldier. *I'll* certainly forget you pretty damned quickly.'

Matt could see Eleanor shivering in the corner, the fear whipping through her with the force of a gale. For her sake at least, perhaps we should get this over with quickly.

'Can you take him with one shot?' Matram spoke without looking around, but it was clear the question was directed towards Godsall.

Matt could see the man examining his options. He was a trained assassin, good at his job. From the detached, curious expression on his face, Matt could tell he was studying the angles, judging the force and velocity with which his bullet would smash through Matt's skull, chew into the brain, and shut down the nerves that processed commands from the brain to the fingers.

If you're going to be shot by anyone, Matt reflected with bitter humour, it might as well be the best in the business.

'One shot will be OK, sir,' said Godsall.

'He won't have time to shoot Lacrierre with that gun he's holding in his hand?'

Godsall shook his head slowly from side to side, with the expression of a man thinking through his answer. 'I can't guarantee that, sir,' he replied. 'I'd say the odds were good. This is a bloody powerful bullet at this range. Once it strikes, you don't have many fractions of a second left to you. One-, two-tenths, that's the most. Never a whole second.'

'Damn it, man,' snapped Matram, his tone impatient. 'Give me the percentages.'

'Seventy–thirty, sir,' responded Godsall instantly. 'In our favour.'

Matram looked towards Lacrierre, his eyes focusing upon him. 'You happy with those odds, sir?'

Matt jammed the gun into Lacrierre's head, struggling to decide whether to pull the trigger now while he still had the chance. Godsall was certainly right: the moment the MP-5 bullet struck, he would probably lose all control of his fingers, and even if he survived for a few miserable moments, he wouldn't be able to shoot anyone. Yet fire now, and a rainstorm of bullets would instantly descend upon both him and Eleanor. He might kill Lacrierre, but he would be killing both Eleanor and himself as certainly as if he pressed the gun to his own temple. While there was just the shadow of a chance, he would hold his fire.

'What about the girl,' said Matt. 'She's not part of this.'

Abbott took a puff on his cigarette, blowing the smoke high into the air. 'Sorry, old fruit, we're not negotiating any more. Should have taken my offer when you had the chance. It's going to cost this little muffin her life.'

'Drop him, Godsall,' snarled Matram. 'Drop the bastard right now.'

Matt could see Godsall raising the MP-5 back up to his shoulders. A look of quiet satisfaction had settled on to his face: the look of a man who had made up his mind, and now just had to implement his decision. The word execution, Matt reflected, had never seemed more appropriate.

He had thought about this moment many times. Soon after he'd joined the regular army, a man in his unit had died on a training exercise. Then, of the ten men who had joined up in his year, four had died during the following decade of active service in the regiment, two of them in combat, two of them in training. With men falling around you at that rate, there were many nights spent lying awake in the darkness, pondering your own fate, and how you would meet it when the day came.

Matt held himself rock steady, disciplining every nerve in

his body. Not a bead of perspiration would be visible on his forehead, not a single tremor evident in his fingers.

I will do the one thing I always promised myself I would do, Matt told himself. *When the bullet comes along that has my name on it, I will take it with dignity.*

A shot rang out, its echo reverberating through the room. Matt could hear the explosion of the bullet igniting in the muzzle of the gun, and sense the parting of the air as the solid, deadly lump of hardened steel picked up velocity. Matt had been told about the way time slowed down when you were close to death. He had spoken with soldiers who had been badly wounded on the battlefield, and yet who had managed to pull through: they all told the same story, of how in the last moments before they thought they were going to die, the clocks slowed to a crawl. God's way of giving you plenty of time to list all your regrets, one of them had remarked bitterly.

Matt heard a shriek, a cry, and then a whimper.

He looked up. Godsall was lying on the floor of the carriage, a thin line of blood sparkling like red wine at the side of his head.

TWENTY-SIX

Orlena stepped forward, the one-inch heels of her black leather slingbacks treading carefully over Godsall's bleeding body. Her hair was tied back, held in place by an ivory pin, and her face was covered in a thin film of sweat and dust.

Leaning down, she tapped the side of Godsall's skull with her Marakov gun. A howl of pain erupted from his lips as the hot metal stung the open wound. Orlena paused, a look of concentration on her face, then squeezed the trigger. The bullet smashed into the side of his head, killing him instantly.

If you're going to come back from the dead, thought Matt, do it with a gun in your hand. He looked at her, their eyes meeting. On her face, he couldn't see even the trace of a smile. She stood up slowly, her progress purposeful, yet still cautious, the way a snake moves through the grass.

The Marakov was pointing straight ahead of her, four bullets left in the chamber. Matt could see the clean, sculpted shape of its barrel, another masterpiece of Russian gun design. *Which of us gets the next bullet? Who is she working for?*

'Whose side are you on?' he said.

'Same side she's always been on,' snapped Lacrierre. 'Her own.'

'Absolutely right, sir,' said Orlena calmly.

'How did you get here?' asked Eleanor.

Matt looked across at her. 'Get hold of his gun,' he hissed. 'We don't want Matram getting it.'

Eleanor walked across the floor, picking up the MP-5 nervously. The sweat was streaming down her face, and her hair was wet and stringy.

'I've been on board since Waterloo,' said Orlena calmly. 'I have a key to the train, always have had. One of the advantages of working as special security assistant to the chairman of the company. I thought I would let you and Matt do all the dirty work.' Her eyes rolled sideways, and she let out a long sigh. 'But it seems you've fucked up so badly, I thought I better do something.'

'What do you want?' said Lacrierre.

'Same thing they want,' said Orlena, nodding towards Eleanor and Matt. 'The antidote. *That's what I was doing working for you all along.* I need the antidote.'

Her gun, thought Matt. It's pointing at Lacrierre, not me.

'Your brother, Roman. He fought in Afghanistan, you told me that.' Matt paused. 'He took XP22. And without the antidote, he's liable to go crazy any time.'

Orlena nodded, advancing another few inches towards Lacrierre, the Marakov thrust out in front of her face. 'By now you'll have had time to process all the data we took from the factory in Belarus,' she said. 'So where is it?'

'I thought you were dead,' said Lacrierre. 'Next time I'll make certain.'

A smile started to crease up Orlena's lips, and for a brief moment she almost looked happy. It was always surprising, Matt reflected, how even in the most desperate of circumstances, people still found the strength to take pleasure in their own cleverness.

'You were wearing Kevlar, weren't you? When we went to see Petor, you knew you were probably going to shoot me, or that I would probably shoot you. So you put on a Kevlar vest just in case you took a bullet, so you could fall back into the smoke.' He paused, looking towards her. 'Congratulations.'

'Thank you,' said Orlena. 'A little late in the game, perhaps, but you seem to have figured it out.'

She held the Marakov aloft, jerking it high into the air so that it was pointing straight at Lacrierre. 'Where is it?' she repeated.

Matt could feel Lacrierre give a Gallic shrug: a very French movement of the shoulders that suggested he was ready to concede defeat, and no longer cared very much about the outcome one way or the other. 'In the computer. You'll find a file called XP44. The name is obvious enough. We got enough material from the computer disks you brought back for the lab scientists to build a rough chemical. It's not perfect yet, but it should work well enough. Any soldier who has taken XP22 just has to take a shot of the second drug and it squashes the side effects. They'll be fine for the time being.'

Orlena stepped towards the desk, picking up her heels to avoid the corpse of Harton still lying bleeding on the floor. 'Where?' she demanded.

'Open the files first,' said Lacrierre angrily.

There was a sudden jolt, throwing Matt off balance. He could hear the wheels of the train screeching against the track as the brakes were thrown hard forward, and the carriage rocked from side to side. Matt could feel his shoulders being forced back against the wall, but his grip on Lacrierre's neck remained as tight as ever.

Their chance, he realised. *This is their chance.*

Out of the corner of his eye, Matt saw Abbott start to advance on Eleanor again. 'Back off,' she said, her voice strained. 'Or I'll shoot.'

They all turned to look at her. Abbott raised his eyebrows. 'Don't be tiresome, old girl.'

'I'll shoot now,' shouted Eleanor.

The MP-5 she had taken was held out in front of her, but it was wobbling in her hand. Nerves, Matt realised.

Shooting a man is harder than it looks. Pointing and squeezing the trigger is easy enough. But the will, you either have it or you don't.

She doesn't have it.

The gun fired, the bullet racing through the air, and lodging itself harmlessly in the side of the carriage. She must have missed by a yard or more. Matt watched as Abbott wrenched the gun from her hand, pushing her backwards. Tears were running from her eyes, and her hand was still shaking.

It was too late. Eleanor had lost control of the battle. Abbott was pointing the MP-5 straight at Orlena.

Orlena spun round, the Marakov pushed out in front of her. The bullet was already racing towards her, slicing through the air, the smoke from the gun rising to the ceiling. It hit her in the chest, just above the heart, the force of the impact rocking her back on her feet. In the same instant, her finger pressed instinctively on the trigger of the Marakov, releasing the bullet. She collapsed on to the floor, consciousness ebbing away from her.

Abbott was clutching his stomach, his hands pressed tight against his skin where Orlena's bullet has struck. Blood was starting to seep up through his shirt and jacket, staining the white linen, and turning it a vivid crimson. He started to kneel, then fell face forward on the floor. The cigarette was still in his mouth, and its tip jammed up against his skin, burning the side of his face. He shouted, rolled over on his side, pushing the burning cigarette away. As he did so, his hands came away from his stomach. At least a pint of blood spilled out on to the floor, seeping out across the carpet. A howl rose up from Abbott's throat.

He had taken the bullet just below his chest. The walls of the stomach had been punctured by an inch of hardened steel, severing the intricate web of arteries, causing massive bleeding. Matt had seen those injuries on the battlefield, and although a man could survive them, he had to get to a skilful surgeon quickly. At the very least he had to be patched up with bandages to get the blood loss and pain under control. Without either, he was going to bleed to death: a painful descent into oblivion, accompanied by confusion, headaches and a nightmarish weakness as your blood and your life slowly drained away from you.

At times like this, you rely on your mates. *Abbott hasn't got any.*

In front of him, Matt could see Matram moving towards the front of the carriage. The door leading to the engine opened with a hiss, a blast of fresh air rushing into the carriage.

Matt pushed Lacrierre to the floor, delivering a sharp blow to the side of his head as he did so to knock him out. Eleanor had already picked up Abbott's gun from the floor. 'Cover him,' he shouted towards Eleanor. 'I'll take Matram.'

Matt's mind was working furiously. The forces of law and order would probably soon descend on the train. *If I can't take Matram now, I don't get another chance.*

The doorway was still open. He tried to level up a shot on his Glock pistol, but Matram had almost reached the driver's compartment. The train was still accelerating, and Matt could see Ashford International whizz past. Another few minutes, and they would be in the tunnel.

Matt threw himself forward, but a fraction of a second too late, he realised, as the door slid shut. Matram was inside, by himself with the driver.

The door was locked from the inside. Matt banged hard on the red emergency lever, but it was not responding. Matram must have already shut it down. Matt cursed to himself. There's only one way in. *I'll have to blow the bastard out.*

From the bag of kit still slung to his back, he took one of

the small balls of Semtex Damien had supplied him with. He jammed it in tight to the side of the door, attaching a fuse to it, then stood back: explosives and charges were part of basic SAS training. He'd watched Ivan do this a year ago, blowing up the door of a safe on a boat they were attacking, but even then, the quantity of explosive needed had been miscalculated, sinking the boat and almost costing them their lives. It didn't matter how expert you were, it was close on impossible to calculate precisely the amount of explosive needed to take out a door.

And I'm not even an expert.

He glanced backwards, checking that Eleanor was still holding a gun on Lacrierre. I don't have time to measure the risks, thought Matt.

He ignited the fuse, shouted at Eleanor to get down, then threw himself back down on the floor of the carriage. A five-second delay ticked by before the fuse activated. He counted down the seconds.

The force of the explosion rocked through the train. Suddenly they were plunged into darkness, and Matt realised the explosion must have blown all the fuses, and that as the walls were completely black on either side, they were now inside the Channel Tunnel.

He could feel the wheels wobble and jump as the blast kicked down into the engine, and for a moment he thought it might be thrown clean from the tracks. The air was filled with the thick, gut-wrenching smell of burning rubber but the engine kept turning.

He leapt to his feet, gripping tight on his Glock pistol. He sensed that the door was hanging loose, a mess of twisted metal and severed wires. He pushed forward, holding his gun straight ahead of him. He wanted to fire into the darkness, hoping to hit Matram, but he knew there was no point in wasting ammunition. Just inside the cabin, he almost stumbled over the unconscious body of the driver.

Then he heard Matram laugh.

Matt could hear him but still couldn't see him.

Raising his Glock upwards, he fired it once, then twice. He heard glass shattering, and cursed to himself. The bullets were flying past Matram, and had broken the windows at the side of the train. Unlike the carriages, this glass was not reinforced, and was breaking into shreds as the bullets impacted against it.

'One against one, Browning,' said Matram. 'Just you against me.'

A hurricane of air swept through the cabin, sucking Matt forward. He steadied himself, using his left hand to grip on to the side, keeping his right hand on the pistol. The wind howled around his ears, its deafening roar drowning out all other sounds.

'I'm ready for you,' he shouted, steadying his gun.

A fist from nowhere punched into his hand. The force of the blow was nerve-shattering, like being struck by a ten-iron golf club. Desperately, Matt tried to hold on to the pistol, but another blow landed, this time on his wrist. Matt squeezed the trigger, and as the gun exploded in his hand, it recoiled and fell to the floor.

We have only the weapons we were born with to fight now, realised Matt. *Our fists. And our wits.*

'You're a bloody coward, Browning,' taunted Matram, his bruised and burnt face suddenly looming out of the darkness. 'That's why we didn't want you in the Increment. You don't know how to take a bullet, and you don't know how to deliver one either.'

'I might be a coward but at least I'm not a murderer,' spat Matt.

'Murder?' said Matram. 'The Increment doesn't do murders, it does assassinations. And you know what, Browning? You're next.'

'Give me your best shot, Matram,' snapped Matt. 'We'll

see who walks out of here. And who has to be carried with a bunch of flowers draped over him.'

'You bottle it at the last minute, Browning,' said Matram, looking at him closely. 'That's why you're not Increment material. Not then, not now. Never will be.'

The blow landed hard on Matt's cheek. He could feel the fist colliding with his cheekbone, shattering the nerve ending and sending a vicious stab of pain juddering up towards his brain. Matt rolled with it, absorbing the force of the blow as much as he could. His back crashed into a lever on the control panel, momentarily paralysing his spine. He struggled to get a better grip on what was happening next.

He could see Matram raising his knee, about to kick him in the groin. Matt rolled sideways, and Matram's knee smashed into the softer flesh of his thigh, the muscle deflecting the blow. As he moved, Matt punched Matram hard in the windpipe. Matram's neck wriggled and shook under the force of the blow. Matt moved swiftly, drawing two feet away from him, his hand reaching back, then punching forward, smashing hard into the side of Matram's face.

'Here's a smack that says I might be Increment material after all,' snarled Matt, jabbing another fist into Matram's face.

Matram spun round, his arm flailing outwards as he tried to regain his balance. Matt moved forwards, ready to finish him. A leg sprang out, kicking up towards his groin. The boot lodged into his stomach, sending him a few inches in the air. Suddenly Matt could feel himself falling, his shoulder bruising as he crashed to the ground. A series of blows fell down on him. Matram punched at his face with his right hand, and at his gut with his left.

'I don't think your ticket's valid for this train,' said Matram. 'We'll have to let you off here.'

343

Matt could feel Matram gripping his neck, squeezing all the air from his throat and starting to drag him towards the broken window, pushing him closer to the gaping, jagged hole. Matt was struggling to break free, trying to land a blow that would weaken Matram's grip. But without any oxygen it was impossible to summon up enough strength. His head was sticking out of the carriage now, Matram holding him from behind. As he looked down he could see the edge of the tunnel racing past them. He could feel his hair brushing against the damp wall as it shot past at over a hundred miles per hour.

'Journey's end, Mr Browning,' laughed Matram.

Reaching down, Matt grabbed a shard of glass from the broken window. He gripped it in the palm of his right hand, the glass opening up a cut in his skin, but he held tight, then twisted his arm sideways. With one swift, brutal movement, he stabbed the glass hard down into Matram's side.

A lucky strike. From the howl of agony that opened up on the man's lips, Matt sensed he had hit a main artery. Suddenly blood was gushing out of Matram's body, as if the tap had been turned on, flooding across Matt's back, warm and sticky.

He kicked back, shaking Matram away, and pulling the shard of glass from his body. Turning round and pushing him hard against the window, Matt now gripped tighter on his shard of glass, jabbing it into Matram's left eye. A pitiful wail erupted from his lips as the glass sunk deep into his skull.

For the first time in my life, I feel good about killing a man.

Matt took a breath, letting the oxygen flood into his lungs. The air was still mixed with fumes, and he could feel the tar sticking to his chest, making him choke. He closed his eyes, taking a moment to draw back his strength. He'd watched men die before: seen them shot, burnt, knifed and strangled. But he'd never seen a man take so long about it, nor absorb so much pain and punishment as Matram had just endured without surrendering his last breath. The man had the strength of a god. *Or a devil.*

'This one's for Gill, you bastard,' shouted Matt.

He jabbed the glass hard into the side of Matram's cheek, feeling it rip through the skin and smash into his teeth. Then Matt grabbed Matram's shoulders and yanked him hard, pushing him to the edge of the window.

With one last heave, he hoisted the man upwards, letting him balance for one second on the edge of the train. *Let him see the fate that is about to befall him.*

Matt put all his strength into his shoulders as he thrust Matram's head through the hole in the glass. As it struck the wall, his skull split apart. His torso was stretching, hitting hard against the side of the window, and spikes of the broken glass were piercing his guts and his chest, sending little jets of blood spiking up into the hurricane of air still swirling through the driver's compartment.

Then, as Matram's head was severed clean from his body, Matt suddenly fell backwards, the headless torso lying on top of him.

TWENTY-SEVEN

Matt looked up. The driver was still unconscious, and he had no idea how to revive him. The train was on automatic. Leave it, thought Matt. All we want to do now is get out of this tunnel, and get out of this train. *Our work is done.*

He lifted himself up, and started running back towards the first carriage.

The sound of a scream pierced his ears. A woman's scream.

'Matt, look out!' cried Eleanor.

Matt ran into the carriage and ducked. The pain in his left shoulder was intense, and his left arm was fast turning numb. Above him, he could see Lacrierre lunging at the wall.

A flash of steel caught a ray of light beaming in from the tunnel lights. Christ, Matt realised, he's going for the swords. They might be two hundred years old, but they are still hardened, sharpened steel. And Lacrierre was a soldier once. *In his hands, they will be as deadly now as they were when they were first used by Napoleon's cavalry.*

Lacrierre grabbed the first of the blades. It shook free from the wall, its casing crashing down on to the floor. He lashed it through the air, curling it upwards high over his head. Matt rolled on to his side, sending a fresh jolt of pain up the side of his wounded shoulder. From the corner of his eye, he could see Lacrierre advancing two paces towards him. Using the muscles in his back, Matt drew up his strength, kicking out his legs and jabbing at the man bearing down on him. He kicked furiously, his legs spinning in the air as Lacrierre deftly danced out of the way.

He might be older, but he's still capable of putting up a good fight.

The blade slashed down, and as Matt tried to roll out of the way, it cut into his right leg. The steel tore through the denim of his jeans, and the blade sliced into the flesh at the top of his thigh. The metal felt cold and soft against his skin, digging into his muscle with the delicacy of a surgeon's scalpel. A gash six inches long and half an inch deep opened up down the side of his leg, the skin curling outwards as the wound opened up and started to breathe.

A sharp stinging pain ran along Matt's side. He levered himself off the ground. 'You're going to die for that, you bastard,' he shouted.

But in front of him, Lacrierre had flicked the blade upwards. It was now resting just beneath his chin, poised above the Adam's apple. A surgeon couldn't have placed it better, Matt reflected. One jab, and it would cut straight through the windpipe. *I will be dead within minutes.*

'As far as I can see I am the only man here with a weapon,' said Lacrierre. 'So I'm afraid it's you that is going to die.'

Matt could feel the blade digging harder into the skin on his neck. The blade was polished and sharpened, its edge as clear as a razor. A sword had to be looked after to stay that sharp. Lacrierre kept it on the wall for show, but also to defend himself.

'Finish me now, you bastard,' snapped Matt. 'Matram's dead, that's all that matters to me.'

He could see that Lacrierre's hand was wobbling. His fingers were trembling, and his eyes were dark and fogged. The man is on the edge, he realised. If that hand shakes any worse, he's going to take out my throat.

'Tell that woman to lay down her weapon first,' said Lacrierre. 'Or else I kill you this instant.'

Behind Lacrierre's back, he could see Eleanor advancing with Godsall's MP-5.

'Careful, Eleanor,' said Matt, watching her movements.

Lacrierre stood still, his hand steady on the sword, a look of fevered pleasure sweeping across his face. 'Tell her to drop it.'

'I can handle him, Matt,' said Eleanor.

At that moment, the train raced out of the tunnel. Matt heard the brakes slamming down on the wheels, and felt the train start to slow down. Eleanor was walking to the side of Lacrierre, the gun held in front of her. Matt could see she was releasing the safety catch, but he could tell she had done it wrong. The rifle wasn't going to fire, no matter how hard she squeezed on the trigger. Had Lacrierre spotted that?

The train shuddered to a halt.

'Take your damned blade from my throat,' said Matt. 'This train is in France. If you give yourself up here, at least you'll be in jail among your own kind. With your kind of money, you'll get your own cell. Probably be out in a few years.'

Lacrierre laughed. 'I'm not going anywhere. Not until I've killed you.'

'I can take him, Matt,' repeated Eleanor.

Matt glanced at her nervously. She was certain of what she was saying, but it wasn't true. The blade was still rubbing against his neck, nicking the skin, sending small jolts of pain up through into his head. His shoulder was still throbbing from its gun wound, and blood was still weeping from the gash on his leg. I'm still standing, he told himself. *But there's not much more punishment my body can take.*

'Put the sword down,' she said, looking straight towards Lacrierre. 'Put it down before I kill you.'

A smile creased up Lacrierre's lips. 'Have I not made myself clear?' he said slowly. 'I intend to kill this man.' The sword wobbled dangerously in his hand, as he glanced back at Eleanor. 'Now you put that gun down, or else I will have to kill you as well.'

'Damn you, it's suicide,' snapped Matt. 'One shot to the head and you'll be dead.' Talk him out of it, thought Matt. Let the fear take hold of the man. Let it eat into his soul. *That's my best chance.*

But in the glint in his eyes, Matt could see the hint of madness within his opponent. 'I'm a braver man than I look,' said Lacrierre. 'Your threats mean nothing to me.'

Eleanor looked across at him, a sudden look of professional curiosity on her face. 'You took the drug, didn't you? You took XP22.'

Lacrierre glanced back at her, his eyes suddenly blazing. 'What man wouldn't take it?'

'You don't get courage from a pill,' snapped Matt. 'You've either got it or you haven't.'

Lacrierre jabbed the blade, exploring and probing the skin of Matt's neck, like a butcher deciding the best way to sever a hunk of meat. 'Prepare to die,' he said, his tone soft and gentle, the same voice an anaesthetist might use before putting you to sleep. 'Close your eyes, compose your prayers, and let the pain take you away to a better, gentler place.'

Somewhere he could hear the echo of a gunshot. The reverberations rattled through the confined space of the carriage, and the unmistakable smell of sulphur started to drift under his nose. In front of him, Lacrierre was lying on the floor, a gunshot blast breaking though his hand, leaving a trail of blood on the floor.

Matt kicked the sword free from his grip. He reached down, grabbing it in his fist, then slashing it through the air. The anger was alive within him, and he raised his hand back, ready to cut through the neck of the man lying prostrate before him.

'No, Matt, no,' shouted Ivan. 'We'll deal with him.'

Matt looked up. Ivan was stepping forward, a Glock in his hand and at his side was Sir David Luttrell, the head of the Firm.

'You?' said Matt, the shock still evident in his voice. 'What in the name of Christ are you doing here?'

'Saving your skin, mate,' answered Ivan, stepping carefully across the corpses of Harton and Godsall. 'I told you I'd gone down to Dorset to look after my family, but I actually went to see this bloke.' He grinned. 'I reckoned you might need some help.'

Lutrell stepped after Ivan, trying to avoid getting any blood on his brown half-brogue shoes. He was wearing blue cotton chinos, and a white shirt open at the neck. A snub-nosed Springfield pocket pistol was still sitting in the palm of his right hand. 'It's like a damned abattoir in here,' he said, looking around at the bodies.

Matt looked at Luttrell. 'So you two are old friends,' he said. 'From your time running the Firm's Belfast office. Ivan was one of your agents.'

Luttrell smiled. 'Not friends, exactly. But we played the occasional hand of bridge together.' He nodded towards Ivan. 'He's good, if a little reckless. Sometimes overbid his hand.'

'When I knew Matram was coming after you, I figured you might need some help,' Ivan said. 'Matram and his boys are tougher than they look.' He paused, looking straight at Matt, his expression serious. 'We knew all along there were some rogue elements working inside the Firm and the regiment. We just didn't know who they were exactly, or what they were up to.'

'We?' said Matt. 'For fuck's sake . . .' He was struggling to control his surprise. He had experienced many different forms of betrayal. But not Ivan.

Ivan shook his head. 'My old friend, didn't you ever wonder about the false passports, safe houses, explosives, all the rest of it? Why do you think I agreed to blow up that factory in Belarus with you? I'm not just a guardian angel, you know.' He smiled sadly. 'In bridge, when you win the contract, then you play your partner's hand for him. So, think of it as a game of bridge.' Ivan moved closer to Matt. 'Remember what I said to you? One of these days a little light bulb is going to switch on inside your head, and you'll understand what's really happening.'

'And you would have let me die?'

'No, no, I got hold of Sir David and told him what was happening,' said Ivan quickly. 'There's a safety device on these trains which means they can be slowed down from a radio link that goes straight into the computer that controls the engine. It was built in so it could be stopped if anything happened to the driver. We activated that so we could climb aboard just after it emerged from the tunnel.'

The blade was still hovering in Matt's hand. Down below him, Lacrierre was out cold.

Matt looked back up at Luttrell. 'So this was planned all along?'

Luttrell ran his fingers through his silver-grey hair. His eyes moved away from Matt, as if he was surveying the rest of the carriage. 'Like Ivan says, I suspected Abbott was a bad apple. Flash house in St John's Wood. A cellar full of fine vintage ports. It was more than most of us can afford. I just didn't know what he was doing wrong. I figured if you two were working together again you'd find something out.' A smug grin started to spread on to his lips. 'Looks like the whole thing has worked out quite well.'

'Thanks,' said Matt sarcastically.

'Oh, don't worry,' said Luttrell, nodding. 'We'll make sure the account is paid. The Firm always makes sure its invoices are settled. In full.' He turned round. 'Now, let's get this place cleaned up,' he said briskly.

Across the carriage, Matt could see Eleanor leaning across

Orlena. 'She's still alive,' she said. 'I don't know how, but she is.'

'Kevlar,' said Ivan, ripping open the front of her coat. 'She's wearing a bulletproof Kevlar jacket underneath her blouse. These things are as strong as steel. The force of the gunshot must have knocked her unconscious, but none of the bullets have penetrated. A few bruises, perhaps, but she's going to be OK.'

'Lacrierre's going to live as well,' said Luttrell, checking the pulse of the Frenchman. He paused, looking first at Ivan, then at Matt. 'I'd rather take him into custody in Britain than in France.'

From the floor, Matt scooped up the fallen sword, then walked six paces across the carriage. He stopped, holding the tip of the blade hovering over Luttrell's chest. 'He's staying right here.'

Ivan started to reach out for Matt's arm.

'Back off,' snapped Matt.

The violence evident in his voice brought Ivan to a sudden halt.

'Don't be stupid,' said Luttrell.

Matt jabbed the tip of the sword forwards, cutting a small nick in the cloth of Luttrell's shirt. The button dropped on to the floor, breaking the silence that had fallen across the carriage. 'Take a look at my face, and tell me just how stupid you think I am.'

Luttrell sighed. 'I don't think . . .'

'How stupid?' roared Matt.

'Matt, I . . .' Luttrell allowed the sentence to fade on his lips as Matt twisted the blade close into the few grey hairs sprouting on his chest.

'Lacrierre was working with the Ministry of Defence,' said Matt, as the waves of anger washed over him. 'XP22 was a government-funded project. It went pear-shaped. Badly. That much is clear. And when the crap started blowing up, he paid Matram and Abbott millions to clear it up for him.' Matt paused, becoming more measured. 'But you aren't going to put him on trial. He knows too much. You're going to get him off this train, give him a slap on the wrist, then send him home. But I'll tell you what, he was responsible for the death of my friend, and the death of my fiancée. There's a price in blood to be paid for that.'

'Don't be absurd,' said Luttrell.

'Absurd?' questioned Matt. 'Then what are you doing here?'

'As your friend Ivan says, saving your ungrateful hide,' snapped Luttrell.

Matt shook his head from side to side. 'The Firm doesn't care whether I live or die.' He nodded down to Lacrierre. 'You're here to get him out.'

'Hold your damned discipline, man,' said Luttrell. 'You're a soldier.'

Matt grinned. 'Not for the past two years. I wish you people would get your heads around that.' Then he raised the sword to strike. 'Hold it right there.'

Luttrell's Springfield pistol was pointing straight at Matt. 'If I have to shoot you, I will.'

Matt looked straight at him. 'You haven't got it in you, sir,' he said slowly. 'Some men can give the orders that send men to their graves, and some men can pull the trigger that sends them to the same wretched place. But not many men can do both.' He paused, grinning. 'And you're not one of them.'

'Ivan,' shouted Luttrell. 'Punch some bloody sense into his fat, ignorant head.'

Ivan glanced back at him. 'Believe me, if I could, I would have done it by now.'

Matt lowered the sword. Suddenly they both laughed.

EPILOGUE

A mellow sunset was resting on the horizon, sending a pale orange light across the Mediterranean. Matt wiped the sweat away from his face, and sat down at the bar. His clothes were still dripping from the five-mile run along the beach he had just completed, but he felt cool and refreshed. The wounds to his shoulder and his leg had almost completely healed, and in the last month he had been well enough to start running again.

'I need a beer,' he said, looking up towards Janey.

The clipping from the newspaper was starting to fade, but it still caught Matt's eye as he knocked the cap from the bottle: six months later it still made him smile every time he looked at it. The clipping was pinned to the cork notice-board, along with ads for a couple of second-hand SUVs and one from a Polish girl looking for some au pair work. EUROSTAR SUFFERS TWELVE-HOUR DELAY, ran the headline in bold 48-point type.

A Eurostar was stranded ten miles outside Lille in northern France last night. A train in front was stuck on the tracks, its engine damaged, and trains were halted all day as workers struggled to clear the line. The carriages of the damaged train were empty according to the rail company. They were on a routine engineering exercise, and nobody was on board. Eurostar apologised to passengers for the severe delays that could be expected to the service for the next forty-eight hours while the tracks were checked for any faults.

Officials of the train company blamed the recent heatwave for the accident.

The wrong kind of heat, thought Matt with a grin as he took his beer towards the back of the bar.

There's only one kind of heat, and you can either take it or you can't.

A Christmas tree had gone up at the doorway, and some of the regulars had put presents around its base. A couple of rows of Christmas cards were hung up on some string behind the bar. The Last Trumpet was fully booked for Christmas lunch, and they'd already sold fifty tickets for the New Year's Eve bash. It promised to be quite a party: an Abba covers band was booked, and Janey had dreamt up a couple of new cocktails. Matt took a sip of his beer, letting the cold alcohol soothe his nerves. It was this part of the day he enjoyed the most. He could kick back, let the fresh air rush across his skin and relax, without the stresses of running the bar that filled up the day. And he had a stunning woman to share his bed at night to look forward to.

So long as I can stay awake, things aren't so bad.

A wind was blowing in from the sea, but the skies were still clear, and the sunset was streaked red and blue. A couple of tables away, Penelope and Suzie were sharing another bottle of Chilean white, and dissecting the latest disasters in their personal life. Both of them were talking at the same time, making it hard for Matt to follow what was up, but from the snippets of conversation drifting across it seemed Suzie's new boyfriend had hooked up with one of the fitness instructors at a gym in Puerto Banus, and Penelope's ex-husband had shacked up with someone else and was trying to cut the maintenance for young Liam.

Matt smiled and looked back towards the bar. Bob and

Keith were looking at a two-day-old copy of the *Daily Mail*, competing with each other to complain the loudest about tax rises they didn't pay anyway since neither of them had been back to Britain for a couple of years. Up on the plasma-screen TV that had just been installed, Sky Sports was getting excited about the Boxing Day clash between Manchester United and Arsenal. Match of the season, Andy Gray was proclaiming, although so far as Matt recalled there seemed to be one of those every week.

At the Last Trumpet, not much ever changes.

His eyes drifted out to the horizon. The last embers of the sunlight were starting to disappear beneath the black surface of the waves. The sun never really sets, Matt reminded himself. *That's just an illusion caused by the world spinning round.*

On the CD, a selection of Christmas songs was already playing: 'Let it Snow', followed by 'Rocking Around the Christmas Tree', 'White Christmas' and 'The Little Drummer Boy', until you imagined that reindeer and holly were all lyricists ever wrote about. Matt had tried to take the disk off, but Janey loved Christmas and put it straight back on again. I'm old enough to stop fighting losing battles, Matt told himself. If she wants the music, she can have it.

He opened up yet another Christmas card, and smiled as he read that Eleanor had got engaged to one of the doctors at the hospital. It was good to see that things were working out for her.

'Is this seat taken?'

He looked up and smiled at Orlena, taking the cap off a fresh bottle of San Miguel. She had just returned from a day's shopping in Malaga. She was carrying a Zara, a Versace and a Chanel bag under her arm. 'How was your run?' she asked. 'Those wounds starting to heal?'

There's still some pain in my leg and my shoulder,' said Matt. 'I'll be OK. I don't take bullets as well as you do.' That was one of the things he liked about Orlena. She was a real fighter. She *understood*.

Orlena laughed. The Kevlar jacket she had been wearing on the train had protected her: she had been badly bruised with a nasty swelling beneath her left breast that had taken a month to clear, but otherwise she had not been harmed. Her ability to survive a bullet had become a standing joke between them.

'That time at Petor's house back in Kiev. I would never have shot you, you know.'

Matt looked at her quizzically.

'But if you ever shoot me again,' she said with a smile, 'then I'm going to be really cross.'

'There's something I've always wanted to ask,' he said. 'Why did you shoot Petor that day in Kiev?'

'He developed the drug that damaged my brother. Not just him. Many good men died because of him, lots of families were destroyed. He deserved to die.'

Matt nodded. Right now, one explanation was as good as another. She wanted to kill Petor for the same reason he felt Lacrierre had to die. 'Have you heard from your brother recently?' asked Matt.

'Roman seems to be fine,' said Orlena. 'Did Eleanor give the antidote to the other men?'

'To all the survivors, yes,' replied Matt. 'There have been no more reports of side effects. They all seem to be doing OK.' He smiled, more to himself than to her. 'So some good came out of the whole damned job. Are you staying after Christmas?'

Orlena had arrived three months ago. Her contract at Tocah had been terminated by the new management that took over after Lacrierre's death. Shooting the chairman was not the sort of thing human-resources departments approve of, she'd noted wryly. But they had been generous with the settlement, as big companies always are when they want to cover up an embarrassing incident. At first she had just planned to stay for a few weeks, but that had turned into months.

Matt could see a look in her eyes: her eyelashes lowered, and her lips moved together seductively. 'I wanted to ask you something.'

'I'm just sitting around listening to Christmas songs,' answered Matt.

'Back in the Ukraine. A business proposition. I thought it might interest you.'

Matt smiled and rubbed his shoulder. 'I'm trying to limit myself to one shooting a year,' he said. 'That and eating more home-delivered pizza. Those are my two New Year's resolutions.'

Orlena's hand reached out across the table. Matt could see a ring on her left hand, a sparkling creation of diamonds, emeralds, gold and platinum, all woven together into an elegant crescent design. A few thousand dollars' worth of finger candy, reflected Matt. 'It could be worth a lot of money,' she said softly. 'And we could work together again.'

Matt grinned. He wouldn't say he wasn't tempted. Life was quiet by the sea. He didn't know how things would work out with Orlena but he was happy just to wait and see. 'I just want to run a restaurant,' he answered. 'The only trouble I want to deal with is a dodgy shipment of olive oil.'